52 WEEKS
A PARTY OF ONE

A Novel

by

Bianca Pensy Aba

ISBN: 979-8-9916897-0-0 (paperback)
ISBN: 979-8-9916897-1-7 (ebook)

This edition first published in 2025
Published by Bianca Pensy Aba

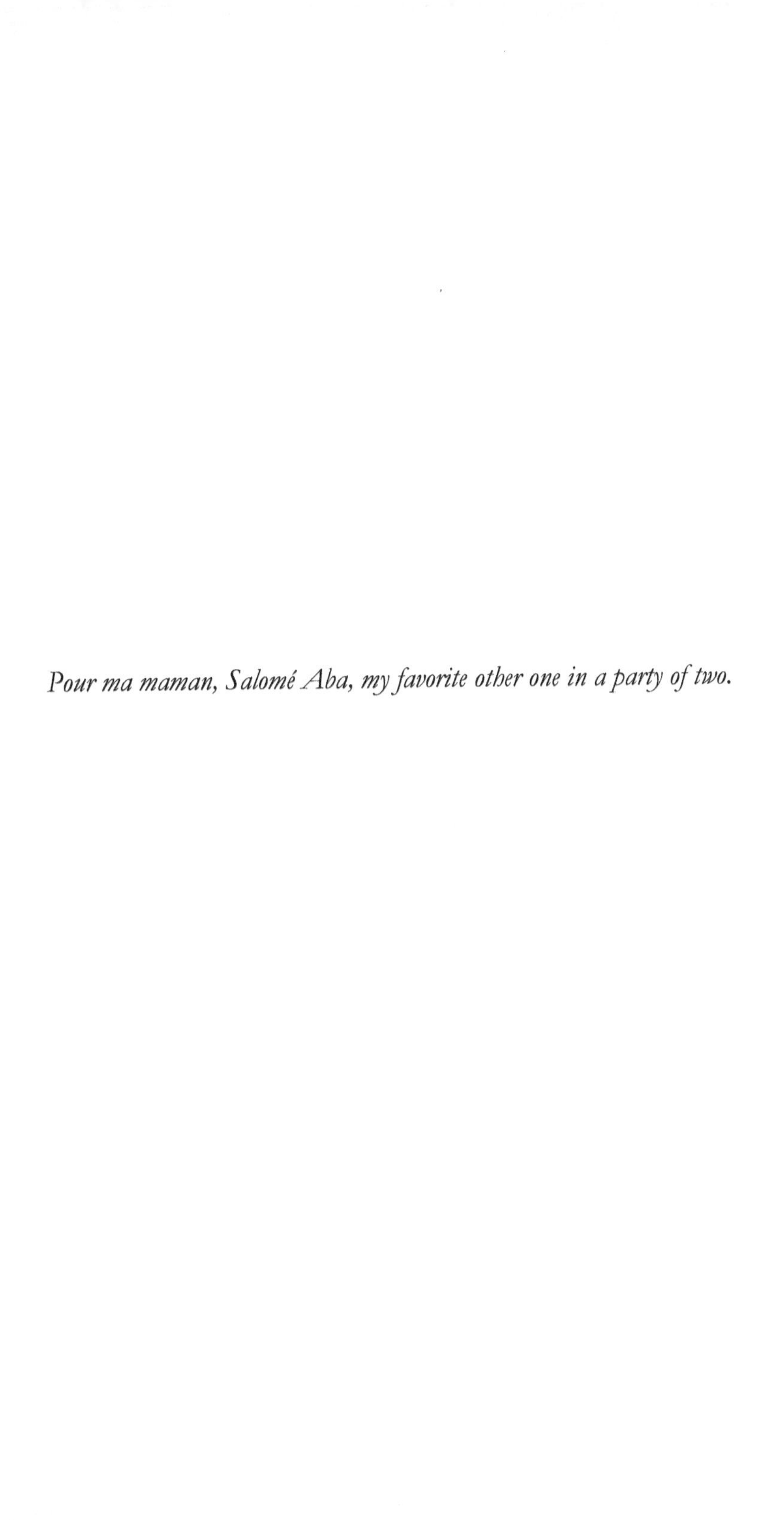

Pour ma maman, Salomé Aba, my favorite other one in a party of two.

PROLOGUE

Aisha walked in on her best friend of six years straddling her boyfriend of two shortly before the clock struck twelve.

"Are you fucking kidding me?" she yelled before slamming the door behind her.

She heard James running after her, screaming her name. "Aisha, please wait!"

She wanted to jump in her car and drive as fast and far away as she could, but she stopped and turned around. He looked even more pathetic than she had expected, his curly hair flattened at the back and sweat running down his face.

"Let me guess," she said. Her eyes were wet. "It's not what it looks like?"

"No, it is," he said, still catching his breath. "I'm in love with her. I'm sorry you had to find out this way…especially today."

Very few things could render her speechless. This was one of them. A few choice words lit up her frontal lobe. She wanted to let them out, free to damage everything in their passage. She wanted to give them full range to shatter his spirit and break him as he had broken her. But was it even worth it? It would take more energy out of her when her batteries were already low. So, she just stared at him. He was wearing the red boxer briefs she had gifted him for Valentine's Day. Was this her karmic justice?

What had she done that was so terrible that this moment was her reality?

"Go to hell," she said at last. Her voice was feeble.

She jumped in her car and left. Without any conscious thought, she drove to her favorite park. When she parked, a message from Sam appeared on her screen.

Sha, I'm so sorry. I didn't want you to find out like this. I fell in love with him. I know you might need some time but please give me a chance to explain when you're ready.

A tear filled with sadness and mostly anger rolled down her cheek. She turned her phone off. She walked to the nearest empty bench and sat down. People were walking around, singing, drinking, dancing, and hugging. Then they all counted down: ten, nine, eight, seven, six, five, four, three, two, one. Fireworks rose above the Denver skyline.

"Happy New Year!" the crowd chanted.

PART I

WEEK 1

The first thing Aisha did the following day was shave her head. She had watched *Waiting to Exhale* and similar movies one too many times. She was now convinced that a significant percentage of one's pain was stored in their hair shaft. So, cutting her hair was the natural first step toward healing.

She looked at herself in her bathroom mirror. She looked exactly like her brother. She looked like Amir with a full head of hair. But with a bald head, she was certain she could clock in at his job, and no one would notice the difference for most of the shift. Her brother was very handsome, according to Sam and everyone else. So, her looking like Amir was a compliment. The thought of Sam, however, made her break into tears. Her head was already shaved, so she had to figure out where the rest of her hurt was stored.

The next thing she did was text James and ask him to not come back home until the following week. Then, she burned all their pictures together. Obviously, bringing everything to ashes was the second step. Fire was cleansing. It pained her, but she could get through flaring all his pictures without pause.

The physically captured memories of the two years they had shared could now be swept into a dustpan. They were gone, unlike her feelings for him. It was shattering, yet she knew she could put the pieces back together. However, what was next seemed unfathomable. Sam had been her best friend for six years.

Six fucking years.

She looked at the picture they had taken just a few months ago by the mountains. Was she already sleeping with her boyfriend then? Sam always had a poker face, but Aisha could've never imagined she could hide this level of betrayal behind her eyes.

She threw all the pictures they had taken together into her fireplace in chronological order. Memory lane was more pungent than ginger, but without the soothing effects. The first picture she lit up was the one they took together at an art gallery the very first day they met. They bonded over their agreement that a red circle inside of a blue square didn't require a five-paragraph explanation. Aisha was the first one to stare at it. Boredom had led her to the gallery, and now she wondered why she had to examine these abstract paintings and pretend she understood their profound meaning.

"Yeah…I don't get this one," a raspy voice rose behind her.

"Me neither," Aisha replied. "Honestly, I don't get most of them. Especially this one." She turned around to identify the person she was speaking to. The woman was about her height and probably around the same age. She had pleasant features: an oval face, dark hair, almond eyes, and a fuller lower lip. A common face. Someone who was probably regularly told by strangers she looked like someone they knew. In fact, the woman vaguely resembled one of Aisha's cousins. That semblance of familiarity immediately made Aisha comfortable around her.

"Right. I mean, it's just a red circle inside a blue square."

Aisha chuckled. "Thank you! But they have an entire essay explanation." She pointed at the description next to the painting. "Apparently, this represents the connection between the physical and spiritual world and the harmony between water and fire."

"It's literally a red circle inside a blue square. I do not accept their explanation. Good on you for even reading that long-ass paragraph," she said, giggling.

"I didn't want to. But I got bored just looking at the square and circle. And the circle started to look like an iris." Aisha winced.

"Like Nietzsche said, if you stare long enough into the red circle inside of the blue square, it stares back." They both laughed loudly, which caused a few annoyed looks from the other people in the gallery. "I'm Samantha, by the way. But I go by Sam." She shook Aisha's hand.

And that's how their friendship began. Even after what she had walked into yesterday, she still recalled those memories with a smile. She couldn't help it yet, but she would. So, she threw everything in the fire. Sam's twenty-fifth birthday celebration, the year of her twenty-seventh. Their trip to Costa Rica the following year after Aisha's father died. She had convinced Sam to go bungee jumping with her.

"Are you crazy?" Sam had asked, slamming her pina colada on the coaster.

"C'mon, you only live once!"

"Exactly! I want to live as long as possible."

But Sam had eventually agreed. Her friend kissed the ground after touching all her body parts to confirm they were intact upon landing. Aisha ran toward her. Tears of laughter were rolling down her cheeks. She took a selfie to *immortalize* the moment: Her laughing until she cried and Sam crying until she laughed. Well, pictures were not gods. They could cease to exist. Now, they were rapidly disappearing from the relentlessness of the flames.

Amongst the ashes, there were pieces of her.

Aisha still felt immense hurt circulating through her veins. She knew the third and final step to heal: time and space. No matter how much action she took in this very moment, only time and space regenerated. She had to leave…for a while. She needed some distance. She needed some time alone to reset.

Over the last four years, Aisha had been house-sitting full-time. It was a low-stress job for the most part. She had established a decent clientele of people who trusted her. They all paid her well to watch after and care for their homes while they were away. She knew how lucky she was, so she didn't want to burn those bridges. However, her sanity came first. She sent an email out to all her clients.

Hello [Name], I hope this email finds you well. I'm reaching out to inform you that I have some personal matters to tend to, so I will not be able to house-sit for the next few months. I'm not quite sure how long I will need to be away yet, but I will make sure to contact you as soon as I know. I'm very thankful you have chosen me to work with you over the last few [time]. I hope this opportunity will still be on the table upon my return.

Thanks for your understanding!
Sincerely,
Aisha Jones

Within a few hours, all her clients replied to her to confirm that the job was hers when she would return. They all wished her well. A few also let her know they would keep her in their thoughts and prayers and hoped whatever she was going through would be sorted out soon. Aisha could feel her eyes water again.

She had a decent amount of money in her checking account. Enough to pay the bills for a few months, but not enough to live on. Some of her father's life insurance had been sitting in a savings account for the past three years. She hated to do it, but she knew it was the only way to sustain herself for an extended period without working. She had promised herself not to touch that money unless it was a matter of life or death. This wasn't a life-threatening situation, but it was dire enough.

Finally, having a father would serve another purpose in her life. Up until now, he had only played a role in providing a sperm cell filled with his DNA. She owed him her almond-shaped eyes, deep dark complexion, and naturally sinewy physique. However, she had only had three in-person interactions with him in twenty-eight years, before he passed away in a car accident three years ago.

Aisha and Amir were shocked when their mother told them they were the beneficiaries of two of his life insurances. She didn't ask her brother how he planned to use his money, but she knew she didn't want to use hers unless it was absolutely necessary. She didn't want her father to contribute anything to her life, even from the beyond.

Yet, at this moment, she had to admit that she needed the funds he left her. Practicality had to override pride. She logged into the savings account and moved some funds to her checking account.

*

Over the next few days, she made all the arrangements for her getaway. She set all the accounts she couldn't cancel to autopay. She logged out of all her social media accounts. Sam and James knew better than to try to contact her too soon, but she knew they eventually would. So, she changed her phone number and only sent the new one to her brother and mother. She just told them she was taking an extended vacation and would keep in touch. They sent drinks and palm tree emojis in response to their family group chat.

She didn't know how to explain what had happened to them. They both liked James. They adored Sam. She had no doubt they would be in her corner, yet she didn't have the strength to break the news to them. Sharing what happened would force her to examine the implications and consequences. She was nowhere near ready to do that.

Now, it was just a matter of figuring out where she would go. She hadn't traveled that much to have a strong preference. She wrote the other forty-nine states on individual shredded pieces of paper. She put them in a bowl and shook it vigorously. She closed her eyes and let her hand search through the papers. She picked the one with the sharpest edges and opened her eyes to read: Texas. She sighed.

She wasn't sure what she had expected, but Texas hadn't crossed her mind. Oh, well. Fate had decided, and she wouldn't go against it. When she thought of Texas, she immediately thought of cowboys (of course). Dallas Cowboys. It wasn't the most sophisticated process, but at least she had a destination. She booked a hotel in Downtown Dallas and packed her bags.

WEEK 2

The drive to Dallas was excruciating. Halfway there, she seriously considered turning around. She was being so dramatic. She had shaved her head, paused her work, and left everything behind because of two people? If the next exit hadn't been for another twenty-three miles, she might've just taken it and returned home. But thoughts also accelerated at eighty miles per hour. James and Sam's affair had been the drop that had caused the glass to overflow, but their little sexcapade hadn't filled the container. Individually, they had definitely poured some water into it, but her father, brother, and mother also had. She had suppressed those emotions for too long, and now they were spilling out. She was capsizing.

She arrived at her hotel early in the evening. The Dallas traffic was ungodly, somehow worse than Denver. She cursed herself for letting pieces of paper inside a bowl decide for her. She was rightfully afraid to trust her decision-making, but that would've been the better course of action. She could've at least done some research and weighed the pros and cons for each state.

Who was she kidding? She was typically not so irrational to go as far as making choices based on the lottery. However, she was a head-first kind of gal. And that had led to her standing in front of a wooded hotel entrance decorated with cowboy and horse statues. Great. She could not get back in her car and drive anywhere right now. She was way too tired to even consider it.

Thankfully, she had only booked the hotel for two weeks. Her original plan was to use that time to look for a furnished apartment. Instead, she could use the daytime to play tourist. Then, in the evening, she could research other places where the roads were friendlier, and everything wasn't screaming "yeehaw" at her. She already felt her body relaxing from knowing she had an exit plan. Having a way out had always given her comfort.

*

Aisha woke up the next day, unable to remember the last time she had slept so profoundly. The kind of sleep that made you question where you were and what day it was when you awoke. From her window, she could discern the skyline on the horizon wasn't the one under the fireworks a week ago. She knew she wasn't home. Though she was over eight hundred miles away, the memories of the betrayal had followed her. How could they? How could she?

How could he?

James had rushed to pick up all her belongings when they had bumped into each other at a coffee shop two years ago. She couldn't believe how cliché their "How did you two meet?" story was. She always rolled her eyes when characters locked eyes after bumping into each other in movies. Yet, there she was, a grown twenty-nine-year-old woman, slowly getting up without breaking eye contact with her future love interest.

"I'm so sorry," the deep brown-eyed man said, handing her back her belongings. "Are you okay?"

Yes, she was okay. More than okay. She was absolutely bewitched for the entirety of their first year together. Then, slowly, quietly, something stealthy happened. At first, it wasn't noticeable enough to cause concerns, but it was perceptible enough to know things didn't feel quite the same. But wasn't that how life worked? Things were meant to change. She figured their love was adapting to their routine, to their inevitable human transformation over time. There wasn't anything to worry about, right?

The glaring sunlight summoned her back to reality. Dallas earned a point for being warmer. She looked around the space. It was so sanitized. There was something alleviating about the impersonality and sterility of a hotel room. Perhaps the lack of commitment and effort required on the patron's end. The exchange was clear. No blurred lines.

She paid for the room, and in exchange, she could come and go as she pleased. She didn't have to add any value to the space. All she had to do was leave it the way she found it. At the very least not damage it. She wished human relationships were that straightforward, but they weren't. The line's demarcation was usually unclear. The exchange was never even. The input was, more often than not, not reciprocal. And it was always damaging. Always.

*

Aisha had been driving around all day, mainly bumper to bumper, even though most highways had five to six lanes. Dallas was enormous, with freeways everywhere. She took random exits at random times to grab some food or use the restrooms. She had neither a plan nor a destination. She might as well have returned to the hotel now to figure out where she wanted to go next.

Aside from the insane traffic, Dallas was perfectly lovely, though. It was a bit boisterous with its infinite roads, overabundant restaurant selections, giant trucks, unnecessarily large buildings, and general loudness. But the city had its charm. People were friendly for the most part, and all the food she tasted seemed to be flavored with pride and industriousness. She just felt like she needed to keep moving.

She made a right turn at an intersection and felt the right side of her car lower to the ground. Her tire pressure icon lit up. She parked at the nearest parking lot and stepped outside of her car. Her front right tire was flat. She sat back inside her car and screamed. She stayed with her face inside of her palms for a solid minute. She knew nothing would change until she did something about it, so she looked for the nearest mechanic shop.

When Aisha pulled into the auto shop, the right side of her car was screaming for help. The place was five miles from the incident, so there was no telling what was left of her damaged tire when she parked her car. She didn't even want to look. She hadn't taken care of any car issues over the last two years. James had. But it wasn't like she didn't know how to handle these things. She was functional and self-sufficient before him. He was simply better at this kind of stuff than her. She hated to admit any of his qualities now, but she couldn't erase her memory. One thing he taught her was to always ask for a quote first, even if she desperately needed a service. It gave the illusion of competency and access to other options.

Aisha held her shoulders back and walked into the lobby. The man behind the counter was surprisingly handsome. Not that mechanics were not attractive. He just looked like he should've been on one of the covers of the magazines spread on the table to his right and not in front of her, wearing a soiled wife beater under an unbuttoned coverall.

"Hello, ma'am. How can I help you today?"

Ma'am? Ugh. "Hello. I have a flat tire. Could you give me a quote, please?"

He looked pensive, his two hands under his chiseled jaw. What was there to think about? The car was parked outside. He finally parted his lips to say: "I've learned that people will forget what you said, people will forget what you did, but people will never forget how you made them feel. Maya Angelou. My favorite quote."

She must have been delirious from exhaustion and his good looks because she laughed. She knew for certain she wasn't in her optimal state of mind then. Under normal circumstances, this type of bullshit would've garnered an eye roll or a sigh from her. But this was her first human interaction of the year that wasn't entirely transactional. She could, at the very least, humor him.

"Good one," she said, still smiling. "Don't quit your day job, though."

He laughed. "Alright, alright. Let me take a look. Please have a seat. Help yourself to some coffee and snacks if you'd like." He pointed at the coffee and crackers next to the magazines.

"Thank you." She watched him walk outside. She had never seen someone so well-proportioned. He had light brown eyes and heart-shaped lips that softened his sharp facial bone structure. *God took his time when he made him.*

He walked back inside as quickly as he had walked out. He gave her the quote. She knew it was fair. In fact, it was cheaper than the last time she had to replace a tire. She nodded in agreement.

"It'll just be about twenty minutes," he said.

"Thank you so much."

"It's no problem." His right eye closed and opened again, while the left remained open the whole time. Did he…wink at her?

Aisha gave him a double take before he walked out. She eventually noticed there were other people around. An older woman and a teenage boy were seated next to a table with various magazines. Other mechanics were working on different cars. They were louder than the engines they were working on. The lobby smelled like sweat, air freshener, and car oil. She grabbed one of the fashion magazines and sat quietly in the corner of the room. She browsed through all the pages to confirm the hot mechanic wasn't moonlighting as a model.

At last, the sound of keys shaking invited her out of the two-dimensional journal and back to her 3D reality.

"All set," the mechanic said. He motioned for her to follow him to the counter.

"Wow, that was quick. You're amazing!"

"I do what I can," he said, slightly flushed. "If you have any other car trouble, here's my card." He paused for a second. "Feel free to reach out to me anytime…for anything."

"Carlos," she read the name on the card. Then she looked at him. "I will."

It wasn't until Aisha returned to the hotel that she realized she hadn't given him her name. The whole exchange was so exciting that she forgot to do one of the only mandatory things required for prolonged human interaction: introduction.

"James, this is Sam, my best friend. Sam, James, the guy that I've been talking about," Aisha had said as they all sat down in her living room.

James and Sam didn't hug. They shook hands. Aisha was the one who had to break the ice.

"You both played basketball in high school." She looked back and forth at them, hoping to establish a common ground. She wanted them to get along and like each other. Her wish was granted with a level of irony only the universe could deliver.

In the present moment, she wasn't ready for anything, let alone dating. Not even a platonic relationship. But a little attention from a handsome man had never hurt anyone, right? She picked up Carlos's card and saved his number.

WEEK 3

Aisha hadn't decided to stay in Dallas because of Carlos. The Southern charm was just working its sweet and flavorful magic on her. A couple of weeks weren't enough to soak it all in. She loved that people made eye contact and smiled when their eyes met. She loved the cheerful greetings when she walked into a business. It was the universal exaggerated and enthusiastic greeting any potential customer got. However, here, the greetings had an additional quality. It was similar to the way the food tasted. She needed that warmth.

She found a furnished apartment a short distance from downtown. She could afford to furnish a space but didn't want to. She wanted to keep things as impersonal as possible so she wouldn't leave any imprints or feel tied down. Aisha knew her commitment issues were merely daddy issues, all grown up. Identifying the root cause of an issue didn't resolve it. And was it an issue, anyway?

Who had decided that sticking with something regardless of the circumstances was a more significant achievement than choosing not to? Her father had decided that being fifty percent responsible for making her a whole human didn't warrant that he should be part of her life. She despised him for it. However, the older she got, the more she understood the appeal of not being bound.

In fact, James had been the one to ask, "What are we?"

Aisha knew the question was coming. She could tell by the way his eyes lit up after they kissed.

She cleared her throat. "Two lovely people who enjoy each other's company." Her grin was too broad, and her body was stiff.

"I need clarity, Aisha. It's been seven months."

She had always found a way to end things before they reached that point. She knew she was vulnerable and raw past it. But like a snake charmer, James had figured out a way to hypnotize her.

She held his hand. "Well, what about a girlfriend and boyfriend who enjoy each other's company?" She pressed her lips against his. He beamed.

Then, she was moving to the sound of his waves, unable to remember why she had fought that soothing feeling in the first place. But now she remembered: Love was volatile, insidious, noncommittal. It lured you in with the promise of forever, took you in an embrace that felt so safe you lowered all your guards, and when you were at its mercy, inside of its arms, it crushed you.

*

There were many art museums and galleries in Dallas. After meeting Sam in one of the galleries in Denver, she had grown fond of visiting them, but not for the appropriate reasons. She especially enjoyed staring at abstract art after identifying the extravagant cost, so she could feel indignant about the lengths people would go to appear sophisticated and enlightened.

Now, Aisha strolled along the narrow halls of a commercial gallery. Colorful paintings, sculptures, and photographs followed her footsteps on both sides. The glossy concrete floor supported bright white walls. A young woman with long pink braids stood a few feet away. She turned to look at Aisha—not in the eyes, a little higher.

"I love your hair," the woman said with a wide grin.

"Thank you! I love yours, too."

Aisha hadn't thought about her bald head that much. She mostly remembered it when the weather decided to sport a breeze. Sometimes, she caught a few looks. She could recognize the primary emotions: confusion, admiration, shock, or, her favorite, indifference. She didn't really care about her new look herself. Perhaps, if she were trying to date, she would. Admittedly, men preferred long hair. Not all, but the majority. It seemed like having short hair was a hindrance that needed to be offset by an outstanding personality. Attraction was epidermic deep. This made Carlos even more intriguing. To be clear, she was far from being the Hunchback of Notre Dame because of her bald head. The style worked for her. Yet she knew her prospects had taken a hit or a cut, pun intended. But again, she wasn't trying to date.

All she wanted to do was look at something objectively beautiful. The painting in front of her wasn't it. So, she pulled out her phone and texted the handsome mechanic.

Hey Carlos! This is Aisha (the girl with the flat tire...you gave me a quote lol) My car is ok but I'm new in town. Mind showing me around maybe next week?

Within an instant, her phone lit up. *Hey Aisha! I was hoping to hear from u. I dont mind at all. Let me look into some fun things we could do & I'll get back to u soon!*

It was the first time she felt excited this year. She put her phone in her pocket and looked back at what was before her. She didn't know which was more outrageous: the price tag or the piece itself. It was worth more than what she still owed on her car. It took her a good five minutes to determine what she was looking at. She didn't read the description because she wanted to figure it out on her own.

After squinting, walking away from the canvas, and then closer again, she realized that she was staring at a large vulva inside a smaller vulva, inside of an even smaller one, and so on, until the smallest one was a dot. She couldn't contain her laughter. She didn't think vulvas were funny, but there was something comical about the way the artist painted them. It was theatrical. The genitals looked extraterrestrial. She understood it was art, yet something told her the person behind this piece wasn't a woman. She looked for the artist's name under the description: David Marshall.

"I knew it!" she said, pumping her fist.

"Knew what?" a deep, sultry voice echoed.

She looked to her right. The man beside her had to be at least ten years her senior. Aside from the colorful scarf he was wearing, everything about him was drab. His skin was pale white, and his blond hair was washed out.

"I knew the artist behind this piece was a man," she said without skipping a beat.

His lips widened in a small smile. "Why?"

"A woman would've been rawer with her depiction. This looks curated, like an opinion. It seems second-hand. It's the way someone views something instead of the way it is."

"Astute." He broke eye contact with the piece and directed it at her. "To whom do I have the pleasure of speaking?"

His formality rubbed on her. "Miss Aisha Jones."

He extended his hand for a shake. "David Marshall. Miss Aisha Jones, it's a pleasure."

She wondered if she looked like a cartoon character with big, widened eyes and jaw on the floor. Unless it was the oddest coincidence, she was speaking to the man who had created the very expensive painting she was just laughing at.

She tried to maintain her composure. "Likewise, David Marshall. Good work!"

He laughed very quietly. "I don't think this one has won you over, but thank you, Aisha."

"No, I love it…" He looked at her like, *you can be honest.* She put her hands on her hips. "Okay, maybe I wouldn't hang this in my living room. But it's definitely intriguing. Tell me, what inspired you to paint this?"

"Lust."

His straightforwardness made her like him a little more. "Now, I can get behind that!"

He laughed harder, yet the sound was still barely audible. "Are you an artist, Aisha?"

"No. I just like looking at interesting stuff."

"Well, we have something in common." He was still smiling. "I have an expo in two weeks. I'd like for you to stop by if you're free, of course. I'm interested in hearing your take on my other pieces." He handed her a card and a flyer.

"David, I must tell you, I'm not an expert. I don't know how valuable my opinion would be."

"You have a sharp eye, Aisha Jones." He started walking away. "I hope to see you there." He finished without turning around.

She sighed. She hadn't come to Dallas to collect men's business cards. She had driven eight hundred miles away to be alone and heal from the pain that had been growing inside of her. The one she had ignored for years until it was bigger than anything else inside of her, tightening her vital organs until she couldn't ignore it anymore. Perhaps she shouldn't further her interactions with Carlos and David.

She would be lying if she said she wasn't intrigued by both men. They both seemed to be interesting human beings. And for the nth time, she wasn't interested in dating. She just wanted to get to know some nice people along her healing journey. The two men probably weren't interested in her in *that* way either. They were merely decent people. Furthermore, she had no ties to this city. If things got too overwhelming, she could leave.

*

That evening, she made a reservation at a steakhouse just a short distance from her hotel. She finally felt like dressing up. She had been wearing her go-to knee-high boots, sweaters, and leggings over the last couple of weeks. Since her mood had slightly improved, she reckoned time and space were starting to do their job.

However, she had actively avoided thinking about the event that caused her to be in the state where everything was bigger—including the cowboy boots she wore that evening. She had kept herself busy and had found something to do anytime the thoughts of New Year's Eve decided to haunt her. She knew she'd eventually have to face those ghosts. She just wanted to postpone that encounter as long as her mind could pretend they weren't in the attic.

Aisha walked inside of the restaurant.

"Hello, miss. Do you have a reservation?" the hostess asked her.

"Yes, for Aisha Jones. 8:30 PM."

"Is it just going to be you this evening?"

"Yes."

"Alright, party of one coming in," the woman whispered into a walkie-talkie. "Please follow me," she said to Aisha.

WEEK 4

Her new seven-hundred-square-foot apartment was very generic and beige, precisely what she wanted. To ease her mind, she had signed a month-to-month lease agreement. She was only contractually bound for four weeks. She could handle that length of commitment. After unpacking, she looked around the apartment. The stainless-steel appliances, the granite countertops, the wood coffee table, and the beige sofa were new and shiny.

At the very least, this would be her home for the next four weeks.

When she finally settled in, lonesomeness did as well. Sharing a hotel with other guests had shielded her from feeling completely alone. Even though she didn't speak to a single person for the duration of her stay, seeing people before walking inside her empty room filled a void within her. Now, she'd have to figure out another way to pour into that space.

Lonesomeness was, in almost every regard, a black hole. She was stuck inside of it and couldn't find a way out. It sucked everything out of her except dejection. Those feelings were not new to her, but they intensified in Dallas. Everything was indeed bigger in Texas.

Even when Aisha's life was at its fullest, there had always been a sneaky presence within her. An emptiness hidden somewhere below her breastbone. A greedy void that demanded space only to fill it with nothing. She had busied her life with all the people and activities she could handle to cover it. But all a cover did was put something on top of something else. The thing was still there, underneath. All it took was a little wind to blow the covering away and be exposed.

She recalled sharing those feelings with her brother a year before their father's fatal car accident.

"Can I talk to you about something?" she said after sitting on Amir's red futon. She bit her lip and tapped her foot on the hardwood floor.

"Uh-oh. What's going on, little sis?" She was two years older than her brother. "Talk to me," he invited while patting her knee.

"I don't know. I just feel off. The whole thing with Mom…" She paused. She couldn't handle talking about what happened with their mother. "I guess Albert not giving the smallest shit to even stick around for me or you. I feel like it's all getting to me." Amir was listening quietly. She glanced at her brother's faux brick wall, then looked back at him. "Do you ever have those feelings?"

"Yes. It was really bad for a while. It's better now. Mom and Dad were really young when they had me, and even younger when they had you. He's not a monster, you know. Just a flawed human being."

"Since when do you call him *Dad*?" The word felt foreign coming out of her mouth. It left a bitter taste she wanted to brush off. "I thought you hated him."

"I know, but it was eating me alive. I couldn't go on like that. I've been talking to him more often. And you know often for him isn't even the frequency of the Olympics." Amir smiled. Aisha didn't. Her brother continued. "He's just fucked up, Sha. I feel sorry for him."

She huffed. "I'm sorry, what? *You* feel sorry for him? Are you kidding? News flash: he abandoned us, not the other way around. He does not get a pass because of whatever bullshit excuse he fed you." She didn't speak for a moment. Amir didn't say anything. She shook her head. "I can't believe you've been talking to him without telling me."

"I knew you'd react like this. Little sis, listen to your big brother. You can't go on like this. You'll have to forgive him or at least let go of this anger."

Usually, Amir's "little sis, big bro" gimmick softened her, but not this time. "Whatever," she said and rolled her eyes.

Aisha was hurt. Her brother was the only person who understood the root of her pain. The only person who had shared it and lived it. She felt less alone when he felt the same way she did. Someone could relate. Someone got it. Not anymore.

Now, Aisha shook her head. She needed to get away from her intrusive thoughts. There was a beautiful two-in-one bookstore and coffee bar near her place. She had driven past it a few times. This was the perfect day to spend there.

From outside, *Libros & Libations* looked like a farmhouse. She was transported back to the eighties when she walked inside the book café. Colors yelled at her eyes in a manner that managed to be endearing, like an old wise guy in a Scorsese film. There were vinyl records on the opposite side of the books. The bar was somewhere in the back.

She didn't know what she was in the mood to drink, but she knew what she wanted to read. A thriller would keep her mind occupied. When deciding what to read, Aisha always judged a book by its cover first—like everyone else. She picked up a few books. Neither the covers nor the blurbs resonated with her. They were not dramatic and catastrophic enough. She needed something objectively worse than her circumstances, so she continued her search.

At last, at the bottom of the shelf, she saw the one: *Between the Riverbank.* The cover illustrated a dark-haired woman sitting at the edge of a dock, under the moonlight, looking at the horizon at a hand sinking below the water. The description on the back cover confirmed she had found what she was looking for. The protagonist, Jane, couldn't fight her past, so she decided to embrace it. The consequences promised to be deadly.

Aisha walked toward the bar with the book in her hand. A huge sign let her know her second drink would be on the house if she purchased a book. She was planning on buying the book anyway. She hadn't planned on getting more than one drink, but free stuff made you change your plans. She ordered her non-free drink.

"One Irish coffee," the grunge bartender yelled to no one.

She sat on one of the couches by the vinyl records. It was midafternoon on a weekday, so the place wasn't bustling. Just a few college-aged people, a group of women enjoying some mimosas, and an older man with round glasses so deep in his book she was afraid it would swallow him whole.

Aisha began sipping her hot beverage as she turned the pages. Jane's turbulent upbringing didn't waste any time introducing itself. Alcoholic parents. Foster homes. Homelessness. Aisha wondered if Jane would be the murderer or the sinking hand. She ordered her second drink and charged the house. She was now competing with the old man with round glasses to see who would get swallowed by the pages first. She looked at him. The spaces between his glasses and his book had severely tightened. He would absolutely disappear first. She chuckled at how little it took to entertain her. Before she could plunge back into *Between the Riverbank*, the front door of the book café opened.

The man who walked in could fit into a 6x2 rectangle. Every step he took was tight and precise. He was dressed casually in a white sweater and blue jeans, but his demeanor was polished and formal. His dark skin was clear, his cut was low and perfectly lined up, and his shoulders were broad and square. When Aisha realized she had stared at his entire entrance, she quickly looked back at her book. She held her breath, hoping it would erase her lingering stare. Then, she felt the breeze from his walking past her. Before she could exhale, the man spoke.

"Great read," he said.

She looked up. His face had a candor she hadn't expected. "Yes, I just got started."

"You'll enjoy it." He grinned, then walked away.

She exhaled and plunged back into the pages. The old man with round glasses left when she was a hundred pages in. Later, there were more groups of women, though they were drinking wine then, not mimosas. The college-aged people had multiplied. More people around her age were also spread around. Polished Guy was gone, and she wasn't sure when he had left. To be fair, Jane had found out her second husband had another family thirty miles away in Little Rock.

Aisha had been so lost in the pages that everything that happened in the coffeehouse in the meanwhile was a mystery harder to solve than the disappearance of Jane's first husband. When Jane started stalking the mistress who had borne her husband's children, Aisha knew she would be the murderer. She just wasn't sure whether she would kill her husband or his mistress. She laid her bookmark on page one hundred sixty-eight and closed the book.

*

The next day, she woke up to a message from Carlos. She thought it was too early to text until she saw that it was almost noon.

Good morning Aisha, he wrote. Instead of punctuation, he used a sunshine emoji. *There is a fun dance festival Downtown this weekend. We can dance on the streets walk around grab some food & drinks. How does that sound?*

She stretched out loudly before replying, *That sounds like my weekend plans!*

The day she met Carlos he looked even more handsome than she remembered. How was that possible? She figured being *wife-beaterless* helped. He was wearing a fitted overcoat and a beanie. Aisha's hair had grown about half an inch, enough to protect her scalp from the Southern elements, so she only wore a light jacket and leggings.

"You're not going to be cold?" Carlos said.

"I'm from Colorado."

"Ah!" He nodded. "So, how long have you been in Dallas?" They were strolling down the rowdy avenue. People were strolling or pacing past them. It was a long street with restaurants, coffee shops, ice cream shops, bars, food trucks, and other businesses on both sides.

"About three weeks."

"Oh, so you're brand new!"

"Yes." She smiled at his excitement. "What about you? Where are you from?"

"Born and bred in Dallas, Texas," he said with an exaggerated twang. "What brings you here?" he asked with his normal tone.

Betrayal. Hurt. Gloom. "Just needed a change of scene." She looked down.

"I see." He looked to his right and halted his steps. "Have you had some tacos and frozen margaritas yet?"

"Not yet."

He grabbed her hands and led her to the closest food truck. A few people frowned or shook their heads as they cut through the crowd to make it to the food truck on the street corner. Thankfully, the line wasn't long, so their orders were ready within fifteen minutes. They sat on a picnic bench to eat. Aisha wasn't a fan of tacos, but those made her reconsider her stance.

"Pretty good, huh?" Carlos said when he saw her empty plate.

"Not bad." She licked her fingers.

Music started playing somewhere above them. People sang and danced wherever they stood. Aisha yelled above the sound. "How long have you been working at the mechanic shop?"

"Seven years," he said just as loud.

"Do you like it?"

"It's a job. Well, a family business. I inherited the shop when my father passed away."

She regretted asking the question. The fact that they both had a dead dad who had left them an inheritance didn't make her feel good. It made her feel like the universe was having, yet again, a great time at her expense.

"I'm sorry."

"It's okay. It's been a while."

She could tell it wasn't okay, but she couldn't help but pry. The concept of *father* was so foreign to her that whenever someone shared a story about their male parent, she attempted to live victoriously through it to hopefully graze a piece of the unconditional love she wasn't granted.

"Were you two very close?"

His features shrunk. "Yes, he was my hero." He drank the rest of his margarita in one gulp. "Let's dance!"

Before she could agree, he lifted her and began twirling her around. Loosened from the drink and filled up from the delicious tacos, her body didn't resist. They danced for hours as the people seated on the picnic benches around them left, and new people took their place.

Shortly before the sun went down, she saw a spark in Carlos's eyes. A light that was too pure, too hopeful. The way he looked at her made her feel both nervous and happy. She shrugged her worry away and enjoyed the rest of the night. She had so much fun. In fact, Aisha had such a great time with Carlos that when she got home, she decided she wouldn't see him again.

WEEK 5

The vibration of her phone woke Aisha up. It could only be two people. Well, three. However, she doubted Carlos would already be contacting her. She was hoping he wouldn't do it all. She hated that she would have to ignore him if he did. He was a nice guy. His life didn't need to be tainted by the dirty mess that was hers.

She looked at the name on the screen. "Hey, Mom. Good morning."

"Good morning?" Her mother laughed. "You must be having a blast on your extended vacation. Where are you, anyway?"

She sat up. "I'm in Dallas."

"Oh, I bet the weather is nice over there right now!"

"Yes."

"Are you okay? You don't sound well."

"I'm fine. Just tired."

"Okay." Her mother cleared her throat. "Make sure to drink lots of fluids."

"Okay."

"Oh, how's Sam? I haven't heard from her since you left."

"She should be fine."

No one spoke for a moment.

Her mother broke the silence. "Hmm…okay. And How's James?"

"He's fine." Aisha's voice was monotone.

"Alright, that's good. Well, I just wanted to check on you. I haven't heard from you in a while. Glad to hear you're fine."

"Thanks."

"Well, okay. I'll let you get back to it then. Bye-bye."

"Bye."

Aisha exhaled the moment the call ended. She still hadn't forgiven her mother. She thought time and space would've naturally healed the wound by now, but they hadn't. She could still feel the tear on her heart, deep and intact.

She took another breath and checked the weather on her phone. It was even nicer outside today. It was ideal for a nature walk. She wasn't the most active person, especially since she had been blessed with genetics that falsely portrayed vigor. Her frame rarely fluctuated, no matter what she did or didn't do. She looked in her closet and picked anything that looked to belong on a hiking trail. Then, she drove to the closest trail near her apartment and started walking.

After Aisha ignored the burning sensation in between her thighs, at the center of her chest, behind her knees, around her ankles—let's not even talk about her lower back—the walk began to feel decent. Eventually, she remembered that she had a mouth, so she opened it to help the air flow in and out. The burning simmered down. Her heart rate evened out. Then, the sun caressed her skin as if congratulating her for not giving up—a measly prize, in her opinion.

Everyone else looked fine. Hikers passed her, chit-chatting as if walking wasn't an activity that required their full attention. Runners didn't even seem human. They floated away at five miles per hour, probably heading back to their planet. Bikers flashed by her left side, using their calves as engines. Yet nature was calm and steady, containing it all.

Aisha sat on a bench to stretch before driving away. Though she was tired, she felt better than before her stroll. She would do this more often—okay, she would try to. She stood up and extended one leg on the length of the bench, attempting to create a ninety-degree angle. She was about twenty degrees from her goal when her muscles and bones begged her to remember who she was. She conceded in pain. She put her hands on her lower back. The effort contorted her body.

"Are you okay, girl?"

She turned around very slowly. "Yes, thank you. It's been a while since I walked this much. Maybe at the mall, but the clothes are a good distraction not to notice."

The woman laughed. Her smile was bright, and her face was open. Her energy matched the peaceful nature around them. "I hear you, girl. Well, get you some good rest. You deserve it."

"Thank you. Enjoy your walk!"

"Thank you!" The woman smiled and then resumed her fast-paced thread. Her honey-brown curls were bouncing at the same speed.

People were so friendly in this city. Aisha was glad she had decided to stay. Now, she desperately wanted to return to her apartment and lie on her bed. She was exhausted, but her stomach growling rose above the fatigue. She hadn't cooked a single meal over the last month. Wow. It had already been one month. It wasn't as if time had flown by, though. She could feel it every single day, accumulating on top of her shoulders, lowering her posture. Her resolve.

When Aisha arrived at the restaurant, she stood by the "Please wait to be seated" sign. She ate out ninety-five percent of the time. She wanted to be alone but surrounded. She wanted to hear banter, laughter, crying, arguing, life. She wanted to get a glimpse of what was awaiting her at the end of the healing tunnel.

The host greeted her with a formal nod. "Hello, ma'am. How can I help you?"

"I'd like a table, please."

"How many people in your party?"

"Just me today."

The host cracked a small smile. "Please follow me."

*

The flyer David Marshall had given her was resting on her kitchen counter. His expo was in a couple of days. Given that she had decided not to engage with Carlos further, she wondered whether she should go to David's exposition. She didn't want to make a habit of building bridges, only to immediately light them on fire. The difference was that the exchange with Carlos had a hint of flirtatiousness from the very beginning. She had barely exchanged two words with the Vulva Artist. He was merely curious about her opinion of his art. And she had enjoyed having an attentive ear to appreciate her "sharp eye." A little human interaction couldn't hurt.

Two days later, she drove to David's expo. The difficulty of finding a parking spot let her know David Marshall's event was no small matter. She finally squeezed her compact car between two giant trucks. The gallery wasn't very large, yet it was more crowded than a New York subway in the early evening. She knew it for sure because she had been in one that year she spent Thanksgiving in the Big Apple with Sam's family.

"How are things going with you and James?" Sam had asked under a tall stranger's elbow.

"Good, actually. One month as an official couple, and I don't feel the feral urge to flee yet."

"Aw! My little stray's getting domesticated. I'm proud of you. You know, at first, I wasn't sure about the guy, but I like him now. He's good for you."

"What made you change your mind?"

"The way he looks at you when you're not looking. He loves you."

Aisha's eyes doubled in size. It was one thing being girlfriend and boyfriend, but love was an entirely different beast. "Slow your roll there, sis. We can revisit that love talk in seven to twelve business months." Sam and the tall stranger chuckled. Aisha smiled. "Anyway, when are you ending your dating fast? I'm ready to laugh at some ridiculous online dating profiles again."

"Sorry, your entertainment will have to wait another four business months. I'm going for the full year."

Now, Aisha walked down the gallery, looking for a piece with the least amount of people staring at it, whispering about texture, color palettes, lines, and how it somehow explained the meaning of life. In one corner, a piece was by itself. It was one of the only non-abstract paintings. Just a regular human woman lying on the grass and looking at the sky. And for once, Aisha would agree that life's meaning was somewhere on the canvas, existing in the sky's reflection in the woman's eyes.

The more she noticed the details in the woman's irises, the more emotional she became. The woman didn't look spectacular. Nothing about her was remarkable. Aisha knew the moment she would walk away, she would forget the woman's face. But she would never forget the contentment and peace in the woman's eyes. How could she get there? A tear rolled down her cheek.

"I had a feeling you'd like this one." The sultry voice warmed her skin.

She didn't move an inch. "Why?"

"Because it appears simple, almost cliché, until you focus on it. Then it hits you. The eyes. And you can't stop looking at them because not only is the sky reflected into them, but so are you." The man got closer. "You don't like frills, do you, Aisha?"

He was right, but she disliked when people thought they had her figure it out. "Who does?"

David smiled. "Thank you for stopping by. I was hoping you'd come."

She wanted to ask why but feared that the answer would force her to never see him again. "You didn't tell me you were a big shot. I almost had to park in a random apartment complex and risk getting towed to make it here." David laughed in that almost inaudible manner of his. Aisha got a step closer to the painting. "So far, my ranking is *The Sky in Her Eyes*, then *Vulva Wormhole*."

He blinked and looked at her like she had grown a second head. "Have you looked at any other paintings yet?"

She tittered. "No, but I feel very strongly about those two."

"Well, why don't we grab a drink afterward, and you could catch me up on your latest ranking."

Well, it was nice knowing you, David Marshall. "I won't be able to do that today. I actually have to head out soon, but I have your card."

He smiled and maintained an intense stare. Somehow, it didn't make her feel uncomfortable. It made her feel observed.

"Yes, you have my card." He turned around. "*The Sky in her Eyes*, I can make my peace with. But *Vulva Wormhole*? I expect better from you, Aisha Jones."

They both laughed as David walked away. Her laughter swallowed his. When he disappeared into the cheering crowd, Aisha left through the back exit.

WEEK 6

What's goin on, Sha? Sam sent me a cryptic message indirectly askin where you were and if you were okay. Is everything alright? Amir texted her.

Please don't tell her where I am and do NOT give her my new number. I'll explain later. She hit the letters on the keyboard like they were her opponent in a boxing ring.

Fine. Can you at least confirm that you r okay? This is for internal use only

She laughed. *Yes big bro. Fine as cream gravy.* She added the emoji with the cowboy hat at the end.

Lord

What's up with you? How are things with Thomas?

We broke up last month

Aisha almost dropped her phone. On one hand, she was hurt that her brother didn't tell her about the end of his three-year relationship. On the other hand, she had still not told him about the simultaneous end of her two-year relationship and six-year friendship. Amir didn't know that, though. He was the better sibling. The one who had dealt with all his trauma. He shouldn't act like her. She called him while tapping her foot on her living room's hardwood floor.

"What, cowgirl?"

"Why didn't you tell me about Thomas?"

"I don't know. I guess I was waiting for the right time."

"What the hell happened? You guys were perfect together."

"You're not the only commitment-phobe, Sha. It got a little too real, so I panicked."

"What? How? Why?"

"I saw that he was looking at rings on his laptop. I freaked out. I didn't tell him I saw it. I just started making comments about marriage just being a piece of paper blah blah blah. Like the smart man he is, he got the hint. We got in a big fight, and yeah, we're over."

Aisha sighed. "What the hell is wrong with you?"

"The same thing that's wrong with you."

"But you're better than me."

"I thought I was too." He laughed dryly. "I guess I'm not."

She wanted to go on and tell him how wrong he was, but the beam in her own eye was too damning. "I'm sorry," she said. "Are you okay?"

"I'll be fine."

"Don't keep anything else like that from me, you hear me. I'm your big sister."

"What's going on with Sam?"

"I promise, I'll tell you. Just not right now."

"Hypocrite."

"I know. I'm working on it."

"Whatever, Sha. I gotta go. Bye."

Before she could say anything else, the disconnect tone forced her back into her remote reality. The emptiness enveloped her with its tight grip, leaving her immobile. Growing up, Aisha and Amir used to tell each other everything.

She immediately let her brother know when she figured out Santa was their mom. He didn't believe her. Their mother couldn't last a day at the North Pole—she hated the cold. So,

Aisha woke Amir up late on Christmas Eve to show him the irrefutable proof. He gasped, hidden behind the wall, when their mom tiptoed into the living room to put all the presents they had requested from Santa under the tree.

After his first week as a high schooler, Amir ran to her room to tell her he had found the love of his life. She hugged him tight and immediately demanded details. They both broke into laughter when Amir admitted he didn't even know the boy's name.

Later that year, she quietly walked into his room after their second encounter with their father. Her brother looked at her, and she looked at the floor. He ran toward her, and they cried into each other's arms. They didn't know the words for what they felt. All they knew was that they had each other.

Somewhere along the way, Amir healed his wound without her. His fissure was closing and cementing like a paved road. That road distanced them. Aisha watched him drift further and further away, but she was too ashamed because he had done what she couldn't. So, she let him go. She didn't want to be a burden. Now, she regretted not being by his side. Obviously, her brother didn't have it all figured out. She wished she could help him. She wished she could tell him all the right things. But how could she when she didn't know what they were? How could she help him find the path to wholeness when she had never left the hollow?

Her phone screen lit up.

Hey Aisha! How are u? Lets grab drinks this weekend if u free. I know a great spot Downtown u'd definitely like

She read Carlos's text and immediately put her phone away. She didn't want to make up a lie to explain why she couldn't hang out, so she didn't reply. He would eventually get the message. A handsome guy like him wouldn't have trouble finding another woman to spend time with. He would forget her in no time.

She didn't leave her apartment the rest of the week, sustaining on delivery food and Netflix binges. Carlos messaged her again two days later.

Hey...is everything ok? Did I do something wrong? I'm kinda worried. If u dont want to hang out again I understand. But please just let me know u okay and I wont bother u again.

She read his message with tears in her eyes. She didn't even have the decency to humanely part ways with someone who had been nothing but kind to her. She had used him to fill a void. And the moment his presence hinted at happiness, she discarded him. She couldn't risk any part of her happiness to be provided by anyone except herself. It was too risky.

Her heart couldn't take more shattering.

I'm okay, she finally replied.

He sent a thumbs-up emoji and nothing else.

WEEK 7

The main reason she finally decided to go outside was the weather. It was sixty-five degrees in the middle of February. It would've been a crime to stay inside. The other reason was that it was Valentine's Day. If she didn't get some fresh air, she knew her thoughts would transport her back to James chasing her on New Year's Eve in the boxer briefs she had gotten him the last time the fourteenth day rose on the shortest month of the year.

She forced herself not to think about that night. She found her hiking gear and drove back to the trail she had walked almost two weeks ago. She didn't want to explore anything new. She wanted to revisit something she knew.

Her thighs, chest, knees, ankles, and back didn't burn as badly as before. They recognized the path. It had a hint of familiarity, so they knew what to expect and how to engage. She decided to challenge herself. She walked faster and further. She could feel her lungs expanding, inviting air. She had been walking for almost an hour when she saw a dock overlooking a lake. The timing was perfect. In the last five minutes, her body had given her hints that she was doing more than it could manage. She slowly sat down at the edge of the dock. The sunlight was reflecting on the lake, crystalizing the water.

For a solid minute, it was complete silence. It was just her, the dock, and the lake. Somehow, her thoughts didn't intrude, recognizing the beauty of the scenery. Then a raft of ducks swam by in a perfect line. She looked at them with a smile. She admired their confidence and unity. They knew where they were going, and they knew they had each other. A giant bird she couldn't identify flew in the water. Its beak disappeared for a fraction of time and emerged back with a fish. She looked back at the ducks. They were all perfectly lined up, not fazed by the entire ordeal.

When she finally soaked in the view, she realized she was the personification of *Between the Riverbank*'s cover: a lone woman sitting on a dock. Well, minus the sinking hand. She looked at the horizon to confirm no one was drowning in the distance. She hadn't opened that book since she last went to *Libros & Libations*. Perhaps she should make that a thing. She could read there, which would give her a reason to leave her apartment. And when it was nice outside, she could walk the trail. The more consistent she'd be, the more it'd become routine and familiar.

Familiarity seemed to be one of the most competent opponents against the hollow. It was just as sneaky and covert. It gradually made you feel safe and comfortable, eventually filling the void. The problem was that she was afraid to let things get too familiar because she knew if those things went away, the hollow would come back meaner and emptier. Yet she had to take a chance and do something.

She got up from the dock. On her way back to her vehicle, she recognized a shapely silhouette in the distance. The woman was stretching gracefully, her golden curls bouncing in the direction she was leaning toward. She had such an inviting presence, so Aisha walked toward her.

"Hey, there! Working hard or hardly working today?" she said.

"Oh hey, girl! Hardly working today." The woman grinned. "It was just so beautiful. I had to get out. It's good to see you again."

"You too." She thought about walking away. Their brief small talk should fill her daily need for human interaction. But she stood still and said, "Are you just getting started or finishing up?"

"Just getting started." The woman stopped stretching and gave Aisha her full attention. "What about you?"

Aisha stretched her arms out and exhaled. "I'm done for the day. Now, it's time to eat!"

The woman laughed. The sound came straight from her belly, loud and unfiltered. "I wish I could fast forward to that part of my day." She looked at the trees and the clear sky. "I guess it's worth it being out here right now." She turned back to Aisha. "My name is Dahlia, by the way."

"That's a beautiful name. I'm Aisha. Nice to formally meet you."

Dahlia waved off the formality. "Do you walk this trail often?"

"Not as often as I should, but that's my goal."

"Well, I come here at least three times a week. Maybe we can meet and walk together whenever we're both here if you're down?" She didn't wait for Aisha's answer and took her phone out. "We can text whenever we plan on coming out. What's your number?"

Aisha's thoughts began to race. The thing she was even more afraid of than romance was friendship. She knew she would be able to recover from the cut James had carved way before she could start to examine the damages Sam had caused. Sam was the only person who knew her better than Amir. And much of what her brother knew was because he was there when it happened. However, she had volunteered all her most guarded secrets to Sam. Aisha had willingly opened the door to invite her in. But like a vampire at dusk, Sam had gotten inside only to suck what was left of her life force. *Bitch.*

Still, Aisha had to try to step outside her comfort zone. The goal wasn't to find a replacement for Sam. All she needed was familiarity and connection. Dahlia appeared to be a kind person. All she offered was to meet for a walk, that was all. Aisha knew she had a bad habit of thinking of the worst-case scenario, too far into the future while the present was still unfolding, then slowly becoming her past.

"You don't have to give it to me if you don't want to," Dahlia said with her broad smile and no hint of bitterness, bringing Aisha back to the present. "I'm sure we'll run into each other again."

"No, no. I definitely want to." Aisha typed her number into Dahlia's phone, and Dahlia did the same.

"Alright then." Dahlia began her thread. "I'll catch up with you later, girl. Enjoy your lunch!"

"Thank you. Enjoy your walk!"

*

On Sunday, she went back to the coffeehouse. Although she had only been there once, Aisha had missed the atmosphere of *Libros & Libations*. She was excited to sit on the couch by the vinyl records and catch up with Jane. She ordered an Irish coffee just like the first time. The bartender who was there wasn't as eccentric as the first one. She didn't yell out her order to herself like he had done. She was disappointed. She had looked forward to that part of the order.

When she sat on the couch, she looked on the other side of the room. The old man with round glasses was there. She almost let out a celebratory sound. He didn't look that invested in the book he was reading. Old Man with Round Glasses would've been immersed in the pages if the story was good enough. She smiled and turned to page one-hundred and sixty-eight.

Jane was unraveling. After weeks of stalking the mistress, she bought a Smith & Wesson. Aisha was amazed at how well she maintained a façade. Internally, she was crumbling. On the surface, she was a solid block—her family's rock. Though Jane was putting on an act until she could construct a solid alibi for whoever she was going to kill, Aisha admired how she maintained her external composure. She had always envied people who could mask the way they truly felt. Not being able to hide her emotions was one of her greatest weaknesses. Anybody who stared at her for more than five seconds could have a good gauge of her internal monologue.

"What is it, Aisha? You don't want us to move in together?" James had asked her. His feet were resting on *her* rustic coffee table.

"What makes you think that?" She tried to maintain an expressionless exterior.

"Aisha, we've been together for fourteen months. I know you. It's written all over your face."

She wanted to lie, but she wasn't good at it. "I don't think I'm ready for that step."

He dropped his feet on her hand-knotted rug and sat up straight to face her. "I don't want to rush you, babe." He grabbed her left hand and held it between both of his. "I just need to know this is going somewhere. I love you."

Aisha wanted to scream, not from happiness but from fear. It was the first time he had said those three words to her. She wasn't afraid because she didn't feel the same way. She was afraid because she did. The vocalization of those words destroyed her escape route and closed her exit. She was bottlenecked. And if things didn't work, she would be stuck in the devastation lane for a while.

Yet she couldn't lie. "I love you too."

She shook her head and snapped back into the present. She couldn't help but look at the front entrance of the coffee shop after every chapter. She was hoping Polished Guy would walk in. She didn't want to actively interact with him. She just wanted to watch his perfectly angled movements.

Seven chapters later, he still didn't walk in. Old Man with Round Glasses left. He looked dissatisfied. Aisha tried to catch the title of the disappointing book he was reading, but he was too far away. She read a few more chapters of *Between the Riverbank*, hoping Polished Guy would eventually come in and punctuate her evening outing. By page two hundred and forty-three, she knew Jane would kill her husband. She also knew Polished Guy wouldn't come, so she left.

WEEK 8

Aisha wanted to go to the hiking trail but didn't. She told herself it was because the weather wasn't as nice, but that wasn't true. She didn't want to go because she didn't want to run into Dahlia. She wanted to walk with her and get to know her eventually, not just yet. So, she went to grab brunch instead.

She sat in the corner of the L-shaped wooden bar counter to avoid telling the hostess she was alone. The place was packed with families, friends, and a handful of people dining alone. It was so loud that the bartender had to lean over the counter to hear her order. Aisha noticed that she had two nose rings: a stud on the left and a hoop on the right.

Two attractive women were seated next to her. They were laughing while looking at something on their phones. Aisha glanced at the screens and recognized one of the dating apps Sam had used before her dating hiatus.

"Okay, it's been a full year," she had said to Sam then. "Are you ready to get back on the market?"

"I don't know. I might go another six months." Sam opened her fridge and grabbed two water bottles. She threw one to Aisha from her kitchen counter.

Aisha didn't catch it, and it landed in front of the TV. They were watching *Insecure*. She stood to pick up the bottle and then turned back to face Sam. "Still not over Blake?"

"Oh, I very much am, trust. I've just been able to get so much shit done when I'm working at home. I can spend as much time as I want at the gym afterward. Dating is going to affect my productivity. Also, I don't want to waste my time anymore. The next one has to be the last. He's not getting away, believe me."

"Damn, Black Widow, don't hurt 'em!" Aisha laughed. Sam had that look she could never read. Her friend didn't look upset, but she didn't look amused either. Any other emotion could've been assigned to her face. Aisha always reverted to seriousness when she looked like that. She took a sip of water and sat back down. "I understand where you're coming from, though. You'll know when the timing is right. I'm glad you can get more things done in the meantime."

Sam walked back to the living room and sat on her gray couch. She finally nodded, and her expression loosened. "I see myself more as a praying mantis than a black widow."

Aisha relaxed and resumed the laugh she had interrupted. "Why?"

"Praying mantises consume black widows with almost no effort." She joined Aisha and laughed even louder than her. It was kind of scary.

Now, the bartender placed her croque madame and second mimosa on the counter. One of the two attractive women looked at her. "That looks really good," she said.

Aisha took a bite and confirmed, "Yes, it's pretty good."

The woman smiled and looked back at her friend. They continued to talk and laugh. The need for friendship stung Aisha like a bee, so she messaged Dahlia.

Hey Dahlia how are you? Looks like it's going to be really nice on Thursday. I think I'll go for a hike. You're welcome to join if you're free

The answer lit up her phone a few minutes later. *Hey girl, I'm great! Hope you're having a lovely day! I would've loved to but I'll be out of town that day.*

At first, she mistakenly thought the emotion she felt was relief. However, she quickly recognized that it was disappointment. Her initial attempt to get out of her comfort zone was met with denial—a clear sign that it was too early to build any new friendship, right?

Another text came in. *I'm planning on going next Monday if you're free then. It won't be as nice as this Thursday but it should be nice enough.*

She exhaled. *Yes I'll be there!*

See you then!

She focused back on her lukewarm croque madame. For the first time, she voluntarily recalled what had happened on New Year's Eve. She vividly remembered hearing James' footsteps behind her. His calling for her to stop and hear him out so he could tell her the great news: he was in love with her best friend. *Woohoo!* Then Sam messaged her to double down: *I fell in love with him.*

How?

When?

She couldn't have been so oblivious. She was even more outraged that Sam had asked her to give her a chance to explain when she was ready. As if she was certain forgiveness would be on the table, and it was only a matter of time until it was served. Aisha wasn't quite sure why Sam believed she was so forgiving. Nothing in her history reinforced that. Or perhaps she thought their friendship was too special not to be salvaged.

"But not special enough to not fuck my man," she said out loud.

She suddenly remembered she wasn't alone. Though she had tuned out the chirping from the two women seated next to her, it was clear their discussion had halted.

"Hell *nah*! They did what?" the one with the red lipstick asked.

They both put their phones down and looked at Aisha in delighted shock, like noblewomen in a period drama, waiting for elaboration.

"Who fucked your man?" the one with the nude lipstick chimed in.

Aisha entertained the thought of coming up with a lie, but what was the point? Again, she was a terrible liar. Furthermore, she would never see these two women again. Talking about this aloud could be helpful, especially since they were strangers with no stake in the matter.

"My best friend of six years slept with my boyfriend of two," she said. The two women gasped. Their eyes and mouths widened in disbelief. Aisha wanted to see how much more their features could expand, so she added, "I walked in on them on New Year's Eve, a few minutes before midnight. Happy New Year to me." She raised her glass.

They didn't say anything for a few seconds. She could see a million thoughts running through their stunned faces. The one with the nude lipstick spoke first. "Please tell me you beat her ass!"

The one with the red lipstick interjected, "Beat *her* ass? What about him? He deserved the brunt of the ass-whooping."

"Are you okay?" Nude lipstick furrowed her brow. "The betrayal is worse on her end. They were friends longer."

"She was in a committed relationship with him for two years."

"Chicks before dicks."

They both cackled, which was all it took to clear their disagreement. Aisha laughed as well. She wanted to be part of the moment, even if the laughter was at the expense of her reality.

"I should've beat both of their asses," she said, "but I just left Denver instead. And here I am."

"You left legal pot because of them?" Nude Lipstick said earnestly.

"Jesus. Weed is not that damn serious, Jane." Red Lipstick shook her head and chugged her drink.

Aisha smiled, got up, and without any explanation, she covered her tab and left. The two women just stared at her silently. They resumed their conversation when she was a few feet from the bar. For some reason stripped of logic, the fact that the woman was named *Jane* healed a fraction of the pain inside of her. Not enough to make her feel better, but enough to make things seem fated. She was where she needed to be, doing what she needed to do. She also remembered that she had packed some marijuana in preparation for her departure from Colorado. She knew when she'd get home, her thoughts would welcome her in to disrupt her evening. She had a green remedy to shoo them away.

Aisha didn't smoke weed very often, but when she did, she liked to be so high she couldn't discern what was real and what was a figment of her inebriation. As soon as she made it home, she lit up one of the pre-rolled joints that had been hidden in her bedroom drawer since she had moved in.

A few inhales, and she envisioned herself as Jane. Not the one from the bar, but the one from the book. Then, somewhere between inebriated awareness and stage one REM sleep, she was stalking Sam during the day and wiping her Smith & Wesson in the evening. She was making hateful, sweaty, animalistic love to

James at night while simultaneously thinking about how large a trash bag needed to be to work as a body bag. Then, the bag was in her trunk. Inside it was a lifeless body. The person who deserved the brunt of her ass-whooping. Then, she drove to the hiking trail. She parked by the dock during the wee hours. The moment she was ready to throw the body away from the riverbank, it was dawn.

Her car was gone.

The body was gone.

She was now walking with Dahlia, who was telling her how grateful she was that it didn't rain. Then, the water from the potential raindrops became her tears. She laughed at how ridiculous her stream of laced consciousness was. She inhaled more smoke from the devil's grass.

Now her father was walking with her. Not as fun of a thought. He tried to make her laugh. How pathetic. She willed her mind to erase him. Her wish was partially granted. Her dad became a tiny creature in her left palm. She flicked him away. Then, her mom appeared. She made her into a tiny being, too. However, Aisha didn't flick her away. She put her mom in her pocket.

Then, she was a pre-teen, laughing with Amir about something she couldn't articulate. Although she had already forgotten what it was after the next puff, she still cackled. The sound was a sharp and loud wheeze, which made her laugh even harder. Now she felt cold, so she pulled her blanket closer. Then it was too hot. She stuck one foot out, and it was finally perfect.

She fell asleep while her lucid thoughts waited in the corner till dawn.

The next morning, she woke up to a message from her mother. *Hey sweetie, just checking in. Hope everything's going well. Call me when you can. Miss you.*

Hi mom. Yes everything is great. I will

It hurt her that this was the state of their relationship. Sporadic check-ins when her mom worked her hardest to get anything out of her. Her mother was the hopeful farmer, and she was the hardened soil. Aisha thought time, space, and the watering of their relationship would've been the ground breaker. Almost four years had passed, and she was still a compact, unforgiving block.

Some words simply couldn't be taken back.

She wanted to forgive her mother, but she didn't know how. Whenever she thought she was ready, the words echoed in her mind, bringing her back to ground zero. She missed her mom. Before the incident, not only did Aisha adore her mother, but she also looked up to her.

"I'm so proud of you, Mom!" She had thrown her mother's graduation cap in the air and immediately jumped to catch it.

Helen cried and opened her arms out. Aisha and Amir, both in their mid-twenties then, ran toward her and cried like they had just exited her womb. "If I had to do it again, I wouldn't change a thing. You two are my biggest achievements. I love you," she said.

"We love you too, Mom," Amir replied, still inside the embrace.

"Yes, and we're so proud of you, Mom. You're a fucking rockstar!" Aisha said.

Her mom lightly tapped the back of her head for cussing. They all laughed. Special events justified special behaviors, though. "Damn right!" Helen said. She was laughing, crying, and twirling all at once. The other graduates and their families cheered behind them.

Now, Aisha sat up. Another day without a plan. Another day alone.

She slept through that day and the next few days. She only woke up when she couldn't force herself to fall back into Morpheus's shielding hands because her body stupidly required awareness and movement. She only got up to use the bathroom or grab a bite of her refrigerated days-old take-outs.

She exchanged messages with Amir a couple of times to make sure he was doing better than she was. All his responses were short. She was too tired to demand more. One day, she slept sixteen hours straight. She wondered if she had broken some type of record. She didn't bother to look it up.

She had to stick with the schedule: eat, use the restrooms, and go back to sleep. Somehow, she was even more tired now. How ungrateful was her body? What would it take for her to feel rested? What would it take to feel at peace?

What would it take to let go?

When the sun rose on Sunday, her body demanded fresh air. Her apartment was suddenly too small and stuffy. She felt like the walls were closing in on her. She had to step outside to breathe air that hadn't witnessed her life—or lack thereof—over the past few days. She wasn't sure what she wanted to do.

She didn't want to go to *Libros & Libations*. She was going to the trail tomorrow to meet Dahlia, so she had no intention of hiking even one step further than what she had already signed up for. The thoughts of interacting with humans made her want to break her sixteen-hour sleep record. Still, she wanted to see life. Animals, perhaps? *Yes.*

It was too chilly to be outside today. She was definitely acclimating to the Dallas weather to think today could be considered a cool day. Anyway, she chose to go to the aquarium instead of the zoo to be indoors.

Aisha bought her ticket online. She showered and wore a blue sweater, leggings, and knee-high boots. She got on the road.

The Aquarium was forty minutes away. Halfway there, a sedan barely larger than her compact car cut her off on the slow lane. Three cars could've fitted both in front and behind her, yet the driver decided to almost graze her car at fifty-five miles per hour (the speed limit was thirty-five). Dallas's drivers were reckless.

Trailing behind, she rolled the window down to flip him off. Then she blasted her horn. To her delight, the red light stopped his mania. She could hear his engine roar in an attempt to beat its destiny: a stop. *You can't outrun your destiny, darling.* She pulled up next to him and made sure their cars were perfectly lined up. She stared at him. She wanted to see his face. He looked straight ahead, both hands on the steering wheel. *Yeah, bastard. You know what you did. Fucking moron can't even look at me.*

She managed to hold what she knew would be a very loud cackle if let out. He looked even dumber than what he had done. The moment the light turned green, he flew away. She broke into laughter and didn't stop laughing or drive off until the car behind her honked twice.

Something about that unrestricted laughter made her turn around. She'd go to the aquarium another day. The pass was good for one month. Today, she'd be fine not seeing marine life. She wanted to save the experience for a day she'd really need it. Thanks to Dumbass on Wheels, today wasn't that day. The best remedy combo against the hollow was slowly but surely coming together: familiarity, laughter, and, of course, time and space.

She was on the right track, the path toward feeling whole.

WEEK 9

Aisha got to the hiking trail a few minutes before the meetup time. She wanted to ensure her body was prepared to keep up with Dahlia. With every stretch, she heard her body complain with loud cracks. *You have been sedentary for almost a week. No amount of stretching will make up for that.* She tried to shut it up with some jumping jacks. A mistake. She didn't have to see herself to know she looked like she was dangling off a puppeteer's strings.

"Wow, that's a serious warm-up. I don't think I'm prepared for this walk," Dahlia called behind her.

"What do you mean? I'm trying to make sure I'm prepared to keep up with you!"

They didn't hug or exchange greetings. Something about Dahlia's demeanor wrapped Aisha in an invisible soft blanket. When she smiled, Aisha thought it was the sparkle in her eyes. Dahlia was probably three to five years older than her, but there was an ingenuous light in her gaze, something from childhood that had never been affected.

"Girl, you're fine. I prefer to stroll anyway, to take in the scenery."

"I stroll because my joints don't allow me to speed up, but yeah, the scenery, too."

Dahlia threw her head back and laughed. Aisha was trying to think of anything else she could tell her to keep her laughing. Perhaps she could tell Dahlia how she left legal pot because her best friend slept with her boyfriend. It worked with Jane and

Red. She didn't care to see those two again, though. So, Aisha didn't say anything else and looked around instead. Then she took a deep breath.

"There you go," Dahlia said, then did the same thing. "This is so therapeutic."

Then, without any notice, Dahlia began to walk. Aisha followed behind and eventually caught up with her. For the first few minutes, they didn't say anything. They just looked around and smiled at each other. Runners and bikers flew by their left. Other hikers smiled or nodded as they passed them. The ground was cold under their steps. Plants were stiff and flowerless, yet there was a quiet understanding they were fine. They were taking on the form they needed to get through the season. They'd bloom again when the timing was right, and the climate allowed.

Aisha broke the silence. "When did you come back to town?"

"Yesterday. My ex and I share joint custody of our daughter. He couldn't pick her up, so I offered to drop her off. Thankfully, he's only forty-five minutes away, in Fort Worth."

"How old is your daughter?"

"She just turned eight. Her name is Nia. She's a good kid. We're very lucky."

Aisha didn't know where to go from there. Her only certainty about children was that she didn't want any. Every time people talked about their kids, she felt like an alien sent to Earth to learn about the purpose and appeal of human reproduction.

"That's so sweet," she finally said. The words came out like they were generated from a computer: *That's—so—sweet.*

Dahlia chuckled. "You don't have any kids, do you?"

She smiled. "No." They walked into the non-paved path. Aisha felt the crisp grass under her shoes. The sunlight faded between the thick leaves.

"Do you want kids?"

"No."

"Good for you for knowing and being true to what you want."

Aisha couldn't help but think about the time she had a similar conversation with James after he told her he loved her. The reception wasn't quite the same.

"I wish you would've told me this earlier," James had said. He walked outside to his balcony. The view was a never-ending, loud construction site.

She followed him. "I'm sorry, babe. We never talked about it. I assumed we were on the same page."

He looked at the horizon. "When I picture my future, I see kids."

"I don't." That should've been the end of it. "At least, not in the near future," she added.

He finally looked at her. His deep brown eyes were sparkling with hope. "So, you're open to them, right? Just not right now?"

"I have to think about it, but I'm not one hundred percent opposed to it." She hoped there was some truth to it. The fear of losing him made her believe there was.

"That's all I need to know," he said.

He held her tight, and they kissed. Later, they made love. Aisha made sure he wore a condom. She also made sure to take her pill.

The sound of a branch cracking under her left foot brought her back to the present.

"Thank you," she replied. "I have thought long and hard about it, and it's simply not my path."

"I respect that." Dahlia nodded. "Where are you from?"

"Denver. I've been here for a couple of months. What about you?"

"Louisville. But I've been here for so long that I now claim Dallas. So, just two months, uh? Did you move here for work?"

"In a way, yes. Personal work. I had to get away for a while. I need a reset."

Dahlia looked at her as if she had told her the sky was blue. "I see. And how's that going?"

"It's going…It's definitely a process."

"I get it. I went through something similar when I was going through my divorce. It's not easy, but it'll be okay in the end. Just give yourself time and grace."

"How long did it take for you to…get through it?" They got to a dead end, turned around, and retraced the path they took to get there. Aisha thought talking while walking would require more effort, but it didn't. The two activities paired well.

"It took at least two years before I started feeling like myself again."

"Wow."

"Yeah, it's a journey. But I'm so much better for it."

Aisha wanted to ask what led to the divorce, but she felt it was too early in their relationship to demand those details. Although they had already shared way more than she had anticipated, she still wanted to tread cautiously. She enjoyed Dahlia's company, so the last thing she wanted to do was ruin a potential friendship with premature questions.

"What do you do for work?" she said instead.

"I'm a professional dance teacher. Mostly salsa and bachata. What about you?"

"That's so cool! Right now, I'm taking some time off, but I was house-sitting full time before I left Denver."

It had taken Aisha a lot of time and reflection to say those words without any shame or feeling of inadequacy. Her last interaction with her father had given her the ultimate certainty that she liked her job, regardless of what anybody else thought of it.

"That's awesome," Dahlia said with that sparkle in her eyes. "So, how are you liking Dallas so far?"

"So far so good. I haven't seen much yet, but I like what I've seen." Her voice came out flat.

"I see. Well, if you ever wanted to hang out, I know my way around…well, mostly the dance scene. I think you'd enjoy it, though."

"I have two left feet."

"You can shimmy your little heart out with less." Dahlia interrupted her walk to demonstrate what she meant to Aisha. When she shook her shoulders and let her chest and curls rise and fall to the sound of her internal music, Aisha saw that pure quality from childhood took over her movements. It was so beautiful she almost cried. She caught herself and immediately demanded that her tears remain in whatever dreadful place they resided.

Y'all better not come out! I don't want to look like some unhinged loon.

Uh…but you are.

Okay, but she doesn't need to know that right now!

The tears didn't fall.

"I might just have to take you up on that offer with those moves." Aisha laughed.

Dahlia chuckled and put her hands on her hips. "I promise I'm a little better than this."

They were back on the paved road. The last few steps ended the way they started: silently. However, this time, there was a knowing between them similar to the one that whispered the flowers would bloom again when the climate allowed, an understanding that things were going in their natural order and that the two women had crossed paths for a reason.

"This was fun!" Dahlia said when they made it back to the parking lot.

"It really was. Hopefully, we can do it again soon."

"Yes. And if you ever want to move those two left feet of yours, let me know."

"I will." Aisha smiled.

"Alright, girl. I'll see you later." Dahlia hugged her and walked to her car.

"Yes. See you later."

The hike with Dahlia fueled her batteries for the rest of the week. She did her laundry, cleaned up her space, went grocery shopping, and for the first time since she moved to her apartment, she cooked. It wasn't an elaborate meal, yet throwing the shrimp and the vegetables into the pan affected something inside of her.

The warmth of the home-cooked meal did more than feed her gut. It fed something else inside of her that had been starving much longer. The thing that needed healing the most. So, she told herself with an even stronger conviction that she was exactly where she needed to be doing precisely what she needed to do.

WEEK 10

It was a chilly day in March when Aisha finally decided to call her mother. Even though she still hadn't forgiven her mom, Aisha never wanted her to fret. Helen picked up on the second ring.

"Hey, sweetie! How are you?"

"Hey, Mom. I'm fine. About yourself?"

"I'm fine. It's good to hear from you. I was starting to worry."

"Sorry."

"It's alright. I'm just glad you called. So, how's Dallas?"

"It's fine. The food is good."

"I bet! How long are you planning on staying there?" Helen's voice reverberated.

Aisha waited for the sound to stop. She leaned against her living room couch. "I'm not sure yet. A little while longer."

"It won't be an issue with your clients?"

Aisha could tell by the echo behind the tone that her mother had walked into a different room. "No, I let them know. Where are you?"

"I'm at the salon. One of the girls put in her two-week last Thursday, so I have an interview today."

"Oh, okay."

"How's Sam? I'm kind of worried because she usually texts me at least every other week to say hi. I haven't heard from her since you left."

"Yes, you told me last time," Aisha said sharply. "She's fine."

"What's going on, hon? Did you guys have a fight?"

"I don't want to talk about it." She could tell by the knot in her belly and rapid breaths that she was getting irritated. And when she was irritated, her tongue ruled her mind.

"Okay, I'm leaving it alone," Helen said.

Aisha could hear the sound of papers being rumpled on the other side of the line. "Sounds like you're busy. I can call back another time."

"No, no, I can talk!" her mom yelped. "Otherwise, I'll have to wait another month for my next chance."

Since their exchange, Helen had never expressed her awareness of Aisha's cold treatment aloud. Her mother had quietly taken the very little Aisha had given her, knowing it wasn't enough, but understanding that asking for more would result in even less. This was the first time she had vocalized her discontentment, and frankly, Aisha wasn't sure what to say. So, she didn't say anything.

Helen spoke again. "I'm sorry. That's not what I meant. I just want to talk to you as long as possible. I miss you, sweetie."

Aisha wanted to say it back to her. Not only to appease her but also because it was true. But she felt like telling her mother she missed her meant the beginning of forgiveness. She wanted forgiveness to be on the table, but to put it there, she had to get a hold of it first.

"Hopefully, you can find a replacement soon," she said instead.

Helen sighed. "Aisha, I don't know what else to do. You're going to have to give me something. Am I sentenced to life?"

Aisha felt the weight of her heart sinking near her belly button. "I'll call you again soon," she blurted out. Before her mother could respond, she hung up.

She was expecting a text message from her mother to light her phone immediately, but the device stared back at her with the same blankness that was on her face. Lonesomeness yelped for her to get back into its black hole. It was the most disorienting feeling. It felt like the ground was shaking under her feet. She fought the urge to get in her bed, under her blanket, and force herself to sleep. She wasn't going to let herself get back into the state she had marinated in two weeks ago.

Aisha knew what would cheer her up. She picked up her phone and dialed.

"Yes?" Amir picked up. His voice was hoarse.

"What's wrong?" She sat up straight.

"No, ma'am. You still haven't told me what happened between you and Sam. I'll tell you mine when you tell me yours."

"You're a child."

"It is the only way to reason with you."

"Fuck you." She laughed. No one called her out like her brother, and she loved him for it.

"And you." His voice sounded lighter. "So, speak."

"Do not tell Mom!"

"Now, who's the child?"

"I'm serious. I don't want her to know yet. In fact, I don't want anyone to know. Keep your mouth shut!"

"Jesus. If you're about to tell me about a crime, I suggest you keep it to yourself. I'll fold during the interrogation. I might even unconsciously volunteer some information."

She chuckled. "You're an idiot."

"I'm just saying," Amir said. She heard him move around. Then he said, "Okay, if you didn't kill anyone, your secret will be safe."

"Sam slept with James," she blurted out. She was surprised at how easily the words flew out of her mouth as if they made sense.

The sound of something falling on the ground came from her brother's side. Aisha was startled by the breaking noise. Amir shouted, "No fucking way! What? Are you sure?" He was so loud he sounded like he was sitting next to her.

"Yep. I walked in on her straddling him on New Year's Eve."

"How treacherous. Wow."

"Yep."

"Damn, Sha. I don't know what to say. That's so vile. I'm sorry."

"I know. That's why I left. I just needed to get away. I can't deal with this shit there. I need some distance to…to get over it." She leaned back against the couch.

"No, I get it." His voice suddenly sounded further away when he said, "How are you feeling?"

"You put me on speaker?"

"Yes, I broke a vase. I'm sweeping."

"Sorry. Definitely shattering news." She giggled.

He tittered. "I'm glad you maintained your shitty sense of humor. So, how are you feeling?"

"Not great, but better."

"That's good. So—"

She didn't want to talk about what happened further. "I told you mine, so it's your turn."

"Fine." He sighed. "Someone told me they saw Thomas on something that had all the qualities of a date."

"No way. You guys just broke up!"

"Exactly! Now, I'm questioning everything. If he can move on that fast, I'm wondering if his feelings were even real."

"You know the answer to that."

"No, I don't," he said, sounding closer again. "I thought he felt as terrible as I did, but obviously, he's having a fantastic time."

"You don't know that. You don't even know if it was a date. You know he loves you. Everything he's doing right now is to mask the pain."

"Whatever he's doing, I just need him to find his way back to me a-fucking-sap."

"You have to let him know the path is not closed. You're the one who chickened out when it got real, so you have to let him know that you're on the same page now and make amends."

"Right," he mumbled. "Have you been reading some self-help crap or something? Since when are you so level-headed?"

"I'm your big sister. I've been on this earth longer than you. I've seen some shit you couldn't even imagine. I have—"

"Girl, please," he cut her off. "You're only two years older than me. Talking like you fought in World War One or something."

"Oh, the Great War," she hummed. "So many lives were lost."

"Shut your ass up!" He laughed. "I won't say anything to Mom. And if Sam dares to text or call me, I—"

"Please act like you don't know or ignore her if you don't want to deal with it. I don't want things to escalate right now. I'll deal with them later."

"Whatever you decide to do, I will *not* fold during the interrogation."

They both laughed. She continued to laugh minutes after they hung up.

*

As much as her conversation with Amir made her feel lighter, she was still sensing the weight of the emptiness within her. As much as her walk with Dahlia had filled her up with whatever of that thing she needed, she was still not whole. Aisha knew she would eventually have to address the actual events that led her to Dallas. James. Sam. James and Sam. Her father. Her mother. Even the way she and Amir had drifted apart over the years.

She was just not ready for any of that yet.

And as much as she was sick of telling herself: *I'm not ready to deal with things right now*, as much as it was frustrating to acknowledge that she needed more time to confront what had birthed the void within her, as much as it was difficult to postpone inner peace due to the work required to get there, as much as…as much as…as much as, the delay was mandatory in order to maintain her sanity.

She went on a few spontaneous drives the rest of the week to look at her surroundings. Trees were still stripped of their colors and fullness by the climate. The sidewalks were deserted, save for a few people who were over-layered to combat the "harsh" fifty-seven-degree winds.

She rolled the windows down to hear that *whoosh* sound created by the perpendicular contact of the air against her moving machinery. She felt the urge to hang her head and tongue out like a dog, but she didn't. She had to keep her eyes on the road. She wondered what the appeal of the whole thing was. What was it about the wind hitting their faces that made dogs happy? What about dry eyes and dry tongues made their hearts full? Perhaps a tail was required to understand. The thought made her smile.

She quieted her thoughts and let the *whoosh* sounds of the wind clear her mind.

WEEK 11

On Tuesday evening, Aisha went out to dinner at an Italian restaurant. Her hair stood an inch and a half over her scalp, so she combed it out for a fuller effect. She wore a sweater dress and cowboy boots. She didn't make a reservation, assured there would be plenty of open seats at the bar.

"I'm sorry, even the bar is full," the host told her with an apologetic frown. "I can add you to the waitlist. It'll be about thirty minutes."

Aisha pulled a map of the area in her head. The closest restaurant was about seven minutes away, and its reviews were not as favorable. She didn't feel like getting back on the road to hopefully find a seat at the bar for a lesser-rated meal.

"Yes, please add me to the list." She could see the lips of the young man parting to ask the question she had to answer numerous times. Before he could speak, Aisha added with authority, "It'll just be me."

She gave her phone number and walked outside. There was a nice breeze, so she sat near the entrance on one of the benches. She watched the people who walked inside of the brick house building: couples, families, and friends. Singles were few and far between, mostly middle-aged men. Another couple walked in, and if the man hadn't worn such a colorful scarf, Aisha wouldn't have paid attention to his face.

Her eyes were not deceiving her: David Marshall walked past her with a short-haired, dark-skinned woman with high cheekbones and a lean frame—and probably around her age, too. She wasn't far enough to not be seen, but far enough to hopefully be missed. She instinctively tried to cover her face with the hair she forgot she had shaved. The result was a weird caress of her forehead. Thankfully, the couple didn't notice her. David and her doppelgänger disappeared behind the red bricks.

Aisha got up from the bench to leave and go eat somewhere else. The moment she stood up, she received a text: *Aisha, your table is ready!*

Of fucking course, it is.

The low-rated restaurant seven minutes away didn't sound too bad then. Except, no. She didn't even know the man. What should she feel awkward about running into him? Plus, the restaurant was very spacious and packed with guests. David most likely wouldn't even see her, especially since he would be occupied with his date. And so what if he did? She wasn't going to let the *Vulva Wormhole* artist rob her of a four-and-half-star meal. She walked inside and followed the host to her table.

Aisha was seated at a table for two. Every other table around her was fully seated. The classical music playing competed with all the ongoing conversations. The décor reminded her of the inside of a cathedral. The ceiling was too high, the art was too gilded, and the seats were too wooden and uncomfortable. The food had to be outstanding since the overall reviews were so positive. She received the ultimate confirmation when the prosciutto bruschetta was served, and it tasted like a dance recital was happening on her tongue. She looked around to see if she could locate David Marshall and her twin. They were nowhere to be found. She felt her body relax into the ambiance.

Aisha caught a few glances from a handful of people next to her. They seemed to expect the other seat on her table to get filled soon. They were probably waiting for someone to walk in and tell her: *Hey! Sorry, I'm late. How are you?* When the main course was served, and it was still just her, she caught some furrowed brows.

At first, the looks were a mild intrigue, then a question, and finally sympathy. It was so interesting how some people couldn't fathom that someone—a woman, especially—could go out alone to enjoy a nice meal. As if digestion required someone seated next to her to be completed. As if her body would reject nutrients because she wasn't accompanied.

As if she couldn't possibly enjoy her time because she was alone.

She took a sip of her pinot noir to wash down the lasagna. She looked around in an unfocused manner that made everything look blurry and heightened one's auditory senses. She moved her head to the wavy sound of the piano notes. She closed her eyes. The notes began to sound like her name.

"Aisha Jones?" she heard more distinctly.

She slowly opened her eyes. She knew the night would force this moment to happen.

"David Marshall," she said as if she had said: *Well, well, well.*

He smiled. "What a pleasant encounter. How are you?"

She glanced behind him, expecting the woman who looked like her to be standing there. "I'm well. And you?"

"Very well. Even better now. Are you accompanied?"

Nope. Party of one, baby! "No, just me." She hesitated, then asked, "And you?" She couldn't help but raise her left brow in accusation.

"I was, but it's just me now. Do you mind if I join you?"

The balls on this guy. His date was probably still warming her engine in the parking lot, and here he was, already hunting for his next short-haired, high-cheek-boned, slim, dark-skinned prey.

Relax, Aisha. You're doing it again. Thinking of the worst-case scenario when the man is just being nice. What makes you think he's even interested in you? A pleasant conversation wouldn't be so bad, you know.

"No, I don't mind," she said, pointing at the empty seat.

He sat down and looked at her almost empty glass. "What are you drinking?"

"Pinot noir."

He looked above her head, and as if his eyes were a magnet, the server was instantly next to them. "Two glasses of her pinot noir, please." The server nodded and disappeared as promptly as he had materialized. "How are you enjoying your evening?" David focused back on her.

They had never really faced each other. In the two instances when they interacted, he stood by her side, and they only glanced at each other briefly. It was long enough for her to notice that his features were average and ordinary. However, now that they were looking directly at each other, she noticed the green of his eyes had the quality of a forbidden forest. The kind of gaze that was so intriguing it made the person who wore it alluring, regardless of their other features.

"It's been lovely so far. How about yours?"

"Just fine. Running into you made it a lot better."

I repeat: he's not interested in you in that *way. Just exchanging pleasantries. Chill.*

"Really? Why is that?"

The server came by with their drinks. David waited for him to be a few feet away before he answered. "The opportunity to spend some time with a very attractive and very sharp woman."

I knew it! "Thank you." She could feel her tongue squirming inside of her mouth, ready to say the things her mind wanted to hold. "Didn't you just spend some time with another attractive young lady?"

If he was taken off guard, nothing about his demeanor revealed it. He smiled. "I did. Though I'm even more intrigued by y—"

"Let me stop you right here, buddy." She held her index finger up. "I don't know what the hell you think this is or what you're trying to sell me, but I'm not interested."

He laughed aloud, creating a sound that still remained inside their square for two. "Not trying to sell anything, I promise. There is something about you that captivates me, Aisha. You remind me of a complex painting. I very much would like to peel your layers and examine the raw thing underneath."

Now, she was the one laughing. "Have I drunk my way into a Hallmark movie?" she said. He was just looking at her with those emerald eyes, holding a soft grin. "Please, leave my layers and that raw thing alone." She physically air-quoted "layers" and "raw thing," still laughing. "That was a sexual innuendo, right? Please say yes. I'll be disappointed if you meant that in some deep artistic way."

He chuckled. "I meant it in both an artistic and sexual way. Disappointed?"

"Partly." She took a moment to settle down. "David Marshall, I like your candor. You seem like an okay gentleman. We could be friends. Don't fuck things up by running some weak-ass game on me." She took a sip of her pinot and tasted the noir in a way she never had before.

"Just an *okay* gentleman?" He leaned forward with a smile.

She crossed her arms. "Yes. Weren't you just on a date with someone else who, by the way, looked a lot like me?"

"I'm flattered."

"What?"

"You were watching."

She rolled her eyes. "Please. I caught a glimpse, that's all. Got a type, don't we, David Marshall?"

"Yes, beautiful women."

She wanted to challenge him a little more on that answer. However, her mind stepped in and won against her then slightly fatigued tongue. "Why did your date leave without you?"

"A little jealous, aren't we, Aisha Jones?"

"Oh, don't flatter yourself. Just making conversation."

He bore his eyes into hers. Though his stare was always intense, it had never made her feel nervous...until now. "Do you really want to know?"

She sighed. "Yes, that's why I asked."

She was taking a sip of her drink when he said, "She went to her place to put a butt plug in to prepare for later."

She spat her drink out. Some of the red liquid came out of her nose. She laughed so loudly that she was afraid they would escort her out. She couldn't get herself to stop. The people around them looked her way with an amused look that quickly faded into mild concern. Her heart was beating so fast she had to put her hand on her chest to slow it down. David was staring at her, the corners of his mouth crooked with mirth.

When she finally began to calm down, he put his hand on top of hers. "Are you going to be okay?"

She was breathing like a woman in labor. "Yes...I think so...Oh my God...I'll be fine."

He looked at his watch. "Do you still have my card?"

"Yes," she said when she finally regained her composure.

"As you know, I have to go and handle some *very* important business." He got up and winked at her. "Text me when you're available for drinks. I still want to hear your thoughts on my paintings."

She watched him walk away. "Have fun!" she yelled out. He waved a hand without looking back.

A few minutes later, the waiter came by to tell her that her bill had been covered and invited her to order anything else if she wanted. She ordered a tiramisu. Then her mind wandered off. She imagined that David Marshall and her clone were on top of each other right about now, resembling the dark and white layers of her dessert. That picture led her to wonder where she had placed his card in her apartment.

When Aisha woke up the following day, her stomach was still knotted by the laughter of the previous evening. She didn't think anal sex was funny. She had just not expected David Marshall to deliver that news with such authority and seriousness. His straightforwardness was disarming. Aisha was dying to tell someone about her evening. Then, it dawned on her that the person she wanted to share the story with the most was Sam.

She recalled calling her then-best friend as soon as James had left for work the morning after they had done it five times.

"Goddamn, Sha! Y'all are some fucking animals! Details, now!" Sam had screamed out.

"*Giiiiirl!*" Aisha replied.

"You whore!"

"Fucking right!"

"*Biiiiitch!*"

"I'm still lying down. I don't know if my legs work as we speak!"

Sam laughed. "Lucky you! Meanwhile, I just ordered another dildo."

"If you get back one of the apps now, you can fuck someone tonight."

"I know," Sam said. "But that's not what I want, Sha. I'm about to be twenty-nine years old. I want to get married. I want to have kids. Nothing wrong with casual sex. Hell, you know I had plenty of it. But I'm ready to settle down. I'm looking for someone who looks at me the way James looks at you."

"You'll find him."

Now, Aisha was making some eggs and coffee. She wasn't going to let her thoughts ruin her day, especially after the night she had. She looked through her drawers while her coffee was steaming. David Marshall's card was there, under some ketchup packets. She would contact him before the end of the week. She didn't want to sleep with him. She just wanted to hear about his wild escapades; it was clear he had plenty of them. Plus, she genuinely enjoyed his company. She would be lying if she didn't admit that she also wanted to find out what was hidden behind that forbidden-forest-green gaze of his. Unlike Carlos, it was evident David just wanted to mess around, no strings attached. So, if things escalated sexually—they wouldn't—it would be a very casual and inconsequential fling. No one would get hurt. But again, it wouldn't even come to that. She wasn't going to sleep with him. *Ahem. Sure, Jan.*

Speaking of names starting with j, a, n, it was about time she found out how Jane's story ended. So, she drove to *Libros & Libations* that afternoon, ready to learn how the sinking hand ended up in the lake. The shadow part of her, the side that allowed her mind to entertain dark thoughts, also wanted to know how the murder was executed. Not the emotional part that led to it, but rather the practical way it was completed. It was the same part that had been upset that her father had passed away, not because of the hurt it should've caused her, but rather because he hadn't lived long enough to see how well her life was going without his participation. The part that was furious because he had dared to die before her *Fuck You Moment*.

Aisha painfully recalled their first interaction when she was eight. Her father had spent almost a decade living a carefree, worry-free, child-free life. As if the two human beings he had actively taken part in creating were not breathing and existing, needing his presence, love, and care. Aisha wasn't sure what had triggered him to remember them. Her. He didn't tell her, and neither did her mom. Aisha didn't ask. She was eight.

She remembered reluctantly walking into the living room, led by her mother's grasp of her then tiny, sweaty hand. The man seated on the purple accent chair was a stranger. Yet even then, eight-year-old Aisha recognized the similarity in the way they squinted when they smiled. She was amazed at how his deep brown skin caught the light in the same way hers did, how the glare of the sun contoured their faces in the same corners.

She looked more like Albert than her mother. How stupid or evil was the universe? Her own features were an indelible reminder of the person who had abandoned her before she took her first breath. The person who felt like even though she was made from his cells, she wasn't worth his love. The person who didn't care to such a degree that he was perfectly fine walking away from a piece of himself.

Her mother had prompted her to sit on the couch facing him. Then, she told Aisha the shameful and obvious truth. "Sweetie, this is your father: Albert."

"Hello there, pretty lady!" Albert extended his hand for a shake like they had just concluded a business meeting. *Moron.*

"Is Amir coming?" She turned to her mom, ignoring the man's extended arm.

Her mother whispered while caressing her hand, "I just want the two of you to spend some time together first, then Amir will come down to join you."

Thinking back on it, she realized how ridiculous the whole thing was. What? Grown man Albert couldn't handle an eight-year-old and six-year-old at once? He had to be spoon-fed to digest meeting his own offspring? *We must not startle poor Albert. He was brave and gracious enough to swing by.* And swing by was precisely what he did.

He asked what her favorite color was, what subject she enjoyed learning about most in school, and if she had any crushes yet. She answered 'green, science, and no' without making eye contact. Then, her brother came down and responded to his own "tailored" questions with more enthusiasm: his favorite sport was soccer, his favorite subject was math, and yes, he would look after Aisha and Helen while Albert was away. Amir was six.

From the moment Albert sat on the chair to when he closed the door behind him, the clock had barely advanced forty minutes.

Aisha didn't see him again until she turned seventeen.

Before walking into the coffeehouse, she took a deep breath so the thoughts of Albert could go away. The only resolution that mattered today was whether Jane would get away with murder or not. To her delight, she saw the grunge bartender behind the bar when she walked in. He was wearing an oversized black shirt with red skull drawings and a few intentional holes.

He pointed at her, revealing his black-painted fingernails. "Hey, you're back! Good to see you again. Irish coffee?"

She hadn't thought about what drink she wanted, but she was so happy he remembered her and her last order that she nodded. "Yes, please!"

He yelled to the ghost next to him. "One Irish coffee!"

The couch by the vinyl records was occupied by a couple publicly displaying their affection, so she sat at a table across the room. She skimmed through the crowd. Old Man with Round Glasses wasn't there. She was disappointed, but she figured she couldn't have everything. Seeing her favorite bartender would suffice for the day. She took a sip of her drink and felt the warmth of the beverage traveling from her tongue to her throat and resting inside her belly.

She opened the book to page two-hundred and forty-four.

I will be damned if I let you make a fool out of me, Jane had written in her journal. *You took me for a foregone conclusion; I'm taking your life. I'll be the catalyst of death doing us part.*

Aisha felt shivers going down her spine. She felt like she was chasing behind the words, trying to reach the story's climax. Jane's alibi wasn't bulletproof, but it could take a hit or two. However, Aisha wondered if she even wanted to get away with it. She had scanned her gym card slowly, making sure the front desk people saw her face with her hair pulled back. Then she had circled back out after a few minutes with a hoodie on. She was trailing behind a loud group of friends. Two of them also wore their hoodies over their foreheads, so she blended in—except she was removed from their conversation, a couple of steps behind. She drove back to her house: the future crime scene. A diligent eye would catch it, and Jane knew that.

Aisha turned the pages frantically until she reached the *bang*. One shot straight to the chest. On the floor, a lifeless body—the person who deserved the brunt of *her* ass-whooping. Jane cleaned up the blood and put the warm and heavy body that used to be her husband in the trunk. She drove to the lake as the twilight took over the sky.

When the full moon shone brightly over her head, she threw the person who had been careless with her heart away from the riverbank. She sat down on the dock and watched the body sink with a blank expression. One week later, she was arrested for the murder of her husband. *Now that we're even, I've forgiven him*, was the only answer she gave when asked if she had anything to say.

After Aisha read the book's last sentence, she considered whether murdering James and Sam would make her feel better. This was a serious thought for a full minute. She ran everything in her mind at maximum speed, like Doctor Strange in *Infinity War*. She wondered if her head was bobbing in every direction like his. If it were, she would've paid good money to see herself. That thought made her chuckle. But all the alternative realities where she killed her ex-boyfriend and her ex-best friend landed her in places where the appropriate dress codes were a straitjacket or an orange jumpsuit.

As much as she despised what James and Sam had done, they didn't deserve to be killed. Moreover, she didn't deserve to ruin her life because of their carelessness. Murder was off the table. *It is the only way*, she quoted Doctor Strange internally. She laughed aloud.

When her laughter settled, she saw him across the room. Polished Guy. She immediately felt self-conscious. How long had he been there? She prayed he hadn't seen her cackle like a buffoon for the last few seconds. She straightened herself in her chair. She was planning on leaving after she finished her book, but running into someone you were attracted to had a way of interfering with your schedule. She could allocate thirty minutes of her day to try to make eye contact with him. It's not like she had any urgent business to tend to anyway.

Aisha stood up with her book in her hand and walked toward the bar. Polished Guy was about thirty feet away, to the right of the wooden counter.

"Another Irish coffee?" the bartender asked while dancing to the pop song playing in the background.

"Let me try your house cab."

"House cab!" he yelled out.

Aisha smiled and glanced to her right. As if he had been waiting for it, Polished Guy looked up. Their eyes met. She fought the urge triggered by fear that screamed at her to look away. She held his stare. He smiled and waved. He remembered her! She grinned and waved back. When the bartender handed her the overfilled glass of red, she held her shoulders back and walked toward Polished Guy. She didn't know what she wanted out of the interaction. All she knew was that she wanted to talk to him.

"Hello," he said when she was close enough.

He was seated in the corner of the room, and no one was around him. The only other people in the coffeehouse were a handful of scattered individuals staring at their screens and the couple on the couch who needed to take their business to a hotel room.

"Hi," she said. "I just finished *In Between the Riverbank*." She held the book up as proof. "You were right. Excellent read."

"I'm glad you enjoyed it. I was hoping Jane wouldn't get caught."

The open dialogue felt like an invitation, so Aisha sat down. "Same! She's been through hell. I would've preferred a more ambiguous ending, you know, where her fate was up to the reader."

He nodded with a smile, and his face brightened, which made him look like a boy. It was only when she noticed how square and wide his shoulders were that Aisha remembered that she was talking to a handsome, grown adult male. His skin was darker than hers, with a sheen that belonged in a lotion commercial.

"I couldn't agree more," he said. "I'm Marcus, by the way." He extended his hand. She shook it. He had a firm and confident grip. The one of a man who was probably told regularly: *Great presentation, Marcus! We'll be in touch very soon.* If she took a guess, she'd say that he was working in finances, sales, or marketing.

"I'm Aisha. Nice to meet you." She grinned.

"Likewise. So, what are you reading next?"

"I'm not sure. Any suggestions?"

"What are you in the mood for?"

Revenge. Payback. Slap a bitch. "I could do another thriller."

"Hmm." He tapped his index finger on his cupid bow. "I read another book by the same author, *What Do You Know About Her?* I think you'd enjoy it."

She was most likely not going to read that book. She just wanted to keep the conversation going, although she still didn't know what she wanted out of it. "Thank you. I'll check it out." She looked at the papers spread to the right of his laptop. "What are you working on?"

"I'm writing some notes for a sales presentation I have to make at the end of the week."

Knew it! "What do you sell?"

"Medical devices."

"Intense." The word came out before she knew it. Out of all the words that existed, she wasn't sure why that one chose to sneak out.

Mercifully, he smiled. "I suppose."

She was expecting him to also ask her what she did for work. Something about the way he was seated, very straight and square, made her wish she was a physician, a teacher, an accountant, or whatever other job was respectable and formal. Being a professional house sitter couldn't possibly fit into his neat rectangle. Not that she wanted to fit into it.

"Do you come here often?" he said instead.

"Not as often as I would like to. About once or twice every other week."

He looked at his watch. "I, unfortunately, have to head out. But I'll be here same time next week if you'd like to hang out."

"Yes, that'd be nice."

He gathered his stuff. He stood up in a smooth and clean motion without making any noise or bumping into anything in his tight corner. "Great. I'm looking forward to it," he said. Before he walked away, he looked at her and smiled. "Have a good evening, Aisha."

"You, too." She waved goodbye as she fought the urge to giggle like a teenage girl.

*

When Aisha got home, she thought about her lack of progress. She hadn't been very productive. She hadn't taken any actionable steps toward her goal. Instead of narrowing her focus on the wounds she had traveled twelve hours to heal, she was doing everything in her power to avoid thinking about them. But perhaps that was the most crucial part of the healing process after all: detachment. Though she had to admit she was nearing avoidance. Obviously, she was still hurt by everything that led her to Dallas.

However, the cut the pain had carved didn't feel as deep. It was very much there, but it felt different. She could already see a faint and distant glimpse of something on the horizon: the light at the end of the tunnel. To get there, she knew she couldn't continue to ignore her issues much longer. She needed to address them head-on. And she would. Soon. Eventually. For now, she was content sending her text message.

Hello David Marshall, this is Aisha Jones. Let's do drinks next week?

WEEK 12

On Monday morning, Aisha received a notification announcing that her aquarium ticket was expiring soon. Her Wednesday was reserved for *Libros & Libations*—mainly Marcus. David Marshall had confirmed reservations for them on Friday. The forecast for the day was clouds. It was too gloomy to be outdoors but too depressing to stay home all day. It was the perfect day to go to the Aquarium.

Her phone lit up again. *Hey girl! The sun should be out tomorrow. Wanna meet for a hike?* Dahlia texted her.

Yes! How's 5?

Perfect! See u then

Aisha was excited about her week. She could get used to her life in Dallas and away from what led her there.

Why did everything need to be addressed, anyway?

Was sweeping things under the rug so bad if what was underneath was never uncovered? How bad could it be if no one knew about the filth underneath the mat? What was the problem with putting everything she didn't want to see inside a room and keeping it locked?

Except she knew what was under the mat, behind the door, inside of her. If she kept it hidden and unaddressed, she was the one who risked being hurt the most.

As much as Aisha spoke her mind, she had never been the most eloquent when it was time to talk things out. It had been especially true during her arguments with James.

"What do you want me to say?" she had yelled out one afternoon. "I can't move at the same exact pace as you. I'm not a fucking robot!"

"Oh, you're not? Some days, I can't tell. It's like, you don't fucking care. Do you even want to be with me?" James shouted while he stood behind his white marble kitchen island.

"Oh. My. God. I can't keep having the same argument with you. What will it take for me to make you believe I want to be in this relationship? News flash: If I didn't want to be with you, I wouldn't be." She stood a few feet away from him, in front of the sofa.

"Here goes Aisha Jones, the cynical reporter, with her damn news flash. Well, I got a couple of announcements to add to your report. I had to beg you to make it official. I had to squeeze an *I love you* out of you. I'm begging you to plan a future with me. A family. Obviously, that is too much to ask. So now, I'm just asking for the nth time to please move in with me because I love you, and I want to be with you. We've been together for a year and a half, but it's still too damn much for you. You know what, I'm sick of begging you." He caught a breath and lowered his tone. "If you don't want this, please tell me now. I don't want you to be in something you don't want to be in." His voice broke at the end.

She was afraid of what moving in together preceded. One more step toward becoming one and closer to completely baring her soul. She was scared to give her all to another human being because of the risk it created. The moment she let all her walls down, she'd become a target in an open field. Then, it would be a clear shot to put a hole at the center of the chest.

She was afraid someone she loved could decide at any moment she wasn't worth sticking around, and when they left, they would take a piece of her with them. But as much as she feared that her heart could get shattered, she was more afraid to lose James. She loved him.

"I want this," she said softly, closing the gap between them. "I want you. I love you. I want to be here. I want to wake up every morning to your horrible snoring."

He let out a single chuckle. "Are you sure, Sha? I don't want you to feel obligated. I want you to do what makes you happy."

She pressed her lips against his. "You make me happy, roomie."

Now, Aisha was rubbing her hands up and down her face as if the friction would wipe her memories. She forced James out of her mind and pictured what she wanted to wear to the Aquarium instead. Her go-to sweater, leggings, and knee-high boots would do. It was only 1:00 PM when she got on the road, but it was so dark outside that it looked like happy hour was at its tail.

She had no issue finding a parking spot at the aquarium. It was early afternoon on a Monday, so it made sense the place wasn't crowded. The aquarium was very blue and smelled like fish. Every sound seemed to adhere to the water's flow. While there, her worries were trapped in a container that stayed outside the aquarium, allowing her to fully enjoy the moment.

Aisha looked at all the sea creatures in awe. She was fascinated by how gracefully they floated above and next to her. She was envious of their peace and carefreeness. She admired the state of their evolution: some concerns were simply a non-factor for them. She was a human, so she couldn't replicate their lifestyle. She had bills, responsibilities, relationships, and emotional wounds. But there had to be a way to apply the peaceful ways of her marine mates to her human existence. She didn't know what it was yet, but she would do her best to figure it out.

When Aisha returned home, she still felt like she was floating. Flowing. For the first time, she physically felt that over half of her being was made of water. She felt connected to the universe. She just didn't know where to go from there. Though she felt lighter and fluid, her pain hadn't been washed away. When it came to healing, one couldn't cut corners. The work had to be done. Things had to be addressed. So, she picked up her phone and group messaged two phone numbers she knew by heart.

Hey this is Aisha. I'm not ready to talk yet but I might be soon. Please don't text me back. Just like the message to acknowledge that you received it. I'll contact you individually when I'm ready to talk.

James immediately liked the message. Sam followed a few minutes later.

That night, it didn't take as long for her to fall asleep. It took almost three months, but she finally took one actionable step. She wasn't sure when she would be ready to have a conversation with either of them, but for the first time in a long time, she felt like it wouldn't take everything in her to do so.

The next day, she arrived at the hiking trail with a little boost of energy. Dahlia immediately noticed Aisha's upbeat mood. "Hey girl, you're radiant!" She hugged Aisha.

"Am I?" She felt her cheeks flushing under her brown skin. "Thank you! You're always glowing, so nothing new there."

Dahlia smiled. "Thanks, girl! It's coconut oil." She threw her head back and laughed at her own comment.

Aisha couldn't help but laugh with her. Her laughter was contagious. When they settled down, they began their walk. They took a narrower path than last time. Dahlia led the way with confidence. Aisha followed behind her with no hesitation. They didn't speak for a while, breathing nature in a comfortable silence. The bright sun created lengthy shadows behind them. The ground was slightly moist, making their steps hollow.

"What have you been up to?" Aisha said at last.

"Busy with work. I took another class during the week."

"How many students do you typically have per class?"

"It varies. I have a handful of regulars, about five to ten new people each time, and some folks who come by sporadically."

"It sounds fun." Aisha moved a branch that was in her way with the back of her hand.

"Yes, it can be. It just gets very repetitive having to teach the same basic steps every week and not seeing most people progress because they're inconsistent." Dahlia waved a gigantic bug away without flinching. Aisha's eyes widened at that sight, but she didn't say anything. Dahlia continued, "My goal is to hopefully start teaching more advanced classes by the end of the year."

"What would it take for you to get there?"

Dahlia didn't speak for a moment, thinking of her answer. "Someone to get fired, I guess. Or I might have to apply at another studio." She laughed. The sound was different, dryer than her usual laughter.

"You don't think it'd happen at your current studio?" They passed a sign that read, "*Beware! You might encounter snakes and poison ivy beyond this point.*" Dahlia continued to walk, unfazed, as if the sign had read, "*Welcome! It's very safe beyond this point. March on!*"

"It's not likely. It's a family business. The owner's son and daughter also teach there. They're not as experienced as me, but apparently, blood is thicker than credentials, so they're next in line." She sighed. "Anyway, how are your wounds healing?"

Aisha smiled at the segue, ignoring the speeding of her heartbeat caused by the potential reptile and poisonous plant encounters. "It's fine. I honestly haven't done much. I'm hoping time does the heavy lifting."

They mercifully came to a cul-de-sac and turned around. They walked back over the footprints they had created on their way there. "I get it. Time will definitely help a lot. Just take it day by day."

"Yes, that's what I keep telling myself." Aisha didn't want to talk about her situation further. Perhaps she would elaborate another time. "How's your daughter? Nia, right?"

Dahlia smiled from ear to ear. "Yes, good memory. She's great! She spent the weekend with her dad. She's always a ball of energy after she sees him. She worships the ground he walks on." Aisha nodded quietly, hoping not to trigger her negative thoughts about Albert. Dahlia continued, "You spend nine months baking a human being, and they come out looking like a spitting image of their dad. That's some bullshit, I tell ya." She laughed out loud, covering the sound of the birds chirping above them.

Aisha wondered if her mother felt the same way. "It's great that you guys can co-parent amicably," she said.

Dahlia nodded. "Yes. It took a minute, but I'm glad we're finally in a good place." Aisha wanted to ask what caused the divorce, but she didn't know if it was appropriate at the stage of their relationship.

Dahlia continued like she had read her mind, "Finding out the man I was married to for ten years had a five-year affair broke me in such a deep way I thought I was irreparable. I didn't think I would ever feel whole again. But two years, a lot of tears, and a hefty therapy bill later, here I am in the woods, very much alive and full."

There was the universe doing that overdone bit again. Boy, was it getting old.

What are you trying to tell me this time?

Here is someone lively and happy after being cheated on and hurt, just like you. She was able to heal, and so will you. Stop worrying and trust the process.

Fuck off!

Aisha didn't need her circumstances mirrored as proof of a potential positive outcome. She didn't need other people's success stories thrown on her path as some kind of incentive not to give up. It wasn't encouraging. It was quite the opposite, actually. All it did was shed a light on the very long path still ahead of her. It was even longer, narrower, and more hazardous than the trail they were now walking out of.

"Wow," Aisha finally said. "I'm sorry you went through that. But I'm happy you came stronger and better on the other side."

"Thanks, girl! I'm sure things will work out just as well for you." They were back on the hard concrete ground. Dahlia opened her mouth to say something, then closed it. She opened it again and said, "I feel like I talked the whole time, sorry." She looked at her watch. "Next time, I'd like to hear more about you if you're open to sharing."

Aisha half-smiled. "Yes."

Dahlia looked at her for a few seconds but didn't speak. Her stare made Aisha feel warm and seen. Dahlia hugged her. "You'll be fine, girl. I promise."

A tear rolled down Aisha's cheek. "Thank you." She wiped her cheek as discreetly as she could behind the embrace.

"Hopefully, we can meet again soon. I really enjoy walking with you. It makes time go by much faster," Dahlia said when they parted from the hug.

"Seriously! Hopefully, next week?"

"Yes, just text me whenever you're free." Dahlia walked to her car and waved goodbye.

Aisha did her best not to think about what Dahlia had shared with her when she made it back home. It's not that she disagreed that she would be fine at the end of this. It was similar to watching a thriller or horror movie and knowing the protagonist's fate. It was evident the film was engineered for them to make it out alive.

Right before the credits rolled, they would be seated on the stairs, blood painted all over their body, quietly waiting for the police to arrive. The loud sirens would deafen their thoughts. They would absently answer the cops' questions with a blanket wrapped around them.

Yes, at that moment, after facing and defeating the antagonist, they would've come to terms with their reality. At that moment, they would be okay. But it wouldn't erase everything they had to go through to be there. It didn't change that they had to give up some parts of themselves to remain alive. That was the cost of survival. The scarring exchange. Yes, they were fine now, but they would never be the same, for better or worse.

To silence her internal monologue, she texted Amir. *What's up big bro?*

Her phone rang a few minutes later. "Sha, I'm scared!" Amir whispered.

Aisha's heart began to race. She could make it to the Dallas Fort Worth airport in half an hour. A non-stop flight could land her in Denver in a couple of hours. If she booked an Uber as soon as she landed, she could immediately get to wherever Amir was. "What's going on? Are you safe? Where are you?" she asked the three questions in one breath.

"I'm at this…thing," he murmured. She heard him move around. There was some indistinct music faintly playing in the background. "They're all wearing white, with flowers wrapped around their heads."

"What?" She frowned. "Are you safe?"

"I don't know. Someone told me Thomas might be here, so I decided to come to hopefully run into him, but now I'm freaking out."

"Why? What are they doing?" She was getting irritated because her brother wasn't clear about the situation. She had to book a flight immediately if she needed to be there.

"It's fucking strange. They're all just smiling non-stop. They're dancing to this weird ass music. They're all high as hell. Like, there isn't a single conversation that makes sense. I tried to join several."

Aisha laughed out loud. "Oh my god, I was so scared! I thought you were in danger, but you're just at some bohemian party or something."

Amir's voice rose one decibel. "No, this isn't just some hippie get-together! Next thing you know, they're all going to line up to jump off a cliff, on some *Midsommar* shit!"

She laughed louder. "Is there a cliff nearby?"

He sighed. "No, but that's not the point!"

"What's the point?"

"This shit's weird as hell!"

"Then you should fit right in." She was still laughing.

"Fuck you!" He finally laughed. "I'm sharing my location with you. If I'm in some forest in the next few hours, you better do something, or I'll haunt you first!" His voice lowered again. "Oh my God. Thomas's here. Gotta go. Love you. Bye!"

She continued to laugh long after he hung up. It was the furthest away they had ever been physically, yet it had been a long time since she had felt so close to her brother. So, she went to bed with the conviction that things would work out for the better when the credits rolled to punctuate this chapter of her life.

The next day, Aisha arrived at *Libros & Libations* an hour before Marcus was supposed to get there. Her favorite bartender was there, wearing ripped jeans and a cropped top that drew a line below his belly button.

"Hey!" he yelled when he saw her. "You're a couple of Irish coffees away from becoming a regular."

She laughed. "Well, I might just become a regular today, then."

He let out a sound that was indisputably laughter. However, it was closer to the sound a washing machine made at the end of a cycle, which made him even more endearing. "What's your name again?" he asked.

"Aisha. And you?"

"Zac with a C." He formed the letter C with his fingers. "One Irish coffee for Aisha!" he yelled to himself. The two people seated at the bar looked at each other, then looked at Aisha and smiled. Clearly, everyone enjoyed Zac's antics.

She grabbed her Irish coffee and sat at the table where she had arranged the rendezvous with Marcus. She looked around and recognized a few people who had been there at least one of the other times she was there. Old Man with Round Glasses wasn't there. It wasn't the same without him. She smiled at that thought.

She sipped her drink slowly while she waited for Marcus. The first sip was hot, warming her throat on the way down. By the time she took the last sip, the beverage had cooled down, and there was an entirely new set of people at the coffee shop. An hour and a half had gone by. Marcus should've been there half an hour ago. She walked up to the bar and fulfilled her contract to become a *Libros & Libations* regular with her second order.

"Another Irish coffee, please," she said. Zac nodded and immediately made her drink.

She drank the second coffee whiskey beverage even slower, hoping Marcus would walk in at any moment. But he didn't. When her phone confirmed she had been there for almost three hours, she accepted that he wouldn't show up. She was disappointed. Hanging out with him was what she had looked forward to the most this week. The feeling was obviously not reciprocal. It's not like she wanted to date him or anything like that. He just looked like an interesting guy, with some interesting things to say, an interesting smile, some interesting shoulders, and some interesting lips...*Jesus!*

What the hell was wrong with her?

She was all over the place. She finished her drink and left. It was probably for the best that Marcus didn't show up today. For once, the universe worked in her favor to prevent her from doing something stupid. He most likely wasn't even interested in her in that way, anyway. Obviously not, since he hadn't cared to show up. He probably forgot about the whole thing because hanging out with her was an insignificant grain of salt in the sea that was his very busy life.

It took her a while longer than usual to fall asleep that night. And when she awoke, the message on her phone lowered her spirits even more.

Greetings, Aisha Jones. Could we reschedule our reservation for next week? Something came up. My sincere apologies. I was very much looking forward to seeing you on Friday. Please let me know what day would work better for you.

If Marcus had shown up yesterday, David Marshall's message wouldn't have affected her as negatively as it did. The things she was excited about and was using to define her social progress in Dallas were merely an afterthought for the people on the other side of it.

Aisha was again reminded of why she couldn't allow any piece of her happiness to depend on anyone but herself. She wasn't going to shut down completely, though. She understood the importance of socialization. However, she wasn't going to rely on it for her happiness. For that, she could only count on herself.

Hi David Marshall. No worries. I can do next Tuesday or the following Friday

The sooner the better, so let's do next Tuesday!

She stayed home the rest of the week. She wasn't sad. She was apathetic. One could argue the latter was worse than the former. She checked in on Amir. Thomas had ignored him at the *Midsommar* party. She could tell how hurt he was—and how much he had cried—by the hoarseness of his voice. But when she asked him to share more, he told her he wasn't ready to talk about it.

Like sister, like brother.

WEEK 13

There had to be some clues, some signs, something which hinted at James and Sam's betrayal. Aisha knew she had probably dismissed it because she trusted them both. But no matter how hard she tried, she couldn't recall any occurrence in which they had behaved in a particularly suspicious manner. She remembered how pleased she had been when they finally started to get along and tease each other like old friends.

"Whatever," Sam had said to James. "I saw your little high school highlights. You have Shaquille O'Neal's shooting range. No way you can beat me at *horse*."

Aisha chimed in, "What's *horse*?"

James replied behind her, "You essentially go back and forth taking shots. If you make the shot, the other person has to make the same shot in the same way, wherever you took it. You spell out *horse* for each shot made, and the person who gets to the letter 'e' first wins."

Aisha nodded. It was simple enough. Sam gave him a golf clap. "Great explanation, James. If you had taken as much time practicing your free throws as you did explaining *horse*, you might have gone more than twenty percent from the free throw line."

Aisha giggled. She must not have fully comprehended all the basketball lingo because James laughed harder than she believed the comment deserved. He took a few steps toward Sam, leaving Aisha on the other side of their kitchen island.

"Even if I was zero percent from the free throw line, you couldn't beat me at *horse*. Wanna bet? Let's put twenty dollars on the line." He extended his hand to make the deal official.

Sam stood up from the counter stool. She looked directly into his eyes and spoke with confidence. "Make it fifty, and you got yourself a deal." He nodded, and they shook on it. Sam broke James's stare and directed her gaze toward Aisha. "Sha, I know I told you things have been a little tight since my roommate moved out, but you didn't have to do this."

Aisha frowned. "What are you talking about?"

Sam looked back at James. "You didn't have to ask James to find a way to give me fifty dollars."

They all laughed at once. Aisha noticed James and Sam were still holding the handshake. They were both very competitive. She couldn't be at their *horse* game because she had to house-sit on the day they scheduled it. That evening, James came back home in a very cheerful mood. Aisha figured he won the game.

"Well, I'm out fifty bucks," he said. Then he gave her a peck on the cheek.

Was that when it started? Basketball required a lot of contact. Was that how it happened? Their skins grazed. They sweated from the effort. Sweat, in the proper context, was an attraction lubricant. James was conventionally handsome, in good physical shape, and had beautiful brown eyes. Sam was attractive in a more unassuming way, which one could argue was more dangerous. Her disposition lowered guards, and when people felt comfortable and safe, their inhibitions exited stage left.

Was that what took place? Perhaps they continued to banter after the game. They talked about things they had in common, things Aisha couldn't relate to. Then one story led to a laugh, one laugh led to a look, one look led to a touch, one touch led to a kiss, and one kiss led to Aisha walking in on them fucking on New Year's Eve. *Life can be a bitch, amirite?*

*

She didn't leave her apartment that Monday. She texted her mother to say hi and let her know she was okay. She wasn't ready to talk with her on the phone, especially given how they had left things the last time they spoke. As expected, her mother replied that she was glad to hear Aisha was doing well and hoped they would talk soon.

The next day, David Marshall texted her around noon to confirm they were still on for their evening reservation. She re-read the message he sent her last Thursday to cancel their meetup.

Greetings, Aisha Jones. Could we reschedule our reservation for next week? Something came up. My sincere apologies. I was very much looking forward to seeing you on Friday. Please let me know what day would work better for you.

The petty side of her wanted to reply to his check-in text today with: *Greetings, asshole. Could we reschedule our reservation for never? Something came up (a nap). My insincere apologies. Could you lose my number now or immediately? Please let me know which option works better for you.*

She was sure the thing that "came up" when he had canceled on her was some lubed butthole. But she couldn't be upset at him. He didn't owe her anything. Plus, he had reached out early enough to let her know about the change of plan.

Aisha was confident David Marshall wouldn't be a significant part of her life, even for a brief period. This was someone she could have fun banter with. After a couple of drinks, she might even throw in a dash of flirting. And if he said the right things, whatever they were, she might even consider tasting a spoonful of his lips. Some harmless fun to add some spice to the very bland mixture her life had been over the last three months. Unlike Sweet Carlos, she would feel no remorse if she had to completely cut contact with the artist at any point. That would probably save him the trouble of finding an excuse to move on to the next layers he wanted to "peel."

Thinking about Carlos created a pinch that traveled throughout her lower abdomen. She hadn't treated the man kindly. She owed him an apology. Though she wondered if he still cared. He had most likely forgotten about her completely. The best service she could offer him was never to contact him again.

The weather remained in the low sixties that evening. She wore an off-the-shoulder, long-sleeved black dress that drew a line above her knees. She paired it with some black pumps that hadn't seen the light since she unpacked her bags. Her hair was long enough for tiny finger coils, so she twisted the kinky strands around themselves to create the style. She looked in the mirror and smiled. She looked good. The night would go wherever she felt like taking it.

David Marshall stood when she arrived at the restaurant. She walked with her chin parallel to the stone vinyl floor and her shoulders held back. Their table was in the middle of the room, surrounded by the other guests—mainly couples—who were seated so close to each other that they created a single shape under the dimmed lights.

"Aisha Jones," he said when she was close enough. "You look splendid, breathtaking." He hugged her. He smelled like bourbon and vanilla. She held the embrace a little longer to inhale the warm scent.

She looked directly into the green of his eyes when their bodies parted. "Not breathtaking enough, since you're still standing." She smiled only with one corner of her mouth.

He laughed in that contained manner of his. "I don't know for how much longer," he said when they sat down.

The waiter came by to hand them the food menu and take their drink orders. She ordered the cabernet with the fanciest name, *Château Pape Clément*. The slightly widened eyes of the server and silent nod told her she had butchered the pronunciation. David ordered an Old Fashioned. The server repeated their order and took it as his opportunity to correct her politely.

"So, one Old Fashioned for the gentleman and a glass of the *Châ-teau Pa-pe Clé-ment* for the lady." She hadn't been that far off. A little more stress on the "eau" and the "*é*," and all she needed was a beret and a baguette to book her flight to Paris.

David nodded. "Yes, thank you." When the waiter walked away, he said, "Aisha, you are so stunning. I must say, you make me a little nervous."

He's not wasting any time, uh? You're going to have to work a little harder than that, my friend. "Thank you. Did you invite me here to hit on me or talk about your art?"

He smiled. Then he looked at her so intensely she felt like the material of her dress was thinning. "Both, and I think you know that."

She crossed her arms over her chest. His stare made her feel naked, and though she didn't mind, she wanted to let the night unfold before anything happened...if it came to that. "Well, I'm here to give you the feedback you requested on the two paintings I looked at. And I'd like to hear about your creative process. This is a professional meeting." She patted his hand. "Behave."

He pressed his lips together. "I'll try."

The server came back with their drinks and took their food orders. It was a steakhouse, so Aisha and David ordered a porterhouse and a filet mignon.

Aisha took a sip and nodded approvingly. "So, about the two paintings, what inspired you to create them?"

He answered without any pause, "The first piece you saw was driven by my sexual desire for women. The beauty, depth, and warmth of their parts. It was overwhelming my thoughts, so I wanted to illustrate how I viewed it on a canvas." He spoke slowly while looking at her in the eyes, then gazing at her lips and back at her eyes.

She felt her breaths speeding up, causing her chest to rise and fall just as fast. She hoped the lights were dimmed enough to hide her reaction.

"Interesting," was all she said in response. If David said anything else about women's warm and deep parts, she couldn't guarantee that her own increasingly heating parts wouldn't be warming his face before the red meat was served.

"What about the other painting?" she said before he said anything else about vulvas.

"When I saw your reaction to it, my interest in you grew even more," he said. She nodded but didn't speak. He continued, "I'm a bit of a nihilist, Aisha. So for a while, I struggled to find any meaning in life. The only way I finally concluded that life made sense was by experiencing beauty." He leaned forward and spoke in a lower timbre. "That's what inspired me to create *The Lady on the Grass*. The satisfaction and peace in her eyes when she looked at the sky was my own. Her eyes are for anyone to see through. It's one of my favorite paintings, yet not many people are moved by it as much as I was when I put the brush down. But you were."

She swallowed the knot clogging her throat. "Yes."

"Tell me more about yourself, Aisha."

"What do you want to know?"

"Whatever you want to share."

"I won best Halloween costume in eighth grade."

He laughed. "What was the costume?"

"I was simultaneously Scooby-Doo and Shaggy."

He laughed the hardest he had since she had met him. "I have so many questions, so I will ask none."

She tittered. "Smart decision."

Their meals arrived, smelling divine and seasoned just the right amount. After one bite, she asked one of the questions she had been thinking about for a few days.

"So, how was your evening after we parted ways last time?" She raised one eyebrow as she took another bite of her medium-rare steak.

He took his time to swallow his rarer cut before he answered. "Very enjoyable."

She asked the other question on the tip of her tongue. "Is that why you canceled on me last time? More *enjoyment* scheduled?"

He didn't answer for a few seconds. He just looked at her with a tight-lipped smile, as if he was searching for something on her face. Then he stared at her lips like he had found whatever he was looking for. "Yes," he said. He took another bite of his filet. "Does that bother you?"

She rolled her eyes. "Why would it bother me?"

"Some people are very territorial."

She put her utensils down. "I'm not territorial. And even if I was, you're not my territory to guard."

He took a sip of his drink. "Wonderful. Possessiveness is a turn-off for me."

She snorted. "I don't care what your turn-offs are. I'm not trying to turn you on."

"Why not?"

"I'm not interested in you in that way." She hoped that she sounded convincing.

He leaned forward. "I am."

She could feel her blood pumping faster and faster. "Well, that's…that's not my problem."

David found her hand on the table and caressed it with his index finger. Then he moved his hand away from hers to take another sip of his drink. A drop of the liquid rolled down the corner of his mouth. He slowly wiped it with his middle finger. He looked back at her and said, "Don't fight your urges, Aisha." His voice was so sultry she began to perspire. He moved his chair closer to hers.

Aisha watched him in silence. She thought she would be the chauffeur for the evening, but clearly, she was the passenger, and she would be lying if she said she wasn't enjoying the ride.

She finally managed to speak when they were shoulder to shoulder. "What do you think you're doing?"

He didn't answer. He looked at her first in the eyes, then focused his stare on her lips, chest, and back at her eyes. She saw a hint of the wilderness behind his gaze. It called for her, and she wanted to answer. Now David was staring at her with a desire that darkened his irises.

He wanted to fuck her. She wanted to fuck him. *So, fuck it.*

David leaned forward and kissed her like he had heard her internal concession. The kiss was so passionate she had no idea how much time had passed when their lips parted. The server must've been waiting for them to finish because he immediately took the opportunity to drop the check. David held her hand under the table while he covered the tab with his free hand. Then he brought her hand to his lips and kissed it softly.

"Would you like to get out of here, Aisha?"

She just nodded in response. They walked outside without speaking. He led her to his vehicle, a very sleek black sports car parked in the back of the almost empty parking lot. His mouth opened to say something, but she shut him up with her lips. Everything that happened tonight confirmed that David was someone she wouldn't be interested in having any meaningful relationship with.

Clearly, he was a hedonistic rake. He was only interested in consuming what he considered to be beautiful. She was the latest thing that had sparked his sensual desires. The moment he would get sexual access to her, his interest would fade. She had no desire to entertain any romantic relationship at this time, but she was horny. David was the perfect match for her current circumstances.

With her lips still against his, Aisha jumped to wrap her legs behind his lower back. Her arms were circling his neck. She found his mouth again, then bit his lower lip lightly. He groaned, and she felt his erection against what he had described earlier as her "deep" and "warm" parts. He walked toward the car's passenger side with Aisha still wrapped around him. He gently put her down and opened the car door.

He searched through the glove compartment and grabbed a condom. Aisha stepped in front of him. She sat on the red leather passenger seat. She was facing him as he stood by the car door. She took her panties off. Then, she stood back up and smiled at him with a new spark in her eyes. He bit his lip. She turned to face the car seat and leaned forward. She raised her dress, bent down, and used the red leather seat for support. She heard him move behind her. She turned her head to look at him. He put the condom on.

Everything that followed was well done, compliments to the chef. She felt the same way a famished person would feel after a great meal. They knew anything would be satiating since they were starving. Yet even through hunger, they recognized the quality.

After they both climaxed, she put her underwear back on. David leaned against the car, panting. "You're a marvel, Aisha," he said between breaths.

She grinned. "Thank you for dinner…and for this." She gave him a peck on the cheek. "Have a good night."

He smiled. "You too."

She walked to her car without looking back. She drove away and saw David enter his car through her rear mirror. When she parked her car at her apartment complex, she was surprised to receive a text from him.

Made it home safe? he asked.

Yes

Have a good night then!

Good night

The following day, she considered blocking David's phone number. She projected that their arrangement would last a few weeks at best if she decided to make him a sort of acquaintance with benefits. Between her reluctance to any form of commitment and his thirst for novelty, she couldn't predict which one would tap out first. She wasn't thinking about ending things with him mid-genesis because she feared feelings could grow. It just seemed redundant.

Last night was fun. However, when it came to sex, an emotional connection always enhanced the experience for her. The intimacy the feelings created made the act more pleasurable.

However, she had to admit that last night was great. There were no emotions involved, just a raw and primal connection. It was different. It wasn't her number one preference, but it was fulfilling in its own right.

And if Aisha was going to try to mirror the sea creatures from the aquarium to find inner peace, what was wrong with tapping into her animalistic side for her sexual desires? It would provide her with a temporary outlet for release, and when things would inevitably end, no one would get hurt. It was an ideal arrangement.

Aisha picked up her phone to message Dahlia. This was the one new relationship she was interested in nurturing. So far, Dahlia had been delightful and vulnerable—the quality she admired the most in others. She had voluntarily shared so much about herself that Aisha was somewhat comfortable telling her more about what brought her to Dallas. For some reason, the need to share pieces of her story with Dahlia felt very urgent now.

Hey! Would you like to meet for a hike this week?

It took about four hours for Dahlia to respond. *Hey girl! Unfortunately I cant. I have a lot going on this week. But I'll text you next week.*

No worries next week's good. Hope you have a good rest of your week!

Aisha was disappointed. The one week she felt like opening up to someone whom she believed worthy of moderate confidence, the opportunity wasn't on the table. She realized how irrational her thought process was. She could wait another week, and if the need to talk became more pressing, she could call Amir.

She was just more comfortable sharing her feelings with someone who didn't know her that well. The feedback would be more objective. Plus, Amir was still withholding details about what happened with Thomas. She wanted to leverage the details of her issues to access his. She was sad her conversations with her brother now resembled a prisoner swap, but she had to do whatever she had to do to maintain some kind of intimacy with Amir.

Aisha spent the rest of the week alone, only opening her mouth to say, "Hey," "Good, and you?" "Excuse me," "Thank you," "You too," and other platitudes mindlessly thrown out when someone stepped outside of their home. She only left her apartment to run errands or grab food.

On Thursday, the cashier scanned her items and spoke to her without making eye contact. "How are you?" the woman said.

"Good, and you?"

On Friday, she went to the first floor of her apartment to pick up her mail. Someone was in her way, too focused on a phone conversation to notice her. "Excuse me," she said as she passed her obnoxious neighbor.

She felt like dressing up on Saturday, so she made a reservation at an upscale Mexican restaurant. The maître d' greeted her with a wide grin.

"Aisha Jones?" the man called. "I'll walk you to your table. Please follow me."

"Thank you," she said.

David texted her on Sunday. *Hey! Just wanted to say hi. I hope you're having a lovely day.*

Hey thank you. You too

WEEK 14

Aisha hadn't spoken a single word out loud that Monday. Even on the days she didn't interact with anyone, she spoke to herself aloud. It made her feel less alone. Her favorite monologues were delivered when she watched horror movies.

Yes, please go in there. Go investigate. Dumbass. No, yeah, walk inside the dark tunnel. No, that's great. Sure, follow that weird voice in the forest. No, you're doing amazing, sweetie. Keep going! Your head's not going to get chopped in about fifteen seconds. Oh, now you wanna run? No, go back there and try to talk to that thing to understand its story. Idiot. Oh my God, that little ass branch got you on the floor? Yeah, you're dead.

But that day, she watched two scary movies silently, only mildly chuckling when the designated to-be-murdered characters inevitably tripped on a branch or a rock while running away from their gruesome scripted death. She only opened her mouth to brush her teeth, eat, and drink. She wanted to feel the bluntness of her loneliness. She wanted to challenge the hollow, and it was up for the task, as if it had been waiting for the opportunity to tell her how empty she really was deep down. Everything she had done over the last three and a half months was a frail cover that one quiet day alone with her thoughts could easily blow away.

It didn't matter how many miles she had hiked.

It didn't matter what new friendship she thought she was building with Dahlia.

It didn't matter how much she had enjoyed her Irish coffees at *Libros & Libations*.

It didn't matter what great sex she had with David.

It didn't matter how close she believed she was growing back to Amir.

It didn't matter how proud she was of herself for finally reaching out to Sam and James to hint at a future conversation.

It didn't matter that she was no longer that uncomfortable being a party at one at diners.

It didn't matter how much progress she believed she was making.

When she was alone, without distractions, she was still that eight-year-old seated across the purple accent chair, looking away from where her life had originated. The child who had stared at the floor to not face the river her stream was sourced from. She was still that little girl who needed her father to water her so she could grow into a filled-up woman. And if he couldn't do that, she wanted to know why! If, at the very least, her father cared enough to tell her why he didn't care about her, that would've given her something to grasp.

But he didn't.

She would have to scream at him to get anything useful. But now she couldn't even find Albert to demand answers because he was dead. How could she get any resolution from someone who was no longer here? How could she get closure when she knew that even if he were still alive, he wouldn't have the tools to fix the void he had carved within her? How could she share the DNA of such a careless human being?

If genes had passed Albert's physical features down to her, it was inevitable they also shared similar character traits. She resembled the person she despised the most. That conundrum had fed the void his absence had created.

By Wednesday, she had still not spoken out loud. When Dahlia messaged her to ask if she wanted to meet for a hike the next day, she replied that she couldn't meet this week and would reach out the following one. Her desire to share some of her story with Dahlia had been swallowed by the same ebb and flow that had temporarily taken her voice.

On Thursday, she ignored her mother's call. After the ringing stopped, she messaged her to let her know she would reach out soon. As much as she despised her father, she also questioned her mother's judgment because she chose him. Aisha was convinced that feeling would've evaporated if it hadn't been for the incident that had damaged their relationship. While she admired her mother for single-handedly raising both Amir and her—and sacrificing a whole lot in the process—it still didn't excuse what she said.

On Friday afternoon, she declined David's offer to meet for dinner that very evening. She wasn't in the mood to see him, and a four-hour notice wasn't acceptable. Even if they were only going to be sex buddies, a certain amount of decorum was still required.

Amir was the one person who could get her out of her silent spree. However, when she called him on Sunday, he didn't answer. After the ringing stopped, he messaged her to let her know he wasn't in the mood to talk and would call her back when he was.

WEEK 15

The sun was so bright when she opened the blinds that Aisha stepped outside on her balcony. She never spent much time on it because it was very small and looked brittle. Also, there wasn't anything interesting to look at out there. As she stood with her elbows against the railing, she was nervous the whole thing could collapse at any moment.

Thankfully, the spring had given her something interesting to look at. A flowerless tree she had only given an unfocused glance at when she moved in was now an exuberant bouquet of white magnolias. Aisha was still for a moment as she stared at the flowers blooming about ten yards away from where she stood. She was in awe of the beautiful life that had always been there, even when she couldn't see it in its totality.

Finally, she spoke. "Wow."

When she walked back inside, she immediately picked up her phone and dialed. Her mother answered on the second ring. "Hey, honey! How are you?"

"Hey, Mom. I'm doing well. You?"

"I'm doing fine. I miss you. How's Dallas?"

"Good. The weather's beautiful."

"Oh, I bet."

No one spoke for a moment. Aisha was used to her mom asking back-to-back questions for the duration of their calls.

Aisha broke the silence. "How are things at the salon?"

"Good. The new girl's picking up quickly. I was really nervous when Leslie put her two weeks. I relied on her a lot, probably more than I should've more recently. I knew it would be hard to make up for her absence, but the new girl's doing well."

"That's good. Did Leslie tell you why she decided to quit? I thought she loved working there, and all the clients loved her too."

"They did. More than me, apparently. A lot of them started to come only when she was here. So, when she told them she was opening her own salon, quite a few decided to follow her."

"I'm sorry, Mom. That's kind of messed up."

"Yes, sweetie, but there's not much I can do about it. I just have to be more present at the salon to maintain a great rapport with all my patrons. That way, the next time one of my employees decides to open their own business, I won't lose twenty percent of my clientele."

Aisha considered her next words before she let them out. She knew tact could sometimes be lacking in her delivery. "Mom, I thought the hair salon was your top priority. What's taking your time away from it?" she said measuredly.

Her mom cleared her throat. "I don't know if you've been talking to your brother more often than you and I have, but…he's not doing great since he broke up with Thomas. He's not handling it well…to say the least."

Aisha's chest tightened. "Did something happen? Did he try to hurt himse—"

"No, no! Nothing like that! Don't worry, honey. It's not that bad. I just have to check in on him more often and spend time with him a little more frequently, that's all. He's doing a lot better now, but I still go see him at least every other day for my own peace of mind."

"Should I come back? I didn't know it was that bad."

"Baby, it's fine, I promise. I would've told you if it was cause for concern."

"You'd tell him if I needed to be there, right?"

"Of course! He's just heartbroken, but he is slowly putting the pieces back together. Your brother's tough. He took the breakup really hard, but he'll be fine."

"Okay, I'll call him today."

"That's a good idea. Please don't tell him I told you how sad he is. You know how he can be?"

"How's that?"

"Like you, hon." Her mother laughed. "I gave birth to two of the most prideful and hard-headed human beings on the planet."

Aisha chuckled. "True."

"I miss you, sweetie."

She took a moment to answer. "I miss you too." She heard her mom's exhale behind the line, which made her smile. "I'll call your bullheaded son now. Bye, Mom."

"Bye-bye, sweetheart."

Aisha wasn't sure how to handle the information her mother had just shared with her. She wasn't sure what hurt her the most: the fact that Amir was doing so badly that her mother had to spend time with him on an almost daily basis, the fact that her mom lost her best employee and a good percentage of her clientele taking on what Aisha believed was *her* responsibility, or the fact that all of it took place without her knowledge.

Why was she still in Dallas?

She could avoid James and Sam in Denver. Frankly, it might be more convenient to deal with her mom, Amir, and even her father's situation there.

It was time to go home.

Before Aisha drove back to Denver, she had to catch up with everything she had missed. She sat down on her beige couch. She redownloaded and logged back into her social media accounts. Facebook led her way too far down memory lane, sharing updates of distant family members and high schoolmates she no longer cared to keep up with. At least no one had died. One of her acquaintances from college who had previously overshared all the details of their then amazing relationship was now sharing a post listing the "Top Ten Signs You Are Dating a Narcissist!"

Instagram had more relevant updates. Someone got a puppy. Someone got their dream job. Someone said yes. Someone shared a throwback vacation photo captioned "Take me back," as if she had financed the initial trip. Someone felt cute and might delete later.

Someone was expecting.

Aisha stopped scrolling. She read the name under the sonogram over and over again until her eyes watered: *Sam.McMiller1411*. With her eyes widened and moist from stupefaction, she scrolled through the one hundred and four people who *liked* the picture. And there, casually, as if she had never mattered at all, *James_____Ashton__* had left a heart.

Aisha logged out and deleted all her social media apps. When her phone was cleared from the medium that had shown her the unforgivable, she put her head inside her hands and let the tears fall. The reality was limpid, yet she needed absolute crystal-clear clarity.

She messaged the group chat she created a couple of weeks ago. *Are you pregnant? Are you the father?*

Sam replied first. *Yes*

James followed. *Yes.*

Aisha saw the bubbles forming next to Sam's and James's names. They were writing something she didn't want to read, elaborating when nothing else needed to be said. She had the only two answers that mattered, so she didn't want to hear anything else from them. Ever. She blocked both of their contacts in a hurry. She didn't delete the messages, just in the event that she would wake up one morning and question if any of it had been real.

She could've lay on the couch and closed her eyes. Morpheus would've absorbed some of the pain. Not the brunt of it, sure, but enough to buy her some time to accept the reality. The person who knew all of her, who she had allowed the closest to her heart, was expecting a child with the only person she had ever been in love with and had planned to spend the rest of her life with. That was the naked, crystal-clear reality.

Closing her eyes and escaping her reality was a short-lived but appealing option. She could sleep and dream and sleep and dream until it wasn't clear what was real and what wasn't. But no matter how long she kept her eyes shut not to face reality, the truth would still be there. It would continue to grow until it took its own unassisted breaths when it reached full term. How could she ever forgive or even look at Sam and James again when the reminder of their betrayal had taken a life of its own?

Aisha gathered all those thoughts to the best of her abilities and moved them into a hidden compartment inside her mind. She locked them in. She knew they wouldn't stay there quietly. She knew they wouldn't politely wait for her to let them out when she was ready to deal with them. They would barge out at the most inappropriate time and probably ruin something that had nothing to do with them. She knew that very well since she had previously practiced this faulty self-preservation method. She was well aware that it was a band-aid placed over a gunshot.

Yet she calmly patched the adhesive bandage on top of the deep bleeding hole. *Making do.*

Aisha grabbed her phone and walked back to her tiny balcony. She sat on the floor and dialed. After a few rings, a drowsy voice picked up.

"Yes?" Amir said.

"Hello, Sleeping Beauty. Don't you have to be at work?"

"I took a sick day."

"Are you sick?"

"Duh."

"Sick sick or don't-feel-like-being-at-work sick?"

He cleared his throat. "Both."

"How are you, Amir? Like, really. Don't bullshit me."

"I've been better."

"How can I help?"

"Tell me something really fucked up or really funny." His voice sounded a little clearer.

Without skipping a beat, she said, "Sam's pregnant." She waited for a reaction, but Amir was silent. So, she added: "James is the father." Not a single sound came from the other side of the line. Aisha looked at her phone screen to make sure Amir was still on. "Did you hear me?"

"Y-yes. Jesus. I heard you. Fuck. That's really fucked up indeed."

"You asked; I delivered."

"Damn, Sha. I'm sorry I haven't been checking in on you that much after you told me about them. I know how you like your space and whatnot, but damn. If you told me about this, I would've made sure to call more often. I mean, I'm not doing great with the Thomas thing, but this is some next-level fuckery." He whistled. "Are you okay?"

"I haven't processed it yet. I just found out today."

"They told you?"

"I logged back on Instagram and saw that Sam posted a sonogram. James liked the pic. I texted them to confirm it was their baby, and they both said yes."

Amir whistled again. "I knew I did the right thing by blocking them. My IG account would've probably gotten suspended if I saw that shit," he said. Aisha chuckled. Her brother spoke again. "So, what are you going to do? Are you just going to stay in Dallas now?"

"Before I saw that picture, I decided to come back home. I mean, I really miss you and Mom, too. It's not like I was planning on just forgiving them and moving on, but at least before I found out, it was fathomable, you know. We could've possibly had some type of courteous relationship in the distant future…but a kid? Like, I don't even know where to start. I don't know what I'm gonna do. It feels like I have to put the pieces of a puzzle back together, but I don't know where the puzzle is to begin with."

"I understand, sis. I'm so sorry. Is there anything I can do to help?"

"Don't keep me at arm's length. Call me if you need me. Reach out to me if you need anything. Talk to me when you're not okay. Talk to me when you're okay. Let me be there for you."

Amir sighed before he replied. "I promise I will do that under one condition."

"Let me guess, I should do the same?"

"Obviously."

"It's a deal," she said with an upbeat tone.

"You promise?"

"Have I ever lied to you?"

"Bitch?"

She laughed. "Fine, I promise."

"Good. I miss you, Sha."

"I miss you too."

They both didn't speak for a while. She was crying. It was clear from the sniveling echoing in her right ear that Amir was crying, too.

He broke the weeping first. "This is gross." He chuckled between sniffles.

She cackled and cried at the same time. "Agreed."

"Thank you for calling. I feel a lot better now."

"Me too."

"Love you, little sis."

"Love you, big bro."

They checked in on each other the next day. And the next day. And the day after. She was so happy things were going back to the way they used to be that she didn't think it would be necessary to address the quiet distance that had grown between them after their father passed away. The wound was healing, so there was no need to figure out what had caused it.

Some stones were better left unturned.

Aisha spent the rest of her week at home but didn't feel as dejected as the days prior. The thing she had found out about Sam and James was still locked in a box inside her mind, and so far, it seemed it was quietly dwelling in the hidden place. At first glance, at least. The reality was a little different. The progress she had made by finally telling her mother that she missed her, rekindling her bond with her brother, and forming connections with new people in Dallas was leaning against the door where the box was locked.

The truth box was banging on the door like cops with a warrant. The enhanced relationships with her mother and her brother and her new potential relationships with Dahlia, David, and even Marcus were holding the fragile door in place with all their might. The door was fragile, and the lock was weak. The moment anything would slightly weaken any of those relationships, the truth box would break free, damaging anything on its way to her sanity. Aisha knew it. But as if she were a pirate, she voluntarily put on an eye patch and turned a blind eye.

WEEK 16

It was so interesting how different people were depending on the meals they were eating out. The breakfast people were often in a hurry. If they sat to eat their bagels or drink coffee, they usually checked their watches frantically and/or worked on something on their laptop while taking an unfocused bite. This meal wasn't meant to be enjoyed. It was meant to give them the fuel to get through their day.

The brunch people were Aisha's favorite. These folks were most likely off on the day they decided to hang out with the eclectic love child of breakfast and lunch. They leisurely strolled to their seats, laughing on the way there. They asked if the mimosas truly had no bottom and broke into laughter mid-question. They took their time swallowing their chicken and waffles. This meal was social. It was meant for catching up and smelling the roses.

The lunch crowd was intriguing, somewhere between the beginning and the end of their day. They were excited because they were finally halfway through their shift, but they sighed as they waited for their meal because they were only halfway through their shift. They ate at a moderate pace. They were trying to enjoy the block of time that gave them back the full humanity that professionalism stripped away.

The dinner people, who were also the happy hour enthusiasts, were fun. They had run to their cars at the end of their workday because the *somewhere* where it was five o'clock was theirs. This meal was meant for unwinding. They had dealt with uncooperative customers, pointless meetings, irritating phone calls, horrible traffic, sick patients, chaotic children, and everything under the sun all day. They ate, drank, laughed, and enjoyed their evening while trying not to think about the fact that they'd have to deal with everything that made their dinner so enjoyable by comparison all over again the very next day.

Aisha was often in the corner of the room, looking at the different crowds and observing the changing dynamics. Sometimes, she stayed in the restaurant so long that the coffees became mimosas, then wine or liquor. She had learned to bring her laptop to give the appearance that she was working on something very important. The electronic device lessened the number of sympathetic looks typically thrown her way. If she was busy working on something, it apparently justified her being alone.

When she left the restaurant that Monday afternoon, her phone rang. It was an unknown number, so she didn't answer. A few seconds later, she saw the notice that a voicemail had been left. It was probably someone who wanted to let her know about her car's extended warranty.

She pushed play. "Hey Sha, it's Sam…" She immediately stopped the recording, deleted the voicemail, and blocked the number. Hearing Sam's raspy voice had made the liquid that circulated through her veins cold and icy. However, a conflicting warm feeling lay below the ice and attempted to melt it. The same feeling one had when they ran into a person they hadn't seen in a while. The way someone felt when they went back home after they had been homesick. The invisible imprints that years of memory left below the skin. Aisha knew she could never forgive Sam, but it didn't erase their six years of friendship.

As she walked to her car, she remembered the day she told Sam she could see herself spending the rest of her life with James.

"I'm shocked," Sam had whispered. They were in an art gallery Sam had read good reviews about. "I knew you had strong feelings, but I didn't realize you thought he was your person."

"I know," Aisha said. "I'm shocked, too. With all the bullshit with Albert, I honestly didn't think I could ever envision spending the rest of my life with a human of the male variety. But I love James." Aisha paused after she said that. She stopped to notice the ease with which the words came out. Her body was relaxed, and her mind was clear. Her feelings were even clearer. "I love him, and I want to spend the rest of my life with him."

Sam stopped walking. They were in front of a geometric optic illusion. A design that changed shape depending on the angle at which one looked at it. From where they stood, it was a triangle.

Sam held her hand. "Sha, are you certain? Like, one hundred percent?"

Aisha looked at the three-sided figure and then back at her friend. "One hundred percent!" She grinned.

Sam smiled. Her eyes shone with tears that didn't roll past her long eyelashes. She didn't say anything. She hugged Aisha. She held her so tight Aisha could feel Sam's heart racing. Aisha closed her eyes and cried. She had found the love of her life, and she was even luckier to have a friend who shared her happiness with no inhibition. They walked away from the geometric design when they parted from the embrace. Aisha looked back and saw that the triangle was now two lines that met and stopped at a point. The third line was a spiral.

Now, she cracked the door in her mind where the truth box was locked, and she attempted to throw the memories of Sam into it—mission unaccomplished. Aisha started her engine and took a deep breath. To avoid thinking about her sad memories and because she wanted to, she texted Dahlia.

Hey! The last few days have been crazy but I'm thinking of going to the trail tomorrow around 12 if you're free to meet. She hit sent and drove off.

Dahlia replied when Aisha made it home. *Hey girl, same! Yes tomorrow is perfect. See you then!*

*

When Aisha arrived at the trail the next day, Dahlia was already there. She was stretching in that elegant and breezy manner she always did. When Aisha was a few feet away, Dahlia spoke without looking up from her hamstring stretch.

"Hey, girl! Do you want to take the hard path today?"

Aisha frowned. *The hard path?* What did that mean? The last path cautioned to beware of venomous snakes and poison ivy. What was worse than that? Potential bear run-ins? "What's on the hard path?" she asked behind her locked teeth.

Dahlia was still looking down. She must've heard the nervousness in Aisha's tone because she laughed before answering. "Don't worry," she said as she looked up, "no werewolves. It's just a bit hilly and lengthier, that's all."

Aisha tried to hide her relief with exaggerated enthusiasm. "Oh, okay! Sure, then. Let's take the hard path!"

With the habituality of leap year, the behavior of things that do not happen that often but manage to remember patterns, their steps immediately aligned as they took the hilly path. They hadn't walked together for almost one month, yet there was no awkwardness because of how much time had passed since they last met. There was no discomfort because they hadn't made much effort to communicate until they met again today. Their reunion felt like the most natural thing in the world. It felt like the green leaves, the blooming flowers, and the birds singing because the spring was here. Their relationship had the texture of the ground below their footsteps: not too deep, not too shallow.

"What have you been up to?" Dahlia said as they started ascending.

Before the pregnancy news, Aisha was ready to open up slightly. She wanted to reciprocate the trust Dahlia had granted her when she shared details about her work situation and the cause of her divorce. She wanted to crack the door and give someone new a chance to peek through and see her. The pregnancy news made her even more hesitant to trust anyone. And if Dahlia didn't have that ingenious lightness emanating through her pores, Aisha would've reverted to her default response. She would've slammed that door shut, double-bolted. She would've forced their conversations to resemble the ones that primarily existed in hospitality lobbies and long checkout lines until it became so insufferable and banal that Dahlia would justifiably have to excuse herself. But the cadenced way the hips of the woman walking next to her flowed from side to side, washed away some of her resistance. She wouldn't make Dahlia pay for Sam and James's actions. She was going to proceed with caution, yes, but she was going to proceed, nonetheless.

"I've been resting," Aisha said, "and catching up with my family and things going on back home." Her breaths accelerated to adjust to the new altitude. The hill wasn't anything compared to the mountain trails in Colorado—though she was mainly speaking from other people's experiences—but it was challenging enough to justify its higher ranking compared to the *Beware of venomous snakes and poison ivy* path.

Dahlia took a moment to catch her breath before she spoke. "Phew. I've not walked this trail in a long time. I forgot how it was." She wiped the sweat from her forehead with the back of her hand. "So, how's everyone doing back in Denver?"

"Okay." Aisha exhaled, both to catch her breath and to give herself the strength to share. "My brother's going through a breakup. I'm trying to be there for him, but it's tough being eight hundred miles away."

Dahlia nodded. "I'm sorry to hear that. How long were they together?"

"Three years."

Dahlia nodded again. "Continue to check in on him as often as you can. It's tough, it's hard, but it'll be fine in the end." Dahlia said the words with confidence, as if it were a promise she was in charge of fulfilling.

Perfect. Aisha had completed her confiding quota for today. Sure, what she had shared wasn't directly about her, but it was about someone very dear to her, so it counted. "Thank you," she said before looking down to ensure her foot didn't hit a big rock on her right. "What about you? What have you been up to?"

"I'll tell you in a little bit. Knowing me, I'll start going on and on for half a mile like last time. Today, I want to hear more about you. You don't have to go into details unless you want to, of course. But tell me, what did you travel twelve hours away to work on?"

Welp, here goes nothing. "I lost my best friend and my boyfriend," Aisha said. Dahlia's eyes widened in shock. Aisha immediately understood how Dahlia heard it, so she clarified. "Oh no, they're not dead! Well, they're dead to me."

"That's terrible. Losing a best friend and partner is…man. I mean, I don't know which one is worse. Again, only share as much as you're comfortable with, but how long were the respective relationships?"

"I was with him for two years, and I've known her for six." She could hear the truth box banging in her mind. She clenched her fist to fight off the emotions that wanted to overpower her.

They turned sharply into an open field where the sun shone without any obstacle, and the grass was the height of their ankles on both sides of the dirt path. Dahlia glanced at Aisha. She opened her mouth, then closed it. She took one breath in and one breath out. Finally, she said, "Were the losses…related?"

Aisha didn't answer. She just looked down at their uniformed steps.

"I see," Dahlia said. "How's the healing coming along?"

"Trailing."

"Anything I can do to help?"

Aisha looked at her. Then she looked around them. Finally, she opened her arms like *Christ the Redeemer* on top of Mount Corcovado. "This helps."

Dahlia extended her arms out in a similar fashion. "Doesn't it?" She let her arms fall gracefully, like a ripe fruit off a tree. "Nature keeps me sane. I needed this, too."

"How's everything been for you?"

Dahlia sighed. "The last two weeks have been…what's the best way to put it…interesting."

"You don't have to tell me all the details if you are not comfortable, but wha—"

"My ex wants to get back together."

Aisha halted her steps. "Your ex-husband?"

Dahlia continued to walk. "Yes."

Aisha caught up with her. The open field tightened back into a narrow, pebbly path framed by tall trees full of green leaves. "How do you feel about it?"

"I don't know. I was definitely caught off guard. He told me when I dropped Nia off at his place two weeks ago. He's been acting differently for the last three months, but I was not expecting that." She wasn't looking at Aisha when she spoke. She was looking straight ahead at the endless greenery.

"How has he been acting?"

Dahlia finally looked at her, but only for an instant. "It's hard to explain because you don't know him. He's not someone who observes, hmm, how do I put it? Formalities. To the point that it might seem rude to someone who doesn't know him.

"So, when he started asking if I'd like a drink when I dropped Nia off or if I wanted something to eat, it made me raise an eyebrow. I thought he needed a favor. But then, the co-parent hand-off that used to last less than ten minutes stretched to about half an hour because of him, and I'm the talker." She chuckled, then continued, "He asked how things were going at the studio one week, and the next one, he followed up on my previous update. He listened attentively to anything that came out of my mouth. He hasn't behaved that way since we started dating twelve years ago. Then, two weeks ago, he finally told me. He said that he still loves me and is willing to do whatever it takes to fix what he broke." Dahlia didn't tear up, but her voice broke at the end.

Aisha knew what her response would've been if she were in Dahlia's shoes: *Take that "love" of yours, get some lube, and shove it there.* Gone were the 'You don't have to tell me if you don't want to.' She wanted to know. "What did you say?"

They took about ten steps before Dahlia replied. "I told him to give me some time to think about my answer. If he told me that two years ago, I would've immediately flipped him off." *Attagirl!* "A year ago, I would've said, 'Are you out of your mind?'" *I'll allow it.* "Six months ago, I would've reminded him of how much he had hurt me before telling him it wasn't a good idea." *You're losing me.* "When he told me two weeks ago, I thought a 'no' would immediately come out of my mouth. I waited, but I couldn't get it out. I don't know when things changed for me and I could even consider what he said, but that's where I am." *Yep, you lost me.*

Aisha didn't have a poker face. So, when she nodded with what she hoped looked like an understanding smile, Dahlia said, "I know, I know. After what he put me through, I'm silly for even considering this. I know. I've put so much work into healing from the hurt he caused me. I'm healed, yes, but I never completely stopped loving him. Twelve years is a long time, you know. And I'm thinking about Nia, too. I'd love for her to grow up under one roof. She deserves to have that."

Before her tongue could curate her mind's words, Aisha said, "And what do you deserve? How can you forgive someone who did what he did to you?"

Dahlia looked at her the same way an eyeglass wearer read fine prints without their glasses. "I deserve what makes me happy and full. I forgive if the apology is meant and the actions back it up. People fuck up. Life's not a straight line. Shit happens."

Aisha's body tensed up. Dahlia didn't sound upset, but her usual warmth was absent from her delivery. Aisha knew she had spoken out of turn, and quite frankly, she was projecting. "I'm sorry, not my place at all. I apologize." She took a breath. "Thank you for sharing that with me. Honestly, I admire your willingness to forgive. That's something I'm working on."

"No apologies necessary." Dahlia patted Aisha's shoulder. "I appreciate how outspoken you are. That's something I'm working on."

They smiled at each other. They walked silently for a while as they inhaled the light air, soaked in the bright sun, and enjoyed the conversation of the birds. Aisha loved how comfortable the atmosphere was between them. And every time Dahlia looked her way and grinned, Aisha knew she felt the same way.

When they made it back to the parking lot, Dahlia said, "If you're still up for a little shimmy, there's a nice event coming up. It's in less than two weeks, the first Saturday of May. If you're free and up for it, I can get a ticket for you."

Aisha flapped her wings. "Free as a bird, baby!"

Her new friend laughed. "Should I expect similar moves on the dancefloor?"

"Worse."

"Shit."

They both laughed. Before they parted ways, Aisha leaned forward and hugged Dahlia.

Dahlia smiled. "I really enjoyed this, Aisha. I'll send you the ticket next week."

"I did, too! Thank you so much. Can't wait for May!"

*

Aisha woke up in the following days still running off the ancient medicine nature had administered her. The chemistry that existed in plants, in the air, and shone through the sun. An alchemy that couldn't be grasped at random but only mastered through years of work. The state of being of the selected ones who had found inner peace through trials and tribulations.

She knew it would wear off soon, so she took advantage of it while it lasted. She used it to cheer Amir up by sending him

130

the funniest memes she could find. She used it to deep clean her apartment. She also used it to spontaneously check in on her mother—something she hadn't done in months.

Hey mom I hope everything's going well at the salon. Just wanted to say hi

Her mother was, of course, delighted and confirmed that everything was well and that she missed her very much. As the ancient medicine effects faded away, she used the last of them to reach back to David. He had asked that she let him know when she'd be free to meet.

Wonderful, he replied to her text. *See you next Tuesday!*

WEEK 17

What made this day stand out wasn't its caressing warmth, the beautiful white magnolias blooming across her balcony, or even the loud, obnoxious music from her neighbors permeating through the walls. This day stood out because thirty-four years ago, in Colorado Springs, James had cried for the first time when his lungs adjusted to their new environment. And he had kept the tradition going for the two birthdays she had spent with him.

On his thirty-second birthday, Aisha had made reservations at his favorite Thai restaurant. She invited his family, friends, and a handful of coworkers. Sam and Amir had helped her put the event together.

She had to omit rather than lie to get James to dress up. "I'm taking you out on a fancy date tonight, so wear something real nice for Mama," she said behind him while he was brushing his teeth. She circled her arms around his torso and laid her head between his shoulder blades.

He laughed as he rinsed his mouth. He turned around to face her. Her arms were still wrapped around him. He looked down and cupped her face inside of his hands. "Oh yeah?" he said. She nodded with a mischievous smirk. He spoke again with a similar smile. "What else is Mama going to do for me?"

Aisha pulled his shirt that she was wearing over her head, led him to the bed, and did something for him. That evening, when they arrived at the restaurant and James saw his family and friends, he cried like the day he was born. Still teary-eyed, he walked up to Aisha after greeting everyone who had shown up to celebrate with him, and he told her how much he cared about her with his lips. Then, he told her that he loved her with his eyes.

When he turned thirty-three, she did something more intimate. In the weeks leading to his birthday, they had fought about moving in together and what their future would look like if they got married. She had eventually agreed to move in with him. However, her decision to not have kids wouldn't change.

The only reason she was even thinking about the topic was James. He wanted to be a father. She didn't want to be a mother. She hoped they could find a satisfying middle ground. They paused the discussion on the subject because they couldn't figure out a solution that didn't lead to one person compromising too much of themselves and ending up resentful. So, for his birthday, she just wanted to spend the evening reigniting the playful flame that had sparked at the beginning of their relationship.

When they awoke that morning, his back was facing her front under the covers. She wrapped her leg and arm around him. He slowly moved away and sat up on the bed. She was still under the sheets.

"Around what time do you think you'll be back home today?" she said.

"Sixish. Why?"

"Well, it's your birthday. Mama has something nice planned for you." She smiled and moved the covers below her waist.

He looked at her for a moment with no expression. He finally cracked a smile. "I'll be back around six, Mama." He gave her a peck on the lips and walked away to the bathroom.

When James returned to the apartment, Aisha had a four-course meal ready. For the hors d'oeuvres, she had followed a deviled egg recipe, which, given her skills, was a little sinful at best. She had purchased some spinach artichoke dip for their appetizer. She thought about making it from scratch but soundly decided against it.

For the main dish, she put her apron back on and (hopefully) sauteed some shrimp and pasta. The final product looked like the picture at the end of the recipe. The taste was fine. For the sweet course, she played it safe and bought his favorite dessert: Cookies 'n' Cream ice cream.

James put his keys down on the entryway table and approached her. She took her apron off. She was wearing a lace negligee.

"It smells good," he said. He looked at her for a while, so long she thought he wouldn't say anything else. He finally spoke again. "You look beautiful."

She hugged him tightly. "Happy birthday, babe. I love you."

He broke the embrace first and kissed her on the cheek. "Thank you, Aisha." He looked away at nothing in particular, then looked back at her. It was very quick, but long enough for her to notice. "Love you too," he said at last. He teared up after the three words.

She wanted to say something and ask him what that look meant, but it was his birthday, so she didn't want to ruin the mood. She wiped his face gently, and they kissed. It was an intense kiss, though it didn't feel like it was generated by passion, but rather by habit.

Today was James's birthday.

That was why this day was different. And that was why she went to the drawer where the dried leaves were stored. She didn't have the strength to fight her thoughts alone today. So she lit up the joint, inhaled the soothing fumes, and faded into oblivion. In a moment of fleeting awareness, she replied to a text Amir had sent her hours ago, asking how she was doing today—given that it was James's...you know.

yeS IM FIND, she wrote back.

Amir sent a laughing face emoji first, then a text. *Are u drunk?*

She only sent him the cloud emoji in response. She laughed out loud. Then, without any proper transition, she put her phone down with a sudden urgency and passed out.

When she woke up the next day, her body was very relaxed. Her thoughts, however, resembled scribbles that didn't make any sense at first glance. She didn't want to analyze them to understand what the patterns meant. It was better that way, at least for now. She was going to focus on the present moment: her evening rendezvous with David. Though what happened in the past had very much informed her decision to entertain a primarily sexual relationship with the artist, she still didn't want to think about said events yet.

There was a certain effectiveness born out of procrastination, right? When one postponed something until it physically couldn't be delayed anymore, it somehow energized them to get whatever they needed to be done in a substantially shorter period and with an arguably similar level of quality. Did the person put their mental and even physical health at risk? Sure. However, the effects were minor compared to the successful results produced in a considerably fractionated amount of time.

Theoretically, she should've tackled everything she had come to Dallas to address with a mathematical frequency from day one. Practically, her batteries were running so dangerously low that anytime she received any boost of energy, it was just enough to get her through another week, at best.

That evening, Aisha silently got ready for her date and drove to the address David had sent her with all her car windows rolled down. The artist was already there when she arrived. He was wearing a dark sweater with horizontal stripes and a multicolor scarf with vertical stripes. In addition to his usual look, he was also sporting a boater hat. The whole thing worked for him. He was the kind of guy who could pull anything off because he didn't give a shit just the right amount: not enough shit to get away with it, just enough shit not to be an asshole about it.

Though the restaurant was pretty empty, David was seated in a green booth in the corner of the room. He walked a few feet away from their seat and stood before a vacant table for four to greet her.

"Hello, Aisha." He hugged her like an old friend. The embrace was so platonic that Aisha slightly frowned in confusion. "How are you?" he asked as they walked to their booth and sat down.

"Hi, David. I'm great. Love the hat. How are you?"

"Even better now that you're here." He looked at her in the undressing manner he had last time. The relief she felt caused her an equal amount of shame and concern.

Don't you dare to develop any fucking nothing for this man, you hear me? You have enough on your plate as it is. Get your shit together, thank you.

"Is that right?" She raised a brow and smiled with one corner of her mouth.

"Aisha, why do you ask questions you know the answer to?" He winked at her.

They barely looked at the waitress when she took their orders. Aisha didn't even speak. She just pointed at what she wanted. She was too busy staring at David to hear what he had ordered. This thing with him was so urgent, irrational, and volatile that she couldn't help but want to grasp it while it was still within her reach.

David repeated something he had said for the third time. He didn't mention the fact that he had to repeat himself. He simply smiled without breaking eye contact and asked again, "You're not from here, are you?"

"No. I'm from Denver. I've been here for about four months. What about you?"

"I'm from a very small town in Iowa. I've lived in Dallas for half of my life. The weather brought me here. The art made me stay," he said. His eyes were sparkling. He took a sip of a drink the server had put on their table during some magical interval of time Aisha hadn't been privy to. She acknowledged his answer with a nod. He continued, "So, what brought you to Dallas?"

She narrowed her eyes. "It's not necessary that you know that. It wouldn't help for…our purpose."

He tittered. "And what is our purpose?"

She shrugged. "Fun. Sex. Art."

"And you believe our getting to know each other more intimately would deter us from those things?"

"To a certain degree, yes. We don't need the sad shit. Let's keep it light. Let's make this canvas pure delight."

He raised his drink. "To pure delight, then." They clinked their glasses.

"So, David, I'm curious: how many women are you currently…entertaining?"

"Not as many as you think." He was holding a permanent smile.

"I'm not thinking anything. I'm just curious," she said. *Lies! It has to be at least five, excluding me.*

He cocked his head. It was clear he didn't believe her, which amused him apparently. "If you must know, right now, I'm enjoying the company of four ladies, and that's including you, Miss Jones."

Close enough. The fact that the rules of engagement for their relationship were clear allowed her questions to come purely from a place of curiosity, with no trace of the possessiveness he apparently oh so despised. "How do you keep up with it all? And do they all know they're not the only one?"

He tightened the space between them by leaning forward. "Yes, I'm very honest and upfront. And just like you, I imagine, they're also engaging with other people freely." For the first time since she had met him, he frowned. It was so faint that she would've missed it if she wasn't staring at him. He continued, "I just don't understand how people can voluntarily limit their capacity to care and love to only one partner. It's so limiting and suffocating. It absolutely destroys romance. Most people would be happier if they didn't restrict themselves in that manner."

She was intrigued by what he had said. An academic intrigue. If he didn't look so revolted by the mere thought of monogamy, she would've considered his take to be the typical Don Juan's horseshit. She would've thought: *Sure, dude. Gather 'round, folks! Real hero over here, ladies and gents. Sleeping with multiple women on a weekly is really ethical and eco-friendly. It's right up there with recycling. Thank you for your service, kind sir!* But the way his features had shrunken as he spoke let her know he truly believed everything he said.

"Are you speaking from experience?" she asked.

"I am, actually, yes. I was married for four years, a lifetime ago. I was madly in love with her. Then, I saw how the fun, excitement, and mystery of love were drained out of us by that kind of union. We were like birds in a cage. If we allowed each other to fly and experience the world freely, it would've only strengthened our love."

Is that how James had felt? No. He definitely preferred monogamy, just not with her anymore. Aisha cleared her throat. "Although I prefer to only commit to one person, I respect your perspective." She drank the remaining of her beverage in one gulp.

"I wouldn't expect any less from you, Aisha." He looked at her empty glass. "Would you like to order some food?"

"No, thank you, but I'll have another glass. Last one for me."

He looked toward the bar, and his magnetic gaze immediately pulled the waitress their way. They both re-ordered their original drink, and he asked for the check. "I'm surprised you're not leaning more toward polyamory, Aisha," he said when the server was far enough from their table.

"Why is that?"

"I don't know, just a hunch. You don't strike me as someone who would prefer to commit to only one person."

Getting warmer, Columbo. Except that is not the number of partners to commit to that's the issue for me, my friend. It's the commitment itself. She didn't want to reveal too much of herself to him, so she waved the comment off. "Okay, David. The one woman I saw you with looked like my kin. Do all your partners have a similar look?"

The server came by with their drinks and the bill. Aisha finally broke her stare from David and noticed the waitress's beautiful dimples and fresh face.

David took a moment to answer. "I never thought about it until you pointed it out last time, but yes. They all have relatively similar features, I suppose."

"Is it by design?"

"What are you really asking?"

She raised an eyebrow. "It's a very specific look."

"Are you thinking I have some kind of…fetish for slender women of a darker hue?"

"Do you?"

He blinked and shook his head. "Of course not."

"Your date at that restaurant really looked like me, to an uncanny degree."

"What can I say? I'm a sucker for beauty."

She frowned slightly. "It's such a specific look, David. Does your ex-wife have similar features?"

He took a moment to respond. "Yes."

Aisha sighed. She took a sip, then put her hands under her chin. "David, I'm not interested in—"

He gently took one of her hands away from her face and held it. "Aisha, rest assured, this is not some sort of…substitution for my ex-wife. I just like what I like."

She tilted her head to the right so he could only see her profile. She gave him a long side-eye. "Sure," she said. She turned her head back to face him and held one eyebrow very high.

He smiled. "Why so skeptical?"

"Why so suspect?"

"Why so apprehensive?"

"Why so provoking?"

"Why so intriguing?"

She looked at his scarf, then at his sweater. "Why so many stripes?"

They both laughed. David took her other hand. "Aisha, I promise. I'm interested in you for you, that's all."

She still had some doubts as to his motives, but did it really matter? The clock was already ticking on whatever this was. "Fine, David, I believe you." She finished her drink. "Why don't we get out of here?"

He covered the tab and stood up at once. "After you."

When they were about to pass the family restrooms, she grabbed his hand and led the way to the small cubicle space. He followed without objection. They made sure the door was locked, and then they used the room for all the things it wasn't intended for. After the imprints of the deed were left on the countertop, the mirror, and the door, Aisha walked out first.

David met her in the parking lot by her car. "We can go to my place if you'd like," he said.

What for? We already had sex. She gave him a peck on the cheek. "Maybe next time." She got inside of her car. "As always, I had a good time, David. Thank you."

He closed the door for her. "So did I, Aisha. Text me when you're free again, okay?"

She winked. "Okay."

"Drive safe."

On her ride home, she thought about why she didn't want to go to his place or have him come to hers. It would be too intimate. *Better keep your guard up, soldier.* She didn't think there was any possibility she could feel anything for David. But on the off chance the universe felt like trying a new bit, she would keep him at arm's length. This thing with him was worth it because it was a good distraction. Plus, the sex was great. She just had to make sure not to allow her fragile heart to believe it was anything more than what it was: a diversion until she was ready to face the ghosts in the attic.

At the end of the week, Dahlia sent her the ticket for the dance event scheduled for the following Saturday. Looking at it generated conflicting feelings of excitement and concern within her. Next week was May. The year was close to his mid-point. Time was advancing and running away from her while she stood still.

Stagnant.

WEEK 18

*L*ast night was fun! Miss u already hottie. Sam had texted her one morning.

Girl what? Aisha replied the moment she read the text. *Are you seeing someone?!!*

Sam took almost twenty minutes to respond. *I didnt mean to send that to u.. oops*

No shit! Why didn't you tell me? Im calling you right now pick up!!

Aisha was upset Sam hadn't told her about her secret lover, but she was even more excited her friend had finally met someone. Sam must've had good reasons to keep it hidden from her.

Sam picked up on the third ring. "Sha, it's nothing. Just some guy I met last night. I didn't tell you because I was kind of ashamed."

Aisha huffed. "What? Why the hell would you be ashamed? You met someone and had a great time."

"I know, I know. But I've been telling you that I'm ready to find my forever person and start a family, and here I am, sleeping with some rando I met at the bar."

"First of all, I'd never judge you or not be in your corner. Second, even if you don't end up marrying the guy, you still had a good time. And he doesn't have to be a rando forever, you know. Let me check the transcript." She read Sam's text, "*Miss you already, hottie.*" She giggled. "This is what great love stories are made of."

Sam laughed quietly, and her voice sounded off when she spoke. It might've been the connection. "I don't know, Sha. I don't know if it's worth it."

"You don't think there is anything there?"

"There is. And that's the scary part."

"Just go for it!"

Sam didn't speak for a moment. "Okay," she said at last.

"Oh my god! I'm so excited for you! I can't wait to tell James when he gets back from his work trip."

Now, Aisha stepped outside on her balcony. She looked at the white magnolias with tears in her eyes. Memories were now visiting her randomly, like a neighbor needing a cup of sugar. The truth box was still where she had locked it, but what good was that when the thoughts of the people who had created it roamed freely in her mind?

Perhaps she was making connections that didn't exist to make sense of *when* and *why*. She felt like an oblivious fool. How could she have missed it? James was out of town for "work" the same weekend Sam had mistakenly texted her and admitted she had met someone. Then, the thought that anything suspicious was going on hadn't even crossed her mind. Now, it was the most obvious thing in the world. But why?

I'm in love with her.

I fell in love with him.

She needed something familiar and immersive to distract herself. A book and an Irish coffee at *Libros & Libations* would do the trick. She got dressed and drove to the coffee shop. When she walked in, she went straight to the romance section. She was in the mood for delusion. Today, she'd judge the book by its title. The more cliché, the better. She walked from the right side to the left side of the first shelf, reading all the titles. And just like Rafiki held Simba on Pride Rock, the chosen one rose above the crowd.

Her eyes sparkled with eagerness when she read the title: *I Always Knew It Was You*. The degree of the platitude almost made her roar with laughter. She couldn't wait to roll her eyes as the childhood sweethearts ran into each other in another city (oh so conveniently) and reignited their love by breaking up with their current respective partners. Poor idiots never stood a chance.

"I'm so sorry, Susan," the male protagonist would probably say. "I never stopped loving her."

"What does she have that I don't have, John?" (There was a ninety percent chance he'd be named John.) Poor Susan would cry out, "I've done everything right!"

John would take a moment to think of the best answer. The one that could simultaneously cause the least hurt and make the breakup final. He would, of course, not deliver on the hurt part. "You're amazing! You would make any man happy. You're just not her.*"*

Then, the story would cut to the female protagonist (Aisha felt like she would be named *Emma*), delivering a very similar monologue to her love placeholder. *Greg* was no *John*, regardless of how fantastic his chin dimple was. And then, a couple of heartbreaks later, *John* and *Emma* would live happily ever after…unless there was a sequel where they actually had to be together. That was the magic of the happily ever after: the ever after wasn't told.

Zac wasn't there today. Bummer. She grabbed her drink from the unremarkable bartender du jour and sat on the couch by the entrance. She finally skimmed around the room. *Oh. My. God.* Old Man with Round Glasses was there! A smile lit up her face. He was the most focused he had ever been on his reading. He was turning the pages rapidly, sipping his drink every few minutes. His presence made her feel like a soft blanket had been wrapped around her. She sat on the couch, crossed her legs, and began reading *I Always Knew It Was You.*

She was immediately proven right on almost all her assumptions, except the characters' names. *Hunter* and *Hunter* (*Yes, people! It's worse than we thought!*) had run into each other in New York after leaving their small hometown in Nowhere, Kansas. The rest of the story was progressing exactly as expected. Aisha rolled her eyes or said, "Yeah, right," or "Umph" every few pages.

She was so focused on her hate read that she didn't hear him the first time.

"Hey, Aisha," Marcus repeated.

She looked up, fighting the urge to rub her eyes to make sure she wasn't hallucinating. "Oh, hey," was all she was able to say.

"Can I sit here?" He pointed at the available seat on the couch.

She nodded. He smiled broadly, which made him look like a kid in a candy store. When he sat down and filled his half of the loveseat, Aisha felt goosebumps rising on the top layer of her skin. The contrast between his boyish face and his sturdy figure was a dangerous mix. A face that made you want to squeeze his cheeks. A body that made you want to cover said face with *your* 'cheeks.' *Whew.*

But no matter how fast her blood was pumping at this moment, she couldn't forget that he stood her up a few weeks ago. Sure, it wasn't an official date, but still. She closed her book and looked at him intensely.

"Long time no see," she finally said with no effort to hide her bitterness.

He slowly shook his head up and down. "I'm sorry about last time. I was looking forward to hanging out with you, but something came up, and I couldn't make it."

Something snapped within her.

Frankly, Aisha was sick of being on the other side of "something came up." She was sick and tired of being the person who had to be rescheduled because a better option was available. She was tired of being the backup plan, the placeholder until they found something better. Until they found what they really wanted.

I'm in love with her.

I fell in love with him.

BANG! BANG! BANG!

One hard knock after the other, she heard the truth box undo the locks that kept it away from her mind. Away from the little shell that remained of her, the frail piece of sanity that kept her sensible enough. All this anger and resentment honestly hadn't much to do with Marcus. Yes, she was annoyed because he hadn't shown up last time, but they were nothing to each other. He didn't owe her anything. And again, they hadn't scheduled an official date or anything of the sort. It wasn't his fault she was trying to hang on to any semblance of hope to stay afloat.

Are you pregnant? Yes.

Are you the father? Yes.

BANG! BANG! BANG!

The door caved in, the ship capsized, and everything rushed out. The person seated beside her didn't deserve to be the victim of this unexpected hurricane. But no matter how much we tried to forecast and prepare, the weather was unpredictable. Nature always had its way.

She glared at him. "Oh, fucking, please. I waited three hours here like an idiot, hoping you'd show up. Why make promises you can't keep? You could've just said, 'Nice to see you again. Till next time.' But you just had to make me hang on to some hope and expect more. We would've run into each other again, eventually. But *nooo*, you had to promise more when you knew you couldn't deliver. You had to make me envision a future you knew you didn't want to be a part of. I was here, alone. I was waiting for you. You left me here all alone. You abandoned me. You never cared!"

She stood up at once, grabbing all her belongings in one swift motion. The few people there were staring at her in shock. Marcus was sitting, immobile and stunned. Before she walked out, she gave a final look to Old Man with Round Glasses. Her outburst hadn't made it past the wall of pages in front of his eyes. He was focused on his book. What a gem. She would miss seeing him.

Obviously, she'd never show her face at *Libros & Libations* again after what she had just done. For a moment, her anger overpowered the embarrassment that rightfully hid underneath, waiting patiently like a sniper. As soon as she closed the door behind her, the first shot hit her lower half. Her legs began to tremble with shame.

Oh my God. What just happened? Why did I do that?

What did you think was going to happen? You have been suppressing things since—

She found her own I-Don't-Give-A-Fuck weapon. She shot the low voices of reason and rationality still hanging on for dear life. She heard them fall over. Drown. Washed away. Gone.

Poor idiots never stood a chance.

Now, it was just her and all the feelings she had been trying to suppress, and they surrounded her. She was outnumbered.

PART II

WEEK 19

The difference between the hollow and the chaos was that the former sucked everything out, only living enough for functionality. The latter gave it all with no restraint or order. The hollow was greedy. The chaos was overgenerous. Yet the end of their respective roads led to the same exit: stagnation—just from a different angle. If Aisha had to choose, she preferred the chaos. The anarchy it generated did a much better and more entertaining job of masking the lack of progress.

Aisha had ignored Dahlia's text last Saturday morning asking her to confirm that they were still on for their dance night out. She hadn't replied to Amir's texts checking in on her. She had left her mom's calls unreturned. But she was ready to deal with everything when she woke up on Monday.

She messaged Dahlia when she was confident in her lie. *Hey Dahlia I'm so sorry for not answering on Saturday. I was very sick and couldn't get out of bed (food poisoning). I'd love to meet sometime this week whenever you're free*

Dahlia replied about half an hour later. *Oh no, I'm so sorry. Hope u feeling better. I would've loved to but I'll be in Fort Worth all week. I'll text u when I get back in town. Rest up!*

She hated to lie to Dahlia, but it would take too much effort and context to explain what really happened. She would've to start all the way back when Albert was seated on that purple accent chair over two decades ago. And from what her new friend said, she wasn't making good decisions either. Her ex-husband was the one in Fort Worth. So clearly, Dahlia was going there to be with him. But Aisha had retired her robe and gavel after last week's outburst. She was in no position to judge anyone.

After she ate some leftover pasta from the Italian diner down the street, she sat on her couch and called Amir.

"Hey, big bro!" she said.

"I was about to call 911. Why are you ignoring my texts?"

"I'm sorry. Last week was a lot."

"What happened?"

Before all her emotions took control of the ship last week, she would've only given her brother the Cliff Notes. Well, there was a new sheriff in town who wasn't afraid to tell it like it was. "How much time do you have?"

"Enough."

"I met this cute guy at a coffee shop a few weeks ago, and we chatted for a bit. He had to go, so he suggested we meet the following week to hang out. But he didn't show up. So last week, we finally ran into each other again, and I went off on him."

"What did you say?" Amir said in between chewing something very loudly.

"Ew. What are you eating?"

"Girl, I'm on lunch break. Don't worry about what I'm eating. Hurry up! I want to hear how this ends."

"Well, I basically projected all my frustration on him. I told him that he abandoned me and made promises he couldn't keep. Like, all kinds of wild shit that had nothing to do with him." She shook her head. "Poor guy. He just sat there confused and didn't say anything. I feel so bad."

Amir laughed. "Sis, you were bound to snap. You can't hold shit in forever. I feel bad for him, too, but I'm happy you let it out."

Aisha wanted to tell her brother there was a lot more where that came from, but she felt good having him think she was making substantial progress. "Anyway, that's what I have been up to: yelling at innocent strangers. What about you?"

"Still heartbroken. Thomas blocked me on everything, so I created a fake account to stalk him on IG. I accidentally liked a picture of us he hadn't deleted from thirty-seven weeks ago. I unliked it as soon as I noticed, but I guess it was too late."

"Damn."

"Yep. He deleted that picture, went private, and blocked my fake account. In that order."

"Oof."

Amir was silent for a moment. Then he chuckled. Aisha almost joined him until he spoke again, and she heard his uneven voice. "I don't know what else to do, Sha. I thought he just needed space, but it looks like he's moving on. I fucked up, and I can't fix it."

Last week, she would've told Amir to give Thomas more time and space. Fight for what they had. Do whatever he could to make it right and fix what he had broken. But the thing the chaos loved more than disorder was company.

"You know what," she said, "the hell with him! If he's not even going to give you a chance to apologize and talk to him, fuck him. Does he expect you to grovel? Okay, you made a mistake, but you've been trying to correct it. If he doesn't think what you guys had is worth not giving up on so easily, the hell with him. You deserve better than this!"

To be fair, a part of her genuinely believed Thomas was too unforgiving. *Pot, meet Kettle, much?* But in all honesty, the loose pieces of her that took over her ship wanted to undo anything in their course that was uniform, solid, and intact.

"Maybe you're right," he whispered.

"Louder for the people in the back!"

"You're fucking right! Screw him. I'm done," he said as loudly as he could in the break room.

She put her phone on her lap, turned the speaker on, and clapped into the microphone. "That's my little big brother!"

"Thanks, big little sis. You're the best," he said with a lighter voice. "Okay, if I'm going to live my best life, I need to not get fired. So, let me clock back in before they come and get me. Talk to you later!"

"Bye!"

She stayed seated after he hung up. She didn't feel quite right that most of her wanted Amir to go buck wild with her. She wanted them to share the same experiences so they could continue to relate intimately as they had done growing up. She wanted them to be hand and in hand when they jumped off a cliff, on some *Midsommar* shit.

She tried to hang on to the fact that a minuscule part of what she had told him came from a genuine and unselfish place. She loved Amir, and she truly wanted the best for him. She just needed someone—truly, everyone in her orbit—to let loose and become undone with her. It would be more bearable that way.

Aisha didn't feel like talking to her mother yet, so she texted her instead. *Hey mom sorry I haven't returned your calls. It's been pretty busy here. Anyway hope everything's good at the salon. Miss you. I'll call you as soon as I get a chance*

She no longer felt any unease telling her mother she missed her for two reasons. First, she did. Second, as opposed to what she had believed, it didn't prompt them to talk about what had happened. If anything, it bought her some time. She could postpone that dreadful conversation for later since she gave her mom something to hold on to.

As expected, Helen's reply was cheerful. *Hey Honey, no worries. All is well here. I miss you so much. Talk to you soon!*

Aisha had this new boost of energy after last week's outburst. It was so interesting how sometimes giving out energy could fuel instead of consume. The week she broke her record for the longest sleep, she felt exhausted instead of recharged. And this week, following her blowup, she was feeling electricity circulate through her veins and lighting her up.

The only issue was that she wasn't energized to deal with any of her original problems, the things that moved her south. Suddenly, they all seem secondary to any other random thing that would potentially cross her mind. She wanted to do everything else. She wasn't even sure what "everything else" was yet. All she knew was *everything else* mattered more than those old ghosts in the attic.

Aren't y'all tired of haunting me yet?

Boooooooooo!

Oh hush! I don't care anymore.

Aisha decided to go for a drive because it was a beautiful day outside. The clouds painted the sky a wavy white. She missed being close to the mountains, but the way the Dallas sun caressed her face made up for it. She rolled the windows down and turned the radio up. She sang along to the songs she knew and mumbled through the ones she didn't.

When she stopped at the red light, she didn't turn her volume down or stop singing loudly. She met the stare of the driver on her left side. The woman rolled her eyes, then looked straight ahead. Aisha turned her volume to the maximum and mumbled even louder. The woman drove off as soon as the light turned green. Aisha laughed as she put her foot on the gas. The moment she did, her engine light came on.

"Fantastic," she hissed.

She looked at the sticker on the top left corner of her windshield. Her oil change was due over two thousand miles ago. Her car was braking slower than when she left Denver. Her alignment was messed up. Her car badly needed to be serviced. Before James, she mainly took care of her car after a light came on or when her engine sounded like the drunkest guy at the party. When she got with James, he made sure that she stayed on top of her auto-care.

"Sha, your oil change is due pretty soon. I'll call my guy to book an appointment. What day would be good for you?" he had said one evening.

Aisha had noticed that he had called her *Babe* less frequently over the last few weeks. And it wasn't like she enjoyed pet names more than the next girl, but he had started it. Why change now that she was finally getting used to it—and kind of liked it?

"Thursday or Friday would work. Thanks, babe," she said.

He nodded and picked up his phone to call the mechanic.

The following day, she called Sam. "Something's off with James," Aisha said.

"What do you mean?"

"I don't know. He seems distant. We haven't had a fight in weeks, so I don't know what it could be."

Sam didn't speak for a moment. Aisha could hear her breaths distinctly. "Maybe he's stressed at work?" her friend said. "I remember you told me they raised his quota or something."

She gasped. "You're so right! That's probably it. I wish he would just talk to me, though. He used to tell me everything without me having to ask. Now, it's like pulling teeth to get anything out of him."

Sam sighed. "Just be patient with him. He has…I'm sure he just has a lot on his mind, and it's not all about you."

She frowned. "Did he tell you something? I know you two have gotten closer over the last few months. I'm happy about that, but I hope you'd tell me if he told you something about our relationship."

Her friend spoke faster and louder. "Of course, Sha! I'm loyal to our friendship first. I would've told you if he had shared anything with me. I really think it's the work thing. Just ask him about it."

Aisha shook her head. "You're probably right." She cleared her throat. It had been tightened by the same lingering pull that had knotted her insides for some time now. That gut feeling with the unknown birthday, probably two to three months old. Her intuition was alerting her of something, but the signal was too vague and scattered to determine its origin. So, she just ignored it. "What's going on with you, Sam? I feel like you haven't told me much lately."

"Because there is nothing to tell. Unless you want to hear the latest reason a family canceled their life insurance policy?"

She chuckled. "I'd love to, actually."

"Simple: we're all going to die, anyway, so why bother?"

"No lies were told."

"And with that truth, my bank account lost a dearly beloved eight hundred and sixteen dollars. Rest in peace."

Aisha giggled. "Sorry, girl. Those chargebacks are no joke." She tittered before her segue. "Speaking of charging your back, how's your secret lover doing?"

Sam laughed hoarsely. "You worked hard for that one, so I'll give it to you." The next sentence came out smaller and hesitant. "He's fine. Still too soon for an introduction, but he's fine."

"Can I at least get a first name?"

"J-John."

Same initial? She wasn't even trying that hard to mask her betrayal. At the time, alarm bells didn't go off to wake Aisha up. Only that ancient humming in her belly. The ancestral warning that recommended caution. The genetic code from the lineage of people before her who had also been betrayed whispering something she couldn't translate. Then, it was just a bunch of undistinguishable and confusing emotions. Now, the truth was staring at her: identifiable and nameable. Her best friend was having a full-on affair with her boyfriend.

After driving aimlessly for over an hour, she returned to her apartment. She would deal with her engine light later. She had more urgent matters to tend to.

She texted her favorite artist. *Hey David let's meet soon.* She punctuated her text with a wink emoji.

He replied after a few minutes. *Hello, Aisha. I was just thinking about you. I already have some commitments this week, so how about next Tuesday?*

She needed her urges satisfied sooner than that. *Okay that works*

Wonderful!

After she read his one-word reply, she downloaded the Tinder app. She added three of her most flattering pictures. One wearing a décolleté. One revealing her toned legs. One with her two-piece bathing suit. No point in beating around the bush. She was there for a good time, not a long time. And according to most of the bios she glanced at, so were most of the men there. *Perfect.* She swiped right until she ran out of matches. She only read the bios of the men she matched with. Not because she wanted to learn more about them, but to weed out the ones who might show up to her place with a knife, or worse, hoping this could lead to something more serious.

That evening, she slept with the six-pack surfer dude. *Rad.*

The next day, she slept with the forty-something finance bro who was very likely cheating on the wife he claimed to have recently divorced. *Dangerous Liaisons.*

On Thursday, she met the fine-ass retired NFL athlete who couldn't stop talking about his professional career—he had warmed the bench for two years and bragged about his "time in the league" ever since. At any rate, his bedroom performance was superb. *Touchdown!*

On Sunday, she felt secular. She invited the loud and proud atheist over. She let him ramble on about Darwinism while she smoked a pre-roll. When he was done, she asked him to put his mouth to better use. He did. *Big bang!*

When he left, she was satisfied enough to sleep peacefully. The pleasure numbed the pain and hurt still residing yonder.

WEEK 20

If not for her car screeching at every stop, Aisha would've continued to ride with her engine light on. She knew that sound very well. So, she was aware that if the issue wasn't fixed soon, the later bill would make her jaw drop ground-level, like a Looney Tunes character. It was just a matter of where to go to correct the problem, and suddenly, she missed being with James.

She missed that he had completely taken this kind of concern off her plate. This wasn't her domain of expertise. She didn't want to go to just any shop and risk being taken advantage of because she couldn't name more than a handful of car parts—and their functions. She could picture the scene from here.

"Hey, sir, my car has been making weird sounds, and the engine light came on. Can you fix it?"

"Have you gotten the code read?"

The little crickets would fly from her left to right ear.

The mechanic would titter. "I see. Let me check it out. Please have a seat."

He would come back twenty minutes later. "The plug light and the machetes stopped firing. We need to replace the Uno shields…It'll be fifteen hundred and sixty dollars. I'll add a discount for you, so it will only be fifteen hundred and twelve dollars."

Absolutely not. She wouldn't go through that song and dance, spend days going from shop to shop to hopefully get a fair estimate at last. She needed someone who would give her an honest quote right away.

"I've learned that people will forget what you said, people will forget what you did, but people will never forget how you made them feel. Maya Angelou. My favorite quote."

Please don't. I know you are in this I-don't-give-a-fuck era or whatever, but please leave that nice man alone.

But I need my car fixed, and I don't want to get ripped off.

Girl, please. He's not the only honest mechanic in town. You just want to have an excuse to see him.

You're wrong! My car can break down at any time. I don't have time to drive around for days to hopefully find someone else. He's my best bet. This is purely professional.

Whatever helps you sleep at nigh—

SHUT THE FUCK UP!

And with that, she was on the road to Carlos's auto shop. The voice was right. Her car could probably handle another week of riding around to find an honest mechanic who would give her a fair price. But why not kill two birds with one stone? She could simultaneously get her car fixed at a reasonable price and amend things with Carlos.

When Aisha pulled in, she was more nervous than she had expected. This was a bad idea. Their last interaction ended with a thumbs-up emoji from Carlos after she ghosted him. Perhaps he'd still be upset and tell her that the machetes and Uno shields needed a little two-thousand-dollar adjustment; for her, only nineteen hundred and eighty-five dollars. She took a deep breath when she got out of her car. Carlos was an honest man. Even if he was still upset—which she doubted—he would be fair. Plus, she wouldn't mind staring at his beautiful face for a little while.

Yeah. This is 100% professional. Okay, girl.

Oh. My. Fucking. God. SHUT THE—

Fine, whatever. Don't come crying to me when it goes to shit.

She rolled her eyes and walked inside of the shop. And just like the first time, Carlos was standing at the counter looking as dazzling as the sun above them. His overalls were buttoned to the top, but she could still trace all the chiseled muscle lines underneath. He was typing something on the computer. It took him a few seconds to notice her.

"Hello! How are y..." He paused when he recognized Aisha.

"Hey, Carlos. I was looking to get a quote." She cracked a small smile.

His formal grin faded at once. He spoke evenly, "What's the issue?"

She looked around the lobby. An older man was sitting in the corner of the room. He was staring at his phone, utterly uninterested in anything that wasn't on his screen. She thought about Old Man with Round Glasses and half-smiled. She looked back at Carlos. "Well, I'm not sure. I definitely need an oil change. Probably some air in my tires. I think an alignment, too. And probably other stuff. My engine light came on the other day."

"When was your oil change due?" His voice was monotone, and he made a point to stare at his computer screen.

She clenched her teeth and grimaced. "About two thousand miles ago."

He didn't smile, but he finally looked at her. "I see," he said. Then he put his hand out toward her.

Was that a white flag? The cold treatment was finally over. Her heart rate sped up in excitement. She grabbed his extended hand and shook enthusiastically to accept the truce.

He tittered, then immediately composed himself. "I wanted the keys."

Her eyes widened. "Oh." She searched through her purse. "S-Sorry about that. Here you go." She handed him her car keys.

His features loosened slightly. "It'll just be a few minutes. Please have a seat."

Aisha watched him walk away. When he was far enough, she facepalmed before looking back at him. She couldn't stop staring at the sweet Adonis she had ghosted a few months ago because she had too much fun with him. Like, how dumb was she? And how arrogant to think he would inevitably fall in love with her and get his heart broken.

She peeked through the glass door. He had parked her car inside one of three stations under the garage shed. He was under the chassis. The upper half of his coveralls was unzipped, and she could glance at his biceps contrasting as he twisted his wrist to undo whatever mysterious items were under her car. She fully turned around and rested her chin on her fist to watch him work.

Oh, what would she give to be her car right now…she shook her head and sat straight. No. She had done enough damage. She was here to get her car serviced. She wouldn't mind getting something else servic—*Stop!*

She grabbed a random magazine to distract her mind. She turned the pages aimlessly until she heard the side door swing open. Carlos waved at her to come to the counter. He had unfortunately buttoned his coveralls back up. She walked up to him and tried to meet his eyes.

"Luckily, it's nothing too serious," he said, typing and staring at the screen. "You severely need an oil change, new air filter, spark plugs replacement, air in your tires, alignment, and a few other small tweaks. Again, nothing critical. But you should try to at least get your oil changed on time to avoid more serious problems in the future."

"I know." She nodded. "What's the financial sentence?" She smiled, still searching for his eyes.

He looked at her with a straight face. "If you want to get everything taken care of, it will be four hundred and some change. I'll throw a promotion in there, and you'll be right under four hundred bucks. Honestly, you should take care of everything if you can. Most of this stuff is way past due."

Aisha knew it was true because of how awful her car had been sounding and shaking most recently. She also knew someone else would've quoted her double the amount for less work. Carlos was a fair man. But obviously, he was still upset—rightfully so—and he wanted her to know. And as much as she had wished to kill two birds with one stone today, just the one severely-needing-oil-change-birdie would have to do for today.

"Okay. Let's take care of all of it. Thank you for adding the discount; I really appreciate it."

He nodded and looked at her in an unfocused manner. "I have one car in front of you, so it'll be about three hours." He finally focused on her brown eyes. "You're welcome to hang out here, or we can call you when it's done."

She looked down. "I'll hang out here."

He looked back at his computer. "Okay."

She walked back to her seat. Carlos called the man in the corner of the room. The old man put his phone in his back pocket and strolled to the counter. The two began to speak in the car language in which her fluency was the Spanish equivalent of *Mi casa es tu casa, Donde es el baño?* and *Gracias.* She opened another magazine and turned the pages mechanically.

She needed to apologize to Carlos. She had been so rude. She really thought she could come back here with a smile and a callback and immediately get him to look at her the way he had earlier this year. And what did she even want out of this?

Friendship? An arrangement similar to the one she had with David? That was her problem, wasn't it? Jumping headfirst with no plan and no endgame, changing the game rules in the process, and not giving a shit about the other players who had followed them all along.

"So now you're saying you for sure do not want to have kids? One hundred percent?" James had said while massaging his temples.

"Yes." She sat next to him on the couch and folded her arms.

"You told me you were open to it."

"I said that I wasn't one hundred percent close to it."

He dropped his arms to his side and looked at her like a deer caught in headlights. "What the hell is the difference?"

"One is positive, one is negative."

"Fuck syntax. I thought you were open to having kids when the timing was right. I thought that if I proposed and we got married, that would be our next step. That was bait-and-switch on your part."

Aisha stood up at once. She cocked her head and glared at him. "Bait-and-switch? Are you fucking serious? You think I trapped you in this relationship under the pretense that I wanted kids? Maybe I didn't express it perfectly every time, but you knew that being with me, kids might never be on the table. Don't say I baited and switched you. That's not fair." She exhaled loudly and spoke more calmly. "I don't want you to be in something that you don't want to be in. If you don't want this, please tell me now."

No matter where it started, their arguments always ended somewhere along these lines: *If you don't want this, just tell me.* And whoever was on the receiving end would immediately counter that this was what they wanted. They were exactly where they wanted to be; how could the other even ask?

But for the first time since they became an official couple, James didn't do that. He didn't move and just stared at the floor. An excruciating thirty-seven seconds crawled by before he spoke. "I love you, Sha. I do. I just have to think some things over."

She didn't ask him what he meant by that. She didn't want to know the answer.

Two hours and fortyish minutes later, Carlos walked back inside the waiting room. His coveralls were completely soiled, and he was covered in sweat. He looked like the May picture on the sexy Blue-Collar Calendar.

He waved her car keys to alert her. "You're all set."

She met him at the counter. Now, it was just the two of them in the room. "That was quick. Thank you," she said.

He nodded and only looked at his screen. "Alright. After the promotion, your total is three hundred and eighty-two dollars."

She gave him her credit card, and he only looked at her hand to take it. She sighed. "I'm sorry about last time, Carlos. I shouldn't have done that."

He ran her card and gave it back to her. "It's all good." He tore the receipt as soon as it was printed out. "Please sign here." He pointed to the line she needed to endorse.

She wrote her initials absently and looked back at him to ask a question she knew the answer to. "Are you mad at me?"

He finally met her eyes. "No. We just don't have anything to talk about outside of your car needs. Your car's fine now. Again, just try to keep up with your oil change."

She shook her head in surrender. "I understand...thanks."

He stared at her for a moment. She was standing still with her head down. When she looked at him, it seemed like he wanted to say something. But after a few seconds, he walked outside and got under a G-Wagon. Onto the next thing, bigger and better things. She walked to her small compact car and drove away. She confirmed that one bird had indeed been killed during her drive back home. Carlos was good at his job. Her vehicle was running smoothly.

When Aisha walked inside her apartment, she broke into tears. It was difficult to accept, but sometimes it was simply too little too late. Even when one's heart was in the right place and remorseful enough, some things couldn't be taken back or repaired. That was how she felt about her relationship with her mother. Being on the receiving end of unforgiveness made her feel more empathy toward her. Being completely denied a chance to make amends was harsh and bitter. It was a hard pill to swallow. At any rate, Aisha wiped her eyes and took her medicine.

*

The next evening, she cheerfully got ready to meet up with David. Fuck Carlos—*if only*. She wasn't going to let his denying her of a chance to make things up with him rob her of her new I-don't-give-a-fuck attitude and all the fun that was on her horizon because of it.

Her hair was officially a TWA—Teeny Weeny Afro. She used some conditioner and gel to coil it. She wore an emerald one-shoulder dress, which drew a line on her collarbone. Even after sleeping with all those guys last week, her desire for David hadn't lessened. She felt uneasy admitting it, but it wasn't only about sex with him. To be clear, she didn't want anything that could be considered "serious" with him. However, she did enjoy his company for non-genitalia-involved activities as well. She just had to make sure the line between what this was and what this wasn't remained solid, and that the marking didn't wear off with time.

When Aisha entered the restaurant, David greeted her with a dramatic hand kiss. "What a vision," he said when his lips detached from her hand.

"Why, thank you, David."

He pulled her chair and sat facing her. The place was packed but intimate. Each party was distanced enough from the next to maintain privacy. The capacity was at most fifty. Apparently, their mojitos were fantastic. In fact, they had a menu just for their different takes on the minty drink. The wallpaper was even covered in mint leaf drawings.

"I'll try the mango mojito." Aisha smiled at the server, who was wearing a green bow tie.

"Just a regular mojito for me," David said, then handed him the drink menus back.

"Regular? I expect better from you, David Marshall."

He half-smiled. "Not feeling very adventurous today, I guess."

She cocked her head and squinted. "How come?"

"My daughter's upset with me." Now, David was the one narrowing his eyes as he waited for her response.

So many thoughts flooded Aisha's mind. David was a dad? She had never thought to ask because everything about him led her to believe that he had decided in his early teens that he didn't want children. So, he had gotten a vasectomy as soon as the clock struck twelve on his eighteenth birthday.

David should've told her that he had a child. She sure as hell wouldn't be sitting here, smiling at the green-bow-tied-wearing server as he gently put her mango mojito on the table.

It was only when the waiter asked her if she needed anything else that Aisha snapped out of her thoughts. How long has it been since David spoke?

"I-I'm good, thank you."

The server nodded and walked away. She finally looked at David, who had been waiting silently. "How many kids do you have?" She tried to sound casual, but her voice came out croaky.

He chuckled in his restrained fashion. "Just one. She's not quite a kid anymore. She is twenty."

She sighed and took a sip of her drink before she spoke. "Why didn't you tell me before?"

He seemed to be searching for something on her face. "It never came up." He leaned forward and rested his head in his hand. "Is that an issue?"

"Well, I'm not interested in dat..." She paused. They weren't dating. They were barely meeting twice a month to have sex in a public area. The fact that David had a twenty-year-old daughter did not impact their arrangement. They had no future together. If anything, his having a child completely closed off any crevasse she might have missed. Now, there was truly no chance any unexpected feelings would arise.

She straightened herself in her seat. "No, it's not an issue at all." She smiled. "Why is your daughter upset?"

He tapped the tip of his fingers on his cheekbone and smiled. "What just happened?" he said.

"What do you mean?"

"Aisha, why do you love asking questions you know the answer to?" He was still smiling. "You were ready to walk out because I have a daughter, but you had an internal monologue and decided against it. What did you tell yourself?"

She smirked. "My thoughts are a private domain." She leaned in. "All you need to know is that it's not an issue."

He raised his hands in surrender. "Alright, alright, the prosecution rests."

"That was your best shot? You'd make a shitty lawyer."

He laughed. "I agree. I'll stick to my paintbrushes."

She nodded. "You're a smart man, David. So why is your daughter upset?"

He lay one hand on the table. His fingertips were lightly tapping the wooden surface. "She doesn't agree with my lifestyle." He looked away at nothing in particular, then back to Aisha. "She called me a libertine."

Without meaning to, she let out a single tee-hee. "I'm sorry." She cleared her throat. "Do you disagree with that description?"

David looked at her intensely, as if he were turning the pages of a book written in a foreign language. "Not entirely, honestly. I do, however, disagree with her judgmental tone. I find self-righteousness distasteful."

She nodded. "What led her to say that?"

He didn't respond immediately. He rubbed his eyes in a circular motion. He kept them close for a second or two, and when he opened them, his expression was different. He finally spoke. "Let's keep this canvas pure delight, right?" He raised his glass.

She didn't raise hers. "David, I know I said that, but it doesn't mean we can't have more serious conversations."

"No, you were right. We don't need the sad shit." He winked at her. "There is enough of it everywhere else. Let's talk about something fun!"

She wanted to counter but didn't. Those were the rules she created. She was fine with them when it got her out of talking about something she didn't want to share. However, now that it was David's turn, she wanted to call the referee to double-check the rulebook.

I think there is foul play here, sir!

Let me check the replay…Ah, yes. Yeah. This is clean, ma'am. 1-1.

She sighed. "Fine. What would you like to talk about then?"

"I would like you to pose nude for me."

Aisha's face was now ninety percent eyeball. "What?"

He smirked. "You heard me."

She shook her head frantically and crossed her legs. "I don't think so."

He tittered. "Don't worry, it'll be somewhat abstract, so no one will be able to recognize you. I'll just capture your essence."

She took a sip of what was left of her drink. She noticed how the mango now overpowered the mint. She squinted her eyes and raised one brow. "Between pilling my layers to get to the raw thing underneath and capturing my essence, I'm starting to think you're some sort of maleficent creature after my life force."

Under the table, he inserted his foot between her legs to part them. He stared at her eyes, then at her lips. He created even more distance between her legs with his foot. "Maybe," he said.

And just like the last time they met, their "dessert" was savored where other guests had expelled theirs. David met Aisha in the parking lot after they were both satisfied.

When he was next to her, he took a deep breath. "Although I enjoy fucking you in the restrooms—I really do—next time, I'd like for you to come to my place so we can be more comfortable."

With David announcing his lifetime membership to the Fatherhood Association, she saw no problem with going to his place. "Okay."

"And think about my proposition. We would have a lot of fun."

Absolutely not, Cowboy. "I'll think about it."

She kissed him on the lips and got inside of her car. She looked back at him before she drove off. He was standing still, and he blew her a kiss when their eyes met.

*

On Friday, she woke up to five missed calls and a text message from Amir that read: *Aaaaaaaaaaaaaaahhhhhh!!!!!!!!*

She knew what that message meant and called him without getting up. Her brother answered on the first ring. "Guess what?" he screamed into her ear.

She turned around in her bed. "Can you, like, not yell? It's too early for that volume."

"Bitch, it's twelve o'clock *your* time. You need to get a job or volunteer or something." He chuckled. "Anyway, I have some great news!"

She sat up, understanding she wouldn't be able to go back to sleep after this conversation. "You made up with Thomas?"

"Alright, good news then. He unblocked me on all his social media accounts!"

Aisha could hear the excitement and giddiness in her brother's voice. A feeling of profound desolation rose within her. When she spoke, her voice was cold. "That's it?"

"What do you mean, *that's it?* That's huge! That means he's slowly opening the door back for me."

She sneered. "I wouldn't get my hopes up if I were you. Maybe this is part of a sick little game to hurt you even more." She softened her tone to sound caring, but she could hear how patronizing her speech echoed. "I mean, he completely cut you off for months because you expressed an understandable hesitation about a lifetime commitment. He ignored you at that boho party. He blocked you because you made the grave mistake of liking an old picture of you two. And the second he does the bare minimum, you're ready to forget everything? C'mon, big bro, you're better than this! You deserve more than this."

It was completely silent for a long time. Aisha could only hear her own A/C blowing above her head. Knowing Amir, this could go two ways. He would either figure out that she didn't have his best interest at heart and tell her the absolute fuck off. Or he would believe her and self-condemn. She wasn't sure which one would make her feel worse.

When Amir finally spoke, all the enthusiasm was drained from his voice. "You're right, sis. I'm such an idiot. This is so pathetic, I know. I'm grasping at straws and actually acting like breadcrumbs are a four-course meal." He sighed. "I don't even recognize myself. I run to get my phone every time it rings, hoping it's him. I go to all the places I know he frequents, hoping to run into him. I've created several fake accounts to hopefully get the smallest glimpse at what he is up to. Like, I only think and talk about him. Hell, I got a little promotion at work, and I don't even care. I didn't even tell you or Mom because Thomas is the only thing that matters. This is so pathetic, I know. I've lost my sense of self." His voice broke. "I feel like I'm nothing without him."

This made her feel worse. She could stomach his yelling at her and cussing her out. She'd prefer if he were upset with her and not with himself. She didn't want him to be one hundred percent happy, so they could trauma bond about their *ain't shit* boyfriends. She didn't mean to trigger his feelings of unworthiness.

"I'm sorry, Amir. You were right to be excited. I shouldn't have said that."

"No, you were right. Thank you for bringing me back to Earth. I should probably get back to work, though."

"Are you okay?"

"Yes, I'll be alright."

"Congratulations on the promotion!"

"One of us has to work. Learn from me, sis!" He sounded lighter, but Aisha knew it was for her sake. "Alright, I gotta go now. Love you. Bye!"

"Love y—"

Disconnect tone.

Aisha closed her eyes and forced herself back to sleep.

WEEK 21

Aisha hadn't heard from Dahlia all last week, so she messaged her Monday morning.

Hey Dahlia how are you? It's been a while! I'm planning on going to the trail tomorrow do you want to join me?

Dahlia answered a few minutes later. *Hey girl! It has. Yes let's meet around 11 if that works for u?*

11 is perfect. See you tomorrow

Frankly, Aisha wasn't really in the mood to hike. It was merely the easiest way to reconnect with Dahlia after kind of ghosting her a couple of weeks ago. Per her new friend's lighthearted response, she had bought her food poisoning excuse. Thank goodness, because this was the one new relationship Aisha didn't want to light on fire like Angela Bassett did with her husband's clothes in *Waiting to Exhale*.

She really enjoyed Dahlia's company and wanted to build a friendship with her. Plus, it looked like her local friend was making decisions that could compete with hers in the *How Dumb Are You Olympics*. She was fighting hard for that gold medal by considering getting back with her treacherous ex-husband.

Aisha was the first one to arrive at the trail the following day, which was good because she needed time to warm up. The only times she had been active since she had last hung out with Dahlia were under the sheets. She walked to a big rock a few yards away to sit and stretch on. She was already breathing loudly by the time she made it there.

Just a few weeks of inactivity and her body had forgotten all the miles and hills she had walked not even a month ago, yet all the memories she had actively tried to erase for months—hell, even years for some—were safely stored and preserved like the remains of a Pharaoh. Mummified. Locked in a box. *Well, I say: "Let my people go!"*

She chuckled, then stood up slowly. She moved her hips clockwise and counterclockwise. She extended her left leg on the rock, then her right. The sun was blazing above her. Summer was still a few weeks away, but the air was already wavy and thick. She adjusted her sunglasses and exhaled.

"Hey, girl!" Dahlia waved as she approached. She looked even more radiant than usual, with long ombre braids that rested just below her hips.

"Love the hair!" Aisha yelled though Dahlia was almost next to her then.

"Thank you." She hugged Aisha. "I got it done last week. This shit took nine freaking hours." She shook her head. "I think you got it right," she said, pointing at Aisha's short hair.

"Seriously." She grinned. "At first, I was anxious for it to grow back, but I don't know. I'm kind of feeling the short look now."

Dahlia smiled. "It suits you."

And just like that, the last month without contact felt inconsequential. It was so easy with Dahlia. No judgment. No pressure. *Space.* This was honestly the only way any of Aisha's relationships could thrive.

"I'm going to sleep in the guest room tonight," she had told James one evening.

"Okay," he said, without looking away from his phone.

Then, she had convinced herself that was all they needed. *Space.* Living on top of each other for that long would inevitably lead to arguments. That was what the last months had been about. Not the kid thing. Not how they were growing apart. Not the fact that they had no desire to be intimate with each other. No, those were not the real issues. The apartment was just too small, that was all. They needed some space to miss each other. Yes, that was the real problem. She had cracked the case. *Elementary, my dear Watson.*

Denial was one helluva drug, wasn't it?

She shook her head and focused back on her new friend. "Thank you! I'm in my Lupita Nyong'o *hair-a.*" She chuckled, then looked ahead. "If you don't mind, let's take the easy path today. It's been a while."

"Nice wordplay!" Dahlia smiled. "And I don't mind, girl. It's been a little while for me, too."

Remembering the way, Aisha took the first steps. "So, how have you been?"

"Busy but good. The dance event was fun! I'm sad you missed it."

"Me too." She clenched her teeth. "Stupid Taco Bell." She forced a laugh and looked at the ground.

"Taco Bell?" Dahlia gasped. "You're living on the edge, girl."

"Yeah, the edge of the toilet."

Dahlia cackled over the chirping of the birds. "You're funny! Anyway, I'm glad you're feeling better, but you were kind of asking for it."

"I know, I know." Aisha shook her head without looking up. She wasn't a good liar, and she especially hated being dishonest with such a genuine person. "Enough about my adventurous food choices. What have you been up to?"

"Well, since you couldn't make it to the dance party, I ended up going with Mark."

Aisha was confident Dahlia had never mentioned her ex-husband's name, yet she was sure that was who her friend was referring to.

She confirmed solely because she wasn't sure what else to say. "Your ex?"

Dahlia gently waved a branch away from her path. "Yes."

Aisha looked ahead as they walked into an open trail framed by colorful blooms. Butterflies were flying from flowers to flowers, noncommittal and free. "How did it go?"

"It was lots of fun, actually." Dahlia bent down to pick up a spent sunflower and continued to walk with it anchored between her thumb and index finger. "When I didn't hear back from you, I thought I'd just go by myself. I mean, that's what I do ninety percent of the time they have this event anyway. I already know most people who go there, so I don't mind going by myself. But I don't know, I didn't feel like going there alone that night." She threw the sunflower back on the ground. "Nia was at my parents', and I knew Mark would be home, so I asked him to meet me there if he was in the mood to dance. I thought he'd make up some excuse and say no because he's not the best dancer and doesn't want to learn. But he was so excited I invited him, and he showed up in his Sunday best. It was sweet." She looked at the horizon and smiled.

Aisha was so mad at herself for not going to dance that day. If it weren't for that, Dahlia wouldn't have spent that evening with Cheating Mark. As much as she wanted to blame herself for the obvious rekindling of Dahlia and Mark's relationship, she knew that based on their last conversation, it was bound to happen sooner than later—with or without Aisha's help.

"How are things between you two?" she said.

"Good." Dahlia was still smiling. "Really good, even. I stayed at his place for almost two weeks." She bit her bottom lip.

Aisha wanted to grab and shake her until she came back to her senses. But she remembered she was in no position to be judgmental. Plus, she didn't know how their relationship was before the affair. As far as she was concerned, unfaithfulness was an unforgivable offense. However, Dahlia and she were two different people. Sometimes, what's good for the goose isn't good for the gander. And she had to admit: Dahlia was glowing.

"You look happy," Aisha finally said.

Dahlia looked at her with a sparkle in her eye. "I am! I didn't know how much I had missed him. It's like we're twenty again. Everything is light and fun. It's so effortless. It just…makes sense." Aisha didn't mean to do it, but she slightly furrowed her brow. Dahlia smiled at her expression, then said, "I know, it's all happening so quickly, and it's moving so fast. But I spent some time alone after we were together, and honestly, I feel really good about this. No alarm bells are ringing. Nothing feels off. It feels right."

They were back on the narrow path again. The birds resumed their song above them. The tall trees completely shielded them from the sun. "So, are you, like, back together?"

"Not officially. We're just going with the flow, I guess. Letting things happen when they are ready to."

"Wow. Okay. I'm happy that you're happy."

"Right." She tittered. "I promise, I'm not just thinking with my heart and vagina. My head's in the game, too. He really has changed, and it's obvious he has done a lot of personal work. I think it's worth a second try, just dating. No serious commitment yet. He'd have to be consistent for a while for me to consider that." She increased her volume when saying *a while*.

There was so much Aisha wanted to say. *He'll be consistent until you take him back and a little longer after that. Then, boom! He has to work late. He has to be out of town longer than expected. Why do you nag so much? That's not what he signed up for!* She held her tongue. As if she was a robot malfunctioning, she repeated her previous sentence. "I'm just happy that you're happy."

Dahlia chuckled. "Enough about me, girl. What have you been up to?"

Aisha sighed and took a moment to decide what she wanted to share. "I'm on Tinder."

"How many dick pics?"

"I stopped counting after ten."

Dahlia laughed. "Met anyone you like so far?"

She shook her head. "No, and I'm not looking for anything serious. Just some good ol' fashioned no strings attached fun."

"Cool. I'm happy you're having a good time." To demonstrate the kind of fun she figured Aisha was having, Dahlia humped the air and smacked its light booty. Aisha giggled. Dahlia spoke again in a more serious tone. "And the healing?"

"Tinder's part of it, I think. So, I guess I'm making *loooots* of progress." She raised her eyebrows up and down repeatedly.

"Good for you! Do whatever you gotta do, girl." They walked silently for a moment. They were approaching the parking area now. "I like you, Aisha. We should hang out more often."

Aisha felt her chest and cheeks warm up in excitement. "I feel the same way."

"I'll be in Fort Worth over the next few days." Dahlia winked at her. Aisha wanted to flick her eyelid to wake her up. *No judging,* she remembered. The sun was shining on Dahlia's face when she said, "Let's do drinks next Monday or Wednesday, maybe?"

"Either day is good for me." They were now standing in the parking lot.

"Okay. I know a spot that has amazing happy hour drinks on Wednesdays. I'll text you the details."

"Sounds like a plan."

"Yay, can't wait!"

They hugged goodbye.

Aisha wasn't sure whether it was her conversation with Dahlia or nature, but she felt a new energy flowing through her veins, so she called her mother the next day.

"Hey, sweetie! How are you? It's been so long! How's everything?" her mom said the moment she picked up.

Aisha let out a muted sigh. Perhaps she didn't have enough energy to deal with her mom's relentless enthusiasm after all. "Hey, Mom. All is well here. How's everything on your end?"

"Great! The new girl is crushing it! Apparently, some of the clients who followed Leslie are not satisfied with the quality of her salon, so they are slowly creeping back here. I honestly can't complain, honey. I just really miss you."

"I'm happy business's back to normal. I knew your clients would come back. You and your team really do an amazing job." Aisha meant every single word. She used to get her hair done at her mom's salon. They deserved ninety percent of the credit for her then-full and long hair. She suddenly realized she hadn't told her mother she shaved it all.

Because of that telepathic connection between a parent and a child, Helen said, "Where are you getting your hair done now, anyway? I know you're not even detangling it by yourself." She giggled.

Aisha hadn't told Helen because it would obviously lead her mother to ask why. She was still not ready to tell her mom the true reason. And again, she wasn't a good liar. Her mother, out of all people, could sniff out her attempted bullshitting before she even finished a sentence. "I shaved it," she finally said.

Helen gasped. "Because you couldn't find a good salon?"

Aisha chuckled. "No. I'm not that helpless."

"Then, why? You just wanted a new look?"

"Something like that." Her voice was a little drier because she didn't want to answer more questions about why she cut her hair.

Helen knew her well, so she left it alone. "I'm sure you look beautiful. Send me a picture if you can. You know, I used to wear my hair very short back in the day, and let me tell you, I didn't have a shortage of suitors."

Aisha smiled. "I bet."

It was quiet for a moment.

"No rush, baby, but I'd like to have a conversation about what happened whenever you're ready."

"I'm not ready."

"Yes, I know. Again, no rush. I just wanted to throw that out there because it's been a while. But no rush, baby. Send me a picture of your haircut whenever you can. I love you."

"Love you too. I have to go. I'll talk to you later, okay?"

"Alright, sweetie. Have a good day. Bye-bye."

"You too. Bye."

As soon as she hung up, Aisha took a picture of her hair and sent it to her mom. Helen texted her back immediately. *You look gorgeous, honey.*

A tear rolled down her cheek. She felt horrible about the way she was treating her mother. Why was she so unforgiving?

Why was it so difficult for her to let go? She knew her mother loved her. Everyone made mistakes. At the very least, she could give her a chance to explain, talk it out, make amends. Why did she want to hold on to hurt so damn bad? Did she enjoy harboring pain on some unconscious level? Was there a part of her that enjoyed feeling uneasy? Was her holding grudges a way of hiding an ugly truth about herself? If she was too busy feeling restless, she wouldn't be still long enough to see who she truly was: Albert's abandoned daughter. Helen's inconvenience.

There. Finally, she had allowed herself to flesh out that feeling. Perhaps she should now take a moment to ponder on it. Get granular. *I don't know, pick up a fucking notebook and write that shit down, bitch.* Get her feelings on paper. On her phone. Somewhere. Anywhere. If she needed to talk it out, call Amir. Use this moment when she finally had the courage to spell out her thoughts to dig deeper. But as if she were the diametrical opposite of an expandable character in a horror movie, she decided to not open *that* door to investigate further.

Instead, she opened the Tinder app and began swiping right.

WEEK 22

After replying *Yes* to a text from David asking if she was free tomorrow evening, she called Amir.

"Long time no talk," she said the moment he picked up.

"And whose fault is that?" He yawned.

"Am I boring you?"

"Yes, but that's fine. You woke me up."

She smiled. "Why are you sleeping at 6 PM?"

"What's with the third-degree?"

"I only asked two questions."

"*Bruh*. You woke me up for this?"

She laughed. "I just wanted to check in on the new team lead."

"I swear to God, if anyone else escalates some psychotic ass customer to me, I'm going to quit. Like, how hard is it to plug something out and plug it back in? Humans are devolving."

She tittered. "You got it, bro. They promoted you because you were the best man for the job."

"Girl, please. They promoted me because I was the *only* man for the job. Anyone who would've lasted more than six months would've been considered. And turns out I'm the only maso who stuck around."

She laughed. "It's that bad?"

"Yes, but it's alright. I just mute them when they go on their little rants. Anyway, what's going on with you? Still hoeing?"

"Yep."

"I'm about to get on that train soon."

"Really?"

"Yep. You opened my eyes last time. I'm over here putting my life on hold and waiting for Thomas to give me the smallest hope when he has clearly moved on. I mean, he unblocked me, but then nothing. I followed him again on IG, but he didn't follow me back. I'm sick of his little games. I'm over it."

A part of her echoed yonder: *You know you're not over it. Give him some time. More importantly, give yourself some time to heal. Getting under the next man will only numb the pain. It's just a cover. All that hurt will still be there under all the noise. You need to be strong enough to do the actual self-work.* But just like an echo, the words became smaller and smaller and traveled further and further away until they were completely swallowed by the ether. Gone, like they never existed.

Also, people who live in glass houses.

So, all Aisha said was, "About time. Welcome to the club, baby!"

Amir chuckled. "Thanks." He yawned again. "I'm going to meet with Mom for dinner. You spoke to her lately?"

"Yes. Last week."

"Okay, that's good. Alright, sis. I'll talk to you later."

"Love you."

"Love you too. Bye."

That evening, Aisha made a reservation at an interesting sushi restaurant with raving reviews. The full experience required turning your phone off before entering the premises. Her eyes slowly adjusted to the dimmed lights when she walked in. The hostess welcomed her with a smile brighter than the room behind her.

"Hello, miss. Do you have a reservation?"

"Hello. Yes. 8 PM. Aisha Jones."

"Party of one?"

"Yes."

"Did you get a chance to turn your phone off?"

"I did, yes."

"Wonderful. Please follow me."

She sat Aisha in the corner of the room. Everything was scarlet. There was a small red vase with two red roses on her table. The menu cover was red. The place was packed, but just as quiet as the lighting. She could see that people's lips were moving, but she couldn't hear a thing. Typically, when she went to restaurants alone, she always caught a few sympathetic looks. *Aw, poor girl is alone.* And though some were pity stares, it made her feel seen.

But tonight, in the dark red room, no one looked at her. And perhaps it was that or the fact that the place was practically silent. She had no distractions. No phone. No entertainment. No escape. All she had were her thoughts, and she felt profoundly alone.

She felt like her existence was insignificant. Her presence or absence didn't move the needle in either direction. She felt weightless. Whether she did everything right or everything wrong, ultimately, it wouldn't matter.

Why try to fix things if, in the grand scheme of things, it was inconsequential? Why unearth stuff that had grown roots within her? It was honestly too dangerous to go so deep within, below the dermis, to such an unknown territory. She could destroy the very structure of her being. And for what? To hopefully fix things that would ultimately not matter when the dust settled. Years of work. Years of healing. Years of rebuilding. And then someone else would come along and raise it all to the ground in a fraction of time. Then, she'd have to start all over again. For what exactly?

Look at Dahlia.

Poor girl had done years of therapy and self-work to get over her husband. And just within weeks, she was right back where she started. Doing the same thing and expecting different results because, hopefully, enough time had passed, and things *might* turn out differently. Aisha couldn't take that type of risk. She respected the strength it took to put one's heart on the line repeatedly, knowing it might get ripped to shred with every single try. It was admirable, sure, but mostly stupid, honestly.

Look at Amir.

He had done "the work" too. He thought he had gotten over his abandonment issues and became a well-balanced individual. But when it came down to it, he sabotaged his relationship because of the fear of commitment he thought he had worked through. And now he was back on the same starting line Aisha had never left. All this effort only to get back where he had started. What a waste of time. What was the point, really?

Aisha ordered some sake and sushi rolls. She drank and ate quietly. She was going to use her time on Earth wisely. She was going to do whatever the hell she wanted, whenever the hell she wanted, and with whomever she felt like doing it with.

Fuck healing.

Hopefully, with time, some wounds would close naturally. But whether they did or not, she would make sure to be too busy and inebriated by life to notice.

She waited for her inner voice to come back with some smart-ass remark and try to speak some sense into her, caution against her reckless decision, and talk her out of it. But just like the rest of the room, the voice was utterly silent.

*

The following day, Aisha woke up to a text from David. *Good morning, Aisha. I'm looking forward to seeing you this evening. I've missed your company.*

Good morning David. So have I - see you tonight

She walked outside to her balcony, stretched her arms out, and exhaled. The sun was gentle today, caressing her skin and the white magnolias in front of her. The light gave the flowers two equally stunning tones. She hummed a familiar song: *My Girl* by The Temptations, one of Sam's favorite songs.

Aisha recalled when Sam had sung her lungs out, screaming, "*My giiiiirl*" as they were headed to the Rocky Mountain National Park.

"If you're going to replay this song a million times," Aisha said, "can I at least listen to it and not you for once?" She rolled down the driver's side window so the wind would cover Sam's scratchy vocals.

"*My giiiiiiirl*," Sam replied, holding an imaginary microphone.

Aisha chuckled and listened to her friend sing the song twice from beginning to end. By the time she was done "singing," all the windows were rolled down.

"Okay, I think I'm done now. You can play something else," Sam said, breathless.

"Thank God."

Aisha put her R&B playlist on shuffle and turned the volume down. "Someone's in an amazing mood. Does your secret lover have something to do with this?"

"Yes, ma'am." Sam looked at the blurry landscape flashing to her right.

"Okay, I'm getting offended now. When am I going to meet John? What's with the secrecy? Is he an ex-con or something? I promise I won't judge."

"And I promise, I'll tell you in due time. I just want things to stay the same right now. I don't want to ruin things by changing them. I promise, when I'm ready, you'll be the first to know."

Aisha rolled her eyes. "I better be." She looked at her friend. Sam was blushing. "Wow. I've not seen you like this since the early days with Blake. You're in love, my friend."

Sam covered her face. "Not, I'm not!"

"Oh my God. You are, aren't you? *Dear John,* must be one hell of a catch." She patted her best friend's thigh. "I'm happy for you, Sam. You deserve this."

Sam cracked a small smile. "Thank you."

Now, Aisha was staring at the white flowers. The sunlight was no longer shining on them. She walked back inside and slid the door closed behind her.

That evening, she was the first to arrive at the bar David had chosen for them to meet. She wore a strapless dress that contoured her body like a chalk outline. She didn't wait for him and ordered a cocktail. Might as well get this party started. She had listened to *Drake* on her way there, and tonight, she was absolutely going to be on her *Worst Behavior.* She knew David would enjoy it.

When he arrived, Aisha already felt light and loose. The place was packed and rowdy. She was seated in the center-right of the lounge. As David walked up to her, she stood up to hug him, making sure to press her chest against him.

"Hello, handsome."

He grinned. "Hello, beautiful." They sat down. He looked at her almost empty glass, and his smile widened. "I see I have some catching up to do."

She tipped her head back and swallowed the remaining of her cocktail. "You do." She winked at him.

The waiter walked to their table. He was older, and his eyes had fine lines on their corners imprinted from years of smiling. With that smile, he spoke to David. "Hello, sir. Are you ready to order?"

"Yes, I'll have what she's having. And another glass for her, please."

Aisha double-tapped the stem of her glass and looked at the server. "Please make it a double."

"Yes, ma'am," the man said, then walked away.

"Are we celebrating something tonight, Aisha? You're in a very festive mood."

She raised her empty glass. "Yes, we're celebrating life!" She only realized how loud she had spoken when some people around them paused their conversation and directed their collective gaze toward her.

She almost felt embarrassed, but then someone in the section beside them raised their glass and yelled. "That's right. To life!"

Glasses clinked and laughter echoed. "To life!" their side of the room chanted.

David joined them with a fist in the air. "To life!"

Then, the room resumed its original cadence. David and Aisha looked at each other and burst into laughter. "You, Miss Aisha Jones, are the life of the party this evening."

She shimmied. "You got that right!"

The server materialized next to them and placed their drinks and some water on the table. David raised his glass. "To the life of the party!"

She lifted her drink. "Cheers!"

"I'm dying to hear what you've been up to, Aisha. Please tell me everything."

She spoke at once. "Just living life, you know." She took a big sip and then crossed her legs. "Life is ephemeral, David. Meaningless, really. I realized I was taking it too seriously. It's all a moot point, isn't it? I mean, we spend our entire lives trying to figure out our shit and understand why we're fucked up. We try to fight our demons. We try to understand where all our traumas come from."

She looked around the room, then looked in David's direction, but not into his eyes. "Then, miraculously, some of us actually figure our shit out. We have a respite. Finally, we get to enjoy the fruits of our labor. But then some other shit happens, and boom, we're back where we started. Then, we die." She took another sip and uncrossed her legs. "I don't want to spend my time on Earth this way. Life's too short for that, David. It's best to ignore it all and just have fun. You understand me, right?"

He was just gazing at her. Aisha finally maintained his stare, and she immediately knew without a shadow of a doubt that if eyes were hands, she would be sporting her birthday suit in the middle of this noisy lounge on a random Tuesday evening. "I understand you, Aisha. I really do," he said at last.

"Good." She extended her arm and took a sip of his drink without breaking eye contact. Her lipstick left a red print on the glass.

He smiled, grabbed his glass back, and carefully aligned his lips where hers had left the red mark to finish his drink. "Have you given any thoughts on posing nude for me?" he said when he put the glass down.

She left electricity traveling through her upper body and settling in between her thighs. She had no idea what he had just said. "Can you repeat the question?"

He laughed. "Have you given any thought to posing nude for me? Again, it'll be quite abstract, I promise. No one will be able to tell it's you. You will, of course, be compensated for your time as a model. It's been a long time since I've felt inspired. Lately, nothing and no one has sparked my creative interest…until you, Aisha. Please consider it. I've missed the urge to grab my brushes. That passion. That fire and tightening in my guts!"

"Have you considered laxatives?"

He laughed so loud that he looked slightly different, somewhat juvenile. Aisha took a good look at him. She hadn't focused on his face very much tonight. His blond hair was a little longer. He had let his facial hair grow, too. He had some light dark circles under his eyes. He looked like he could use a nap.

He drank some water after he settled down. "This is what I'm talking about, Aisha. You must pose for me, I implore you. Be my muse. We would have a blast!"

She pursed her lips. "How abstract are we talking?"

"Even you will have a hard time telling it's you."

She didn't speak for a moment. She tapped her top lip with her index finger. "If I can tell, you'll have to destroy it, okay?"

He nodded rapidly. "Absolutely. Even if you can't tell and you don't want me to showcase it anywhere when it's done, I won't. I'll get rid of it if you want. Just creating it will get me out of this slump. Get my creative juices flowing."

"Fine. We have a deal." She grabbed his hand and shook it. "Now, why don't we go to your place and get my juices flowing."

David frantically raised his hand and waved at someone. Aisha looked behind her and saw their waiter pacing toward them. "Yes, sir?" the old man said.

"Can we have the check this instant, please?"

The man glanced at Aisha and then back at David. He smiled. "Absolutely." He left and returned within seconds with the bill. "Have a lovely rest of your evening!" He grinned.

They both smiled at him, then at each other.

The next thing Aisha knew, she was following behind David. They drove for about twenty-five minutes until the houses they flashed by became bigger and bigger and stood further and further away from the road. At last, they pulled inside the gates of a modern villa. Based on his art expo and his sports car, she knew that David was doing well for himself, but she could've never imagined that he was doing *this* well.

His estate had to be about four thousand and five hundred square feet. The roof was flat, with a spacious balcony sitting atop. The structure was cubic and asymmetrical. The exterior was made primarily of charred wood. The whole thing was stunning.

She didn't think David would be living off the grid or anything like that. This was just more extravagant than she was prepared for. Was this why he was so insistent on her coming to his place? Was he trying to impress her with his nice house so she'd be more susceptible to do whatever he wanted? Perhaps he was hoping his painting could be less abstract. Thinking she'd be too blinded by the luxury to say no to his demands? If that were the case, he was up for a rude awakening—emphasis on *rude*.

Her questions were answered the moment they walked in. David didn't comment on the obviously expensive art lining his wall. He didn't say anything about the onyx kitchen island. He didn't tell her the history of the French Empire chandelier hanging from the ridiculously high ceiling. They walked on the longest runner rug she had ever seen, past three rooms, up a spiral staircase, and he only asked her what she wanted to drink.

"Any red you got," she said.

"Cab? Pinot? Merlot?"

"Dealer's choice."

They walked into an entertainment room with a pool table and other games leading to the balcony. "Make yourself comfortable out there. I'll bring a bottle."

She walked outside and sat on the teak swivel chair beside a large sectional. It was too dark to get a good peek at the landscape before her, but from the sound of it, they were surrounded by nature, far from the city. Suddenly, she panicked. She was God-knows-where, with someone who—all things considered—was still a stranger.

Obviously, his goal wasn't to impress her. He just wanted her to come to his place so he could be in a more intimate setting…to murder her. It was so obvious now. He knew she was far from home, with no family in town. No one would find out for a while, and he'd have plenty of time to cover his tracks. Her heart rate began to race. She looked around to find the easiest way out. She walked up to the ledge and looked down. It was about a twenty-foot jump. With enough adrenaline, she could clear that with minor injuries. She sat back down, ready to fight for her life.

David walked outside with two glasses in each hand and a bottle tucked under his arm.

"Voilà," he said as he put one glass on the wooden table in front of her. He sat on the edge of the sectional and put his drink in front of him and next to hers.

"Thank you," she said, controlling her breathing. She pointed at a large naked woman statue by the balcony ledge. "Did you make that?"

The moment David's head was fully turned to the left, she quickly switched the drinks. And if she had to, she would grab that wine bottle and slam it in his face. *Please, try me.*

"Oh no," he said, then looked back at her. "I wish I could take credit for it, but I bought it at an art fair. A very talented young lady. If she had some name recognition, she could've sold it for ten times what I bought it for."

Something about the way he spoke so softly and looked so pensive made Aisha realize David wasn't planning on killing her. When he took a sip of his drink, a part of her still expected him to pass out, but he didn't. Instead, he leaned toward her. "You seem distracted. Is everything okay?"

She shook her head. "Yes." She finally took a sip of her drink. "*Soooo*, you're rich," she said.

He smiled. "I wouldn't say that, but I guess I can't complain."

"Unrelated, but my nude modeling fee has increased recently due to high demand. I meant to tell you earlier."

He laughed. "Understandable. Thank you for penciling me in."

She crossed her leg. "It's no problem. My agent will email you the contract." She broke into laughter, and he joined her. "But seriously, you have a beautiful home."

"Thank you. I don't have much to do with it. My architect and interior designer did the heavy lifting." A weird smile suddenly cornered his mouth. "I saw you switch the drinks, Aisha. I want to be offended, but I can't say I blame you. You can never be too careful these days."

She felt her cheeks flush. "I'm sorry, David. Intrusive thoughts."

"You don't have to apologize. It's okay, I really get it," he said earnestly. Then he smirked. "Let's say I did want to hurt you. What was your plan?"

"Knock you over the head with the bottle of wine, then jump off the ledge and run away to my car."

He laughed. "Try to grab the bottle," he said with a sparkle in his eye.

She furrowed her brow. "You think I can't do it?"

"Try."

She extended her arm as fast as she could to grab the bottle, but he was quicker than her.

"Shit," she said.

He drank from the bottle, then winked at her. "Good thing I only want to fuck you and not hurt you. I mean, I do want to spank you, but I'm pretty sure you'll enjoy that."

She snatched the bottle from his grasp. "Prove it."

He did just that. Spanked her, kissed her, bit her, and fucked her on the balcony for the better part of the night.

She passed out before him on the sectional. She woke up at dawn. He was still asleep. She walked to the ledge and looked at the horizon. Trees were still a bright green, resisting the summer heat that aimed to brown them. She looked at David. He looked so peaceful. For some odd reason, she wanted to kiss him on the forehead. *Jesus.* She shook the feeling off and left. She texted him when she made it back to her apartment.

Good morning David. Sorry I had to run. Last night was fun. Let's schedule our first session soon xoxo

He replied two hours later. *Good morning, Aisha. Last night was amazing. Absolutely. I'll text you to put something on the calendar.*

She was on cloud nine all morning. Around noon, she heard her phone vibrate. She hated to admit it, but she hoped it was David texting her to say that he couldn't wait till next week and wanted to see her again tonight. She looked at the message. It was Dahlia.

Hey girl I'm SO sorry but I have to take a rain check for tonight. How's next Wednesday for you?

She was a little disappointed. She was looking forward to hanging out with Dahlia that evening. She wanted to tell her about her amazing sexcapade. She also wanted to hear what her friend had been up to. But she couldn't be upset. Unlike her, Dahlia had the courtesy to give her a heads-up.

Hey no worries! Hope everything is okay and yes next Wednesday works for me

Aisha spent the rest of her week thinking about her night with David, smoking weed, drinking wine, swiping through Tinder profiles, and making good use of a sex toy she purchased online. She almost didn't think about all her "stuff."

Almost.

Whenever the smallest thought about her past made it past the walls she was building, she looked at the bruises David had left on her thighs, rolled a blunt, poured some vino, swiped right, and turned her vibrator on.

WEEK 23

The second time Aisha saw her father was on her seventeenth birthday. She knew something was wrong when her mom walked into the kitchen. Helen looked like she had seen a ghost because she had. The color was gone from her face. She looked so pale Aisha thought she was going to faint. Aisha ran up to her mother and held her.

"What's wrong, Mom? Are you okay?"

Her mother glanced at her like she couldn't make out her face. She teared up. "Your father is outside. I didn't let him in. I don't know if you want to see him, especially today."

"What?" Aisha let go of her mother.

"Do you want me to send him away?"

"What the hell is he doing here?" she screamed out.

Amir ran downstairs. "What's going on?" he said, looking at Aisha, then at their mother.

"Your father's outside, at the front door," Helen replied. She leaned against the kitchen counter and put her hands over her face.

Amir ran to Aisha and hugged her tightly. "Do you want me to kick his ass?" he whispered to her.

She looked at her brother with tears in her eyes. "Do you want to talk to him?"

He didn't reply. He didn't have to. Aisha knew how much Amir wanted Albert to be part of their lives. A quiet part of her did, too. The loudest one was angry, hated him, and never wanted to see him again. But more than she despised Albert, she loved Amir.

Aisha looked at their mother. "You can tell him to come in."

When Albert walked in, Aisha sensed a knot clogging her throat, growing bigger and wider the closer he walked to her. Her stomach was a tightening fist, tightening more and more when he looked at her. Her heart was beating too fast and too loud. And when her father gently laid his hands on her shoulders, she was paralyzed.

"Wow. You're almost a woman now," he said. "Beautiful, just like your mother."

Aisha was at a loss for words. She wanted to string the foulest sentence together. Words that would undo him. Words that would echo, vibrate, and break. But she couldn't think clearly because she was stunned. It was the sheer audacity that took her off guard. The lightness of his delivery and the light in his eyes. How comfortable he was.

Like, it was just another day.

Like, he was coming back home from work to celebrate his daughter's birthday with his family.

Like, his showing up unannounced after almost a decade of living God-knows-where, doing God-knows-what with God-knows-who wasn't a big deal.

The Prodigal Father. *How much we've missed you. We were worried sick. Where have you been? You know what, it doesn't matter. We're just happy that you're here.*

"Thanks," was all she was able to mutter.

Albert smiled at her, then turned to Amir. "And you, son. You're bigger than me now!" He patted Amir's shoulders. "Look at him, Helen," he turned to their mother, "he's going to be quite the ladies' man."

Amir moved away from him and closer to Aisha. "I'm gay."

Albert puckered his lips and nodded. "Oh, alright. Well, quite the gentlemen's man then." He winked at Amir.

Their mother was standing by the front door. She walked up and stood next to their father in the middle of the entryway. Aisha didn't like that sight at all. What the hell had their mom seen in this man?

"Hmm...uh...okay," Helen said, "why don't we all take a seat at the dining table and start Sha's birthday dinner."

Albert rubbed his hands together and made his way to the living room. "I like the sound of that!"

Behind him, Aisha and Amir looked at each other. Amir raised one eyebrow and let out a single, quiet: *hmph*. Aisha shook her head. They smiled at each other, knowing that no matter how this night turned out, they'd have each other in the end. Then they walked to the dining table and sat down.

For a moment, it was just them and their father. Their mother was in the kitchen, prepping the food. Albert stared at them with a stupid grin on his face. He looked genuinely happy, and it infuriated Aisha. He truly had no remorse, no guilt. He thought he could just show up after nine fucking years and pick up where he left off—which was nowhere. Aisha could feel her blood boiling and her temperature rising. It was only a matter of time until she exploded. Her brother looked at her and held her hand under the table.

Amir broke the silence. "So, hmm, what…have you been up to?"

"Retracing my roots, son." Albert beamed. "Exploring Africa: Congo, Chad, Benin, Niger, Cameroon, Ivory Coast, Nigeria, Angola, Mali." He raised his fist. "So rich. So enriching. So vital. I don't know if your mom told you, but my father was from Cameroon. I mean, going there and exploring his hometown, Ebolowa. God, I just felt like I belonged. It was hard to leave."

This was the moment Aisha heard something snap within her. The compact frame that held the loose pieces of her together and contained her. Filtered what she thought versus what she said. Just then, their mother walked toward the table, holding two pots. Helen looked at her daughter, and Aisha knew her mother saw it was too late. The bullet was already in motion inside of the barrel.

It went out. "What the fuck is actually wrong with you? Are you insane? Are your neurons still firing? Are you stupi—"

"Aisha!" her mom yelled with the pots still in her hands.

"No, it's okay. Let her go on," Albert said.

"You damn right, I'll go on." Aisha laughed dryly. "Wait, is this your attempt at parenting? Are you serious?" She stood up. "What the hell did you think was going to happen today? That you'd just show up here and casually catch up? What's the point of this visit? To feel better about yourself? Is it getting harder to look at yourself in the mirror? Stopped by for a little boost of self-worth, uh?"

"I know I've not been the best father, but—"

Aisha looked at her mother, then at Amir—who hadn't moved an inch—and clapped. "Ladies and gentlemen, for the biggest understatement of the century, the award goes to," she drummed the table, "Albert Thompson!"

"You made your point," Helen said.

She looked at her mother. "No, Mom. I haven't. Not even close." She looked back at Albert. "To call yourself a father is an insult to fatherhood. It was hard to leave your father's hometown? Do you hear yourself talk, or are you too far up your own ass for the words to make it there? You left us and didn't look back. *That* was easy. Your children." She broke into tears.

"Then, for whatever reason, you came back when we were kids to ask about our favorite school subjects. You stopped by for not even one hour, then you left. *That* was fucking easy, right? Jesus. And we go on. We moved on. And now, almost ten years later, here you are, back again. Why? To talk about how great and satisfying your life was away from us? Are you actually sick? What's the matter with you?" Her eyes were red and wet. She turned away from Albert, ready to walk away.

Aisha felt his hand on her skin. She hated that she recognized his touch. He whispered. "I'm so sorry, bab—"

She swatted his hand away from her. "Don't touch me!" She ran upstairs to her room.

A few minutes later, she heard the front door close. Then, footsteps up the staircase. Then Amir's bedroom door opened. She stood from her bed and quietly walked into her brother's room. He looked at her. She looked at the floor. He ran toward her, and they cried into each other's arms. Aisha thought she'd never see her father again.

*

Perhaps it was the scorching Dallas summer heat that had caused her to think about that dreadful day. And yesterday, when she made small talk with her neighbor in the elevator, the woman had dared to say, "Oh, sweetheart, it's not even hot yet." If there was truly a hot burning hell, geographically, it had to be somewhere below Texas.

Thankfully, Dahlia had confirmed they were still on for drinks that evening. And given that she had still not heard from David, she was even more eager to catch up with her new friend. She was annoyed at how anxious she was to hear back from the artist. She knew what their thing was. They met occasionally for flirty banter and sex. And soon, they would spice things up by having her pose nude for him. David never pretended he wanted more out of this arrangement, and she was certainly not ready for more. Yet she found herself checking her phone a few times a day, hoping he had finally reached out to schedule their next meetup.

She was probably just bored. She honestly had too much time on her hands. Amir was right. She needed to get a part-time job, a hobby, or a volunteer position. Anything that would force her to leave the house a few times a week and give her a sense of continuity and consistency. She'd put more thought into that later. Now, it was time to call an Uber to meet her friend for happy hour.

When she walked inside the bar, Dahlia greeted Aisha with a long hug. She was seated at a high-top table near the bar. She still had her long ombre braids and looked even more radiant than usual. Her face was clear and brilliant.

"I need the updated skincare routine," Aisha said when she sat down.

"Girl, ain't nothing changed. Coconut oil is just really agreeing with me these days."

Aisha squinted her eyes. "No, there has to be something else."

Dahlia smirked. "Well, why don't we order first, and I'll tell you all about it."

When their discounted cocktails were served, Aisha leaned in. "So?"

"I got a boyfriend," Dahlia sang. "Mark and I made it official last week. He took me on a little getaway to Wine Country in Fredericksburg and asked me to be his girlfriend."

Aisha wanted to share Dahlia's excitement, but she physically couldn't get herself to smile. She felt like Dahlia was moving way too fast. Even if she chose to forgive Cheating

Mark—which, in her opinion, was incomprehensible—she ought to make him work a little harder than that.

Aisha took a sip of her cocktail. "That was quick."

"I know, I know. But I'm thirty-six. I don't have time to play games. I don't have the energy or stamina for that. To me, it's simple. I love him. I forgave him. I want to be with him. What's the point of dragging this out?"

"If you forgive him so easily, don't you feel like he'll think he can hurt you over and over again? He'll just get a slap on the wrist, a little timeout, and then boom: he's back in your good graces."

Dahlia listened attentively and nodded. Aisha truly admired that she didn't take criticism personally. Her friend took a moment to reply. "I've definitely considered that, trust me. But this is not me having a revolving door for him. This is me giving the man I was married to for ten years one more chance. This is me giving the father of my child one last opportunity to make things right. This is me honoring the way *I* feel.

"I understand this might not work out, and there is a chance I'll be devastated at the end of this. But there is also a chance this will work out, and my heart will be full again. I can get everything I've been missing and wanting. And just the chance of that happening, however slim it might be, makes this worth a try."

"Wow." Aisha whistled. "That's admirable. I wish I could do that. I really hope he doesn't hurt you again. And if he does and you need help jumping him, just let me know when and where."

She laughed. "I'll keep that in mind." She patted Aisha's hand. "Enough about me. God, I always do this. What's going on with you, girl? What have you been up to?"

Aisha's face lit up. "I've been seeing this guy. He's an artist. He asked me to pose nude for him." She smirked, waiting for her friend's response.

"What?" Dahlia gasped. "That's so exciting! You said yes, right?"

"Yes, I did." She giggled at Dahlia's enthusiasm. "I wasn't sure at first, but he assured me the painting would be very abstract, so no one would be able to recognize me."

"Why does he even need you to pose nude for him if it won't be an exact full-length portrait?"

"To capture my essence."

Dahlia burst into laughter. "Bullshit! That man's just trying to have you naked as much as possible so y'all can get your freak on."

Aisha sipped her drink, then smirked. "And the problem is what?"

Dahlia high-fived her. "*O-kayyyy!*"

They both laughed heartily, posing to examine each other's faces, then laughing again.

Aisha also wanted to share how anxious she was to hear back from David, and what happened with Carlos and Marcus. She even wanted to talk about Albert and Amir. She wanted to tell Dahlia what her mother had said to her. She wanted to tell her new friend all the ways she was undone. She wanted to let her know she wasn't even hanging by a thread anymore.

She was falling, fast and hard, nearing mental rock bottom.

But when she saw how hard Dahlia was laughing and how her friend looked at her, like she was this adventurous person with this thrilling life, Aisha decided to hold the bad stories. She wanted to be the person Dahlia thought she was. Their friendship would thrive better that way. And maybe, just maybe, she could start over completely and be that person. Perhaps she could truly forget her past if she ignored it long enough.

When they finally settled down, Dahlia said, "I'm happy for you, girl. Keep doing whatever makes you happy and fulfilled. That's what life's about." She picked up her phone and looked at something. "Oh, by the way, they're going to have another dance event on the last Saturday of this month. You need to come. You can bring your lover friend." She winked at Aisha.

"I guess I can ask him. That could be fun."

"It will be!"

They chatted a bit longer, pairing every new topic with a different cocktail. They talked about Dahlia's increasingly unsatisfying work while drinking Hurricanes. She was seriously considering quitting if she found any other dance studio that offered her better pay and a fair opportunity for career advancement.

Later, they sipped two Malibu Sunsets while Aisha asked Dahlia if she had any suggestions on some fun hobbies or places she could volunteer or work part-time to fill up her days. Dahlia told her she would research, ask around, and get back to her.

When the bill came, their cheeks were flushed, and their movements were airy. While they waited for their Uber drivers, Dahlia showed Aisha some pictures of her daughter.

"She's so cute," Aisha said while swiping through photos of Nia at a dance recital, playing in a backyard, with her face smeared with peanut butter, and then with a man who had her round nose and full eyebrows. She turned the phone toward Dahlia. "Is this Mark?"

Her face lit up. "Yes, that's Mark." She bit her lip. "What do you think?"

Objectively, he was attractive: in shape, with beautiful brown skin, and full lips. But all Aisha saw was a cheater. She held that thought to the best of her ability.

"He's very handsome. And I see what you meant; they are twins."

Dahlia grinned and took back her phone to look at them like it was the first time she saw that picture. "They are, aren't they?" Then, she looked in the distance and murmured, "I really hope he doesn't hurt me again. I want this to work…for me and Nia."

Aisha didn't reply. She just held her friend's hand and smiled.

Twenty minutes later, they walked outside to the parking lot as two sedans waited for them.

"I had a blast!" Dahlia said.

"Me too!"

"Are you good to get home?"

"After you showed me that video of your boss twerking," Aisha air-quoted *twerking*, "I very much am, yes."

Dahlia chuckled. "That man's a trip." She hugged Aisha goodbye. "Alright, girl. I'll send you anything I can find about fun things to do in town. I'll ask around about volunteer positions. And don't forget to tell your boo about the dance event in two weeks. I'll text you the details."

"Sounds good. Thank you so much."

"Of course." She walked to her Uber and waved goodbye. "Get home safe."

Aisha opened her driver's car door. "You too."

*

The next morning, she woke up to a text message from her mother. *Hey honey, just checking in! How are you? Hope it's not too hot there.*

She replied after she had some coffee. *Hey mom it IS insanely hot here and people just act like it's normal. It makes no sense lol I'm doing good otherwise. Everything's going well over there?*

First, Helen sent a laughing face emoji. Then: *Yes, everything is fine. Just call whenever you're free. I miss you so much.* She added a heart emoji at the end.

I miss you too

Aisha lay her phone down on the kitchen counter and walked away to put her coffee mug in the sink. Her phone vibrated behind her. She hoped it wasn't her mother asking how soon she could call. She wasn't in the mood to talk to her right now.

Lately, she was rarely in the mood for it. It wasn't because she didn't miss her mother. It was because she knew her mother would be able to see the fissures behind her façade. And out of everyone she was keeping her true mental state hidden from, her mother was the one she wanted to conceal it from the most. There was already so much that needed fixing between them—damages with an overdue work order. For the sake of their fragile foundation, she couldn't bring anything else up. The whole thing would fall apart.

Thankfully, the text wasn't from her mom. It was from David. She read the message with a broad smile that made her cheeks hurt.

Hello, beautiful. Hope you're having a good day! Are you free next Tuesday? We can have dinner then have our first session?

She immediately replied. *Hey David yes I am! Just let me know the time and place and I'll be there*

He texted her back about an hour later. *I was thinking I'd make something for you. I'm a decent cook haha. How's 7pm at my place?*

Okay that works!

David didn't message her again that day. On Sunday evening, he sent her a message only containing his address. It wasn't that she expected him to start every text conversation with *Hello Gorgeous!* and end with *I miss you. Can't wait to see you!* But that would've been nice, that's all.

Before she went to bed, she sent Amir a GIF of a dog humping a teddy bear. He replied with a laughing face emoji. Then, he sent her a meme of a wooden hoe, standing on its handle, with sunglasses photoshopped over the blade. At the bottom, the text read: *You call it sleeping around, I call it weeding through.*

She chuckled and lay under the covers. Knowing Amir and she were finally in the same place again appeased her. No matter how fucked up things would get, Amir would be there. As long as she had her brother by her side, she was okay with falling because no matter how dark and empty it would be at the bottom, at least she wouldn't be alone.

WEEK 24

When Aisha woke up, she immediately reached for the water bottle on her nightstand because her throat was dry. She really needed to drink more water. She sipped from the lukewarm bottle, then she grabbed her phone and Googled, "How much water is in wine?" She beamed when the top answer showed "Approximately 85%."

"Problem solved!" she said out loud.

She went to the kitchen and poured some white wine into a glass. To be fair, it was brunch time. Though, to be honest, perhaps starting the day with some coffee would've been a better idea. To be specific, she didn't have to clock in anywhere, so she could do whatever she wanted. She sat on her couch and drank the wine.

It was funny how the days felt simultaneously short and long. Short because somehow, next week was the end of June. Long because it was only 11:37 AM, and the only thing she had to look forward to was hanging out with David tomorrow.

Surely, David wasn't sitting around trying to figure out how to fast-forward time until he met with her. Surely, he wasn't at home, listless, drinking at 11:30 in the morning so he could go through the day without allowing his thoughts to exist. David wasn't afraid of his own mind. No. He was probably out and about, doing something avant-garde and eclectic. He was out in the world doing life *his* way. How courageous was that? To live out loud.

In the afternoon, Aisha got dressed and left her apartment without any real plan. She drove around for about an hour, then went to the first restaurant by her exit. When she walked in, she headed straight to the bar. She drank a glass of wine while waiting for her food. Another glass with her meal. A final glass with her dessert. To sober up before her drive, she hung out at the bar another hour or so after she was done.

When she made it home, she immediately lit up a joint and poured the remaining white wine into the same glass she had used in the morning.

Here's a fun little experiment: Let's keep this up and see how long you can go on like this before you lose your marbles, sounds good?

Yep.

By the time she went to bed, thoughts were just a breeze. They came and went, gently caressing her with no real impact, and only leaving a faint trace of what they once were on their way to wherever they landed. And all Aisha did was smile because, at that moment, she couldn't see clearly and think straight. The fog was everywhere. And sometimes, the best thing to do when everything was blurry was to close your eyes.

*

The following day, on her drive to David's place, Aisha wondered if she should've been worried about how excited she was. She wasn't developing feelings, right? *No, no. Of course not!* Great laughter and sex were ahead, and David was just the mouth and penis to provide them tonight. It could've been anyone, and it just happened to be him.

She parked on his driveway at 7:01 PM. For some reason, her heartbeat accelerated when she rang the doorbell. She took a deep breath.

"Hello, Aisha." David opened the front door. He hugged her when she walked in.

She had expected a kiss, but whatever. "Hi, David. It smells good."

"Thank you. I made some tacos. Hopefully, you're in the mood for them."

"I am actually." She followed him to the kitchen while looking at the wall art. "Are any of these paintings yours?"

"God, no. Mine are in my studio, upstairs."

They walked quietly for about thirty seconds and finally entered the kitchen.

"Why don't you hang your paintings in your home?" She sat on one of the four green velvet counter stools.

David put some plates and covers in front and next to her. He was barefoot, which turned her on for some reptilian brain reason. And anytime he put something on the marble countertop, he smiled at her. In her mind, she was playing Sex Jeopardy.

Answer: What are my clothes, Alex?

Question: Things that will be on the floor within the next couple of hours.

David cleared his throat. "I need my work to be in a different space. I couldn't imagine walking in and seeing it on my wall. I need some space from it. I only prefer to see it when I need or want to see it. Plus, it seems vain to me."

"I understand."

"What would you like to drink? I have margaritas and wine, or I can make a cocktail of your choice." He mixed some lettuce, tomatoes, and avocados in a transparent bowl.

She crossed her arms. "You make cocktails?"

"Before I could live off my art, I was a bartender for eight years."

"Wow. I would've never imagined, but now that you've said it, I can kind of see it."

He stopped mixing the salad and leaned on the countertop. "What's the tell?"

She uncrossed her arms. "Well, you just seem very comfortable behind *this* counter. You obviously know what you're doing." He just smiled and nodded, but he didn't speak. She continued. "That's impressive, though. From a struggling artist," she said while opening her arms out, "to this."

He resumed the salad mixing. "I always knew I would end up here. When you find the thing you're passionate about and good at, it's just a matter of time and perseverance from there. And I happen to be pretty good at my thing, so it was no surprise when someone bought one of my pieces at what some people had told me was an unreasonable asking price at the time. The person saw what was on the canvas and knew it was worth more than they paid. People who understand and appreciate art know it's invaluable. The impact of beauty in our lives is truly underappreciated. Beauty is medicine."

Aisha could honestly listen to the man talk all day. Whether she agreed with him or not, his words were like water to her. They lubricated her and made her feel good.

"You're very confident," she said.

"Only about the things I'm sure about."

"What are some of the things you're not sure about?"

"The way you feel about me."

She smiled. "That's just one."

He winked. "That's a big one."

She rolled her eyes and smirked. "I'll have a margarita."

He got two martini glasses out. "What are you passionate about, Aisha?"

Ugh. Why did people always have to ask this question?

Was it okay that some people didn't have one specific goal they wanted to achieve? Was it okay for some people to go through life only feeling lukewarm about most things? Was it okay that some people were content with not leaving any significant imprints behind and didn't want to pretend they did?

"Nothing in particular," she said.

He poured the margarita into their glasses and handed her hers. They raised their glasses and took a sip. David looked at her intensely. "Why do you wake up every day?"

"After about eight hours, it just kind of happens."

He shook his head and smiled. "How do you do life?"

"Jesus. I need a few more drinks and your finest Mary Jane, and I promise I'll give you an answer that'll blow your mind."

He laughed. "I can't wait to hear it." He walked to her side of the counter and kissed her. Then he sat next to her. "First, let's eat."

Her legs felt like jelly. He smelled so good, like bourbon and vanilla. The more she looked at him, the more attractive he became. It was bound to happen. It was law: *Time + Amazing sex = Growing attraction.*

She stopped looking at him to examine the food. Everything was laid out beautifully: the salad, the meat, the lettuce, the diced veggies, the salsa, the guacamole, the tacos.

They put all the items they wanted on their plates. She took a bite. "I'm very impressed, David. This is excellent," she said.

"Why, thank you. I'm glad you like it."

"So, what's the plan for tonight? When do I need to clock in?"

He laughed in his quiet way. "Let's just enjoy our evening, and I'll tell you when it's time. Just make yourself comfortable and let me know if you need anything, okay?"

Jason Momoa, Idris Elba, or whoever was considered the sexiest man alive these days could walk in, and she wouldn't notice. She swallowed the knot in her throat. The one that always preceded the devil's tango. Then, she finally said, "Okay."

After eating, they moved to the lengthy off-white sectional in the living room. *You know what time it is, baby!* She smiled and took her shoes off. David got up to refill their drinks. Before he sat back down, he looked at her.

"Why don't you take your clothes off? I need to look at you and see how you move when you're nude."

She smirked. "Is this dirty talk?"

He chuckled and sat down. "No, I'm serious. This is for the painting. Now, I'm not saying I won't enjoy it, but this marks the beginning of our collaboration."

She stood up and slowly took her clothes off. "Whatever, David. I was going to take them off anyway." When she was fully naked, she bit her lip and smiled. "Why don't you join me, Adam?"

Within seconds, his clothes were somewhere on the floor. Aisha expected his tongue to be somewhere on her body the following instant, but David just kept the conversation going. He was actually serious about this shit. She didn't expect him to have any self-restraint, but, by God, he did.

"Give me a minute," he said, "I'll be right back. Make yourself comfortable."

"I don't know how much more comfortable I can get." She winked and took a sip of her drink.

He grinned before walking away. She looked at him until he was out of her sight. He had a nice little ass on him. Good for him. Then she stood up, grabbed her drink, and walked to the glass wall on the other side of the room. It was so intoxicating to stand here, naked in front of this window in

David's beautiful home, while drinking a cocktail. This whole thing felt like a dream. And like all dreams, Aisha knew at any moment it could turn into a nightmare, or best-case scenario: once it got good and interesting, she'd wake up.

She looked at the horizon, but it was too dark to discern anything. It wasn't scary. It was soothing. It felt safe. The world was there, and she was here, away from it and all the stuff in it. Here, in this beautiful four thousand-something square feet box. This private space where she could exist with no inhibition, and where life was so exciting she didn't have to force herself to not think about her past. She just didn't.

"What a stunning sight," David said behind her. "Turn around for me."

She turned around. He was standing by the sectional with one closed fist, about twenty feet from her. She took a step forward.

"Finally—"

"Please, don't move. Don't speak. Just stand there. I'm seeing you."

Her initial urge was to roll her eyes, but she didn't. She didn't move. She didn't say a word. She stood still and allowed him to see who he thought was before him.

They were both silent for a while. She was a statue, and the artist was slowly closing the gap between them. He was examining a different part of her with each step. She dropped the glass in her right hand because she forgot she was holding it. She didn't look down at the broken pieces, and neither did he. He kept closing in on her, and with each step, her heart rate went up a beat. Now, he was here, in front of her. He stared at her face. She could hear her own breaths. He smiled and kneeled. Her heart reached its crescendo.

With his right hand, David put her left foot on his right shoulder. He slowly moved his tongue from her inner thigh to her clitoris. She moaned and cried. She searched for something to hold onto because her legs felt like jelly. There wasn't anything except the glass wall behind her, so she leaned against it. She looked down, and all she saw was David's blond hair and the glass fragments around him.

He held on to her tighter and gently moved her to the floor, on top of the shards of glass. He opened his left fist. Aisha had never been so happy to see a condom because, at the moment, his being inside of her was the most urgent thing in the world. And within an instant, he was. He climaxed first. Then he moved his tongue back between her thighs. She didn't know if it was the contrast between the sharp glass and the soft tongue on her skin, but she had never felt pleasure so complete. She reached her climax.

They lay on the floor for a moment. Her face was resting on his chest, and his arm was wrapped around her. After about fifteen minutes, he stood up. He helped her up. He wiped the pieces of glass that had stuck to her skin. She did the same.

He kissed her. "Still in the mood for Mary Jane?"

"You've read my mind."

"Let's go upstairs."

They walked up the spiral staircase, passing one room and entering his bedroom. Compared to the rest of the place, it was very minimalistic. There was no television and no painting on the wall, just a king bed and two nightstands. The room was very spacious and had a huge balcony, which she could only assume opened to a stunning view.

"The bathroom is there," he said, pointing at a door to her right. "What would you like to drink?"

She sat on the bed. "Water, please."

"Of course, but what else? The night is young, beautiful."

She smiled and got under the covers. "Pinot noir, then."

"Perfect. I'll also grab some chocolate then. I'll be right back."

He went to the room next door and came back with the pinot, two wine glasses, and the chocolate. He poured the wine into the two glasses and handed her hers first; then, he put his glass on the nightstand on the opposite side of her. He opened a box of chocolate and placed it on the night table by her side. He took one of the cubic chocolates and fed her. She could get used to this. He kissed her and then walked to the other side of the bed.

He opened the nightstand and got a blunt out. He sat down, lit up the joint, took two puffs, and passed it to her. He didn't speak the entire time. He got under the covers while she took her puffs and let his tongue do the talking. Aisha loved what it was saying. She could really get used to this.

They smoked, laughed, drank, and had sex until they passed out.

When Aisha woke up, David was already out of bed. Her phone, purse, and clothes were neatly placed on the nightstand. She looked at the time: 9:48 AM. She put her clothes on, used the bathroom, then walked outside to look for him.

He wasn't in the living room or the kitchen. She didn't feel comfortable enough to open random doors until she found him. Perhaps he went for a walk, to his polo game, his hot yoga class, his seated meditation on top of a rock overlooking a stunning landscape, or whatever rich people did in the morning. He was probably out checking things off his to-do list while she was looking for him because she didn't have one. Perhaps she should just leave and text him on her way home. She didn't want to do that, though. She had such a great night. She wanted to spend a little more time with him and kiss him goodbye.

Aisha walked back upstairs. She opened the first door before David's bedroom. It was an entertainment area with a nice bar. She closed it and kept walking. She secretly hoped to find a sex dungeon, his cannabis greenhouse, or something almost illicit. It would be the least surprising thing if she did. This was a massive space for one person. Surely, the extra rooms were not just guest bedrooms. Yet the next two she walked into looked to be just that. One had a large bookshelf that went from wall to wall. Aisha was sure that tilting the right book would open the secret passage to David's *Chamber of Secrets*.

At the end of the hallway, there was a red door. Aisha couldn't help but walk toward it. She had seen enough horror movies to know she probably shouldn't open the red door at the end of the hallway. But like a stupid movie character, her curiosity got the best of her. She paused when she got in front of the door and held her breath. She opened it slowly.

David was there, sitting in the middle of the room, in front of a canvas, and surrounded by other paintings in different completion stages. He didn't move because he didn't hear her. He was toning the canvas an ultramarine blue. She looked at him silently. The passion and attention in each stroke moved her. What was it like to feel so strongly about anything? If she ever felt that way, she couldn't recall. She watched him for a moment. The beautiful and rhythmic dance of the brush and the blue. She wanted to be part of it.

She cleared her throat. "Good morning."

David finished the layer he was on before turning around. "Good morning, beautiful. How did you sleep?"

"Great, thank you. And you?"

"Amazing! I woke up feeling inspired, thanks to my evening with you."

"Really? We didn't get much done."

He put the brush down and stood up. "Yes, we did. This is the underpainting for our collaboration," he said while pointing at the ultramarine canvas. "I saw you last night, Aisha, and that's the most important thing to get this right. This piece is going to be something." He walked toward her and kissed her. "You are something."

She didn't want to leave. If she had to go, his lips had to come with her. "Thank you," she whispered in between her breaths.

"I'll get back to this now. I'm really feeling it! I'm sure you have a busy day too. Help yourself to some breakfast or anything in the kitchen you're in the mood for before you leave, okay? You can even ask Gwen—Gwen's my housemaid—to make you something if you'd like."

Aisha was a little taken aback. It wasn't like she wanted to spend the entire day with him, but she thought he would've wanted to spend as much time as he could with her before she left, especially after the night they had.

"Don't you need the model for the painting?" she asked with a noticeable angst in her voice.

David looked slightly annoyed, as if he had been stopped by a stranger needing direction while he was on his way to something important. "No, not today. I'll just work on the underpainting for now. We can meet again sometime next week, whenever you're available." He gave her a peck, then turned around. Then he made a sudden one-eighty rotation to face her again. "Oh, could you send me your bank details to compensate you for last night?"

She almost slapped him across the face. "What?"

"We agreed I'll pay you for your time as my muse slash model, remember?"

"Yesterday didn't feel like work."

"Yesterday led me to this," he said, pointing at the canvas before him. "This is the most inspired I've felt in months. Us having fun doesn't mean it's not work."

Aisha knew their arrangement, yet she felt insulted. If he had been more excited to see her this morning and had wanted to spend more time with her, perhaps she would've felt differently. But at this moment, the night she couldn't wait to relive in her mind earlier felt merely transactional.

"You know what," she said without looking at him, "you don't need to pay me. It just doesn't feel like work to me."

"Aish—"

"Why don't you just continue to provide the drinks, the food, and the pot, and I'll provide the inspiration."

He smiled. "Okay, beautiful. But if you change your mind at any time, let me know, okay?"

"I will." She stood silent for a moment. She wasn't sure what she was waiting for.

He blew her a kiss and gave her a final glance before sitting back down. "Text me to let me know you made it home safe, please."

She had no idea when she had walked to her car and driven home. On her way out, she waved at Gwen. The old lady waved back absently and focused on sweeping the broken glass by the glass wall. Gwen had probably waved at dozens of women before her while cleaning up the morning afters.

Aisha couldn't believe what had just happened and how terrible she felt because of it. When she made it back to her place, she sat on the couch and looked around. Her apartment seemed unreasonably small now. It was fascinating how quickly we could get comfortable based on presumption. She certainly did not picture a future with David where they were celebrating their tenth anniversary.

However, she wouldn't have minded a few lazy mornings when they hung out and talked and laughed while she was still in Dallas. Obviously, he enjoyed her company, too. She understood and respected his focus and intensity about his work, but how could he be so dismissive so suddenly? How could he turn around and act like whether she stood behind him or not was irrelevant? How come, all of a sudden, she could matter so little to him when last night he couldn't take his eyes off her? How the hell did people do that? Care so deeply one day and not give a fuck the next? Who held the key to this ancient secret, and how could she get a hold of it?

*

The rest of the week was mostly a blur. And when things dared to look a little clearer, she filled her stomach with alcohol and her lungs with the devil's lettuce.

Perhaps they held the key.

WEEK 25

Aisha knew she was attempting to self-medicate with marijuana and alcohol. And what bothered her the most about it wasn't the fact that she was doing it, but rather how cliché it was. How unoriginal. She could've gotten into something weird and interesting like worm charming or ghost hunting. She could've gotten a face tattoo or shaved her eyebrows. She could've hired a professional dominatrix. She could've done anything else.

But *nooo*, she had to go the most predictable route.

She pictured herself without eyebrows, hunting for ghosts, and she chuckled. She could barely handle the tiniest needle when they drew blood at the hospital, so getting a face tattoo wasn't an option. She wasn't seriously considering getting one, shaving her eyebrows, charming worms, or any other random thoughts that had crossed her mind that evening. She just wished she had thought of something else besides pot and alcohol. Something else potent enough to change her body chemistry without causing too much harm; that way, she could feel better without having to do "the work."

As far as she was aware, marijuana and alcohol were still the best team for the job. There was a reason most people resorted to them. Until they didn't work anymore, they worked. So, Aisha decided to ride the high until the wheels fell off. Yes, that crash might destroy her. But those moments in the air when she was floating, when all the ghosts from her past couldn't get to her because they couldn't fly that high, made her feel light and safe. She took two puffs and laughed uncontrollably because up there in the clouds, she saw worms dancing to the sound of her voice.

*

On Wednesday morning, she woke up earlier than usual. The sun was up and scorching. How did people leave their houses during the summer in Dallas? People went about their days as if they were not melting away, like this shit was normal. The heat wave must've made them lose their minds. But who was she to judge? She had started losing hers well before the temperature went up in the Lone Star State.

"I don't know," she recalled crying to Sam, "maybe we just need space. Maybe we moved together too fast. Or it's the opposite. Maybe we need to spend more time together. Maybe I'm moving too slowly. I think if he thought I was ready, he would've already proposed by now. Maybe I should tell him that I'm ready. Maybe I'm ready. Maybe…I don't kno—"

"Aisha, please stop." Sam sighed. "Take a deep breath."

"A deep breath is not going to help."

"Why don't you try?"

She inhaled and exhaled slowly. She rolled her eyes. "Just as I thought, nothing. I just took some extra air for no reason." She sat down on Sam's gray couch. "What should I do? Please, help me. I love him. You know him almost as much as I do at this point. What do you think?"

Sam blinked. "I think you overestimate our friendship. I don't know him that well. We mostly talk about sports and stupid shit."

Aisha straightened up. "Like what?"

"I don't know. Nothing important. Memes. Seriously, dumb shit. We don't have deep conversations or anything like that." Sam stood up to grab something from her fridge. "Would you like some water?"

"No, thank you." Aisha turned on the couch to face her friend. "Okay, fine. You guys are bros, I get it. But as my friend who has seen us together and knows our relationship, what's your advice? Should I give him more space, or should we spend more time together?"

Sam took a moment to think of her answer. She poured the water into a glass and drank it over her sink. "Since you guys live together, I think maybe more space. Maybe one of you should go on a solo weekend getaway to change scenery, and the other gets to have the place for themselves. You see each other every day. So, if you're fighting, I don't know if more time together would help. I think a few days apart to miss each other might be good."

Aisha jumped from her seat and ran to Sam. She hugged her tightly. "See, that's why they pay you the big bucks to be my Executive Advice Giver!"

Sam smiled but didn't say anything else.

Now, Aisha shook her head. What a trusting idiot. While she was gone to Boulder for her solo weekend getaway to hopefully fix her relationship, her boyfriend and best friend were starting theirs.

She stood abruptly and began pacing around her living room to blur her thoughts. She stopped to turn the A/C down to sixty-eight degrees. How high and drunk did she need to be to not think about this stuff? Seriously, what was the exact dosage in grams and liters? If she knew, she would take her prescription in a hurry.

She hadn't heard from David yet, so she couldn't rely on him for distraction. It was better that way; she needed a moment to hit the reset button on that strange new feeling she had for him. She was certain it wasn't love or even fondness. Just something peculiar that only existed because of their sexual chemistry and the mental space she was in.

The dance event with Dahlia wasn't until Saturday. There was only so much observing she could do perched on a restaurant's bar stool before it got boring. Spending time alone was fine when your mind was your friend. But when it challenged you to a duel every time you simply tried to recall something, being alone with your thoughts wasn't very fun. She didn't have the strength to fight today. She didn't want to be alone. So, she called Amir. To her surprise, he picked up on the first ring.

He spoke at once, "I'm on a date that's definitely going to end well, so I'll call you tomorrow."

"And you answered? I'm flattered."

"I'm taking a shit."

"Ew. Why the fuck would you answer? Bye."

He laughed. "Talk to you tomorrow. Bye!"

She chuckled after her brother hung up. She felt a little lighter but still didn't want to be alone. She lit up a joint and logged into her Tinder account. She swiped right on everyone until she apparently exhausted the app. Now, she needed to wait twelve hours to have the privilege of seeing more profiles of men dancing at their friends' weddings or holding fish. She rolled her eyes. Her index finger was getting tired anyway. She looked through all her matches. Three of them were a good fit for her evening's needs.

She sent all three the same message: *Hey what u up to?*

Two replied within minutes that they were not doing anything. What about her? She told them she was bored at home; did they want to come over? The one she wasn't as attracted to replied immediately. He sent the eyes emoji and said he'd love to; what time? Her blunt went out. She found the lighter and lit it up again. She was hoping the other guy would reply. He didn't. The less attractive one messaged her again and asked where she lived. She shook her head. Thirsty much?

You're one to talk.

She waited another five minutes and started messaging the less attractive one her address. Before she hit *send,* the more attractive one finally messaged her back. Yes, he could come over to 'Netflix and Chill.' She sent him her address, and he confirmed he was on his way. The other guy messaged her three question marks. She didn't answer. She got up and opened a bottle of wine.

Her doorbell rang forty-two minutes later.

Anthony was a good-looking guy. About two inches taller than her, very fit, with beautiful dimples and long dreadlocks. She let him in. They made small talk about the weather and the TV shows they liked. They watched *The Office* and laughed. He didn't smoke but didn't mind that she did. Fifty-three minutes after he had entered her apartment, he entered her. The sex was fine. It was just so incredible with David that this little dance paled in comparison. But Anthony was good enough to keep her mind occupied. He left her place two hours after he had walked in.

She felt better for a moment, but the moment didn't last. She messaged the other guy back.

Sorry I had to take care of something but you can come now if you still free

Thirsty Guy immediately answered. *I am address?*

Aisha sent it to him, and Steven knocked at her door eighteen minutes later. *Holy horny dude who can't wait to get laid, Batman!* She had found someone who didn't want to be alone as much as her tonight. Unfortunately, how quickly he came to her place was a snail's pace compared to how quickly he came. He was breathing loudly behind her. She was waiting for the strokes to resume, but he just collapsed next to her and closed his eyes. She was still on all fours. This had to be a record. The man looked very satisfied and genuinely exhausted. She tittered.

He opened his eyes. "Did you say something?"

She sat down. "Do you want some water or a drink?"

He smiled, and his amber eyes twinkled. He looked better in person. "Yes," he said, "water would be nice, thanks."

She went to the kitchen to get some water. Sure, this was the most useless hookup she ever had, but she was okay with that. All she really wanted was some company. They could spend the rest of the night together, and maybe he'd be better the second time. But even if he wasn't, at least she wouldn't be alone.

When she walked back into the bedroom, Steven had put his gray sweatpants and white T-shirt back on. He gently took the glass of water from her and drank all of it at once.

"Thank you, Asia." He put the empty glass on her nightstand.

She narrowed her eyes. "Aisha."

"Oh right, sorry. This was really fun. Do you want to exchange numbers so we don't have to rely on the app next time we want to do this?"

"Do you want to hang out and watch a movie or something?" *Holy desperate chick who can't get a hint, Batman!*

He started walking toward the living room. "I can't. I have to be up early. I'll message you on the app." He looked back at her, and she could see that he was holding back laughter. "Goodnight." He closed the door behind him.

She ran to her phone to unmatch him, but he beat her to the punch. He was truly fast with everything. She wasn't sad about it because she cared to get to know him further. This whole thing just turned out to be a waste of time for her. She felt cheated because it wasn't the exchange she had expected. She knew he wanted sex. He got it. He could tell she wanted company. She didn't get it.

To her surprise, however, the first guy, Anthony, messaged her his phone number. *Text me anytime you want to watch The Office :)*

Aisha saved his number. This night wasn't a complete waste of time and sweat, after all.

The next morning, her phone sang before the roosters. It was Amir.

"You must be dying, or you must've lost your mind. Which one is it?" Aisha didn't recognize her own voice. Is this what she sounded like at dawn? If yes, she needed to never awake before the sun was close to its zenith.

"Lord, have mercy! I'm so sorry to call before this ogre could transform back into a human."

She laughed, then cleared her throat. She didn't sound much better. "So, you've lost your mind, then. What couldn't wait normal hours?"

"I like him!"

"Who?"

"The guy I went on a date with yesterday. Can you keep up?"

"It's six fucking am; no, I can't."

"You're so grumpy." He giggled. "His name's Walter. He's thirty. He's fine as hell, and we have so much in common. We stayed up all night and just talked."

"Though I don't understand why this information needed to be shared at the crack of dawn, I'm very happy for you."

"Sorry, I just left his place. I'm walking to my car now. I'm so excited about this! I couldn't wait to tell you."

The last statement transformed the ogre back into a human. Aisha smiled and spoke softly. "Aw! Amir, that's so sweet. You're really smitten by him. I can hear it."

"I am!"

"What about Thomas?"

"What about him?" he said sharply.

"C'mon."

"What do you want me to say?"

"Are you over him?"

"Of course not, but I'm working on it."

"So, are you just having fun with Walter, or are you open to something serious?"

"I don't fucking know, Sha. I'm just happy I had a good time and met a great guy. I don't need to have all the answers right now."

"Fair enough." She yawned. "I'm happy for you, bro. Just make sure to protect your heart."

"Oh, believe me, I am. That bitch is guarded with barbed wires, a tall concrete wall, an electric fence, and those hot men from the *300* movie. The only way someone could get through is if I decide to open the door and let them in."

She laughed and yawned again. "Could you send me some of your men to protect my heart?"

Aisha heard her brother's car door closing before he said, "How are you, sis?"

"I'm okay."

"Are you sure?" he said softly. Then she heard his engine start.

"I don't even know what I'm feeling, honestly. I'm mostly tired right now."

He hummed. "I know the feeling. Anything I can do to help?"

"You already did. This chat cheered me up."

"You're welcome, Princess Fiona. My job's done here, then. You can go back to your beauty sleep now. Sounds like you really need it. Love you. Bye!"

She chuckled. "Love you too. Bye."

Obviously, she was happy for Amir. Hearing the lightness in his voice made her happy. She wanted him to heal; she sincerely did. She just didn't want him to do it way before she did. She didn't want him to leave her down there all by herself. Rock bottom was too dark and scary for one person.

*

On Friday morning, Dahlia texted Aisha to confirm that she could still make it to the dance event tomorrow.

Yes I'll be there! Aisha replied.

With your sexy lover?

No just me. He can't make it

After the way David acted last time, she didn't tell him about the dance. Clearly, he only wanted their meetups to be about art and sex, and she should never dare overstay her welcome. His behavior had made that crystal clear.

Oh that's too bad. Mark's coming btw! I'm excited for you two to meet!

Aisha just *hearted* Dahlia's message and asked for the address of the venue. Even via text, she couldn't pretend convincingly. She wasn't a fan of Cheating Mark. She had never met the guy, but she knew she wouldn't like him based on his actions. However, she liked Dahlia. So, if Mark made her happy, Aisha could deliver the best acting performance of her life for her friend's sake.

Her phone rang.

If Aisha answered, her award-winning performance might need to be delivered earlier. It was her mother. She knew she couldn't keep postponing talking to her, but she wasn't ready to put up a front. So, she didn't answer. Usually, her mother understood that she didn't want to talk and just followed up with a text message. She waited for the message to light up her phone.

But instead of the usual: *Hey, honey! How are you? It's been so long. I miss you! Please call me back when you have a moment,* her mother called her on FaceTime.

This was unprecedented. Aisha knew she looked an absolute mess. If her mom saw her, she would immediately know something was very wrong with her. Aisha considered not answering. However, her mother's Facetime call was concerning. Something had to be wrong. She decided to pick up the phone. She could blame her appearance on the scorching sun.

"Hey, Mom. Sorry, I was using the bathroom," she said with that weird smile you gave someone you were finally passing in a long hallway.

"Sweetie, what's going on?" Helen frowned. She was seated in front of a yellow wall, with her long, relaxed hair parted in the middle.

"What do you mean?"

"I love you, hon, but can I be honest? You look awful."

She forced a laugh. "Geez, thanks, Mom. It's insanely hot here, you know. It's useless to get dolled up."

Helen sighed. "I wish you would've told me."

"I did! I told you how hot it is here. It's ridiculous!"

Her mother stared at her. "I know Sam's pregnant by James," she finally said.

Aisha's face dropped. She felt like a physical mask had fallen off her visage. She put her hands in front of her face to cover its nakedness.

"Aw, baby," her mother murmured with tears in her eyes.

It was at that exact moment that Aisha lost it. All the tears she had been holding rushed out, and she just cried silently with her phone anchored in her left palm. She hardly made any sound. Every time she looked at her mother, the tears came out stronger. So, Aisha stopped looking at her.

"My baby," Helen whispered again. Her eyes were red and humid.

Aisha wished her mother would stop talking to her and looking at her. She wouldn't be able to regain her composure until then. Aisha turned her camera off, turned her speaker on, and put her phone down. She walked to the kitchen to grab some paper towels.

"Are you still there, baby?" her mother said.

"Yes," she yelled from the kitchen, "please give me a minute."

"Okay."

Aisha wiped her face. She took some deep breaths and stood still for a moment. At last, she walked back to the living room to grab her phone, but she didn't turn her camera back on. Her mother looked so sad and worried. She hated to be the reason for it. That's precisely why she didn't want to tell her. Aisha wasn't sure when she'd get over feeling this way, so the last thing she wanted was her mother worrying about her. They already had enough on their plate.

"Okay, I'm back," Aisha said.

"Can I see you, honey?"

"I prefer to have the camera off if you don't mind. I don't want to start crying again. And I don't want you to have to look at me right now. Like you said, I look awful." She tried to laugh the tension off.

"Why would you keep something like that from me, Aisha?" Helen looked down.

"I didn't want you to worry about me. I'm okay, Mom. I promise."

Helen looked back up and shook her head slowly. "You're my daughter. I'm always going to worry about you."

"Don't. I'm okay. Really."

"No, you're not. You look like a shadow of yourself. You need to be with your family, not alon—"

"I'm fine."

Helen raised her voice. "Please, stop! You can try to lie to yourself, but you can't lie to me. I'm your mother. I know you. If you don't want to come home, I'll come to Dallas. If something happens to you there, I'll never forgive myself."

Aisha's tears rushed back out, stronger and heavier. This round, the waters came from an older stream. Tears meant to be cried years ago, held too long and too deep. And with those tears, an old truth they were anchoring poured out. A truth that had spent too much time in the deep waters, so it was ugly and decomposed.

Aisha yelled out. "Why do you even care? I ruined your life, remember? My existence robbed you of your future, remember? If you didn't have me, your life would've gone so much better, right?"

It was complete silence on the other side. Aisha was breathing loudly. No one spoke for a long time. Now, Helen was the one who looked like a shadow of herself. Her shoulders were slumped, and her hair covered most of her face. Aisha couldn't look at her anymore. Seeing her mother like that broke her heart, so she hung up. Helen didn't call her back or text her.

*

If Aisha were asked to precisely recount what happened at the salsa dance event for one million dollars, she would've walked out empty-handed. All she remembered was that Cheating Mark didn't make it. She was sure Dahlia told her why, but she couldn't recall. Her friend also looked very sad, but she did her best to show Aisha a good time. And to her credit, Aisha had as much fun as she could under the circumstances. She didn't remember any details, but she recalled a moment when Dahlia and she looked at each other, and it was clear that they both knew they weren't okay. They both knew that evening was an island surrounded by turbulent waters, and they smiled at each other because what else were they supposed to do? Whatever they needed to face after the littoral could wait until the next day.

So, they danced the night away.

WEEK 26

The weather app informed Aisha it was ninety-three degrees outside, but apparently, it felt like ninety-nine degrees. Great. When she stepped outside on her balcony, she wanted to yell at the sun and ask it to chill out. As much as the heat and humidity irritated her, they weren't the main cause of her frustration.

She still hadn't heard from her mother.

She wiped the sweat on her forehead with the back of her hand. Somehow, the white magnolias were still blooming, unbothered by the heat. She sat in the lotus position on the floor to look at the flowers and clear her mind. It was a difficult exercise to not think about anything. She remembered reading about some monks and other spiritual gurus who could sit like that for hours, or even days on end, for the really advanced ones. They "observed their thoughts without judgment."

Now that was a fucking head-scratcher.

Wasn't the sole purpose of thoughts to be assessed, examined, studied, and dissected to the bone in the hopes of learning from them? Then judged relentlessly until new thoughts were born? When sober, Aisha automatically did the assessing, examining, studying, and dissecting. She was just falling short on the most important part: learning—defeating the entire purpose. That's why she wasn't growing; she was just ruminating. She chewed and chewed but never ingested, so she never absorbed the necessary intake to grow.

And clearly, breaking down every single thought and memory to their nuclei wasn't the best way to stay sane. But Aisha knew she couldn't just sit there with her eyes closed and not think about everything. If she so much as tried, all the ghosts would just come out of their dwelling to mess with her. The memories would promenade unorderly in her head, and best believe she would judge the hell out of them. Kudos to the monks, spiritual teachers, yogis, and everyone with that much discipline and control over their minds. As for her, she needed some assistance. So, she walked back inside to light up a joint and open a bottle of wine.

Aisha wasn't sure what day and time it was when her phone rang in her bedroom. She had passed out in her living room before turning the lights off. Her utility bill was already alarmingly high since she ran the A/C twenty-four-seven. Lately, she was regularly passing out in random corners of her apartment with the lights on and an empty bottle of wine somewhere in the room. So, when her phone kept ringing that day, she didn't care as much if it was her mother finally calling to talk things out.

She walked to her bedroom to pick up the phone. Any small excitement or nervousness she felt went away when she saw that it wasn't her mother calling—it was her brother. She was a little disappointed. However, talking with Amir always cheered her up, and she could really use a boost.

"Hey, big bro, how goes it?"

"I'm okay."

"What's wrong? It didn't work out with Walter?"

"It didn't, but that's not why I'm calling."

"Oh, no. What happened? Last time, it sounded like things were promising."

"He's a great guy, but I realized I wasn't ready to date. I was trying to use him as a rebound, which wasn't fair to him. I'm not over Thomas, and that's okay. I have to deal with that on my own and not use other people to shield myself from the hurt I'm feeling."

Aisha whistled. "Preach! Someone's back on the therapy couch, I see."

"Yes. You should give it a try."

"I will, but not right now. I'm not ready for that. I need to deal with some things on my own first before I bring in a second party."

"You've been away for six months. When are you going to be ready to deal with anything, Sha?"

"I'm not putting a timeline on it. I feel like time will help sort some of it out for me."

"Time's not some magical thing that fixes everything, you know. *You* have to make the changes. Time just allows you to look back at all the progress you've made and how far you've come. It doesn't make the progress for you."

"Okay, Buddha." She hated how indifferent she was trying to come off because, for the most part, she agreed with him.

Amir sighed. "What happened between you and Mom?"

She froze. "What did she tell you?"

"Not much, but she looked like *The Walking Dead* when I saw her. She just said you guys didn't have a pleasant exchange."

"Oh."

"*Oh?* What the hell happened?"

"Exactly what she told you."

"You're starting to piss me off with your attitude. You're trying too hard to act like you don't care, and you're not fooling anyone. Our mother's not doing well because of something that happened between you two. And if I had to place a bet, I guarantee it's something *you* said to her and not the other way around. Now, I don't want to be in the middle, and I'm not trying to be nosy. Believe me, I have my own fucking problems. I lost the man I love, and customers are pissing me off. But the bottom line is you're in Dallas, and I'm here in Denver with Mom. I need to make sure she's okay. So, it'd be helpful if my sister told me what happened so I could make sure our mother is good."

Another issue with spending so much time alone was that one began to feel like the center of the universe. If no one else was ever around, then no one else really mattered. Whatever Aisha was going through was the alpha and the omega. The world only existed when she opened her eyes, and life everywhere paused when she closed them. Amir's words were a cold bucket of water thrown at her, and even if the effects were temporary, it made her alert.

"I'm sorry," she said.

Amir spoke gently now. "What happened?"

"You remember our fight when she said those…things to me, right?"

"Yes," he said. He took a moment to speak again. "Now, you know she didn't mean any of that. She was stressed about all the student loans she had to take out when she went back to school for her business degree. You do remember that she had to drop out of college before she even got started, right? You do remember that they withdrew her athletic scholarship offer because she was pregnant with you, don't you? She was overwhelmed, Sha, that's all. She was still taking care of us while trying to finally do the things she wanted for herself. She said those words out of exhaustion. Everyone has a breaking point."

Aisha shook her head. "Amir, you know I think you're so much smarter than me—"

"Mm-hmm. Finally, you're making sense."

She chuckled, then resumed her serious tone. "But I think you're wrong here. Sure, she was overwhelmed and exhausted. I know she did everything by herself, and I can't even begin to imagine how tiring that was. But those words came out of a real place. Deep down, she truly believes I ruined her life and messed up the future she had envisioned."

When Amir spoke again, all the lightness was gone from his voice. "And how do you think I feel?"

Aisha blinked. "What do you mean?"

"At least they wanted you. I'm the product of their fight and make up about you."

"What the hell are you talking about?"

"You can't possibly be this oblivious, Sha. The first time Dad came to the house when we were kids, Mom made sure you spent some alone time with him because she knew he really came to see you. I guess she just had me tag along at the end because she didn't want me to feel left out. I think she thought I'd be too young to remember, but I didn't forget."

"C'mon, Amir. The man was there for what? A half-hour? She probably thought he'd be there longer and would spend some time alone with you at some point."

Now, her brother was breathing louder. So much so that Aisha put the phone away from her ear and turned the speaker on. Amir spoke unevenly. "The second time he came was on *your* seventeenth birthday."

"Okay? Maybe he was planning on showing up to yours, but since it didn't go well for mine, he was too afraid. The man was a certified coward."

"Do you remember when Mom asked *you* if you wanted her to send him away because you were so upset?"

"Yes."

"She didn't even consider if I wanted to see him. She was only worried about the way *you* felt about his visit. Truth is, she might've felt like you changed the trajectory of her life, but they both wanted to have you. You're the love child, Aisha. I'm the oops baby."

Aisha was silent.

Amir continued, "I overheard Mom talking to Grandma before she passed. Damn, I can't believe it's already been four years. Anyway, Dad showed up to see Mom when you were like one. He had been gone that whole time, and he just fucking showed up, out of nowhere. Of course, Mom was furious. He broke her heart. She loved him, you know. And somehow, he was able to convince her he still loved her, too.

"He told her he was just scared because they were so young, but he was ready to take care of his responsibilities. He told her he was going to be there, and they were going to be a family, and she believed him. They made love. Then he went to grab some milk or whatever deadbeats say they go to the store for before they disappear. Of course, he didn't come back, and nine months later, little Amir was born."

Aisha was still silent.

Amir spoke with a lighter voice now. "I think both of our names start with 'A' because of Albert. It just might be a coincidence, but that's my theory. I think Mom really thought one day he'd show back up again after he had figured his shit out, and he'd finally be ready to be a father and a partner. She probably thought he'd come back and be happy to find his two kids with his first name's initials. Then, we could finally be the family she had dreamed of."

It was completely silent for a moment. Then, Aisha said, "How come you've never told me any of this?"

"I always had my suspicions, but I couldn't be sure until I overheard the convo between Mom and Grandma. That really fucked me up. I think, on some level, I started resenting you. Like, somehow, it was your fault."

She nodded. "I've felt some distance growing between us over the last few years, but I wasn't sure what it was about."

"I don't think I fully understood it myself at the time. It's a hard pill to swallow, you know. I even made some effort to reach out to Dad and build a relationship with him. He ignored me for the most part, and when he picked up the phone or texted me back, somehow, the conversation always ended up being about you. Like, damn. Here's my dumbass trying to get to know him, and all he wants to know is what his daughter's up to. That shit fucking hurts."

Aisha had no idea what to say, where to begin, what to ask. She took a moment to think about what she wanted to know the most. "So, how come you forgave him?" she said.

"What else was I supposed to do, Sha? The man was a mess. He died not even knowing who he was. I'm not excusing him, believe me. But human to human, I feel sad for him. He's been dead for three years now. At some point, I chose to let go. Hating and resenting him wasn't worth all the effort."

There was something about the way the words freely flew out of Amir's mouth that irritated Aisha. He said those things so casually, as if he was ordering a cup of coffee. Like, it was just that simple. That mind-over-matter crap. All she had to do was decide something in her head, and just like that, the thing would soon become reality. She just needed to make the decision to move on, make sure to visualize it, of course, do it long enough; and boom, those things that wrecked her would suddenly feel small.

How come she didn't think of that?

Except she did, and that would never work for her. Her feelings were visceral. She felt their impact on her body. They led her to look for comfort at the end of random men's dicks. They led her to drink and smoke until she passed out. She couldn't simply "choose to let go." And the fact that Amir couldn't relate to that was frustrating.

"Good for you, bro," she said coldly. "You're a better person than me. Is that what you wanted to hear?"

"What the hell are you talking about? I'm not trying to hear anything. I'm just telling you why I chose to move on."

"C'mon, don't be so humble. Albert mostly didn't give a shit about me, and apparently, he *reaaally* didn't give a shit about you. Congrats, you won the Abandoned Kids Award. Clearly, you were the worst off, yet somehow, you managed to let go and come stronger on the other side. You're a better human being than me, brother. Hats off to you!"

"Wow."

Aisha golf clapped. "Bravo!"

"You need help." Amir's voice was small.

She continued her gentle claps above the microphone.

Amir let out a single dry chuckle. Then he spoke evenly. "I don't need this shit. You're a grown-ass woman. When you decide to pull yourself together and get some help, you know where to find me. Until then, I don't need to hear from you. And if you don't mind, leave Mom out of your bullshit too."

He hung up.

Aisha walked to the kitchen and sat on her counter stool. She put her hands over her face. A single tear rolled down her right cheek, and she immediately wiped it. Then, she stood mechanically to grab a wine glass and a bottle of cabernet. Now, she kept some of the weed in the cabinet by the kitchen sink because it was more convenient.

When she drew *Texas* from the bowl back on January 1st, she made sure to purchase a lot of marijuana at the dispensary before she got on the road. She knew doggone well where she was headed. At the time, she didn't think at some point she'd be smoking almost every day. At the pace she was turning the herb to ashes, she had another three weeks' worth at best. That was a problem. She'd figure a solution out later. Now, her thoughts needed to become foggy. The exchange with Amir was too much for her to process. If she tried, gravity might become stronger and pull her to the ground. This would just have to be one more thing she put inside a box and locked somewhere in her mind.

Hopefully, she still had enough space to hold it together.

*

Sometime at the end of the week, perhaps Saturday—or it could've been Sunday—David sent her a long message.

Hey beautiful! I hope you're well. I'm sorry for not reaching out sooner, but things have been quite hectic over the last week. But it's better now. My schedule is fully open next week. Shall we knock this thing out? That's if you're free, of course.

Here's my offer.

We can spend all next week together, so you can be here to sit for the painting (that way you wouldn't have to drive back and forth). We can be done by next Sunday if we work about 4 hours/day. We'll have so much fun during and in between, I promise. I know this is a lot to ask, so please rethink the compensation. If you're not comfortable with money, it could be anything else. Either way, let me know if this would work for you. We could start on Monday?

You've been on my mind, Aisha.

She squinted her eyes and read the text a second time. The man was something else. He was acting like he didn't give her the cold shoulder last time. She was lying on her bed, looking around the beige room and noticing how empty it was. As much as she didn't like David's morning-after behavior last time, the truth was they were nothing to each other. Just two strangers who had an agreement and some great sex. Nothing less and absolutely nothing more. She had promised herself not to forget that, yet at some point, she did. But now, she remembered.

Aisha sat up and glanced at the room again. She had absolutely zero plans next week. She could just stay here and make her liver and lungs work overtime. Or she could spend the week with David, have some fun, some amazing sex, and not be alone. And for her compensation, what about enough cannabis to last her until the end of the year?

She texted David back and let him know she was in. As for the payment method, she would accept *Mary Jane Express*.

WEEK 27

Aisha didn't pack many clothes. She was going to be naked most of the time, so why bother? She made it to David's place around noon. He wanted her to start sitting that very evening, so he recommended she come in as early as she could; that way, she'd have time to relax and even get in the pool if she was in the mood to get wet. *Ahem, yes. Definitely in the mood for that.* She laughed and parked her car.

It was so good to be outside of her apartment. It was nice to know that, at least for the next week, her days wouldn't feel like a blur. All she needed to remember was that no matter what would happen in this big fancy house, no matter how perfectly David's tongue would answer her body's demands, no matter how much they'd laugh, no matter how ardent and passionate he'd get when he painted her, no matter how lovely their banter would be, and no matter how great of a time she'd have with him, they were just two strangers sharing a very finite moment of time in space. He didn't want anything else out of this, nor did she—okay, even if a minuscule part of her thought it wanted more, she was in no position to start anything with anyone in any capacity.

Just remember all that, and you'll be alright, m'kay?
Okay.

She put her backpack on and slowly walked up to the entrance. The landscape looked stunning in the daylight. Vegetation and blooms were simultaneously left to grow as wildly as they wanted, yet they circled the house's perimeter precisely and aesthetically. She took a final glance at the scenery, then she took a deep breath and rang the doorbell.

David had the biggest smile on his face when he opened the door. He was wearing a cabana set. He hugged her, then he kissed her for a very long time. She knew it was really long because a mosquito was sucking the hell out of the blood in her left ankle, and the bitch was full enough to fly away voluntarily. When they finally parted their lips, he moved to the side so she could walk in.

"I've missed your company, Aisha. I'm very excited about this week!"

She walked in front of him. At first, David was behind her, and then he got closer. He grabbed her shoulders gently, and she felt his breath on her neck. *Damn! Already?* Now, she was very much looking forward to all the sex, but could she at least get a drink, a "What have you been up to?" or something, prior to them looking like they had been cast to play Adam and Eve? Before she could turn around to tell him exactly that, he took her backpack off and walked next to her.

"This is all your stuff?"

She smiled, relieved. "Yes. I figured I wouldn't be needing clothes most of the time." She winked at him.

David nodded with a twinkle in his eye. "Good point." He looked at her intensely before they walked up the staircase. "How have you been, Aisha?" He narrowed his gaze. "Please, be sincere."

She walked in front of him to break his stare. "I prefer not to get into that. No sad shit, remember?"

He grabbed her hand to stop her tread. "Why don't we do away with that rule this week?"

She furrowed her brow. "Why?"

"I think it'd help us both feel better."

His voice was strained. When Aisha finally took a moment to take a good look at him, she saw the dark circles under his eyes and his disheveled hair. David maintained her stare. They didn't smile. They didn't speak. They just looked at each other at the bottom of the spiral staircase. She saw his pain, and she knew he saw hers. This whole thing didn't last more than a few seconds, but that was all it took for them to gauge that, in their own ways and for their own respective reasons, they were in a downward spiral.

"Just this week," Aisha said, then walked up the steps.

"Deal!"

"Now, it's one hundred degrees, David. I'd like to get in the water, have a nice cocktail, and then I'll tell you how I've been, alright?"

He laughed quietly behind her. "Fair enough."

Aisha led the way to the bedroom. Although she had only spent two nights in this house, she already felt comfortable, which scared her. She ignored the feeling and turned to face David. "So, are you getting in the pool with me?"

"Sure. Why don't you make yourself comfortable? I'll go make drinks for us. Just come downstairs whenever you're ready."

She circled her arms behind his neck and kissed him leisurely. "Okay."

He looked at her with that sparkle in his eye, then put her backpack on the bed and walked back downstairs.

Aisha didn't pack a bathing suit. Skinny-dipping was good for the soul. She took her clothes off and walked to the bedroom balcony in her birthday suit. Below her, she could glimpse a small corner of the swimming pool. In front of her, all she could see for miles on end were trees. This level of privacy was rousing. It made her feel like whatever rules existed beyond the greenery didn't apply here. She walked back inside and slid the glass door close behind her.

When she walked into the kitchen in the nude, David stopped shaking the bottle in his hand. He stared at her but didn't speak.

She gave him a lopsided smile and walked closer. "What are we drinking?"

David just looked at her with that light in his eye. He put the bottle he was holding on the kitchen counter and closed the distance between them. He lifted her off the floor and met her lips. They kissed so passionately and for so long that the mosquito from earlier could've invited its entire family to feast on her legs and she probably wouldn't have noticed. If this was his reaction every time her clothes were off, she wondered if they would be able to get anything done this week. She wouldn't mind if they didn't.

After so much time had passed that she couldn't tell which pair of lips were hers and which were his, David gently put her back down. She pressed her lips together to make sure they were still there. He gave her a final peck, then resumed shaking the bottle.

"Aisha Jones," he sang. Then he spoke with a residual cheerfulness in his pitch. "The pool's back there." He stopped mixing whatever was in the bottle and pointed at the hallway to their right. "Just walk all the way down. There's a basket with clean towels by the door before you step outside, and some sunscreen in the cabinet above the basket. There are some hats, goggles, and sunglasses in there as well, if you'd like to wear them."

She smiled at him, did a little twirl, and walked away. "Thank you," she yelled when she was way down the hall.

"No problem!" he called back.

She heard his response while grabbing a towel and the sunscreen bottle. She grinned. When she stepped outside, the view in front of her made her stop dead in her tracks. The pool started at the corner she was in front of and wrapped around the other side of the house. There were palm, hibiscus, and various succulent plants lining the pool. Somewhere in the middle, there was a cabana which looked very cozy. How many angles and secret corners did this house have? How come she never saw any of this? Why did rich people ever leave their homes? She didn't care to get any of those questions answered. She lay the towel on one of the six lounge chairs to her right, covered her body with sunscreen, and dove into the water headfirst.

It was the change of texture underwater she had looked forward to the most, how different it felt, sounded, and looked when immersed. As long as she could hold her breath and stay below the surface, she didn't have to face the reality of things above the water. The heat. Underwater, things were different, and so were their impacts—the water absorbed most of it. She just needed to hold her breath long enough.

Aisha kept on swimming without coming up for air. She went on like that as long as she could until her heartbeat started speeding up. It was so pleasant underwater, so shielding. The scorching reality would hit her in the face the moment she would break the transparent barrier between the water and the surface to gasp for air. She had to hold her breath as long as she could. So, she kept swimming without coming up. She felt pressure rising from her lungs to her throat, and eventually to her nose. Her heartbeat accelerated even more.

Now, she had two options: sink or come up for air.

Before she could choose, David appeared out of nowhere to pull her above water.

"Are you okay?" he asked with widened eyes.

He was still holding her as they stood on the shallower end. The water was circling her waist and his lower back. She was naked. He was clothed.

Aisha took a moment to catch her breath and let some air back into her lungs. She coughed a few times. "Yes…I'm okay…Why?"

"You were underwater for a concerning amount of time. I thought you passed out. I was waiting for you to come up to tell you the drinks were ready, but you never did."

David looked extremely worried, and for some deranged reason, that turned her on. She cleared her throat and took a couple of deep breaths before answering him. "I'm a great swimmer, David. I can hold my breath for a long time. I'm okay, I promise." She smiled and kissed him.

He narrowed his eyes for a second, then he nodded. "Okay." He pointed at the lounge chairs. "I put your drink on the side table."

"Thank you."

She slowly walked outside of the pool. On her way up the underwater stairs, she turned her head. David was standing where she had left him, watching her. She liked that a lot, so she winked at him and strutted to the lounge chair. Then, she bent down in what she hoped was the sexiest movement he had ever seen, to take a sip of her drink.

When she looked back his way, he was front crawl swimming toward her. Before she knew it, he was right next to her. Then, she was lying on the lounge chair. Then, he was tearing a condom wrapper he had kept in his right pocket. Then, he was on top of her. Then, she was on top of him. Then, fellatio. Then, cunnilingus. They were both sweating and moaning from the pleasure—and the heat. She came. He came. Then, they lay on the lounge chair.

Yep, we're not going to get anything done this week.

To her surprise, David was a different man when the evening came. He looked focused and solemn. He gave Aisha a blue velvet robe. She untied the belt as they walked toward the red door at the end of the hallway. He hadn't said a word over the past twenty minutes. It felt like whiplash; how quickly and drastically he changed when he was in that room. Outside of there, he couldn't get enough of her and couldn't stop staring at her with that sparkle in his eye. But the closer they got to the red door, the colder he became.

And when they were inside, she felt like to him she was indistinguishable from the canvas and other random objects in that room. He still looked at her, but she could tell he was no longer seeing Aisha, the person. She became an abstract thing, a concept, a pathway. An object of inspiration, sure, but an object, nonetheless. She didn't like the way it made her feel. She took the robe off and reminded herself: *Just two strangers sharing a very finite moment of time in space.*

"You can sit here or there," he finally said. He pointed at two identical couches, save for the color. One was blue, and one was purple.

Without any hesitation, she sat on the blue one.

"Great choice." David smiled. "Now, please make yourself comfortable. Whatever position comes naturally to you."

He sat behind the ultramarine blue canvas. She lay on the couch. Her right elbow was on the armrest, her head was cupped in her palm, and her back rested against two blue fluffy pillows. Her other arm was resting on the length of her body. She was comfortable. She looked around the room and noticed that they were perfectly centered. He had moved all the other art pieces closer to the wall. Some of them looked complete, and others looked abandoned. The wall was off-white. There was some ambient music playing at a moderate volume above them.

David grabbed a small brush and looked at her. "Perfect," he said.

He quickly dipped the brush in some water. Then he covered its tip with one color, and the brush strokes began. Aisha thought she would be bored, but looking at David in his element and how effortless his movements were was fascinating. He just knew what to do and when to do it: when to change colors, when to wet the brushes, when to pat them dry, when to look at her, and when to focus back on the canvas. Aisha just lay still, as it was her sole responsibility. And suddenly, she felt like it was her duty to do it right, not to move an inch, no matter what. Now, she was proud to be the object of such focus and attention.

Aisha had no idea how much time had passed when David put all the brushes down and stood up. There was no clock in the room. He walked up to her. "We're all done for the day." He helped her up. "Are you sure you've never done this before? You were amazing."

She blinked a few times to reboot her human functions. She stretched her arms out.

"What would you like to eat?" David said.

"I don't know. Whatever you have. I'm not picky."

"Aisha, I don't think you understand what you're doing for me. Any place you'd like to go, whatever you'd like to eat and drink, just tell me. That's the least I can do to thank you."

She pursed her lips and tapped them with her index finger. "Hmm, I like the sound of that. Anywhere, uh?"

He wrapped her arms around her waist. "Yes."

She gasped. "What am I going to wear? I just packed casual clothes."

He didn't skip a beat. "My daughter left some clothes in her room downstairs. You two are about the same size. She hasn't come by in a while and told me I could donate her stuff because she wasn't planning to pick them up. You can wear and even keep anything you find in there if you'd like. She likes nice stuff, so you should be able to find plenty to wear in her closet."

David said the words casually, but he looked dispirited. Aisha held his hand. "Are you okay?"

He half-smiled. "I guess we still haven't talked about how we've been, have we?" He looked at the time on his watch. "It's almost nine. Why don't you get ready and think of where you'd like to go, and we can talk about things over a nice meal."

She nodded and let go of his hand. "Okay."

"Perfect." He kissed her on the cheek. "When you get downstairs, her room is the third door to the left."

When Aisha walked into David's daughter's ridiculously large walk-in closet, her jaw came close to hitting the blindingly white carpet. It was a house of mirrors, a department store, a vanity room. Did his daughter really tell him to donate all this stuff? What did she own that was better than this? Aisha looked down at the spotless and fluffy carpet. She wanted to lie on it and make a snow angel. If she weren't so hungry, she would have.

She looked through the clothes and read the tags. She recognized some designer brands, while others were unfamiliar. She didn't have to know them to be confident that this was some expensive stuff. Though his daughter wasn't flashy at all. A lot of her clothes were monochromatic and seemed unassuming at first glance, until you took a good look at them, felt the material, and noticed the quality and small details. The sort of unspoken and subtle things that let other rich people know you were one of them before you open your mouth.

Aisha picked a form-fitting black dress with an asymmetrical neckline and open-toe black heels. Then she Googled "very expensive restaurants near me."

Clearly, the man wanted to spend some money, so she wasn't going to get in the way of that. It would be fun to splurge on someone else's dime.

Aisha chose an upscale Brazilian steakhouse. Twenty minutes later, they arrived at the place.

"You look stunning," David said when he opened her car door.

"Thank you. Your daughter has great taste."

He smiled faintly. "She does."

The place was packed. Thankfully, David had made a reservation while she was getting ready. The hostess greeted them with a wide grin. Her hair was up in a very elaborate bun.

"Good evening! Do you have a reservation?" She looked at David.

"Yes. Under David Marshall."

She scrolled down her screen for a few seconds. "Perfect. Thank you, Mr. Marshall." She looked up at Aisha and then at David. "Party of two?"

"Yes," he said.

Party of two.

Hearing those three words awoke a new feeling within Aisha. Her skin warmed up while butterflies frolicked in her stomach. She looked at David. The dark circles under his eyes had fainted. And she felt better, too. She hadn't thought about her "stuff" since she had been with him. Aside from his behavior behind the red door, they got along so well. Perhaps they could be more than *two strangers sharing a very finite moment of time in space.* Perhaps they could help each other feel better beyond this week.

The hostess led them to their table. "Your server will be with you shortly!" she said, then walked away to greet another party waiting at the entrance.

Aisha and David ordered the picanha steak and paired it with some Bordeaux. The meat was served on skewers. The food was astounding, and so was the wine. They mainly chatted about the weather until the food was served. It wasn't awkward; it was comfortable.

After emptying his first skewer, David gave her his intense signature stare. "So, how have you been, Aisha?"

She sighed before sipping her "medium-bodied and elegant" wine. She smiled, remembering their server's enthusiasm when he described his wine suggestion. She wasn't clear on what made it so, but the red liquid was elegant indeed. It was something about the way it smoothly danced down her throat.

David gently tapped her hand. "Aisha?"

She finally focused on him. "I've not been well, David."

He leaned in. "I'm listening."

"I came to Dallas to…heal, I guess. To have some space to get better and let go of some hurt. I've been here for almost seven months, and I've done virtually nothing. I haven't made any progress. In fact, things have gotten worse in some ways.

"Last week, I got into an argument with my mom. Well, it wasn't really an argument, mostly me yelling at her because of some things she said to me a few years ago. Then, I got into a fight with my brother. He told me not to contact him until I got my shit together. Good for him; he has boundaries. I'm proud of him. Oh, and my ex-best friend is pregnant with the baby of the guy I thought I was going to marry. I walked in on them fucking on New Year's Eve. So, I'm not doing well, David. That's how I've been. What about you?"

He whistled. "Wow."

"Mm-hmm."

"I don't know what to say, Aisha. I'm so sorry this happened to you. I truly wish I had some insightful feedback, but I don't."

She waved him off. "That's okay. It felt good just saying it aloud." Suddenly, her mouth felt dry, so she took another sip of her elegant beverage. "Your turn. How have you been, David?"

He leaned back in his seat. "I also had a terrible argument with my daughter last week. Her name is Zoe, by the way. We've had our fair share of disagreements, but the last one was awful. I knew we were due for a big quarrel; I just didn't think it would be this bad."

Now, she was the one leaning in. "What happened?"

"Well, Zoe's not fond of my lifestyle, specifically how I engage romantically with women. She believes I'm too careless and evasive. She also thinks the women I date are too young for me and that I should date someone closer to her mother's age. She thinks I should settle down with one woman, that my behavior is tasteless and cliché. Essentially, she loves me as her father but doesn't respect me as a man."

"Oof."

"It's not the moral judgment that bothers me the most, it's her lack of open-mindedness and her self-righteous disposition. I had her fifty percent of the time until she turned eighteen, so I don't know how she ended up so rigid and inflexible. Even her mother is more open-minded than she is. It's very disappointing."

"Some kids want to grow up to be just like their parents. Others do everything in their power to be their diametrical opposite…" Aisha's voice trailed off.

David leaned back in. "What if they are just like their parents?" He caressed her wrist. "Chances are they are. There's no point in fighting our true nature. We always lose. Nature overpowers nurture, every time. And in the process of trying to deny it, we just get hurt and waste precious time."

He was looking deep into her eyes, searching for a reaction. Her throat was dry, but his stare felt like a weapon pointed in her direction, so she didn't move an inch. She swallowed to alleviate the dryness.

"What's your true nature?" she finally said.

"I'm a simple man, Aisha, and I believe life's simple. Humans overcomplicate it because our brains have evolved past our functions. If we're extremely lucky, we have what, ninety to one hundred years here? I believe there's nothing after that. I honestly don't feel strongly about it. Maybe there is something. I don't know. I don't care. I think it's irrelevant. Whatever it is— if it's anything at all—is probably not as big of a deal as we are making it out to be.

"I believe all we have is this time on this Earth, so I'll enjoy mine. I'm going to indulge in things that make me feel good. Beauty makes me feel good. Beauty is comforting, soothing. It alleviates. It's medicine." He paused to grab her hands. He cupped them in his. "You're beautiful, Aisha. Before you came today, I was in a bad place because of the situation with Zoe. And just being with you, looking at you…I already feel so much better. Thank you for sharing your beauty with me."

She noticed how tightly he was holding her hands. Then, she looked back at his face, and he was smiling broadly. His eyes were bright. She was happy to see him like that. It felt nice to positively impact someone else's life. And being with him also made her feel better.

Perhaps they could help each other feel better beyond this week.

She smiled. "You're welcome."

When they made it back to his place, they drank an excellent nightcap, smoked some top-shelf cannabis, and had superb sex.

The following five days went on like that.

David had given his housemaid, Gwen, the week off so the two of them could have complete privacy. They went for a swim in the morning. They talked about everything and nothing in the afternoon. She sat for a few hours early in the evening and watched him paint her. They went somewhere fancy afterward. Then, they came back home to punctuate their day with a nightcap, pot, and sex.

Somewhere along the way, Aisha became convinced that David would be key in her healing. Somewhere between him looking at her with that sparkle in his eye, between him staring at her lips to reproduce the way he saw them on the canvas, between him telling her about his first heartbreak when he was in his early twenties, between her telling him about how devastated she felt not to have been enough for her father to stay, between him anchoring her inside of his arms, between him making her feel a level of pleasure she never had before, between him gazing at her so intensely she felt seen; somewhere between Tuesday and Saturday, Aisha became convinced that these two former strangers were meant to be in each other's life for a significant period of time.

Then, Sunday came.

Aisha knew something was off when she walked into the kitchen that morning.

"I'm getting in the pool now. Are you coming?" she said.

David was looking for something in the fridge and didn't turn around. "Not today. I'm beat. The sun finally got the best of me. You go ahead, though. Enjoy."

She walked down the hallway. Something was up with him. He hadn't even kissed her good morning. Perhaps she was overthinking. It was one ninety-eight degrees, after all. If she lived in this house, she probably wouldn't care to jump in the pool every single day, either. She shrugged her concern off.

But when the afternoon came, instead of their usual long chat, he asked her if they could start working earlier. "I'm almost done," he said. "I just need an additional hour or two today. I promise I'll make it up to you. I've already packed some MJ for you, enough to last you another year. I also added a little surprise. I put it by your stuff. And tonight, we'll go somewhere really, *really* nice. I'm so thankful for this week with you, Aisha."

"I can't believe it's already been a week."

"Time flies when you have fun."

That afternoon in the studio, the artist only looked at her face. David was incredibly focused. He bit his lip very hard and narrowed his eyes while the soft music gently played in the background. They took a small break for Aisha to use the restrooms and stretch. Then, they resumed. Four hours and twelve minutes later, it was done. David took a long, deep breath and smiled. He looked at the canvas, then at Aisha, then back at the canvas.

She sat up. "Can I see it?"

He nodded. "Of course."

She walked toward him, her heart racing. She was way more nervous than she had anticipated. David was a talented and observant artist. Aisha felt so much better and lighter this week, so she hoped the painting would reflect that. David moved to the side so she could stand in front of the piece to examine it.

Everything below the neck was true to life. She was impressed by the accuracy. He even painted the faint birthmark above her knee. Now, the face was the abstract part. From all her time spent wandering in art galleries, she had picked up a few things. She knew she was looking at a geometric abstraction. Her face was deconstructed in all sorts of shapes and figures, which, if put together, wouldn't amount to an actual head shape.

Yet, she could tell it was her. What gave it away were the eyes, and she cried—not because she was happy, but because she was incredibly sad. In front of her was the way David saw her. Her eyes were dull and unfocused. She looked lost, confused, and sad. That was how David saw her. She let the tears roll down her cheeks.

"Wow. What a compliment! I didn't expect you to be moved this much. It means the world, Aisha."

She walked back to the couch and sat down. She wiped her face with the back of her hand. "So, what happens after tomorrow, after I leave here?"

He furrowed his brow. "Same as before. When we're both available, we meet and have a great time. And as promised, no more sad shit from now on."

She looked down at her feet. She needed to clip her toenails. She looked back up at him. "I thought we formed a deeper connection this week."

He walked up to the blue couch and sat next to her. "We did, but it doesn't mean things have to change. We've been having so much fun. Let's not spoil things by changing our dynamic. It's working so well for us." He rested his hand on her thigh.

She loved how warm his palm felt on her skin, but she didn't like what she was hearing. "What if I want more? I'm not talking about a relationship. I just mean us spending more time together. This week was so good for me, and I know it was for you too. We can continue to help each other feel better." She put her hand over his.

He stood up. "I can't commit to continually spending this much time with you, Aisha. I have other people with whom I also enjoy being with. As much as I had a great time with you this week, it was also about completing the painting. I think I was transparent about that." He sighed, then sat back down. "Look, I really enjoy spending time with you, and I hope we can continue doing that. I just need to make sure we're still on the same page."

She was looking at the floor. "What page is that?"

"Fun. Sex. Art."

Without looking at him, Aisha stood up and walked out. She went to the bedroom and got dressed. She grabbed her stuff, the neatly packed weed, and whatever surprise was in the other container and walked downstairs.

"Aisha, please wait!" David yelled behind her.

She stopped and turned around. He looked shocked, his eyes wide. Hers were humid and red. "What am I waiting for?"

"I thought we were on the same page."

She smiled ruefully. "Not anymore."

He blinked. "I'm sorry, I thought we were. I'd love to continue seeing you, but I don't want to lead you on and hurt you." He closed the gap between them. "Aisha, you're an amazing woman. Thank you for the incredible moments that we shared. Thank you for the inspiration. I'm immensely grateful. If you change your mind and want to keep seeing me in the same capacity, I'll always be open to it. If not, I understand. I truly wish you the very best, Aisha. You deserve it. Please know I'm sincere."

Aisha was too exhausted to react in any pronounced way. She wanted to be upset at him, but David hadn't done anything wrong. He had been honest about what this was, and she was onboard the whole time…until she wasn't. She wanted to be angry at herself, but what was the point? Anger consumed too much energy, and she was spent.

She kissed David on the cheek and walked away. She drove home with all the windows rolled down. Between the heat and the loud wind, her thoughts were temporarily muted.

WEEK 28

The first thing Aisha did when she woke up was text Anthony, the Tinder Guy. *Hey wanna hang out tonight?*

He replied immediately. *You've read my mind! I can stop by around 10. Cool?*

Yes see you then

It was a relief to have something to look forward to. She looked at the time on her phone. It was almost noon. She just needed to make it through the day. She sat up and opened the backpack she brought to David's place. The clothes in there smelled like bourbon and vanilla, like David. She immediately threw them in the washer.

She wanted to forget about him as soon as possible. She wasn't mad at him, though. She simply couldn't make space for one more thing to occupy her mind. Unfortunately, that wasn't up to her. So, the memories of her time with David stuck their elbows out, shoved whatever was in their way, and squeezed in to take a seat. Now she had a headache. She sat down on her bed and massaged her temples.

At last, Aisha looked for the weed container in her backpack. David had stuffed three very large Ziplock bags with enough marijuana for her to start a small illicit business in the Lone Star State. In another smaller container, there were some dried mushrooms. She chuckled because, of course, he would give her magic mushrooms. Then, she teared up.

It was hard to accept that one day someone was in your life, and the next, they were out of it, just like that. And even though they were still alive somewhere, in a way, they were dead to you. Because even if you crossed paths again, things would never be the way they once were. Things would never be the same because since you last saw them, you had changed, and so had they. So, all that was left of the past were the faint memories.

"Do you still love me?" Aisha had asked James one Saturday morning. He was eating cereal in the kitchen, and she was eating oatmeal in the living room.

He replied with his mouth full. She hated that shit. The fact that she was still around despite that was all the proof she needed to be certain she loved James. She just needed to know if he still felt the same way. He chewed and answered at the same time. "Where's that coming from?"

"It's a yes or no question, James."

He swallowed and then took a sip of water. "In that case, yes."

She put her bowl on the coffee table. "In that case? What's the answer in another case?"

He sighed. "Why do you have to nitpick everything? You're right; it's a yes or no question. And the answer is: yes, I love you."

"You sound annoyed."

"I am. It's 8:30 in the morning. I had a long week, so I'm just trying to enjoy my breakfast. You ask me this question out of the blue, and I gave you an answer. What else do you want from me?"

She raised her voice. "Out of the blue?" She paused, then adjusted her tone to its regular volume. "Can we level with each other?"

James put his bowl in the sink and walked around the island. He sat on the accent chair on the right of the couch she was seated on. He didn't look annoyed anymore. Now, his face was clear. He looked ready for whatever was next.

"Sure," he said.

"Things have been off with us over the last few months."

He nodded. "They have."

"Be honest with me, James. I love you. Do you still love me?"

He looked at the floor and didn't answer for a long time. Then he stared at her. He still didn't speak, but Aisha saw the conflict on his face. He looked like he was trying to figure out the answer to a calculus problem. And as much as she feared what he'd say next, she was relieved because she knew he'd be completely honest. His delayed answer wasn't because he was trying to come up with an elaborate lie or deliver small bits of truth to soften the blow.

Aisha knew James was taking his time because he had probably not done this exercise in a long time. It was bound to happen in a long-term relationship. You were together for so long that the lines between comfort, familiarity, and love eventually blurred. They weren't the first couple to be in this place and wouldn't be the last. Soon, they would hit their two-year anniversary. Whatever the answer was, she preferred to know before then.

Without any warning signs, James broke down in tears. Aisha stood from the couch and sat on his lap to hug and hold him. She wiped his face and silently waited for his answer. Her heart halted its beating. Her jaws were clenched, and her body was stiff.

He held her hand. "Honestly, I've been questioning it for a little while. We've been fighting so much, and I wasn't sure if we had the same future in mind. I'm still not sure. But I still love you, Aisha. I do. Despite everything that has happened, I love you. You're the one I want to be with."

He rested his head on her chest, and she held him tight. She was relieved, happy, in love. Next month, she would celebrate the New Year with her boyfriend and best friend.

Now, Aisha lit up a joint and lay on her beige couch. She kept the mushrooms in the box and stored them in the refrigerator. She wasn't planning on eating them. If she ever made things up with Amir, she'd give them to him. He was the one who enjoyed a semesterly "trip." Aisha didn't go chasing those kinds of waterfalls; she stuck to the cabernets and cannabis she was used to. The last thing she needed was to see other dimensions or whatever people saw on those trips. *One fucked up reality at the time, please, and thank you.*

*

Anthony knocked on her door at 9:58 PM that night. They barely got through the end of episode three of season two of *The Office* before their clothes were spread on the floor.

The next day, they only made it through half of the next episode.

The rest of the episode was merely background noise the following day.

The day after, the TV wasn't even on.

Tonight, Aisha wanted them to talk for a little while. She knew absolutely nothing about the man and vice versa. The whole point of her doing this with him was to have some company. Now, Anthony was coming later and staying shorter.

He knocked at 10:32 PM. When she opened the door, he immediately lifted her off the floor and closed the door behind him with the back of his foot. He stuck his tongue deep inside her mouth, almost reaching her tonsils.

She spoke inside of his throat. It sounded gargoyle-like. "Wait!" she said.

He stopped the vigorous kissing but continued carrying her bridal style. "Something wrong?"

"Put me down for a moment."

He did as requested, then furrowed his brow. "Is everything okay?"

"Yes, yes. Everything's fine." She held his hand and led him to the couch. "Let's just sit and talk for a moment."

"Uh, okay."

They sat down. Anthony was sitting straight and square like he was in a classroom or something.

"Would you like anything to drink? I have wine, whisky, and beer," she said.

"Just water's cool."

Aisha went to the kitchen to get the water. She handed him a glass, and he took a very small sip.

"What do you want to talk about?" Anthony said.

"I don't know. I feel like I don't know the first thing about you. Where are you from? How many siblings do you have? What's your favorite color? What do you do for work?"

He tittered. "Hmm, alright. Houston. Two. Green. High school football coach."

She laughed. "You're allowed to answer in full sentences. And that's awesome; how long have you been coaching?"

He sighed, then he looked at his watch. "Seven years. I'm sorry, Aisha, I think I need to head out. I actually have a game tomorrow, so it wasn't smart of me to even be out this late." He patted her thigh, then stood up. "Let's catch up next week, alright?"

Before she could answer, he was out the door.

Aisha walked outside on her balcony, sat down, and stared blankly at the thick and warm horizon.

WEEK 29

Why were human beings still dwelling in Texas? Mother Nature couldn't have made her feelings clearer. The sun was screaming, "Pack your shit, and get the fuck up out of here!" But here were the stubborn humans outdoors: hiking, fishing, picnicking, biking, and voluntarily running. She wanted to believe she had more sense than them, but she was among them. What could she say? The barbecue and the frozen margaritas were just that good.

Today, she had to leave the house and get some fresh air. Whatever "fresh" meant when it was one hundred and two effing degrees. At any rate, here she was, strolling by some lake she had driven by a few times. She hadn't heard from her mother, Amir, and even Dahlia since she had last spoken to each of them.

Amir not reaching out was expected. However, the silence from her mother and Dahlia was surprising. She wasn't equipped to have a conversation with her mother yet, so it was better they didn't speak till then. Her mother probably felt the same way. Helen usually tried to smooth things over, but their last exchange called for a lot more than that.

As for Dahlia, Aisha couldn't remember most of what happened the last time she met with her friend at the dance. However, she recalled Dahlia looking just as sad as she did.

Aisha sat on a bench and texted her. *Hey! How are you? It's been a minute. I hope all is well. Let's catch up soon!*

Then, she messaged Anthony. *Hangout tonight?*

Dahlia responded when Aisha was driving home. *Hey girl! I've been better but it's going to be okay. Yes it's been a while. Let's do that! How's Friday evening? Maybe you can come to my place or I can come to yours? Whatever you prefer.*

Aisha could use some time away from her beige apartment. She replied as soon as he parked. *Great idea! I can come to your place*

They agreed for her to come by early Friday evening. Based on Dahlia's behavior, Aisha was sure Cheating Mark had messed things up. That was why she was so hesitant to forgive: someone who hurt you once was liable to hurt you again. That was law.

Anthony didn't message her back until late the next day. *Hey the teams not having a good week so I'll text u next week*

She rolled her eyes and threw her phone on the bed. Suddenly, this team she wouldn't have known about unless she pried was the scapegoat for everything: why he had to go home last week and why he couldn't come last night. She knew the real reason: he was creating some distance because she had dared to try and get to know more about him. She was too exhausted to get on Tinder and look for another normal and reliable person to sleep with.

So she texted him back. *Ok I hope it gets better I'll wait for your text*

He didn't reply or even acknowledge her response with a thumbs up. She would've moved on if she were in a different mental space. But under the current circumstances, she wanted to hang on to whatever was within her reach. She couldn't handle losing someone else who was part of her life, no matter how small of a role they played in it.

*

When Aisha looked in the mirror on Friday evening, she saw the pathetic person David had painted. The only thing that kept her from crying was her hair. Those follicles had a completely different eight months than her. The strands were thick, shiny, and healthy. She hadn't really done much to her coils besides washing and occasionally conditioning them. Some things genuinely thrived when left alone. Clearly, that didn't apply to her.

That evening, the drive to Dahlia's house was quick. Hopefully, they could get together more often moving forward. Now that things were over with David, Dahlia was the only person Aisha had left in Dallas. She considered Dahlia a friend, and now, more than ever, she needed a friend. Suddenly, a lot of weight fell on Dahlia's shoulders. She was now essential to Aisha's remaining soundness.

Unaware of the new duty she had been assigned, Dahlia gave Aisha a big hug when she walked inside her apartment. Dahlia's place was lovely. It was a bit larger than Aisha's but had a similar open layout and stainless-steel appliances. Another big difference was that it was decorated with cute knick-knacks, making the space warm and homey. Aisha's place looked like she was on the run and was taking cover there. If she had to leave, all she'd need to do was pack her clothes.

"C'mon, fro!" Dahlia snapped her fingers. "Your hair looks so good!"

"Thank you!" Aisha smiled. If she hadn't seen Dahlia the last time she was out of sorts, Aisha wouldn't have been able to tell if her friend had ever experienced the emotion known as sadness. Dahlia was glowing. "You always look good," Aisha said.

Dahlia pointed at the mauve sectional for Aisha to sit. "What are we drinking? I have wine, beer, margaritas, and some cheap champagne I honestly don't recommend." She laughed.

Aisha chuckled. "Margaritas, then."

"I made some carnitas, so that's perfect."

Aisha saw some pictures on the wall to her right, next to a thriving Peace Lily. Most of them were Dahlia and Nia together in different locations. They looked like whatever they were doing was irrelevant to how much fun they were having. They were beaming in every single photo.

"Where's Nia?"

Dahlia was grabbing some glassware. "She is at my parents' house. She's spending a few weeks there for the summer break. I'm going to join them for a little while next week. I need some time away."

Aisha nodded but didn't speak. Hopefully, it wouldn't be an extended stay. She was hoping they could spend more time together and help each other get through the end of their respective tunnel.

Dahlia put the drinks on the coffee table and then brought two plates.

"Do you need some help?" Aisha said.

"No, no. Thank you, though. Just make yourself comfortable. Drink up, girl. The night is young!"

Dahlia put the food on the coffee table. Aisha waited for her friend to sit down to taste the margarita. She handed Dahlia a glass, then raised hers.

"To a fun night and a new friendship!" Aisha said.

Dahlia clinked her friend's glass and repeated. "To a fun night and a new friendship!"

Aisha took the first bite, then the second. "This is excellent! You can cook *cook*," she said, then took three more bites in ten seconds.

"And you can eat *eat*." Dahlia laughed. "I'm glad you're enjoying it."

Aisha smiled, then took another bite before speaking. "So, catch me up. What have you been up to? Last time we hung out, I think we were both…not well. How are you? Like, for real."

Dahlia put her drink down, leaned back on the couch, put a pillow on her lap, crossed her arms, and shook her head.

"Oh, shit." Aisha stopped eating and waited for her friend's response.

"Yeah."

"That bad?"

"Yep."

"What happened?"

Dahlia sighed. "Things didn't work out with Mark."

Aisha straightened up. "What happened?"

"He thought he was ready but turns out he isn't."

The margarita must have already gone to Aisha's head because her brain only gave her access to two words at the moment. "What happened?" she said again.

Dahlia smiled, then looked earnest. "I started talking about the future because I thought we were on the same page. It's only been a few weeks since we made it official again, but this is not some stranger. This is my ex-husband, the father of my only child. I didn't think we needed to date for months before we started talking about what was next.

"To me, we weren't starting over, you know. We were resuming. We have history. We have a past. Yes, to a certain degree, it's a new start, but it's not a new thing. I don't know, maybe I was too eager to get my family back, so I wanted to skip to the happy ending. I mean, he's the one who asked me to get back together," she aggressively pointed at her chest when saying *me*, "but when I mentioned the timeline for Nia and me moving to Fort Worth, he looked at me like he saw a ghost or something. Like, what the fuck? And I wasn't trying to move there next week or anything like that, but I thought that's where we were heading."

She paused to take a sip of her drink and continued, "Then, this man had the unmitigated gall to tell me a part of him still wants to sow his wild oats. He doesn't want to fully commit too hastily and hurt me again. Yeah. The reason he wants to take things slow is to protect me because he loves me. I'm the love of his life, and that's why he can't fully commit to me right now...because he loves me so much. Does that make any sense to you?" She crossed her legs and held the pillow closer to her chest. "That's some bullshit."

"Phew. I don't know what to...when was this?"

"The day we met for the dance. That afternoon. That's why he didn't come." She looked away. "I really thought things would be different this time."

Aisha grimaced. Her eyes were humid with anger, but she didn't feel like those were her tears to cry. Dahlia looked so calm, so she didn't want to trigger her friend's emotions. She spoke as evenly as she could. "You could've taken a rain check that day, you know. I would've completely understood."

Dahlia uncrossed her legs, put the pillow behind her back, and moved closer to Aisha. She held her hand. "I didn't want to be alone. I needed to be with a friend."

Then, Aisha lost it. Feeling needed was incredibly gratifying. She was thankful for their friendship and Dahlia's presence in her life. So, she cried. Dahlia joined her. They held each other for a while.

Somewhere deep within, one of Aisha's old wounds got smaller.

When they parted from the hug, Dahlia took a deep breath and exhaled. "I feel so much lighter. Thank you for listening, girl. Really." She grabbed a napkin and wiped her face. "Now, what's going on with you? You didn't look too good last time, either. Talk to me. How's life treating you?"

Like shit! Aisha cleared her throat, though there wasn't anything to clear. "Hmm, I don't know where to start."

"Start wherever you want, I'll catch up." Dahlia winked.

Aisha copied Dahlia and took a deep breath. She felt calmer when she spoke. "I got into a fight with my brother and something similar with my mom. I haven't spoken to them in the last three-four weeks. They are my only family, so it really sucks. There is so much shit we need to unpack and talk about. It's just too much right now. I can't handle it. I can't deal with things right now. I just can't. I need more time. But the more time passes, the wider the gap becomes. I know that. But I feel like if I try to deal with anything right now, I'll make it worse because I'm just not in the right headspace.

"I'm a mess. And then, things ended with the artist guy. I started liking him too much and wanted to spend more time with him. I knew better, too. He has always been clear about who he was, so I should've never let him get so close. But that's what happens when you have a big void inside, you look for anything to fill it up. It's crazy because I know what the problem is, but I don't have the solution or the tools to fix it. And I'm afraid that even when I do, I won't have the strength to use them."

Dahlia was nodding throughout her speech. Her eyes were glistening with understanding and empathy. She held Aisha's hands. "First of all, thank you for sharing this with me. Your trust means a lot to me." She pressed her lips together, then continued. "This is a lot for anyone to try and figure out alone. I think you need to talk to someone. It's not going to fix everything overnight, of course, but it's a great start."

Amir had given her the same advice, though it was delivered with less patience—understandably so. Aisha knew she needed to see a therapist, and she would, at some point, sooner than later. Right now, it just felt like one more thing she couldn't handle. Frankly, she was also afraid because what if it didn't help? What if it didn't *fix* her?

She saw therapy as the ultimate cure in case nothing else worked. What if she sat on that couch and nothing changed at the end? Then, what? What option would be left, then? No, she couldn't face such disappointment. She needed to build some strength and get a little better on her own first. That way, if therapy didn't work out, she wouldn't fall into utter despair.

This she didn't want to reveal to Dahlia, so instead, she said, "I don't know where to look for a good one."

Dahlia's eyes lit up. "Mine is incredible!" She got up to look for something on a work desk across the room. She ran back to the sectional. "Here's her card. And if it doesn't work with her, she'll have plenty of recommendations for you."

Aisha grabbed the card, glanced at it, and put it in her pocket. "Thank you."

"Of course!" Dahlia handed her another card. "And one of my students owns a nonprofit. They help underprivileged kids. They could use a volunteer to help pack food and other stuff for the children. He gave me his card. You can call him whenever if it sounds like something you'd like to do."

Aisha didn't look at the card and immediately put it in the same pocket. "This is awesome, thank you. I'll definitely give him a call."

Dahlia poured more margarita into their almost empty glasses. "Now, what the hell happened with your former best friend and your ex? I just remember that you cut things off with them at the same time. I'm sure I know why, but tell me, what happened there?"

Aisha didn't answer, but she slowly grabbed the margarita container and topped off her drink until the next drop could cause it to overflow.

Dahlia shook her head and whistled. "They got you fucked up!"

"You don't know the half of it." She took a gulp of the tart beverage.

"How did you find out?"

"I walked in on them doing it on New Year's Eve."

"Bastards!"

"She's pregnant with his child."

Dahlia gasped so loudly that Aisha recoiled. Dahlia was frozen for a moment with her mouth and eyes wide open; then she said, "Girl, I'm so sorry. That's beyond messed up. Jesus. What the hell is wrong with people? I'm so sorry. Have you spoken to them since you found out?"

"Just to confirm they were expecting. She was like a sister to me, and I thought I was going to marry him..." Aisha broke down.

She was surprised because the tears came out of nowhere, rapidly and violently. She couldn't control the flow. The stream was too strong and wanted out. It was pointless to try to stop it, so she cried without restraint.

Dahlia cradled her inside of her arms. She was rocking Aisha gently and whispered that it would be okay. She would be okay. Dahlia told her she was there for her and that everything would be fine. Aisha felt immense relief then because she wouldn't have to face the scary ghosts by herself. When the darkness would rise to try and take over the last piece of light that kept her somewhat buoyant, she wouldn't be alone. Her friend would be there to help her win, at last, this war that had been leveling her spirit for far too long. So, Aisha's face brightened with joy and anticipation for the days when the way she currently felt would be a distant memory.

"There you go," Dahlia said. "Sometimes, you just have to let it all out."

Aisha straightened up and grabbed a napkin to wipe the mist the stream had left behind. Though she had cried a river, she knew there was so much more where it came from. "Phew. I don't remember the last time I cried like this. Do you?"

Dahlia also wiped her face. "Girl, this morning." She chuckled. "I make time to cry; it's very important. We hold so much shit in, you know. And sometimes, we ought to scream and cry and laugh like hyenas and stomp our feet and move our bodies in whatever ways feel good to let that shit out. It's not our shit, really. It's just shit. And shit ought to be expelled." She laughed very loudly, then raised her glass. "To expelling shit!"

Aisha laughed, not as loud, but still wholeheartedly. "To expelling shit!"

The rest of the evening was a blast.

Aisha told Dahlia about her fun week with David and her nightly sexcapades with Anthony. Being around Dahlia completely changed her perspective. Now, her time with David was no longer a story with a sad ending, but rather a very fun adventure that ended at the right time. The brief encounters with Anthony were no longer cold sex with no rapport, but rather two pragmatic adults having a great time with no unnecessary attachment.

Then, Dahlia told her how well Nia was doing in school and how smart she was. Her eyes were shining with pride, and it warmed Aisha's heart. She realized how much she missed her mom. She took a sip of her drink to avoid getting emotional. Finally, Dahlia gave her the latest update on her job.

"I think I'm going to quit," she said. "There's no future for me there. He's already training his kids to take over." She shook her head before continuing. "I'm thinking of opening my own studio. I have a little money saved, and I know my parents would invest in me and loan me some money if I gave them a clear and detailed business plan. And I have one. I'll share it with them when I go there next week. I'm kind of nervous about it, but I think it's going to work out."

"I'm sure it will. You seem confident about it. Your own studio. Wow. That's really exciting."

"That's my dream. I love teaching, and I love dancing. I have so many ideas; I just need the space to implement them. My own space. My way. I know it's going to be tough because this industry is very competitive. But this is what I love and am good at, so I'll work it until it works out."

What was it like to feel so strongly about anything? Aisha just listened in awe and admiration. "It'll definitely work out!" she said.

Dahlia smiled. "Thank you." Then she looked in the distance. "I'm excited to be with my parents for some time. I know I'm pretty cheerful right now, but I was a mess this morning. The sad wave will come again, that's just how it goes. I need to be with my family right now. Mark undid something within me. I knew it was a risk, and I've accepted this outcome. It's finally time to close this chapter for good and fully heal from this heartbreak." She looked back at Aisha with a tight-lipped smile. "Some time away in the country with my parents and Nia is just what I need, and more evenings like this one when I come back."

"How long are you planning on being away?"

"I'm not sure. I'm thinking about two, maybe three weeks. One month max. I need the dirt road to hit my face long enough to clear my mind." She smiled at the end.

Aisha was thinking of anything she could say to shorten Dahlia's countryside getaway. "Is there anything I can help you with here?"

She bit her lip. "I don't think so. I think I just need to be away, with my family. Kind of like what you're doing right now. Some time away to reset."

Being implicit wasn't working, so Aisha just said what she was thinking. "I was hoping we'd help each other through this. Tonight's been incredible. I already feel so much lighter."

"I do too, but—"

"I know you need to be with your family for some time but maybe don't stay away as long. I know it's a big ask, but I feel like together we could…fasten our healing."

"Oh, Aisha, I'm sorry. I don't know. I don't think so."

"Please, consider it. I can come here a couple of times a week or as often as needed, and you can come to my place whenever you want, and we can just talk the shit out, expel all the bullshit, and get better together!"

Dahlia grabbed Aisha's hand gently. "I'm sorry, Aisha. I wish I could agree to this, but I don't think this is best for me right now. I really need to be with my parents and Nia. But I promise we can do that when I get back."

Aisha looked down.

Dahlia spoke again. "In the meantime, you can talk things out in therapy. I think that'd be much more helpful than anything I'd say anyway." She gently tapped Aisha's free hand.

Aisha stood up without looking at the person she believed held the key to the door leading to her recovery and who was denying her entry. "I understand," she said. "Where are the restrooms, please?"

"Are you okay?"

"Yes. I really need to pee," Aisha said, still avoiding eye contact.

"Okay. It's down the hall."

Aisha turned on her heel and marched down. In the bathroom, she cried. She cried because no matter how hard she pleaded and begged, no one would stay. She also wept because she couldn't stand who she was becoming, how pathetic and selfish she was. She hated how much she put the way she felt above anything else, but still did nothing about it. How sad and lonely. How disappointing. She let the tears fall until she felt emptied, then she looked in the mirror.

The sight was horrifying.

She looked the way she felt: terrible and gross. She took rapid breaths, hoping they would do something, anything, so she could go outside and meet Dahlia's eyes before leaving. But the only thing the breaths accomplished was to accelerate her heart rate.

She washed her face and tried to practice the smile she'd put on for her friend. All she needed now was some clown makeup, and she could audition for the next *Joker* movie. Her fake grin was disturbing. It was best to go out there and act as normal as she could.

"Are you alright?" Dahlia asked when Aisha walked back into the living room.

"Yes." She finally made eye contact with Dahlia. Her friend immediately looked very concerned. "Sorry, my bladder was full," Aisha said.

Then she parted her lips and went for that smile she had just practiced. It must've been even more terrifying than she thought because Dahlia blinked a few times.

"You don't look okay."

Aisha was standing next to her by the edge of the sectional. "I'm just tired. I think I'm going to head out. Tonight was really fun, though. Thank you for having me over. Text me when you're back in town, okay?"

Dahlia stood up. "Hang on. Why are you rushing out? Are you upset? Talk to me, Aisha."

"I'm okay, I promise. I just need to go to bed." Aisha opened her arms to hug her.

Dahlia spoke inside of the embrace. "Aisha, please don't shut off like this. I'm here now. Tell me how I can help."

Aisha broke the hold. "I'm okay, I promise. Good night."

She walked out without looking back.

The next day, Dahlia texted her to ask how she was doing. Aisha lied and told her she was fine, then thanked her again for hosting their fun night in.

For the remainder of the week, she finished smoking the Denver weed and began enjoying David's gift. Like anything else from him, the quality was outstanding.

Her thoughts remained cloudy and imperceptible.

WEEK 30

Dahlia texted Aisha on Tuesday evening after leaving town to ask how she was doing. Aisha lied again and told her to enjoy her time away and not worry about her; they would catch up when she came back. Now, Aisha was lying down with her eyes wide open, staring blankly at her ceiling. She noticed a tiny spider web in one corner. She didn't react to it and turned around to grab her phone.

Free tonight? she texted Anthony at 11:32 AM. She hadn't heard back from him all last week.

He replied at 9:37 PM. *Yes I can stop by in about an hour*

She was lying down with her eyes wide open then, too. She needed to cut him off. He obviously thought very little of her. She considered not replying and blocking him, but she couldn't bear being alone all night. It was him or some new random Tinder guy.

Ok, she replied.

Anthony knocked on her door at midnight.

She gave him an angry stare when she opened it. "I was about to go to bed."

"Sorry." He grimaced.

"Maybe you should g—"

He leaned in and hugged her. He didn't kiss her or undid her robe; he just held her. And that affectionate gesture absolved him of everything.

She shook her head, rolled her eyes, and smirked. "Okay, you can come in," she said.

He grinned as he walked in. He sat on the couch and patted the cushion next to him for her to sit. "How have you been?"

She didn't sit. She gave him a double take instead. "Who are you, and what have you done with Anthony?"

He chuckled. "Sorry if I've been acting weird. The guys are just playing like shit right now, and obviously, all eyes are on the coach. I'm catching a lot of heat. Shit's just been stressful. But I'm here now, and we're going to have a good time. What's been going on with you, lady?"

Aisha walked to the kitchen and grabbed two beers from the fridge. She handed him one. Then, she sat down. "I'm sorry to hear that, that sucks. But I'm sure you'll turn it around." She cleared her throat. "And I've been alright. Same old."

He raised his brow. "What's *same old*? Work stuff? What do you do, by the way?"

"Well, I'm kind of on a hiatus from doing things, I guess. I just have some personal stuff to deal with, and I moved here from Denver to have some space to do that."

"Right on. When did you move here?"

"January."

"Cool. Making headway?"

"Not so much." She lowered her head.

Anthony moved closer to her and lifted her chin with his index finger. "It's okay, Aisha. It's just like I told the boys: it's all part of the game, trust the process. At the end of the day, it doesn't matter win or lose, if you didn't learn anything. It ain't over till it's over." He lightly tapped her chest. "That thing's still pumping blood, right? Then, it ain't over."

He beamed, and she smiled back just as wide. He leaned in and kissed her. Then they had the best sex they've had so far.

Aisha's head was lying on Anthony's chest now. A few of his locs fell behind her head. His left arm was wrapped around her back. It was perfect. She was glad she didn't cut him off. He was a nice person. He just had a lot going on with his team, but he clearly cared about her a little.

"When things slow down with your season, maybe we could do something during the day," she said.

"I don't know. I have other things going on, too, outside of the team."

She still was lying on his chest, looking at him, and he was looking straight up at the ceiling. "I understand," she said. "There's no rush. You just seem like a nice guy, so I was hoping we could do things outside the apartment."

He slowly sat up and gently moved Aisha's head on the pillow. "I'm sorry, Aisha. You're a nice girl, too, but I don't think we're looking for the same thing. I just want something casual right now, like we were in the beginning."

She spoke fast, "I'm not talking about a relationship, Anthony. We can keep things casual while we get to know each other and do things outside the bedroom."

"That's the thing, I only want the sex part right now. I have too much on my plate. It's nothing about you. You're really cool. I'm sorry, I thought we were on the same page."

Aisha sighed and closed her eyes. Another person she was on different pages with. Again. Evidently, she didn't know which page she was on, and that's why she kept misreading every situation. She kept her eyes shut.

A few seconds later, she felt soft lips landing on her forehead. Then, footsteps. Finally, the sound of the front door being shut. When she finally opened her eyes, the only other living being in sight was the spider in the ceiling corner, resting on its web.

That night, she had a bad dream about Sam and James. When she woke up the following day, she didn't remember the details, which was good because she didn't want to. But that morning, she couldn't help but recall that one day when Sam had behaved very strangely.

They were self-touring the third apartment Sam was considering moving into. Her lease was up in two and a half months. The first two places didn't quite look like the photos on the website. This one did, but the rent was almost two hundred dollars over her preferred budget.

"I like the blue cabinets," Aisha said while opening one. "And everything looks brand new. I know it's a little over budget, but this place is so cute. If you can swing it, I think you should apply."

Sam stared at her in that unreadable way she sometimes did. "I don't know if I can afford to swing things. I'm not like you. I don't have anyone to fall back on if something comes up."

Aisha blinked. "What's that supposed to mean?"

"Were you to be in a bind, you have James. I have no one."

She frowned. "You have me."

"Sure."

She walked closer to Sam, who was sitting on top of the kitchen counter. She lifted herself and sat next to her friend. "What's going on, Sam? Did something happen? Do you need help? I have some money saved if you need help with rent for a little while."

Sam jumped off the counter. "It's not about money. This isn't something you can help me with." Then, she broke down.

Sam rarely cried. The last time she did was when she ended things with her ex. Now, Aisha understood this was about her secret lover. She jumped off the counter and pulled Sam inside of her arms. "Things didn't work out with John, is that it? I'm so sorry." Sam's body tensed up. Aisha rubbed her back. "I'm sorry. I know you were in love with him." Sam began shaking and crying even louder. Aisha spoke firmly. "Fuck him. What kind of idiot would fumble you? I don't need to know anything about the guy to know you're too good for him. He can go straight to hell for hurting you like this."

Sam moved her head back and looked at Aisha. She was angry and stared at Aisha as if, somehow, this was her fault. Aisha was confused for a second but didn't take it personally. She knew a broken heart could cause anyone to behave irrationally. She gently moved Sam's head back on her shoulder and held her tighter. Sam sobbed and wept until Aisha's left sleeve was soaked.

"That's right," Aisha whispered, "let it all out."

Now she sat up on her bed. She felt so alone, so empty. She had no one left in Dallas, and she had still not heard from her mother. As for Amir, she knew she would be the one who had to reach out first. He was just a phone call away. He didn't hate her. He was just upset with her. But she was too ashamed to contact him. What would she even say? Where would she start? She was doing even worse now than the last time they spoke. If she made this move prematurely, she'd inevitably say the wrong thing and make things go from bad to worse.

Those thoughts weighed heavy and took up so much space. She considered getting up to light up a joint, but she was too tired, even for that. So, she lay back on her bed and closed her eyes.

WEEK 31

*J*ust *like this message or say anything so we know you alive. I know you are but mom's worried. If you could at least send me a thumbs up or something a couple times a month so I can let her know you're fine that'd be great.*

Aisha read Amir's text repeatedly and smiled wider every single time.

Hey big bro! Yes please tell her I'm okay. How are you? I'm so happy to hear from you. I've been meaning to reach out but I was nervous I wouldnt handle things correctly and upset you even more. I miss you. How's everything?

If it weren't for mom you wouldn't have heard from me. Id prefer if you two talked directly but for her sake Im okay being the middleman. Just a biweekly thumbs up or something would do.

She bit her lip. *Understood*

Aisha sighed, then opened a bottle of whiskey. The problem with drinking and smoking regularly was that the more often you did it, the less potent it became, and the more you had to increase the intake and frequency to feel the effects. So that's what she did. In the hopes of balancing things out, she drank lots of water and went to her apartment's gym every other day. Hopefully, she could sweat most of the liquor and smoke off.

For a few days, this seemed to work. The weed fully clouded her mind, and the alcohol put her to sleep. This was precisely what she wanted: to be awake as little as possible and to not think clearly when she was.

So, Aisha went on about her week this way and down that road, happy she had found a path that kept her moving, regardless of the destination. But by the end of the week, she came up to a wall, a block made of apathy and bleakness. She looked back to see if she could turn around to retrace her steps, but now it was just this unyielding wall all around her.

And she felt nothing.

PART III

WEEK 32 – WEEK 45

The next three months went on like one homogenous unit of time. One of the reasons for it was the weather barely changing from one month to the next, so it was hard to tell one season from the other. It was only when she was woken up by a loud leaf blower one Wednesday morning, the third week of September, that Aisha realized the summer was over. Though the temperature remained between the mid-eighties and low nineties during the day.

One evening, she came back home from the store, and that one neighbor lady she always ran into was in a great mood because: "It's so nice outside!" The sun must've fried her brain. It was still eighty-four degrees, for crying out loud. Perhaps Aisha wasn't noticing the fifteen-degree drop because she stayed inside her apartment ninety-five percent of the time. She only stepped outside to run errands.

Occasionally, she sat on her balcony to get some fresh air and look at the magnolias. Unfortunately, just like the leaves blown away from the road every Wednesday morning, the white flowers had disappeared. Aisha was a little bummed out by that sight, but she shrugged the feeling off.

That was her reaction to everything lately: *It is what it is*. She wasn't being stoic, she knew that. This behavior didn't come from deep insight and introspection. It wasn't a decision she made after careful consideration and graduating from the School of Hard Knocks. She simply had no energy left to care.

Nothing interested her.

Nothing upset her.

Nothing made her happy.

She was just going through the motions of life to maintain a heartbeat. Everything she did was out of habit and memory. Even drinking and smoking stopped providing her relief because there wasn't anything to be relieved from. All the pain and hurt she had felt were frozen somewhere behind the wall of apathy and bleakness she now lived within.

When she first began feeling this way, she thought it was a good thing. All the painful and hurtful memories no longer affected her. Nothing did. That was good news, right? She quickly got the answer to her question. At least when she was upset and sad, she felt alive. Now that nothing could make it past her wall, she struggled to justify her existence.

What was the point of this?

Why was she waking up every morning?

If she didn't care about anything, what was left for her to do here?

And she had moments when she allowed herself to explicitly consider the path her mind was pointing at: the end of everything. But she never could go there. She never would go there. It was a passing thought she'd never act upon because she wasn't ready to face whatever was on the other side of her last breath.

At least here, even as aimless as she felt, she knew what to expect. And that comfort, as minimal as it was, fastened her on this plane. Though she was settled on living, this wasn't a good life. She could certainly try to blame her parents, her ex-boyfriend, and her former best friend. She didn't end up here at random after all. But as much as they caused some of the wounds and scars that she had initially traveled to heal, she chose not to do anything about them at some point. She chose this path and marched on until she reached a point of no return.

She went from needing some space to pushing things off, then to avoiding, ignoring, burying, and finally, when it was too much to hold on to, she shut off. Now that nothing moved her, it was easy to admit that. Even in those moments when she was objective about her state and acknowledged how terrible things had gotten, she still didn't feel like doing anything about it. It was such a weird place to be in. It was as if she was falling off a cliff, not concerned about the imminent crash but rather fascinated by Earth's gravitational pull.

Now, her state was somewhat of a morbid interest, as if she was detached from her own existence. She wondered how long she would go on like this until her next phase. And what would the next phase be? Would she experience with hard drugs? Would she become more promiscuous? Would she join a cult? Would she end up killing James and/or Sam? The possibilities were dreadfully endless. This appeased her; to let herself believe that her own life was out of her control and there wasn't anything she could do about it, except watch it unfold.

Aisha knew she could do a few things to better her state. She could call her mother and Amir to finally talk things out. She could meet with Dahlia, who was back in town and had offered to meet and catch up with her. Aisha had suggested they meet at a later date because she wasn't in the mood to talk to her—she didn't give Dahlia a reason. Speaking to a professional first would probably be best anyway. She could call Dahlia's therapist and set up an appointment. But even that felt like too tall of an order.

She'd have to dial, talk, set up an appointment, put it on her calendar, get ready on the day off, get out of the house, drive, park, and walk to her office. Even if she did it virtually, there were still too many steps. She didn't feel like doing any of that. She didn't want to talk to anyone. So, she turned her phone off. All she wanted to do was lay on her couch and watch TV.

She wanted to interact with other people only when absolutely necessary. She wanted to be immobile as often as she could. She wanted to sleep as much as her body would allow.

Sounds like you're quite depressed, my friend.

Yeah.

Are you going to get some help?

No. It is what it is.

After Aisha shut her phone off, she couldn't keep track of her days. She only knew when it was Wednesday because of the leaf blower. That became the one thing she looked forward to, and it was also her reminder to step out on the balcony and get some air.

However, one day, she realized a lot of time had passed since she last heard the leaf blower. She picked up her phone and turned it on to confirm the date: November 1st.

She gasped.

Today was Amir's birthday, and her mother's birthday was last week.

She turned her phone back on and texted *Happy birthday* to Amir and *Happy belated birthday* to her mother. She immediately shut her phone off again to not see their responses, or lack thereof. Up until then, Aisha had kept her promise and texted Amir a thumbs up every two weeks to confirm she wasn't dead.

This was the first time she had directly connected with her mother since they last spoke in June. Jesus, was that how long it had been? She was surprised her mother hadn't contacted her since then or even driven to Dallas to find her. Apparently, there was only so long you could give someone the cold shoulder before the person could no longer ignore the ice and walk away to warmer pastures.

Which made Aisha think of the last time she saw her father.

Albert had texted her out of nowhere one afternoon. He had probably gotten her new number from her brother. She knew Amir talked to him a handful of times every few years. And that was only because her brother went out of his way to get a hold of the man. She honestly didn't understand why her brother went to such great lengths to convince this stranger to be part of their lives when that was clearly the least of his concerns.

Amir had put in so much effort over the past ten years, and the result was—drum roll—he had seen Albert as many times as Aisha had since her infamous seventeenth birthday celebration, which was zero time. It pained her to see Amir's disappointment when his calls went unreturned and his messages unanswered.

Aisha got the message when Albert first walked out of their home when she was eight. He didn't care about them, and she wasn't going to convince him to. As much as she tried to put up an unbothered front and act like she had made peace with it, that eight-year-old girl with sweaty hands felt a void within caused by her father's absence.

Though years had flown by, and she was now twenty-seven, she seamlessly recalled the very first time she saw Albert and how striking the resemblance was. She was very curious about him then. She wanted to see how he moved, how he talked. She wanted to know what he liked and what he didn't like. But the man stood up from the purple chair and left before she could learn anything about him.

When Albert showed up again on her seventeenth birthday, Aisha was furious. She had been diligent about forgetting his face and erasing him from her memory. But here he was, smiling and looking just like her.

As her anger boiled up until eruption, the curiosity about him, which had been lying dormant at the bottom, also made it to the surface. And while aloud, she was screaming at Albert and telling him how awful he was, silently she wondered: *How was your father's hometown in Cameroon? What did you do there? Do we have family there? Did you like it better there? Why did you leave us? Why don't you love us? Why don't you love me?*

And because she couldn't say any of this out loud, it made her fury greater. It was only after she wept into Amir's arms—who was also sobbing—that she finally calmed down. That day, she promised herself never to allow Albert or anyone else to hurt her like that. And if that meant building an impenetrable wall no one could ever get through, so be it.

When she received that text from Albert that random day, she believed her wall was sturdy. There wasn't anything the man could say or do to affect her. She also chuckled because she noticed the frequency of his apparitions. He popped up about every ten years, like the U.S. census, to be accounted for. At that time, she didn't care if he lived or died. What difference would it make for her either way? She just wished he'd keep away from her life for good. In fact, the reason she agreed to meet with him was to tell him precisely that.

Aisha didn't tell Amir about this meetup. She figured her brother had already met with Albert or would meet soon. She didn't want to talk to him about this because she wanted to move on. She was walking into that hotel lobby to close this empty chapter. Blank pages that would forever remain unwritten.

It was time to focus on the next chapter.

Albert was seated in the far back corner of the brightly lit lobby. He stood up and waved as she walked toward him. He looked old. He was only in his mid-forties, like her mother, yet time had already curved his back and left deep lines on his face. Aisha wished her immediate reaction was to think: *That's what you get!* But it wasn't. She felt a quick pinch to her heart. She was equally surprised and annoyed by that. She shook that unwelcomed sentiment off and sat across Albert without making contact.

"It's so good to see you, Aisha. How are you?" he said. She just nodded in response. He smiled and stared at her. "If you didn't have my face, I wouldn't have recognized you. You're a woman now!"

"Yeah. That's what ten years do to a teenager."

"Right." He half-smiled. "I don't even know where to begin. Hmm, so, what do you do for work?"

She narrowed her eyes and gazed at him. "I'm a professional house sitter."

He raised his brow. "Oh, okay. Is that a side gig, or something you're just doing until you find something else?"

She furrowed her brow. She didn't come here to talk about her job. "No. That's my full time job. That's what I do."

Albert looked confused. "It just doesn't seem like a viable career path. Not that everyone must climb the corporate ladder and stick to the standard lane, but don't you have a dream or something that you're passionate about? Something exciting you want to do down the road?"

Now she was getting upset because who was he to tell her anything about her choices? But for whatever reason, she also felt defensive. "I like what I do and get paid well for it. I plan on staying put," she said sharply.

"I'm sorry. I didn't mean to offend you. You are so smart, I just thought you—"

You are so smart. Those four words created a fissure in the wall she believed, not even fifteen minutes ago, was impenetrable. How did he do that? How could he be so casual and comfortable, like twenty-seven years were negligible? How dared he act like he knew anything about her? Where did he get off thinking he could have any input on her life?

Aisha knew whatever she felt inside was always painted on her face. She could tell Albert saw it. Before she could say anything, he spoke again. "I'm sorry, Aisha. You're doing something you enjoy, and that's the most important thing. I'm so happy to be here with you. I don't want to upset you. I just want to spend some time with you."

"Why?"

"It's time to right my wrongs. I want to get to know you, Aisha. You're my daughter."

She cocked her head. "Why now? I'm twenty-seven years old. Why now?"

He sighed. "I've been running away since I was a young man. Looking for purpose, belonging, meaning, and not caring about who I left behind. I've always felt uprooted, like my home was somewhere else, and I've been looking for that place I hoped would grant me inner peace. I've been traveling and exploring, always on the go, and it took me decades to figure out that place was you. You and your brother, wherever you are. I just hope it's not too late to come home."

A tear rolled down her cheek, then she broke, and so did the wall. "It took you twenty-seven fucking years to figure that out? What do you expect me to do? Just to let you into my life? Twenty-seven years, and this is all you got? Do you know how hard this was for Mom? How hard it was for Amir? For us? So, you got to live the life you wanted, and now that it's no longer fulfilling, you crawl back here with this sob story? And what are we supposed to do, anyway? Open the door wide open and invite you in? How can we trust you'll not leave again the moment this is not whatever you've imagined? How can I trust anything that comes out of your mouth? I don't know you."

Albert's eyes were wet. He held Aisha's hand and spoke unevenly. "I know…I know. I'm sorry. I know there's nothing I can say right now to make you believe me. But please, give me a chance to show you with my actions. I'm planning on moving to Denver to be close to you two. I'll do whatever it takes. I know the trust won't be built overnight, but I'll do whatever it takes for however long it takes to earn even the tiniest place in your life." Then, he broke down. "Please…give…me…a chance."

People walked past them on their way to their rooms. Some slowed down to glance at them with a sympathetic frown. Aisha and Albert were sniveling and wiping their damped faces with the back of their hand, with the same cadence. Genetics was nothing short of sorcery. She understood why she physically resembled him. But how the hell did she have the same mannerisms as this man she had spent less than two hours with her entire life? This realization leveled any part of the wall still standing.

As much as she disliked Albert for how careless and absent he had been, he was still her father. Some parts of herself that she didn't quite understand and thus didn't have access to could be unlocked by his mere presence. Plus, the man looked sincere and lost. As much as she was upset with him, she also felt for him. She didn't think she could ever trust him, but she wanted to give him a chance to prove her wrong.

She patted her cheeks with her palm and took a deep breath. "I didn't think I was going to cry."

"I knew I would." Her father smiled.

She smiled back. His face lit up, and a fresh tear fell down his eye. She patted his hand and said, "You have my number. The ball's in your court. I'll give you one chance. One. If you miss it, I'm done."

He almost jumped out of his seat. "I won't miss it! I won't miss it!" He stood up at once. "Can I give you a hug, please?"

She got up. "Sure."

Then, they exchanged their first and last hug.

Aisha didn't hear from him until the following week.

Hey! I'm sorry, I had to drive back to Chicago to handle some things. I don't know why I chose to drive and not fly. I think I thought I'd see something interesting on the road but I didn't lol. How are you?

She was happy to finally hear from him. *Hey glad you made it safe! I didn't know you lived in Chicago. I always wanted to go there*

He replied four days later. *Yes, you should visit sometimes. I think you'll like it. When things settle down for me, I can get two tickets for you and Amir. Work's been crazy!*

She was a little annoyed by his texting pace, but not everyone always kept their phones with them. She texted him within minutes. *That'd be fun! I know Amir will be thrilled. Hopefully things slow down for you soon*

She didn't hear from him for the next two weeks, so she messaged him. *Hey how are you? Hope things have slowed down a bit for you at work. What do you do by the way?*

Albert replied to her text a week later. *Hey! Sorry, it's our busy season but it's usually not this bad. I'll start looking for tickets. It might be easier to catch up over the phone. When can I call you?*

Anytime today is fine

Okay, let me wrap things up here and I'll give you a call in a few hours, ok?

Ok

Albert didn't call her that day, the next day, or the following one, so she called him. He didn't answer. On her third attempt, it went straight to voicemail.

She never heard back from him.

Aisha was hurt. She was also disappointed in herself for allowing this to happen, for letting this person who always left convince her he'd stay. Why did he do it? Why did he come back to sell her this pipe dream? Was this some sick, twisted game? Was he just trying to feel better about himself? Or did he sincerely want to try but just couldn't be present? Was it his inherent nature to run, and no matter how hard he wanted to stay, he just had to go? Or was it something about her and Amir? Or just her?

Perhaps she wasn't someone worth sticking around for.

A year later, a tearful Helen let Amir and Aisha know their father had passed away in a car accident. He had put them down as beneficiaries for his life insurance. For Aisha, this was the coup de grace. The man was a coward, plain and simple. There was no big mystery to uncover. He ran away until he crashed. Then, he had the audacity to list them as beneficiaries to fuck with their heads beyond the grave; to make them wonder if perhaps he had cared all along.

He thought this final act, unexpected and staggering, would absolve him posthumously. Well, he was dead wrong. As far as she was concerned, he could be getting his heavenly wings, his eternal damnation, his atonement in purgatory, his next reincarnated life, his access to Nirvana, his oneness with

Brahman, his seat on the ancestral plane, or nothing at all; but he'd never get her forgiveness.

And Aisha carried that stance with her until the present moment. Forgiveness wasn't a luxury she could afford to splurge on. Someone who hurt you once was liable to hurt you again. Therefore, she never gave anyone else a second chance.

Now, this decision was challenged by her love for her mother. She knew Amir was right; her mother didn't mean what she had said. Of course, she didn't wish that Aisha wasn't born. She knew her mom meant that ideally, she hoped things would've played out differently, that she could simultaneously raise Aisha while pursuing her own goals. As a young single mother, Helen knew getting things done would be a lot more difficult for her; all she asked was to still be granted the same opportunities. But that didn't happen. So, Helen had to put her dreams on hold to raise her children.

That gloomy day Helen told Aisha her life would've turned out so much better if she didn't have her could never be erased from her memory. Aisha could still recall the raindrops' rhythm and the thunder's sharpness. She could see that her mother was at the end of her rope. She looked pale, overworked, overwhelmed. She was leaning against the window.

Helen had never gotten the privilege of being selfish and doing whatever the hell she felt like doing. At no point could she take off and move to a different city indefinitely to clear her mind and heal from all her pain, to have the space to fully acknowledge how wicked it was that the man she loved had just up and left her with the fruits of their intimacy. And because she was the parent who stayed *and* a woman, it was expected that she'd naturally step up with her maternal instinct and cover the space Albert was supposed to fill.

It was expected she should put all her dreams on hold, no questions asked, to do the needful. It was expected she shouldn't make a big deal about it—perhaps vent to her girlfriends occasionally, but that was enough. Many women had successfully taken on this task and many more would continue to do so. She wasn't doing anything revolutionary; no need to make a scene or ask for praise. That was what she was supposed to do. Eighteen years would fly by, and then she could resume the full pursuit of her heart's desires. Helen never had the space to process any of this because it was always about Aisha and Amir.

As a woman, Aisha had tremendous empathy for Helen. As a daughter, she had been deeply hurt by the words her mother uttered. She didn't want to hold on to that bitterness much longer, though. It was hardening her heart and souring her insides. She wanted to let go—she truly did—but she didn't know how to, and she had no energy left to learn.

*

Aisha went on about the rest of her week with the same tempo. Her body was on autopilot, knowing how to take care of her basic needs. So, she just observed from yonder, from within, wherever she was, as the days went on and time lost meaning. Some days, she smoked a small amount of weed and had a glass of wine. But even those things were done out of habit and not desire, as there was no desire left in her. She was only aware of the weight of her eyelids opening and closing.

The following week, on Tuesday or Wednesday, Aisha looked through her freezer for something to throw in the oven. In the back, under something very frozen and unrecognizable, she saw the magic mushrooms David had given her in the small container. She had completely forgotten about them. She grabbed the container and stared at the dry fungi. She hadn't planned on eating them. She had planned on giving them to Amir at some point, if they hadn't gone bad by the time she saw him again, whenever that would be. Her brother had told her about a few bad trips he had taken, and it sounded like scenes from a horror movie. So, Aisha had entirely written mushrooms off.

However, after spending weeks in her apartment merely going through the motions, she was tired of feeling nothing. She wanted to feel something, anything. She would've preferred ecstasy and bliss, but perhaps seeing something terrifying that felt real in the moment would shock her enough to reboot her system. Also, Amir had told her about the amazing trips, when things were beautiful beyond words, and he felt anew once he returned to his normal state. She was okay with either option—any emotion, any feeling, whether positive or negative, would be better than this ubiquitous nothing.

Now that Aisha had decided to eat the mushrooms, she was equally nervous and excited. Doing something new lit a small fire within her. Perhaps it was just the adrenaline. Whatever it was, she was happy to already feel something. She got the mushrooms out of the container. Just gauging their size and weight in her palm, she figured it was between three to four grams. She let them thaw, then ground them.

Then, without further thought, she threw the fragments in her mouth. She immediately grimaced. She might as well have gone out and gotten a handful of dirt to swallow. This wasn't a taste she would ever want to acquire. At any rate, the deed was done. She grabbed some water, a blanket, and a banana. Then she sat on her couch and waited for something strange to happen.

Half an hour passed, and Aisha didn't feel much difference. She felt slightly more relaxed, but it wasn't anything to write home about. She had felt ten times more zen five minutes into lighting a joint. She knew psychedelics took longer to kick in, so she turned the TV on and waited. Another hour went by, and not much had changed. Things looked slightly brighter, and the TV sound was a little sharper, but that was all. She was disappointed. She wasn't expecting the mushrooms to solve all her problems, but she thought she would, at the very least, have a cool experience to break the monotony.

She turned the TV off and walked out to her balcony. The sky was dark and starless, and the moon was waning. The crickets were having a pleasant conversation, and there was a nice breeze. She would've preferred to be tripping balls, but this was fine, too. She turned around to walk back inside. She didn't understand how Amir had all those crazy experiences. She was fin—

Suddenly, she was very aware of her body. Now, the breeze hit her a little too hard, it was too dark, and she wanted the crickets to shut the fuck up. She quickly walked inside and locked the door behind her. Her apartment looked and felt different. She wasn't sure how at first. She stood in the middle of the living room and looked around to determine what changed. It was the walls.

The walls were moving.

They were wavy.

And they weren't just regular beige now; there were sassy beige, whatever that was. And all the colors had that new quality about them.

The stainless kitchen appliances were so shiny that she squinted her eyes to diffuse their sheen.

Then, Aisha realized what was happening, and she laughed. And she laughed and laughed like that for a long time, standing in the middle of the living room. Finally, she sat down because she wanted to be more comfortable to continue her laughter. Apparently, that was a mistake. Changing her position also shifted her mood. Now, she was nervous. She was anxious because of the damn walls. What were they up to? Were they after her?

Her heartbeat quickened. She took a sip of water to cool down. Then, she took a deep breath in and exhaled.

"You're just tripping, that's all. Relax," she whispered to herself.

She sat straight and wrapped the blanket around her. The material was soft, and it appeased her. Now, she wanted to be one with her blanket. She wanted to be a blanket. She wanted to be soft and gentle. She wanted to exist as any material, exist as anything except who she was. She knew she couldn't be anything else, so she cried. She felt powerless and trapped. She didn't know what to do, how to get out of the maze, how to be a blanket. So, she curled up and sobbed. She could feel how heavy and dry her eyes were.

After a while, she was tired of crying—not mentally, but physically. She wanted to move. She stood up and turned some music on, and she screamed along regardless of whether she knew the songs or not. She jumped and danced and sang until she was tired of that, too. Now, she had to pee.

When Aisha walked into the bathroom, she was staggered by her reflection. She looked ghastly. Her eyes were bloodshot, her hair was flattened on the left and thick and wild on the right, and her lips were chapped. It was truly an awful sight, which made her laugh the hardest she had all night. So, she peed and laughed. When she stood again to wash her hands, she caught another glimpse of that horrendous thing in the mirror. Now, she was back to crying. What in the actual hell was happening? She would never eat mushrooms again.

Eventually, she passed out on her couch with a banana peel by her feet.

*

When Aisha woke up the following day, her head was throbbing. This was almost as bad as a hangover. Though she had a mean headache, she felt noticeably lighter. She cried profusely last night, so it made sense. She didn't feel anew, though. If she had any profound realization at some point, she couldn't recall.

However, she felt a general sense of calmness. She most likely had some mist of the fungi in her system still, so that, too, made sense. The feeling that rose above everything else was claustrophobia. Perhaps it was all the jumping and screaming, but that morning, her apartment felt very stuffy and small. She needed to get out of there. She needed some fresh air. She put on some shorts and tennis shoes, grabbed some water, and drove to the trail.

It was a beautiful day outside. The temperature was in the mid-seventies, the sky was clear, and the trail wasn't crowded. She began her stroll. She was walking extremely slowly. An old lady with a very large hat walked by her left. Then an old man who advanced like he was powered by the sun was next to her for one moment and a small dot in the distance the next. She maintained her snail's pace. She wanted to soak in outside. It had been so long since she had been out in nature.

Although she was moving leisurely, her thighs and lower back were still on fire. The months of idleness had left their mark. Even though she was tired, she didn't take a break. But she slowed her pace even more. Her goal was to make it to the lake and sit on the dock.

It was a quiet walk. Not only was nature surprisingly silent, but so was her mind. She didn't question or try to analyze why; she just kept walking. And eventually, she made it to the lake. The view was as stunning as she remembered. She sat on the edge of the dock with her feet dangling over the edge.

The sun was right above her head, creating a golden glint on the water's surface. She was surprised no one else was there because it was such a beautiful scene. She just stared at the water for a few minutes and appreciated the warm breeze on her skin. The gentle wind created small waves moving in her direction.

Then, Aisha wondered: what if she jumped in the water? What if she dove in and let herself sink? How far would she make it down before the water was in her lungs? How far would she make it before it was all over?

Or would she have the sudden realization, as she was letting herself drown, that there wasn't anything for her to see on the lakebed? Would she understand, at last, that she didn't need to hit rock bottom to propel herself back to the surface?

Would it be too late by then?

The waves kept rocking in her direction. Then, she felt a strong current from within herself, moving toward her surface with an uncompromising wrath. If it made it out, it would be devastating, so she had a decision to make.

She could use all her might to push it back down to the abyss it originated from. She could continue down the same path she had been on over the last few months and act like it wasn't down there. She could continue to avoid facing it because she was afraid. She could come up with other distractions and other ways to delay their encounter. She could even live the rest of her life that way and keep running from it until the very end. Or here and now, seated on this dock, she could finally see its ugly face and let it hit her.

She chose to let it.

And it came out with a vengeance because it wasn't supposed to be down there that long. It was supposed to be released into the ether years ago. It wasn't supposed to stay in the deep dark as long as she had held it. So, it grew into a monstrosity and was out to collect the sorrow it was owed. The Big Sad. Here it was. And she saw it completely: grotesque, savage, and forsaken.

Then, it hit her, and she fell apart.

She wept for everything. All the pain she had endured and all the pain she had caused. Everything she had done and everything she hadn't. Who she was then and who she was now. All the people who had hurt her and all the ones she had hurt. The time passed, and the time left. The stream of tears seemed endless, and there came a point when she wasn't sure what she was crying about. But it didn't matter.

She finally understood that she didn't need to have all the answers at once.

PART IV

WEEK 46

Aisha was surprised that she wasn't immediately sweating when she walked to her car. The temperature was finally below seventy-five degrees. There was a lovely breeze, which gave her an extra pep in her step when she arrived at the trail. She had decided to walk the path at least two times a week, whether she felt like it or not. Hell, she'd drive there to just sit on one of the benches if she had to.

Whatever she did when she made it to the trail was irrelevant. The only thing that mattered was being outside. The last three months taught her that she was a creature of habit. So, if she could get used to laying on her couch and doing nothing, she could get accustomed to driving to the trail a couple of times a week to breathe some nature in.

That was her main goal this week. She didn't want to do too much too soon. She needed to take it easy, slow and steady. The last thing she needed to do was press her foot on the pedal too hard and lose control of herself again. There was no need to rush to the end of the tunnel and risk crashing into the darkness.

No matter how long it'd take, how slow and carefully she had to stroll toward the light, the only thing that would matter in the end was the end. How long it took to get there and how many times she fell and failed would be part of her story, sure, but it wouldn't dim the light at the end of this.

She walked slowly on the concrete path. It was a little more crowded today, and she was happy about that. It was nice to see people out and about, living their lives. Spending so much time alone put her existence at the core of the universe, and it was quite a heavy load to bear. It made living such a grave thing. Her low spirits over the past months weighed even more than they were supposed to because everything she felt was the Earth's orbit. Simply being outside and seeing people talk, walk, laugh, sit, be, relieved her of that burden. Whatever she did or didn't do over the last few months didn't stop the world from going round. That realization lightened her gait.

The old lady with the large hat she saw last week walked past her with an even larger hat. Aisha smiled, then looked in front of her and kept walking. Not many thoughts crossed her mind. She mostly thought about the last text messages from her mother and Amir. They popped up on her screen when she turned her phone back on earlier. Though Amir hadn't sent an actual reply to her *Happy Birthday*. He had just "liked" her message. Her mother had sent a short answer. Her words lacked the warmth Aisha was used to.

Thank you, sweetie. I hope all is well.

Aisha let out a loud breath. This week was about spending time outside of her apartment. Depending on how she felt in a few days, she would contact Amir and her mother to finally talk things out.

She continued to walk for a few minutes. She turned around when she reached a dead end lined with tall trees. Then, she took a moment to notice how even she felt. Her mind wasn't racing with all the ways the two conversations could go wrong and damage both relationships. She still had no idea what she'd say and knew things could derail if she said the wrong thing.

But right now, the breeze was hitting her face at the right angle, the sun had finally chilled out, people were passing her with courteous nods and pleasant smiles, and her lower back wasn't on fire from the one-hour walk. So, whatever happened when she'd talk to her brother and mother felt too distant to affect her.

When Aisha made it back to her car, she couldn't help but pause. She frowned when she opened the door because things were going too smoothly. She felt too good. This couldn't be it. Sure, she had a nice cry last week and let it all out, but that possibly couldn't have fixed everything. She was too calm, too restful, too serene. This shift basically happened overnight. Things that came too easily were gone just as fast. Clearly, she was still in the ebb and flow cycle. She was up now because the breeze was lovely and the sun was gentle, but before she knew it would be dark and suffocating again, and she'd be back down. The other shoe always dropped.

So, Aisha drove home with those negative thoughts. She anxiously walked inside her apartment, prepared for the current to change direction and rock against her. At that moment, she was ready to fight it, push it away, swim away from it, block its flow, and do whatever she had to do to continue feeling good.

Then, she remembered she had been here before. She had done this before. In fact, this was what she had always done for as long as she could remember. This was the behavior that led her here in the first place. She never allowed herself to completely feel good because she was so anxious to feel pain and hurt. So, she preemptively chipped away at her happiness to not feel the brunt of the sadness. Thus, she never felt the full impact of any emotion: happiness or sadness, and anything in between.

Last week on the dock was the first time she had finally allowed herself to feel unaltered pain. And it was so freeing. But here she was, not even a week later, close to falling back into her old pattern. She needed some help.

Aisha walked to her room and found Dahlia's therapist card. She called and scheduled the soonest appointment. The nice lady who answered let her know Dr. Lawrence was fully booked this week and the next for new consultations, however, she was accepting new clients. Aisha confirmed her appointment at the end of the month, on November twenty-ninth. Ideally, she would've preferred to meet with her today, but she was happy to have something set in stone. It appeased her for the time being.

When she put Dr. Lawrence's card back on the table, she saw the other card Dahlia had given her. Her student's nonprofit's contact. Aisha was ready to volunteer and help with whatever they needed. She read the name on the card before dialing.

Marcus Wilson.

She gasped. Marcus? *C'mon! Really?* Surely, it wasn't *that* Marcus. Marcus was a very common name. There was no way this was the guy from the coffee shop she had lost her shit on a few months ago. She shook her head and dropped her shoulders.

Of course, it was going to be him because it was her, and just for her, the universe always had a little jokey joke in store. She hesitated for a moment, but then she dialed. Marcus was doing a good thing, and she wanted to help. He was obviously a better human being than her, so he wouldn't prevent her from volunteering because of what she had done. He would separate the crazy outburst from the person who wanted to help. And it wasn't going to be him anyway. But if it was him, perhaps it was for the best, because she owed Marcus an apology.

The phone kept beeping. She held her breath. Someone picked up on the fourth ring. It was a woman. Aisha relaxed at the sound of her voice.

"Marcus Wilson Association, how can I help you?" the woman said.

"Hey! I'd like to volunteer. My friend told me you might need some help packing food and other stuff. I can help with whatever you need."

"Yes, ma'am. That's wonderful. Thank you so much! We can use some help with packing food especially. When do you want to come by? We have morning, afternoon, and evening shifts all week."

"Tomorrow morning is perfect. I might do afternoons other days if that's okay?"

"Absolutely! Whenever you're available. Just let us know about twelve hours before, so we can add your name to the list. Oh, what's your name? I'll go ahead and add you for tomorrow morning now."

"Perfect! Aisha Jones."

"What a lovely name. I'm Martha, by the way. The morning shift is from 9:30 AM to 12:30 PM. Is that okay?"

"Yes."

"Wonderful! Do you need the address?"

"I think I have it on your card. Is it 2419 Cedar Road?"

"That's it. You can send me a picture of your driver's license today if that's okay, so you won't have to do it in the morning. If not, no worries, you can just bring it tomorrow for check-in."

"I'll send it right now."

"Wonderful! Then you're all set, Miss Jones. Mr. Wilson supervises the morning shifts, and I'll be at the front desk if you need anything. We'll see you in the morning!"

"See you then!"

The following day, Aisha surprised herself when she reached for her foundation. She couldn't remember the last time she put any makeup on. The chances that Marcus Wilson was *Libros & Libations* Marcus were slim to none. But on the off chance it was him, it'd be best if she covered the pimple that had sprung on her chin during her sleep. Did pimples know when you had plans? Three months in her apartment with a clear face, and today was the day this thing decided to make an appearance. She chuckled, then examined her face post-coverage. Unless she could make the zit disappear, this was as good as it'd get.

Aisha walked inside the Marcus Wilson Association at 9:20 AM. Her heart was beating fast. The closer she made it to the front desk, the more she was convinced it was going to be *that* Marcus. Of course, it was going to be him. And he was going to be shocked and perhaps even upset to see the crazy bitch from the coffee shop in front of him. She considered turning around when a beautiful older woman with gorgeous white dreadlocks welcomed her in.

"Hello! You must be Miss Jones. How are you?"

"Yes. Hello. Martha, right?"

"Right. Thank you so much for coming! Sometimes, people sign up but don't show up." She shook her head behind the desk, then she grinned. "Do you need some water or coffee, Miss Jones?"

"No, thank you, Martha. Please call me Aisha."

"Okay, Aisha. I got you checked in already. Please have a seat." Martha pointed at the chairs on her right. "Marcus is in the backroom, and he'll be here shortly to get you guys started."

"Sounds great, thank you," Aisha said.

She sat in one of the eight chairs against the wall opposite Martha. There was one man and one woman in the corner. They looked to be a couple in their early sixties. They waved at her, and she waved back. On the other side of the room was a family of four. The parents were probably in their late forties, and the kids were in their early teens. Finally, there was a young man, wearing a backwards hat, sitting alone in the opposite corner while scrolling through his phone. They all look very comfortable. Clearly, it wasn't their first rodeo.

She looked around the room. The wall was covered with pictures of children from kindergarten to high school senior year. They were playing, studying, eating, dancing, praying, graduating. No matter what they were doing, they all looked very happy and content. It warmed her heart. The lobby was about the size of her living room. Five doors framed the space: two restrooms, two offices, and another room by the backwards hat guy. It was probably the backroom Martha had referred to.

Aisha was moved by the modesty and warmth of the space. She was moved that some people's life work was bettering other people's lives. She felt incredibly selfish and self-absorbed at that moment. She understood that to help anyone else put their oxygen mask on, she first had to ensure she could breathe. She was very clear on that. But now that she could finally feel some oxygen get through her airways—even though her own mask wasn't entirely in place yet—she was eager to fasten it so she could positively impact other people's lives.

The backroom door swung open at 9:29 AM. The phone guy straightened up and put the device in his pocket. The family was playing an incomprehensible name game and paused at "Zuri." The man and woman on her right had barely moved. Aisha was scared to look back up and see *that* Marcus. She was anxious for their eyes to meet and for him to recognize her. She took a quiet breath in and a quieter breath out. She was here to pack some goods for the awesome kids on the wall, so whichever Marcus this was would have to accept her presence.

"Hello, everyone," Marcus said.

Aisha looked up at the unfamiliar voice. It wasn't Coffee Shop Marcus. She was equally relieved and disappointed. It would've been nice to see the other Marcus and apologize. She shrugged all her angst off and focused on Marcus Wilson, who looked just as good, if not better, than the other Marcus. His smile was dazzling, and so was his wedding band. Finally, Aisha focused on what the man was saying.

"Who's here for the first time?" he asked.

Aisha was the only one who raised her hand. Everyone clapped.

"Welcome," Marcus said. "Thank you so much for being here. If you don't mind, could you introduce yourself and tell us what brings you here today?"

"My name is Aisha. My friend, Dahlia, told me about what you're doing, and I wanted to help."

"Ah, yes! She's my favorite salsa dance instructor. I haven't seen her at the studio in a while, though. Is she doing well?"

Before Aisha could answer, the backwards hat guy spoke. "You dance salsa, C?" He laughed. "With your two left feet? I need to see that, please!"

Everyone else laughed, including Martha. Although Aisha was new, she already felt like she was part of the group, so she joined in.

"Aisha, c'mon! Don't listen to them," Marcus said, "I got moves." Then he did the "moves" he was referring to.

For a second, Aisha genuinely thought he was having a stroke. When it was clear that he was dancing, she was the first one to resume the laughter. Everyone else followed.

Marcus finally stopped whatever he was doing and laughed. "Alright, I see how it is. Looks like you're going to fit right in, Aisha." He shook his head with residual laughter. "Anyway, shall we get started?"

"Yes!" they all shouted.

They walked into the back room, which had about seven tables and some equipment in the front. In the very back, a bunch of goods were stored very neatly. Marcus told them what needed to be done today. He took some time to explain the packaging process, and he made sure to focus on Aisha when he explained each step.

Backwards hat guy, who went by "E," told her that she could watch him until she got the hang of it. Everyone else offered to help her or answer any questions she had at any time——even the teenagers. After watching E weigh and bag about three pounds of rice and some veggies, she felt confident and moved to her own station.

Marcus turned some house music on, and everyone worked without interruption. It was a rhythmic and seamless sequence: pick up the goods, weigh them, put them in a bag and seal, throw them in the box, and repeat. She quickly found her workflow and thought of nothing except the task at hand.

When the music stopped and Marcus told them the shift was over, Aisha was shocked. There was no way three hours had flown by so fast. Everyone cleaned their station and walked back to the lobby.

"Nice to meet you, Aisha!" the couple said.

"Great job today!" the parents said.

"Bye!" The teenagers waved.

"See you next time!" E said.

"Thank you so much for your help today," Marcus said. "Hopefully, we'll see you again?"

"Absolutely!" Aisha said.

"Thank you for coming, Aisha," Martha said with that lovely smile. "You can schedule your next shift on the website or just call me."

"Will do." Aisha grinned as she walked out. "See you soon!"

She signed up for three other shifts that week. E was there the second time she returned, so she sat next to him while they waited for Marcus to come to the lobby. There were five other people that morning: two women who were friends or related, and three other people who came separately.

One of them raised their hands when Marcus asked if anyone was there for the first time. Everyone else clapped. Aisha felt proud to be on the clapping side. E wasn't there the third time she went, but the couple from the first time was. They were very happy to see her and told her about the Border Collie they had recently rescued. Marcus gave her a high-five at the end of the shift.

Martha greeted her with a hug during her final shift of the week, and Aisha almost teared up. The family of four walked in right after her and beamed when they recognized her. After they asked how she was doing, they began their name game at "Janice." The game was truly an enigma that could only be understood by members of their family. They shared a beautiful bond, and seeing how close they all were gripped Aisha's insides.

Once upon a time, she, too, shared a similar bond with her family: her mother and her brother. Now, it was a thing of the past. It would be difficult to get back to that remote place where they shared intimate moments no one else was privy to. She profoundly missed her family. It would be a very challenging task to get back to that place, but certainly not an impossible one.

She just hoped it wasn't too late to fix their relationships.

WEEK 47

When she got up that morning, Aisha felt incredible resolve flowing through her veins. She felt strong and rested. Today was the day she would have an honest conversation with her brother. She knew Amir was still upset with her, but she was confident that he would, at the very least, crack the door to hear what she had to say.

After she got a cup of coffee, she picked up her phone to call him. To her shock, her phone rang when she reached for it, and it was her brother. She looked at the screen to make sure she wasn't the one calling him. Her eyes were not deceiving her; Amir was the one calling. Now her heart raced because her brother wouldn't call her unless something terrible had happened.

"Hey…Hello? What's going on? Is Mom okay?" she said, panting.

"Uh…yeah. Are you?"

"Oh…yes. I just didn't expect you to call. I was actually about to call you."

"Sure."

"I was, I swear. I miss you. It's so weird you called today. It's like telepathy."

Amir chuckled. "Do you know what today is?"

"Monday?"

"Lord." He sighed. "It's your birthday."

Aisha looked at the date on her phone. She, in fact, turned thirty-two today. "Oh, wow. I didn't even notice, that's crazy."

"Yeah, it is. So, no plans then?"

"No, I was literally about to call you. That was my plan for today."

"To talk about what?"

"Everything."

"Can you narrow it down? I'm off today, and I'm trying to binge-watch *The Good Place*."

"Well, I was hoping we could talk and get back to…*our good place*." She tittered.

Amir didn't speak, and it was complete silence for a few seconds.

"Amir? Hello? Are you still there?"

He cleared his throat. "Yes. I just wanted you to sit with that terrible joke for a moment."

They both laughed.

"I miss you," Aisha said.

"Ditto. But I'm still mad at you. What you said last time was very hurtful."

"I know. I'm sorry."

"I opened up to you about feeling unwanted by Mom and Dad, and you basically made a mockery of it."

"I know. That was fucked up. I'm so sorry."

"Then, I don't hear from you for four months, except for some thumbs up emojis and a 'happy birthday' text. How do you think that makes me feel?"

"I really messed up, Amir, and I'm so sorry. I wish I could go back and handle things differently. You were vulnerable and open with me, and in return, I was an ass. Truth is, I was in a really bad place, but that didn't warrant my behaving that way. I sincerely apologize."

"Thank you."

"Do you accept my apology?" she asked with a small voice.

"You were really a bitch day. A nasty one. But I could tell you weren't doing well. You hurt me, but clearly, you were in pain, too. You weren't in a good head space, you needed me, and I shut you out. These past months, I was scared you'd lose your mind there and do something stupid, but I stayed cold and distant. That was messed up too." He exhaled. "I accept your apology, and I offer my own. I'm sorry, Sha."

Aisha was crying. "Amir, you don't owe me an apology. I'm your big sister. I'm supposed to protect you. I'm supposed to be a good example. I'm supposed to be there for you. I've failed at all of it. You're always being a better person than me. I'm so proud to be your sister. I don't deserve—"

"Stop. Drop all those heavy expectations you've put on yourself. They've weighed you down for too long. All I expect from you is your love. All I want for you is your well-being…and how are you going to protect me when you're one hundred pounds soaking wet?" He sniveled and laughed at the same time.

"One hundred and twenty-one pounds, thank you very much!" She laughed and wiped her humid eyes. "I love you, big bro."

"I love you too, little sis."

She heard Amir blow his nose. "Ew. You could've hit mute to do that," she said.

"Whatever, *bruh*. You should do something today. Go for a drink? Go to a live show? Anything. You only turn thirty-seven once, you know."

"I turned thirty-two, asshole."

He laughed. "I'm just saying, you should do something memorable. So, what are you thinking?"

"I'm going to call Mom to talk about things."

"Phew. Alright. I would've personally ordered a Veuve Clicquot at a nice restaurant, but to each their own, I guess." He cleared his throat and spoke solemnly. "I think she'll be very happy to talk to you. She misses you a lot. She has been waiting for you."

Amir and Aisha exchanged one more "I love you" before hanging up.

She felt like wings were growing on her back after she got off the call with her brother. She felt them flapping behind her. Though she felt lighter than a feather, something still prevented her from taking off. She called her mother to get that final weight off.

Helen picked up on the second ring. "Happy birthday, honey," she said.

"Thank you, Mom. How are you?"

"Better now. And you?"

"Better too. I just spoke to Amir."

"That's good. He really misses you."

"Me too. Hmm…it's been a while since we last spoke."

"Yes."

She waited for her mother to say something else, but Helen didn't. So, Aisha continued, "So, about our last conversation, I'm sorry for screaming at you like that."

"It's okay. I know you were hurt."

"Mom, about what you said that day…I'm still hurt by that."

"I know, and I'm so sorry, honey."

"Please be honest with me. Did you mean that? Do you feel like your life would've turned out better if you didn't have me? I want you to be honest, Mom. I promise I won't yell or anything. I just want to get to the bottom of this once and for all."

Aisha was hoping her mother wouldn't even let her finish her sentence and immediately affirm that, of course, she hadn't meant it. How could Aisha even think that for a second? She was just overwhelmed with everything at the time but hadn't meant any of it.

However, Helen didn't cut her off and interject with the words and delivery Aisha had hoped. In fact, her mother took what felt like too much time to answer. "You and Amir are the best thing that ever happened to me. Aisha, you're my firstborn. I'll never forget how complete I felt when I held you in my arms for the first time. I love you more than you'll ever know." She paused for another moment and took a breath. "I wish I could honestly tell you I didn't mean a word of what I said that day. I wish I could earnestly say that, but if I did, I would be lying."

Aisha's heart dropped. She wanted to say something that would make what she had just heard null and void, but her lips couldn't move. Her throat was dry.

Helen continued, "Do I regret having you? Absolutely not! Do I think I would've had more opportunities if I didn't get pregnant when I did? Yes."

Aisha's brain carefully filtered all the words her mother uttered to confirm that she loved her and didn't regret having her. Her brain, with all its years of experience, surgically grasped the words that would hurt her the most and made them echo in her head. And it was only because of the new wings that sprung from her talk with Amir that she maintained her posture and let her mother continue.

"I lost my volleyball scholarship because I was pregnant. I had no other way of paying for college, so I had to drop out. I had to put my dreams on hold to take care of you. I ended up getting my degree at forty years old. If I graduated in my twenties and had the chance to open my salon then, instead of just a few years ago, there's no telling how far I would've been by now."

Helen exhaled. "But if I could redo it all over again, and there was even a slim chance that I wouldn't have you, I wouldn't do it again. I wish I didn't lose my scholarship and that people didn't look down on me because I was a single teenage mom. As difficult as it was, if redoing things meant that I wouldn't have you, I wouldn't change a thing. And that's God's honest truth."

Aisha felt the wings grow stronger, lightly lifting her off the ground. "I understand, Mom. I don't know what I would've done if I were in your shoes. I'm a selfish person. I don't know if I would've even put my own kids before my desires."

"You're not selfish, sweetheart."

"Yes, I am. I only think about myself and the way I feel all the time. How I feel is the only thing that matters, and I shut people off if they try to take significant space in my life."

"Sometimes, it's okay to be selfish, baby. Sometimes, you ought to put yourself first. I wish I was more like you when I was younger. Sometimes, I regret not being a little more selfish."

Aisha put her phone in her other ear before her next question. "What did you ever see in Albert, Mom?"

Her mom chuckled. "I know you don't want to hear this, but you have a lot in common with your fathe—"

"No, I don—"

"Let me finish, honey. I know he wasn't present, and you have every right to despise him. I'm not trying to defend him, trust me. But he wasn't all bad. As a father, I'm definitely giving him an F." Helen laughed at the grade, which made Aisha smile. "But as a human being, he had some qualities. At least the man I fell in love with did."

"Like what?"

"He was quick-witted, like you. Charming, like you. And he had this way of being so deep in his own head that made you want to be part of his life. Like he had this whole other vibrant world in his mind. And he marched to the beat of his own drum, like you. He did what he wanted to do and was unapologetic about it, so when he opened the door to let you in, you ran to get inside. He also had a kind of vulnerability about him, like a wounded animal, so even when he did you wrong, you wanted to hold him because you knew deep down, he was in a lot of pain."

"That doesn't excuse him from abandoning us and abandoning you. We all have wounds, Mom. I know you do too. I'm sure you could've run too, but you stayed. He left. I don't care how wounded he was. Then don't have kids! Don't make promises you can't keep. He was a selfish coward, simple as that."

Helen's voice went down one decibel, but her tone was assured. "I don't disagree. Whatever happened to him doesn't justify his behavior. He was a coward, but he wasn't evil. I don't want your dislike for him to take too much space in your heart and stifle you. He did what he did, and that was his cross to bear, not yours to hold on to. He's gone now, Aisha. I think it's time you let go, too."

Aisha was silent for a long time. Her mother didn't say anything else. It was nice. Silence was always nice when it was a deliberate choice, after what had been kept quiet had finally been said out loud. The complete silence made Aisha's air conditioning seem louder. She was still running her A/C twenty-four-seven. Since it was finally cooling down outside, the poor thing would be able to take a break soon.

She switched her phone back to her other ear again. "You're right, Mom. It's time to let go."

"Good. I'm proud of you, baby, and I love you."

"I love you too, Mom. And I miss you so much."

Helen's voice cracked. "I miss you so very much, you have no idea. I'm not rushing you; I know you still need to be away right now with everything that's going on. But just know when you get back, I'm giving you the longest hug in history, and there's nothing you can do about that!"

Aisha grinned. "Well, we might just break a record because I was planning on doing the same thing!"

"I'm just so happy right now, I don't know what to do with myself."

"Me too!"

"Well, it's your birthday! Why don't I send you a little something, and you go somewhere very fancy and spend an outrageous amount on a nice birthday dinner?"

"Mom, you don't have to."

"Nonsense!" Aisha heard some movement on the other side of the line. "The money is in your account now. Get you something nice or do something fun! I can't believe I have a thirty-two-year-old. You know, this really handsome man keeps coming to the salon when he doesn't need much done to his hair. The other day, he told me he thought I was thirty-five. Now, I know he's lying and just been nice, but it's always nice to hear."

"Sounds like someone has a crush on you, Mom."

"You think? He's very attractive. He's a widow. He has three grown kids, two dogs, and one cat. He plays tennis on the weekend. He invited me to play and then grab a bite, but I don't know, I'm nervous. I haven't done anything like that in over a decade. I don't know if I should accept his invitation."

"You should absolutely accept his invite. He sounds like a catch!"

"He does, doesn't it? And he's so handsome! Okay, I'll go." Helen's voice rose with excitement.

"Please keep me posted, okay?"

"Yes!"

"I love you, Mom."

"I love you, baby."

*

That evening, Aisha dressed up and went to an upscale Italian restaurant. She knew it was going to be very fancy and luxurious because the prices weren't listed on the menu. The check was meant to be an expensive surprise that could possibly cause a stroke if unprepared. Thankfully, she was prepared to sit at her table and receive the five-star treatment she came for.

After the doorman opened the tall blackwood door for her, the hostess greeted her under a large gold crystal chandelier. Her smile and her French braid were impeccable.

"Hello, miss. How are you doing this evening?"

"Wonderful! About yourself?"

"Very well, thank you for asking. Do you have a reservation?"

"Yes, under Aisha Jones."

The young woman scrolled down her screen. "Ah, yes. Miss Jones. Party of one?"

Aisha grinned. "Yes!"

WEEK 48

Aisha walked the trail on Monday. She signed up for the afternoon shift at Marcus Wilson Association on Tuesday. She had followed the same routine last week. She walked the trail every other day and volunteered on the days she didn't walk. Though her days weren't packed compared to how busy her mother had told her the salon was and how high the call volume had gotten at Amir's job, her days felt full to her.

When she got home for her walk on Wednesday morning, she thought of Dahlia. Nonprofit Marcus told her that her friend hadn't been at the dance studio in a long time. Aisha wondered if Dahlia had finally quit, had found a better opportunity, or had her parents agree to loan her the money to open her own studio.

She wondered how her friend was doing. She hoped Dahlia had healed from the wound that reopened when she decided to give Cheating Mark a second chance. Aisha was also worried Dahlia might be upset with her. After all, she had returned to Dallas weeks ago and had offered to meet. Then, Aisha was still in the bad place where nothing except bleakness was allowed, so she had kind of blown her friend off. She thought about whether she should text Dahlia now or wait. If she ruminated too long on this, she'd find a reason to wait.

She sent the text. *Hey Dahlia how are you? I know it's been a long time and Im sorry for taking so long to get back. A lot has happened. I'm sure same goes for you. I'd love to catch up soon whenever you're free. Just let me know the time and the place!*

As soon as she hit *send*, she threw her phone on the couch like she was playing hot potato. She wanted to mitigate the angst of waiting for an answer by not seeing her phone, as if she didn't understand object permanence. She picked it back up two hours later, confident that Dahlia's answer would brighten her screen, but there wasn't anything from her. However, Amir had sent her a meme that made her laugh. It was about online dating and read:

No one:

Me after swiping right on all the profiles ever:

Then, the photo underneath was Popeye's forearm.

Amir hadn't spoken to Thomas since they broke up. So, her brother had signed up for all the dating sites. Every single one. She had never heard of most of them. These sites were multiplying everywhere like milkweed. And apparently, some were just as toxic at the roots. Aisha knew Amir was still not over Thomas.

She remembered scoffing at the concept of "The One" until she saw her brother and his ex-boyfriend together. Although she was still skeptical about the idea, their relationship truly felt like two people who were made for each other. It was the way they spoke without talking, how comfortable they were around each other, how they could laugh till they cried at the weirdest shit only they understood, and how they held each other like no one else existed. Their bond had moved her to tears on several occasions.

Still, Aisha believed it wasn't that the person you ended up with was a special being crafted specifically for you. In her opinion, the person you ended up with was someone you intentionally chose based on compatibility and readiness to commit. She recalled that James had furrowed his brow when she had shared those thoughts with him.

"So, you don't believe in soulmates?" he had asked, lying on his side of the bed.

"Not really. At best, I think we might have multiple soulmates, several people who check most of our boxes, and whoever we end up with is mostly based on luck and timing. Like, our paths have to cross when we're both ready to settle down."

James sat up, and the satin pillowcase slightly wrinkled behind him. "So, you think there are people out there that we're both just as compatible with and can be just as if not happier with?"

Aisha sat up as well. She adjusted her satin bonnet that had moved too close to her eyebrows. "I don't know about happier, but just as, sure. But it's irrelevant now, isn't it? We found each other at the right time." She gave him a soft peck on the lips.

"Right." James turned the lights off, lay down, and closed his eyes.

Now, another hour had passed, and Dahlia had still not texted her back. Aisha walked to the kitchen to make lunch. Then she turned the TV on to watch a movie. After the movie ended, she checked her phone again—still nothing from Dahlia. If Aisha had ruined this new friendship, it would be a hard pill to swallow.

If Dahlia had decided to cut her off, Aisha would understand. She couldn't put people on hold indefinitely and expect them to still be on the line whenever she was ready to resume. They had the right to hang up at any time after waiting and waiting. They had the right to move on to people who valued their time. Aisha would be hurt if Dahlia had made that choice, but she'd understand.

When the crickets got louder outside, and the moon was bright, Aisha accepted she wouldn't get a response tonight, so she got ready for bed. Before she turned the lights off, her phone lit up.

Hey girl! Sorry for texting back so late. Today was INSANE. I'm happy to hear from you, I was starting to worry. Yes a lot has happened!! Nia will spend Thanksgiving with Mark and his family tomorrow. I was planning on having a self-care day but I'd love to see you! Why don't we grab Thanksgiving dinner somewhere?

Aisha had forgotten all about Thanksgiving until she went grocery shopping a few days ago, and huge birds weighed down people's carts. Later that same day, Amir and her mother had texted her in their undead group chat to ask what she was doing for Thanksgiving. She told them the truth: nothing. They told her they weren't doing much either, just a little dinner with turkey, mashed potatoes, greens, sweet potatoes, cornbread, ham, mac and cheese, and a small pecan pie for dessert. She considered going home then.

Thanksgiving was their favorite holiday. They always spent it together, the three of them, and whoever else they invited. Last year, they invited James, Sam, Thomas, and one of Helen's new hairstylists who was new in town. They told stories and laughed until everyone had digested their food.

Aisha wanted to go home, but she felt it wasn't time yet. She was so close to reaching the end of that long tunnel. She just needed a little more time to get to the light.

She replied to her friend. *Yes let's do that! How's 6:30ish?*

Dahlia confirmed that the time worked for her, and she sent Aisha three restaurants with Thanksgiving specials. Aisha picked the one that was the closest drive for Dahlia.

Aisha was very excited when she walked into the diner.

She was the first to arrive and gave Dahlia's name to the hostess since the reservation was under her. She sat on the side of the booth facing the entrance. The place was surprisingly packed. She had never eaten out on Thanksgiving and assumed that almost everyone spent that day in someone's home. In front of her was a family of six looking at the menu.

Behind her was a very diverse group of friends: three women and two men of different shades and ages. At the bar, one couple was framed by two singles sitting at the end of the curved counter. The lone woman was swaying to the country music coming out of the speakers above her head while drinking a cocktail in a giant glass. Aisha smiled and pictured herself in her place.

"Hey girl!" Dahlia said. "Daydreaming?"

Aisha rose to hug her. Without any conscious thought, she said, "I missed you!" Her eyes widened because she had meant to say, "Hey!"

Dahlia looked at her and grinned. "I missed you too, girl! It's been too long." She sat down. "You look good!"

"Thank you. So do you!"

They both ordered one of the Thanksgiving specials and a bottle of wine.

Dahlia tasted the wine first, then gazed at Aisha. "Tell me everything. You look like a new woman."

"I do?"

"You do. I was really worried about you last time. I thought about you when I was at my parents' home. I wish I could've been here with you, but I needed to be away. But I was worried about you."

"It wasn't fair of me to ask you to stay here solely for me. I'm sorry. You did the right thing."

Dahlia nodded. "So, what have I missed?"

Aisha took a bite of her mac and cheese. "Honestly, not much. I didn't get out of the house for a long time. I wasn't doing well. It was bad, but I'm better now. I actually started volunteering at Marcus's nonprofit recently. It's been very grounding for me. He's a great guy. I'm inspired by what he's doing for those kids."

"Such a great guy! I'm so happy to hear that, that's great. Have you gotten a chance to speak with Kenya?"

"Kenya?"

"Dr. Lawrence."

"Oh, not yet, but I have an appointment with her tomorrow. I'm nervous but excited. I feel like I'm so close to being more than okay."

Dahlia was slicing a piece of ham. She dropped the utensils to pat Aisha's hand. "You are. I can see it. Keep doing what you're doing."

"Thank you." Aisha smiled. "How was the countryside?"

Dahlia picked up her fork and knife and resumed cutting. "Good, very good."

The waiter stopped by their table. "How's everything?"

"Good, very good," Dahlia said to him.

Aisha smiled and nodded to second that the food was good. The server smiled and walked away.

"Okay." Aisha stared at Dahlia. "Did you share your business plan with your parents?"

Dahlia was staring at her plate now. "I did."

"You don't want to talk about it?"

She finally looked up at Aisha. "No, it's not that. They were supportive, but they couldn't lend me the money. My dad was really sick earlier this year, and I thought their insurance took care of most of it, but apparently, they had to pay a lot out of pocket for his medical expenses." She sighed. "They pay so much for their health insurance, so I don't understand why it wouldn't cover them more."

She took a sip of the wine, then rested her head in the palm of her hand. "Anyway, Dad's better now, which is the only thing that matters, but their savings took a big hit. They have some investments, so unless they're not telling me everything not to worry me, I think they should be okay. But they can't lend me the money. They offered to give me a portion, but I couldn't accept it. I feel like I should be taking care of them, you know.

"I'm thirty-six, and I feel like I'm starting over. I think that's also part of why I was trying to make things work with Mark. With him, I had a foundation, a safety net. Now, I'm an unemployed, divorced mother of one. Oh yeah, I quit because screw them. And I know I'll find another job. I have a little saved to be okay for a few months. The problem isn't getting a job. The issue is that I have this dream that seems so out of reach because it takes money that I don't have to make it happen."

Without skipping a bit, Aisha asked, "How much would you need?"

"Like, twenty to twenty-five thousand to get started. I tried to take out a loan, but I had some hard hits to my credit after the divorce that I'm still working on, so I was declined."

"I can lend you the money."

Dahlia dropped her hand on the table and looked at Aisha like a deer caught in headlights. "What?"

"I have some money saved. I can lend you the money. I don't feel passionate about anything right now to put my money into it. Maybe I will someday. Maybe I won't. Either way, I want to help you pursue *your* dreams. That money's just sitting around. At least it can be put to better use."

Dahlia's head cocked like that girl from *The Ring* who came out of the TV. "Are you serious?"

Aisha tittered. "Yes."

"Oh my God!" She covered her mouth not to scream. "Okay, we'll put a contract together for the payments. I want to make sure you get your money back on time. Oh my God, Aisha! You have no idea what this means to me. I don't know what to say…thank you."

"It's no problem. And no interest, no rush on the repayment, whatever is feasible for you. I believe in you and your dream."

Dahlia stood up and leaped to hug her. "Thank you, Aisha."

When they parted from the embrace, their eyes were redder than the wine in the glasses.

"Okay, let's talk about something else," Aisha said, grabbing napkins from the holder to wipe her face. She handed a few to Dahlia. "How's Nia?"

Dahlia wiped her face and blew her nose loudly. One of the kids from the family of six, in the booth in front of them, stared at her with a disgusted look. Dahlia saw him and made a silly face. Aisha and the kid laughed.

Dahlia stood up and sat back down across from Aisha. "Nia's great. She's such a good kid. We're very lucky," she finally said. "Since she spent last Thanksgiving with me and my parents, she's with Mark this year. They invited me, but I didn't want to go. I'm not ready to be around Mark like that."

"I hear you."

"Do you think you'll ever talk to your ex-friend and boyfriend again, or you've turned that page and don't need an…explanation from them?"

"I don't know. Some days, I think I want to hear what they have to say. Other days, I wonder what the point is. I think talking to Dr. Lawrence tomorrow might help me decide what I need to do."

"That woman is amazing, and she cares. Talking to her will definitely give you some clarity."

Aisha smiled. Then, she got the waiter's attention to order desserts.

At the end of the night, the two friends cheered, "To new beginnings!"

The next day, Aisha dressed up for her consultation with Dr. Lawrence. She knew she didn't need to, but she wanted to make a good first impression, like it was a job interview for which she needed to perform well. As if after talking to Dr. Lawrence, the therapist would shake her hands, smile politely, and tell her she'll be in touch. Then, the therapist would never contact Aisha again because she was too messed up.

Aisha walked into the empty lobby twenty minutes before the appointment. The young receptionist confirmed her information, gave her a form to fill out, and asked her to please have a seat. The lobby was smaller than the Marcus Wilson Association. The pictures on the wall were not of kids, but of nature and positive affirmations. The colors were warm, so Aisha immediately felt comfortable.

Dr. Lawrence opened her door at 3:00 PM on the dot. "Aisha Jones?" she said.

"Yes."

"Come on in." The therapist waved.

Dr. Lawrence was tall and athletic. Her long braids were neatly wrapped in a colorful scarf. She smelled of amber and honey, and the room smelled like her. In one corner, there was a bookshelf. In the other corner was one purple accent chair and a green couch facing each other. Dr. Lawrence asked her if she needed to use the bathroom.

"No, thank you, doctor," Aisha said after she sat squarely on the couch with her hands on her knees.

Dr. Lawrence smiled. "You can call me Kenya." She sat on the chair and crossed her legs. "Please make yourself comfortable, Aisha."

Aisha relaxed and leaned back on the couch.

Kenya quickly scanned the intake form Aisha had filled out with her eyes. After asking some questions about Aisha's medical history and reviewing the therapist-patient agreement, she said, "Why are you seeking therapy at this time, Aisha?"

Aisha thought she'd hold back and save some information for later, but she told Kenya everything. Maybe it was the soothing smell of the room, the comfortable couch, or the understanding nods the therapist gave her, but Aisha vomited everything: James and Sam's betrayal, what had happened with her mother and Amir, how she felt about her father, how terrible she had been for a good chunk of the year.

Dr. Lawrence was nodding and taking notes. "What do you expect from therapy?"

Aisha took some time to think of her answer. "I'm not sure, honestly. I think I need someone to talk to and some tools and tips to improve and get better, hopefully."

The therapist nodded. "How have you been coping with the issues you've mentioned?"

Aisha looked down. "Not well. I've been relying on marijuana and alcohol." Her eyes watered. "Sorry," she said as tears rolled down her cheeks.

Kenya leaned forward and spoke gently. "Crying is a normal reaction." She handed Aisha a box of tissues. "It's okay to cry as much as you'd like."

Aisha cried freely while she told the therapist about the three months when she almost didn't leave her apartment, how bad things were, and how awful she felt. She even told Kenya about David, Marcus, Carlos, and Anthony, and what happened with all the men she met in Dallas.

Dr. Lawrence let her go on, occasionally asking a follow-up or clarifying question while taking notes and nodding. There was no judgment in her eyes. She looked like she wasn't only listening, but she was actually hearing Aisha.

After Aisha was done talking, she opened the bottle of water Kenya had put on the end table next to her. The therapist gave her a sort of recap of everything she heard in a concise and insightful manner, pointing out some of the recurring themes. Patterns.

The first consultation mainly involved getting to know her and finding out what made her seek therapy. They would explore what she shared in future sessions, but this was a great start.

"Please keep a journal of your days and how you're feeling, so we can discuss it in the next sessions, okay?"

"Okay."

The time was up.

"Thank you for being vulnerable and open today, Aisha."

"I know today was just an introduction, but I already feel so much lighter. Thank you."

Kenya smiled, nodded, then shook her hand. "You're very welcome. See you next week!"

"Yes. See you next week!"

Aisha scheduled her next appointment with the receptionist. Then, she slithered out of Dr. Lawrence's office like a reptile that had shed skin.

WEEK 49

Aisha had established a routine. She walked the trail, volunteered, and now had a weekly therapy session with Dr. Lawrence. She spoke to her mother and Amir every other day. She still went out to eat a couple of times a week, but she mostly cooked at home now.

This hump day, she wanted to find a good romance or thriller book to read while drinking a hot Irish Coffee. She knew where to go to get the experience she was looking for. *Libros & Libations* was just a few miles away. She missed the fresh-brewed coffee smell of the place, the bright colors, and Old Man with Round Glasses.

Enough time had passed that people wouldn't recognize the unhinged woman who had yelled at the top of her lungs at a man frozen on the couch. The man she had screamed out was the one person who would recognize her. Perhaps Marcus had stopped frequenting the book café because he feared Aisha would return to blame him for other things he hadn't done.

The thing was, Aisha really wanted an Irish coffee. She was excited to finally feel like reading. And yes, she could've found another place, but she wanted to go to *Libros & Libations*. Secretly, she was hoping to run into Marcus because she wanted to right that wrong by apologizing. Perhaps he wouldn't want to talk to her—understandably so. Perhaps he didn't care and had forgotten about the whole thing. Or perhaps she wouldn't run into him.

Whatever the outcome, she walked into the coffee shop that afternoon. A small part of her was afraid that some people would recognize her, whisper something to their friends, and shake their heads in contempt when they saw her. But when she walked to the bar, only a few people glanced at her before staring back at their laptops or books.

Across the bar, she saw Old Man with Round Glasses in the very corner of the room. She smiled. He was very focused on a book thicker than the Bible. She was happy to be back in this familiar place. Unfortunately, she didn't recognize the bartender. She hoped Zac still worked there and that she'd see him next time.

"Hey! What are we drinking?" the bartender asked. She had the Cruella De Vil hairstyle but not the red lipstick.

"Are you still doing the free second drink if I purchase a book?"

The young woman pointed at the sign on her right that read, *Buy a book, and your second drink is on the house!* "Yes, ma'am," she said.

"I'll do an Irish Coffee then."

"Okay. I'll call you when your order's ready. What's your name?"

"Aisha."

The bartender nodded, then turned around to make the drink.

"I love your hair," Aisha said before she walked toward the books.

"Oh, thank you." The bartender smiled, and her cheeks flushed.

Aisha slowly strolled down the thriller section. She felt more relaxed now. Marcus wasn't going to show up today. She kneeled to look at the books on the bottom shelves. She judged the books by their covers, then read the blurbs of the ones she was interested in.

After skimming through a handful of books, she saw the novel Marcus had suggested: *What Do You Know About Her?* She had really enjoyed the first book by the same author, and this one sounded even more interesting. The protagonist had started a new life under a new identity after killing her abusive parents. Now, her secret was at risk of being revealed.

"One Irish Coffee for Aisha at the bar!"

She walked to the counter with the book in her hands. After she paid for it, the bartender gave her a ticket for her free drink. Aisha found a seat not too far from Old Man with Round Glasses and started sipping and reading. As she turned the pages and slowly downed the beverage, she felt wrapped in unyielding peace.

When she finally looked away from the pages to order her free drink, it was dark outside. The place was even more packed now than when she arrived. Old Man with Round Glasses was still there, and he had made quite a headway with his reading. The pages flipped on his left were now thicker than the right. He had a large bottle of water on his table, which was almost empty. When Aisha stood up to go to the bar, he looked up.

"I think we've been here the longest," he said with a surprisingly baritone voice that contrasted with his smaller frame. "How's your book?"

Aisha couldn't believe he paused his reading to speak to her. She felt like someone in a crowded concert selected by the artist to join them on stage for a song. "It's very good! It's a thriller. What are you reading?"

"*The Lord of the Rings.* I've read it before. It's one of my favorite books. I reread just about every other year."

"How long is it?"

"Twelve hundred pages."

Aisha's face dropped.

He smiled. "Yes, it's a chunky one," he said as he pushed his glasses up, "but when you find something you really enjoy, it's worth the time, right?"

"Right."

"Well, enjoy your reading!" he said, then looked back at the pages.

"You too!" Aisha grinned and walked to the bar to order her second drink.

If Old Man with Round Glasses is for me, who can be against me? She chuckled at that thought. When she turned to walk back to her seat after grabbing her free drink, she saw the person who might answer her question by the entrance. *That* Marcus. There he was, looking just as handsome, square-shouldered, and neat as the last time she saw him.

Perhaps Medusa had also walked in and was somewhere staring at her because Aisha couldn't move. She just looked at Marcus walking toward her with her drink anchored in her left hand. He recognized her, but somehow, he didn't turn around to leave. He didn't even look upset. In fact, he smiled at her. She had still not moved an inch by the time he was in front of her.

"Hey," he said, "long time no see."

She cleared her alarmingly dry throat as quietly as she could. "H-Hey."

"*Soooo*...last time was—"

"Excuse me," a woman with pigtails said behind them, "I'm sorry, are you in line?"

"Oh, no, sorry," Marcus said. He waved at Aisha to get out of the lady's way so she could order.

Aisha broke Medusa's spell and moved. She could internally hear every single thud as she followed behind Marcus.

"Where are you sitting?" he said.

She pointed at her table, which conveniently had two seats. *How lovely.* She moved her bag so he could sit down.

"So, what happen—"

"I'm so so *so* sorry. You have no idea! I'm so embarrassed. That had nothing to do with you. I was just going through a lot, and you were in the wrong place at the wrong time. I snapped. None of what I said was about you. I mean, I wish you had come that day, but I wasn't upset, just disappointed. But all the anger and screaming were about other things. I'm so sorry, Marcus. That was messed up. I apologize. I understand if you want to leave now or yell at me."

He stood up at once. *"Leaving" going once, twice, sold to the handsome gentlem—*He moved his chair closer to the table and sat back down. "It's alright," he said with that boyish smile. "I figured you were going through something. I accept your apology, Aisha."

She blinked in disbelief. "That's it?"

He laughed. "Well, yeah. Like you said, you snapped. It can happen to anyone. You apologized. You mean it. Obviously, you're doing better now. So, I'm not going to hold it against you."

"How are you not more upset?"

"What's there to be upset about after you've sincerely apologized? You can't change the past."

"I was so rude. I yelled at you for no reason, and then, I avoided coming back here so I wouldn't run into you."

He was still holding that smile that made him look like a teenager. "What do you think I should do, then?"

"I don't know, tell me off and never speak to me again, or at least not for a long time."

"And what good is that going to accomplish?"

"I'll feel bad about what I did and understand the gravity of my actions."

"Don't you already?"

"Well…yes. But I shouldn't be let off so easily."

"You already feel bad. You've clearly done some personal work. You apologized. Unless you reoffend, I think you've paid for your crime." He air-quoted *reoffend* and *crime*.

"It's that simple, uh?"

"It is."

"Thank you for being so forgiving."

He smiled. "It's okay, Aisha. Just let it go. I have, alright?"

"Alright." She fought tears by tightening her fist under the table.

He looked at the book in front of her. "Ah, you took my suggestion. Are you enjoying it?"

"Yes, very much."

"I'm happy to hear that."

A man with a clean-cut style similar to Marcus walked in and waved at him.

"Okay, my coworker's here. We have to go over a presentation. Hopefully, I'll see you again." He hesitated, then said, "I want to give you a date when I'll be here again, but I've learned my lesson." He laughed.

"Ha. Ha." She tried to hold her laughter but broke when she looked at him.

"Hopefully, I'll see you later."

"Yes."

"Alright. Goodnight, Aisha."

"Goodnight, Marcus."

Aisha read one more chapter and finished her drink. She waved goodbye at Old Man with Round Glasses and Marcus on her way out. They both waved back.

The next day, Aisha wrote about how good she felt about both interactions in her journal. She wrote about how much her relationship had improved with her mother—who had finally gone on her first date in over a decade. A date that exceeded all her expectations—and Amir—who had paused the endless swiping because, and she quoted, 'My index finger hurts.' Aisha wrote about wanting to talk to James and Sam and hear whatever they had to say. Then, she shared it all with Dr. Lawrence at the end of the week.

The more she talked and felt heard, the more they unpacked, and the more she felt the warmth of the light at the end of the tunnel on her skin.

WEEK 50

It was the most wonderful time of the year. The lights were up, the Christmas trees were out, the jingle bells were ringing, and the heat had finally clocked out after the longest shift ever.

Also, today was Sam's birthday.

Though her birthday was in early December, her parents always had one big celebration for her with the rest of their family on Christmas. So, Sam always celebrated her actual birthday with Aisha. Sometimes, they included Amir and Helen. The last one, Sam, spent her birthday with Aisha and James at their place.

"Cheers to twenty-nine!" Sam had raised her glass.

They were seated on the kitchen island. They had moved the counter stools to form a triangle so they could all face each other. The birthday girl was in the middle.

Aisha raised her glass first. James followed and said, "Cheers to you!" He smiled at Sam.

"Yes! Happy birthday, friend!" Aisha clinked James and Sam's glasses.

James got up to slice the Marjolaine cake he had picked up at the French bakery earlier. Aisha was surprised when she suggested a triple chocolate cake, but James insisted Sam would prefer the Marjolaine cake.

"You guys," Sam's face brightened when she saw the cake, "this is, like, my new favorite dessert! I met with a client last month whose policy was about to lapse, and to thank me for letting him know he gave me a slice of Marjolaine. Best thing I ever tasted!"

Aisha looked at James, who was focused on cutting the cake. Then she turned to Sam and said, "James is the one who suggested it, actually." She pursed her lips and exaggeratedly raised one brow. "Is there something I should know?"

Aisha was joking, but Sam laughed a little too hard. "I probably told him when we were hooping or something," she said. "And FYI, I've worked things out with John."

Aisha rose from her seat. "And you're just telling me now? I'm mad at you!" She smirked, then moved her eyebrows up and down rapidly. "So that's why you've been glowing lately."

Sam grinned and nodded. Aisha gave her a high-five and then humped the counter stool to demonstrate the source of her friend's glow. Sam laughed while James was still very focused on slicing the cake into equal pieces.

Aisha wasn't trying to ruin Sam's birthday today—*okay, maybe a little bit*—but she wanted to talk to her former friend now. Perhaps it was the memories of all the birthdays past, but suddenly, she felt like she couldn't wait any longer. She wasn't even sure what she wanted to hear because nothing Sam would say could fix things. Things could never be the same between them.

Their friendship was over.

Perhaps Aisha wanted to hear something that'd somehow redeem the beautiful memories they shared. Humanize what Sam did so Aisha could have the license to recall some of the amazing times they had with a smile.

She unblocked Sam and James, then walked to her balcony and sat on the floor. The magnolia tree was flowerless now, save for one tiny white bloom that had blossomed off-season. It was fifty-seven degrees, yet the sun shone bright. She called Sam.

"Hello?" Sam answered, her voice raspy and small.

"It's me."

"Yes. Hey."

"Happy birthday."

"Thank you. How are you?"

"I'm fine. Can you talk?"

"Y-Yes. Give me one second," Sam whispered. Aisha heard rapid steps behind the line, then a door shutting. "Okay, I can talk now," Sam said at last.

"Why?"

"I need you to know that I wasn't trying to hurt you. I didn't mean for it to happen, but I truly fell in love with him. We tried to stop. We really did. We wanted to tell you before you found out, but we didn't know how to. We both didn't want to lose you. And James was in love with both of us at one point, so I tried to walk away. I really did, Sha. You're like a sister to me, but I fell in love with him. I did. I'll do whatever it takes to fix this. If it means breaking things up with James, if that's what it takes to fix this, that's what I'll do. I don't want to lose you. I've been so miserable knowing I hurt you. I'm so sorry, Sha." Sam's voice cracked at the end.

"You're still together?" Aisha's voice was even.

"Yes."

"How old is your baby?"

"Four and a half months."

"Girl or boy?"

"Boy."

"What did you guys name him?"

"James wanted a junior."

"Of course." Aisha smiled and spoke with a lighter voice.

"I know, right?" Sam's voice was also lighter.

"Are you happy?"

Sam took a moment to respond. "Except for not having you right now…yes."

"Look, Sam, I accept your apology. I know you're sincere, and I believe you didn't want to hurt me. But we can no longer be friends. I know myself. Even though I forgive you, and I do, I'll never be able to forget this. Giving you a second chance would honestly not be fair to you because it'll never be a clean slate. No matter what you do, I'll never look at you the same. A part of me will always hold this against you, so you'd be walking on eggshells for the rest of our lives. I don't want you to go through that, and I don't want to go through that…This is it."

Sam was crying now, but she didn't protest when she spoke. "I understand, Sha. I don't know what I'm going to do without you. I'm gonna miss you so much."

"I'm going to miss you too, Sam."

Someone knocked on the door on Sam's side. Then Aisha heard the person whisper, "Hey, can you come for a moment? He's crying. I think he's hungry."

"Take care of yourself, okay?" Aisha said.

"Okay. You too."

"Bye."

Aisha's mind was clear and quiet. She put on some leggings and a long-sleeve shirt and went for a hike. She walked for an hour, and when she returned home, she called James.

"Hey, Aisha," he immediately answered. "It's so good to hear from you. How are you?"

"I'm fine. I spoke to Sam earlier."

"I know."

"Are you living together?"

"No, but we spend a lot of time at each other's places since…the baby."

"She told me you named him James."

"Yes. He looks just like my dad. It's insane."

They were both silent for a moment.

"Sha, I hope you know how sorry I am. I care about you more than you know. I was madly in love with you, and the last thing I ever wanted to do was hurt you. This…just happened. It wasn't planned. I didn't think it'd come to this." He sighed. "I know you. I know you can't move past this, and obviously, you have every right not to. I don't think I would if I were in your shoes. As much as I'd like to have you in my life as a friend, I know it's not going to happen. But for what it's worth, I'm sorry."

"I appreciate that, James. Thank you. Just one question, if that's okay?"

"Of course."

"Was some of this about the kid thing? If I wanted to have kids, do you think this whole thing would've happened?"

James took a long time to think of his answer, and Aisha didn't interrupt. Finally, he said, "Honestly, I don't know. I'm not sure. Probably not. I think it's what you told me about the soulmate thing. I'm more compatible with you in so many ways. Unfortunately, the one thing we're not compatible on isn't something that can be compromised. Now, don't get me wrong, that's not why I…cheated on you. That was its own fucked up thing, and I was a dickhead for that. But if you wanted kids, maybe things would've turned out differently. Maybe. I don't know."

Aisha sighed. "I guess it's all a moot point now."

"I guess so."

"I'll come get my stuff after the New Year."

"Okay," he murmured. Then he spoke with a higher pitch. "You know you burned that picture of me and my parents at the lake. I loved that picture!"

She laughed. "Oh, sorry, I didn't mean to. Collateral damage."

He laughed. "Just let me know when you're planning on stopping by. I can help you pack or leave the apartment if you don't want to see me."

"Okay, thank you. I'll let you know." She took a deep breath. "Take care, James."

"You too, Aisha."

"Bye."

Aisha thought that after speaking with James and Sam, she'd feel a wave of strong feelings, good or bad. But her mood hardly changed after she ended both calls. It merely felt like a completed task, a checked box. Somewhere along the way, she had closed this chapter. The two conversations were simply her walking back to verify that the book was indeed closed and put away.

It was odd, though. Two of the people she cared about the most in this world would be out of her life forever. That was kin to death, wasn't it? Even if they both did their best to avoid her—and vice versa—she'd probably run into them at some point. She wouldn't ignore them. She would say hi and make small talk for a few minutes. But that would be the extent of it.

All they had been to each other might as well be buried six feet under, so it was reason enough for weeping and sobbing. Yet she didn't cry. Somewhere along the way, those tears had been shed, and she had gotten to the acceptance stage of grief. However, there was still a mist of sadness from the losses that might never go away. But at last, Aisha could close her eyes and recall the good memories of Sam and James with a smile.

*

The next day, Aisha signed up for the morning packing shift. She was sad when she walked in and didn't recognize any volunteers. Today was her last day volunteering at the Marcus Wilson Association, since she would be going back to Denver after Christmas. Martha immediately knew something was off when she looked at Aisha.

"Is everything okay?" Martha asked.

"I'm driving home after Christmas, so today's my last shift."

Martha's shoulders fell. "Well, we're just going to miss you so much, Aisha."

"I'll miss you guys, too. And I'll miss seeing the pictures of the kids on the wall. It just made my day."

"Aw." Martha stood up and hugged Aisha in front of the reception counter. "Marcus is going to be so sad. He always talks about how hardworking and positive you are."

"Please don't tell him, okay? I'll tell him at the end of the shift."

"Of course." Martha sat back down when Marcus opened the door. Then she winked at Aisha and focused back on her computer screen.

The shift went as smoothly as usual. Everyone helped each other when needed and completed their tasks while enjoying the nice playlist. At the end of the shift, Aisha stopped Marcus when everyone walked out to the lobby.

"Hey, Marcus. Do you have a minute?" she said.

"Of course. What's up?"

"Well, today's my last day here. I'm moving back home. I'll be driving back to Denver to spend the New Year with my family."

He leaned on one of the tables. "Oh, man. I'm happy for you, but I'm sad too. We'll miss you around here. And thank you, Aisha, for showing up consistently. That means a lot. Maybe it doesn't feel like much but making sure all the goods are packed in time for the kids makes a huge difference. You're good people. Not surprising, though, given who sent you."

"Why, thank you." She looked away, then back at him. "Marcus, how did you know? How did you know this is what you wanted to do?"

"Hmm, good question. I guess I just felt a strong calling for this work."

"Ah. I wish I had that feeling about anything."

"I think it's okay if you don't; not everyone does. Just keep trying different things. Keep helping others when you can. Keep exploring and enjoying life. In the midst of all that, something might pull at your heart. But guess what? Even if it doesn't, you still lived a full life. You still made other people's lives better when you could. You still left a positive imprint on the world. I think when it's all set and done, that's all that matters."

Aisha wiped the one tear that had rolled down her cheek. "Wow. I should've taken less time making fun of your dance moves and more time asking you questions."

Marcus began moving his legs and arms in uncoordinated motions. "Don't get me started, girl. You know I got it!" Then he did his "dance" thing some more.

Aisha laughed. "Thank you, Marcus. Not for the dance, for the advice. I'll stop here every time I'm in Dallas."

He beamed and opened his arms out. "Come here, girl."

In the embrace, she cried. Tears of sadness because she was leaving these great people, but also happiness because she'd see her family soon.

"Alright," Marcus said with a tender smile, "don't make me cry now."

"Sorry." She wiped her face. "Oh, Dahlia is opening her own studio soon," she said. "You should give her a call or something to ask about the opening date."

"Oh yeah? That's great news! I'm getting sick of doing the same steps at that studio, it's not the same without her. I'll definitely call her. Thanks for letting me know!"

Aisha smiled and nodded. When they walked to the lobby, Martha had a box of donuts on the counter.

"Just a little something for the farewell."

Aisha put her hands on her chest. "Aw, Martha, you shouldn't have."

Marcus gently moved Aisha out of the way. "Ah, perfect, more for me!"

They all laughed, and then Martha opened the box. They ate, talked about some of the funny things that happened during some shifts, and laughed until the afternoon volunteers walked in. Aisha gave them a final hug. Finally, she walked away without looking back. She didn't want them to see how hard she was crying. In the car, she made a two-thousand-dollar donation on their website. At last, she drove off.

*

On Friday evening, she met with Dahlia at a twenty-four-hour café to put the contract together for the loan. Aisha let her know it wasn't necessary, but Dahlia insisted. Aisha agreed to all the terms as long as they were feasible for Dahlia and wouldn't put too much pressure on her. They both signed.

"I can't believe you're leaving next week," Dahlia said.

"I know, I can't believe I've spent the entire year here. I didn't know how long I'd stay when I came, but I didn't expect to be here the whole year."

"Damn. I'm going to miss you, girl. You better come and visit! I'll send you pictures of the studio once it's done, but you'll have to see it in person."

"I'll definitely come back here to see you as often as possible. Nia and you are welcome at my place any time, too."

"I'm sure she'll love Colorado. She hates the Texas heat more than you." They smiled and looked at each other. Dahlia's curls were shining, and her face was open and bright. "This is not the last time I see you, right? Cause I'm not ready!" she said. "Do you want to spend Christmas with Nia and me?"

Aisha shook her head. "Thank you for the invitation, but I think I want to spend it alone. I don't know, maybe it's dumb, but I want to reclaim how being alone feels before I leave."

"It's not dumb at all. You've come a long way, Aisha. I'm proud of you, friend."

"Thank you, friend."

"Okay, can I help you pack after your alone time?"

"Please! I hate packing. She doesn't have to help pack, but can you bring Nia? I'd love to meet her before I go."

"She wants to meet you, too! I told her about you, and how much fun we have together and how you're helping me open the studio and what a friend you are, and this little girl's going to say: 'You know, Mommy, I need to meet her because it's hard to *visualize* your stories if I don't know what Aisha looks like.' Mind you, this child is eight." She shook her head and chuckled.

After they finished their coffees, they walked out to the parking lot.

"I'll text you the packing date," Aisha said while getting in her car.

"Okay. Drive safe, and Merry Christmas!" Dahlia said.

"Merry Christmas!"

On her drive home, Aisha admired all the bright and colorful decorations on the commercial and residential buildings. The lights were beautiful and bright, and she felt their reflection illuminate her eyes.

WEEK 51

Are you sure you don't want to spend Christmas here? Helen texted in the group chat on Wednesday afternoon.

Yeah you gonna be tired as hell but you can still make it! Amir followed.

Guys I told you. I'm almost at the end of this healing journey. Please allow me the time to complete the voyage. Aisha added the praying hands and woman in lotus position emojis for gravitas.

Mom, she's going to come back here with a bald head, barefoot, and an orange robe talkin about: huuuuummmmmmm

Helen first sent a laughing face, then she wrote. *Leave your sister alone! lol*

For YOUR information I'm rocking a twist out. Aisha sent them a selfie of her doing the duck lips.

Wow! Your hair has grown a lot, sweetie. Love the twist out!

Yeah the twist out's alright. Couldve done without the kissy face tho. Amir added the upside-down smiley face at the end.

These haters on my body shake em off. Aisha immediately typed and punctuated her text with the music notes emoji.

Ah, I know this one. Helen chimed in. *Lil Ma sings that song: oouuu!*

Yes mom. You got it! Amir replied.

Aisha chuckled. She put her phone away after telling her mother and her brother that she loved them and couldn't wait to see them next week.

Yesterday, Dr. Lawrence had suggested an exercise at the end of their session: to write a letter to her father. Whatever she felt, whatever she wished she had said to him, whatever was still lingering, whatever she had held onto all these years. Then, Aisha could burn the letter when she was ready to let go.

Yesterday was also her last in-person session with her therapist since the holidays were here, and Aisha was leaving next week. Thankfully, Kenya was also licensed in Colorado, so she could continue working with Aisha virtually when she returned to Denver.

Aisha grabbed a notebook, sat down, and wrote.

I don't know where to start. I thought this would be ~~easy~~ easier
I don't know why I still care. It's not like we had a relationship or anything
Like, I only saw you in person 3 times...
Why? Why did you leave? I understand you felt lost in life. But I feel like a family should've anchored you in some way? I mean you told me yourself
<u>Home is wherever Amir and you are</u>. But you left "home" again. And what you did to mom. What kinda fucking man are you?!?! I'm not blaming all of this on you but I know you've messed up the way
I view relationships in some way... Surely, you have. Like, I hate to be a cliché but "daddy issues" hello?!!! Like fuck you for that. God, I don't fucking respect you. Like AT ALL!!!
I think what fucks with me is the fact that in ~~som~~ many ways, I'm kinda like you.

I'm selfish like you. I put myself first like you (which I know can be good but not if it means not giving a fuck about anyone else). I'm scared of commitment like you.

I feel (felt?) lost like you.

I. don't. want. to. be. like. YOU.

This year was rough, but I think I'm on the right track now.

I don't have it all figured out but I think I'm going to be alright. Hopefully.

I wonder if you would've reached out again if you didn't die. Probably.

That loneliness hits you in the face like Myke Tyson, don't it?

You would've band aid the void and guilt by showing back with your tail between your legs 10 years later on some BS

'I'm SO sorry! I was in Madagascar, the North Pole, in Papua New Guinea looking for myself in the corners and cracks of the Earth. But I FINALLY know for sure: I'm nothing without you and your brother. Please forgive me.

I promise that... blah blah blah" Like, STFU. Ugh.

You know what, I'm not even mad at you anymore.

Amir was right. I feel sorry for you.

Why the hell am I trying to find myself through someone who never found themselves?

I don't know what I was even holding on to

I guess if I had you to blame then I had an excuse to not look inwards?

Maybe. I don't know... Good luck Kenya! lol

My hand hurts. And I think I'm over it.

This whole thing with you. I'm over it.

Thanks for the money though. I think I'll look for more causes I believe in and give more away. Continue to help Dahlia.

Shit, look at me. I'm a philanthropist, baby! LMAO

I like that. Helping other people's dreams. Helping their causes.

Maybe that's my thing?

I don't even know what you did for work to leave us that kind of $$$$ but SHIIIIIIIIIIIIIIIIIIIIIT I don't need to know. LOL

Anyway, I think I'm good now.

I'm sure you'll pop up in my head here and there but I think I'll be fine.

And you know what: I hope wherever you are you're finally at peace.

I am.

Aisha ripped all the pages she had written on. Then she grabbed all the pieces of paper, a metal container, and a lighter, and she walked out to her balcony to complete the exercise. Watching all the words and feelings she had put on the paper go up in flames was cathartic. She felt a sense of release. She had let go of most of what she had held onto when she finished writing, and whatever had remained was now turned to ashes.

That evening, she lit up a joint and had a glass of wine on her balcony. It was nice because she wasn't trying to escape anything. She wasn't avoiding feeling, and she wasn't trying to numb herself. It was just the perfect temperature and star-filled night, so she wanted a little extra buzz to enjoy it.

*

On Christmas, she woke up to a *Merry Christmas!* from her mother, Amir, Dahlia, and…David?

Aisha immediately returned the greeting to her brother, mother, and friend. She needed some coffee to decide whether to reply to David or not.

Why did people do that? Use the holidays to try and "spin the block," message something that seemed innocuous but was rather insidious, to see if they still had a chance to hurt the recipient one more time. What kind of creep did you have to be to do something like that—

OMG I messaged Thomas Merry Christmas with my Google number whyyyyyyyyyyyyyyyy. Amir texted her.

Aisha broke into a very loud cackle. *Welp.*

Another text from her brother came in. *And I didnt do the software update or whatever so I can't unsend it. Like it's done DONE! WTF did I do that for?!!!*

Aisha called her brother.

"What do I do?" he said the moment he picked up.

"Well, just wait. That's all you can do. And it's Christmas, so if he doesn't answer today, I think it's understandable. Give him some time."

"True."

"I thought you had moved on…with all the online dating?"

He sighed. "Yeah, I tried, but I was lying to myself. Thomas is the love of my life. I honestly didn't try that hard to get him back. Maybe he has moved on and he's completely over me. And if he is, and he doesn't reply and I never hear from him again, I'll accept it, and I won't bother him again. But I just wanted to give it one more try before the year ends."

Aisha nodded. "You did the right thing following your heart. Either way it goes, I'm here for you, okay?"

"Okay. Thank you, sis. Love you."

"Love you too."

After she got off the phone with Amir, she replied to David. *Merry Christmas*

I hope all is well! The artist texted back immediately. *I have an exhibition on the 28th. Your portrait is one of the pieces. I'd love to see you there and maybe we could catch up afterwards?*

That's great! Thank you for the invitation but I won't be there. I'm excited for you though

I see. Perhaps we could meet another time then?

I think we should leave things the way they are. Now if you end up selling my portrait for millions of dollars don't hesitate to reach out to me to rediscuss the compensation thing alright? Lol

LOL! Certainly. Well, take care of yourself, Aisha Jones.

You do the same, David Marshall.

*

Aisha mostly spent the rest of the week at home. She only left her apartment to hike and, one time, to run some errands. She watched a lot of horror movies. She yelled at the screen and threw her hands up when a side character stepped on a branch to alert the murderous creature of their presence. Some nights, she had a drink. Some nights, she didn't. All nights, she enjoyed herself.

At the end of the week, she looked around her apartment. The seven-hundred-something square feet space that had seen and held her at her worst and provided her with a container to scream, cry, and let go. The space that allowed her to become undone and then put the pieces back together to heal. She would miss this place.

WEEK 52

K NOCK! KNOCK!

She let Dahlia and her mini-me in. She hugged her friend and bent down to greet Nia.

"Hey, Nia! I'm Aisha. Nice to meet you!"

Nia patted her shoulder with her tiny hand. "Hey, I know. Nice to meet you too. You're shorter than I thought. I like your kitchen. Do you have juice?"

Yep. 'No kids' for $500, Alex.

"Please?" Dahlia said.

"Do you have juice, please?" Nia corrected.

Aisha tittered. "Yes, in the fridge. Get whatever you'd like." She only had milk, orange juice, and apple juice in there. She didn't think Nia would try to drink alcohol when they weren't watching, but she figured it was best practice not to have any in her fridge by the time the kid got there.

Nia rushed to the fridge, her curls bouncing. Aisha watched her and chuckled.

"This is what I have to deal with," Dahlia said, tenderly looking at her little girl.

"She's too cute! She looks a lot more like you in person than in the pictures I saw."

Dahlia smiled. "Thank you." Then, to Nia, she said, "Okay, baby, just get your drink and…" She turned back to Aisha. "Can she watch some TV for a little while?"

Aisha nodded *yes, of course.*

Dahlia turned back to Nia. "You can watch some cartoons for a bit; then you can come to help us pack, okay?"

Nia had already spilled some juice on her overalls. She spoke in between gulps. "O-kay!"

Dahlia and Aisha moved to the bedroom and began packing. Nia popped in and out to throw some clothes in a bag.

"You have lots of leggings," the girl said as she threw a pair into a small bag. "I watched the Lu-La-Roe documentary with Mom last week. Those leggings were *soooo* ugly! Yours are fine."

Then, she was back in the living room eating a snack and watching *Karma's World*.

"She's going to run the world." Aisha grinned.

"Tell me about it."

They were almost done since Aisha mostly had clothes and shoes to pack. She looked around her empty room. "I'm going to miss Dallas."

"And I'm going to miss you, girl," Dahlia said.

They look at each other with melancholic smiles. "I'm going to miss you too," Aisha said.

She dropped the hanger she was holding and hugged her friend tightly. They stayed like that, holding each other as they sat on the edge of the bed, and they cried for a while.

"Are you two okay?" Nia said.

"Yes, baby," Dahlia wiped her face with her shirt, "I'm just going to miss Aunty Aisha a lot."

Aisha had made it to 'Aunty' status! Her heart swelled.

Nia walked closer and patted both of their thighs. They were both seated, so she was at eye level with them. She had spilled something else on her overalls, leaving a new stain. Nia looked at Aisha. "Aunty Aisha, have you considered moving here? I know you have to see your family and everything, but maybe later?"

Aisha nodded and looked at Nia. "You know, that's not a bad idea. I'm going to think about it." Then she turned to Dahlia and said, "The thought actually crossed my mind. I feel like I have a lot going on here. Once I'm home and spend time with my mom and brother, I'll have a better sense of where I need to be."

"There you go!" Nia said and marched back to the living room.

Dahlia and Aisha watched her until she was out of sight, then they laughed.

"Whatever you decide," Dahlia said, "I'm just a phone call away."

"Right back atcha."

They embraced each other again.

*

The day before her drive back home, Aisha went to *Libros & Libations*. She wanted to spend one last day at her favorite coffee shop before she left. She was also hoping to run into Marcus again. If she did, she'd ask for his phone number so they could stay in contact.

When she walked in, she recognized a few faces that she had seen at least one other time when she was there. She scouted the corner of the room for Old Man with Round Glasses, but unfortunately, he wasn't there. However, at the bar, she saw Zac. He was sporting a mullet and a colorful tie-dye shirt.

"Hey!" he said when he saw her. "Long time no see!"

"Yes. Love the hair!"

He looked at a mirror behind him, then back at her. "Thank you, me too!" Then, he narrowed his eyes. "Irish coffee, right?"

"Yep!"

He did a spin and shouted. "One Irish coffee!"

Marcus walking in was the only thing missing to make this stop perfect. And because this was the final thing she cared to do in Dallas before she left, Aisha waited for hours until the place was almost emptied, and Zac screamed, "Last call!" before dimming the lights. The last two people there with her gathered their stuff. Aisha looked at the table where Marcus and she had their last conversation.

Finally, she stood up, waved goodbye to Zac, and left.

*

Aisha checked every room the following day to ensure she hadn't forgotten anything. She was all packed, and her car was loaded. She stepped on her balcony and gave the flowerless magnolia tree a final glance. Then, she got on the road and drove back to Denver.

She was disappointed not to have seen Marcus one last time before she left. Perhaps it was better that way. Sometimes, it was best for stories to end with ellipses. Maybe she'd run into him again when she returned to Dallas. He was a good guy, and at the very least, she hoped they could become friends.

Now Aisha had one friend in the Lone Star State. She could've never imagined taking such a liking to Dahlia after what happened with Sam, but she did. She trusted her new friend and was grateful to have her and her daughter in her life.

Though she was leaving a place and people she had grown to love, she was overjoyed to see her family soon. She had been gone a whole year. It took twelve months, but the woman switching lanes to take the next exit wasn't the same woman who had sat on the bench fifty-two weeks ago when people were chanting the countdown to the New Year.

Did Aisha have everything figured out and fixed? No.

But whoever did? And was that even the point?

She was at peace.

She was looking forward to waking up. She was curious and excited about her future. She was open to opening her heart, even if it meant she could get hurt. Her foundation, at the core of who she was, felt sturdy, so no matter how many people would walk in and out of her life, she wouldn't completely fall apart. *That* was healing.

That was the end of the tunnel.

*

When Aisha exited her car, she ran toward her mother and brother. They met at the end of the driveway and stood there, holding each other in tears.

That night, Helen invited her date, Charles, to the New Year's Eve party. They were sitting on the couch, talking and laughing. A few of her brother's friends, three of her mother's hairstylists, and a handful of family relatives stood and sat across Helen's living room as the clock approached midnight.

Aisha was wearing a very thick coat, and Amir had a jacket on as they stood outside, against the railing, on their mother's verandah.

"Still nothing from Thomas?" she said.

Amir shook his head no. "I mean, I was hoping he'd answer before the end of the year, but I guess deep down, I knew he wouldn't. It sucks, but I just have to accept it and work on moving on, I guess."

She looked at his visible breaths slowly disappearing into the atmosphere. "I'm sorry, bro. Well, at least you tried. And I don't know, the year's not over yet." She patted his back.

He shrugged. "It's okay, I'll be fine." He put his hands in his pockets. "Maybe I need me a little Southern getaway, too. It's not that I didn't believe you, but, like, whatever you did really worked. I'm proud of you, sis." Then he raised one brow. "It was Ayahuasca, wasn't it?"

She laughed. "No. I actually started seeing a therapist, and at some point, I decided to be honest with myself. I cried a lot, *bruh*. It was crazy. Oh, but I ate mushrooms one time. That shit was insane."

He chuckled. "I told you."

Aisha rubbed her hands together and blew some air in her palms. She missed Texas' warmer weather. "My therapist gave me an exercise: to write a letter to Dad. About how I felt, just anything, then burn it. It was powerful. I don't know if you're still holding on to anything there, but if you are, or even for anything else, I think it might help."

Amir smiled and nodded, but he didn't say anything.

"They're going to start the countdown soon," Helen said. She slid the door close and stood in between her children. She rested her hands on their right shoulders and brought them closer. "I love you two so much, you know that, right?"

"Yes, Mom. We love you too!" They both said, resting their heads against hers.

Someone slightly slid the door open behind them so they could hear the countdown.

"Ten, nine, eight, seven, six, five, four, three, two, one…Happy New Year!" voices echoed in the living room.

The three of them held each other tighter. "Happy New Year!" they all said.

Helen walked back inside and gave Charles a very long hug. Aisha and Amir turned around to watch them. Aisha cocked her head, and Amir pursed his lips. They both grinned. Their mother was happy. Then Amir's phone lit up.

Her brother showed her the text, his mouth agape. *Merry belated Christmas and Happy New Year to you.* From Thomas.

Amir screamed and jumped in the air. "Oh. My. God. I can't believe this! This year is off to a great start. Let me go grab two flutes and that nice bottle of champagne Charles brought. I'm getting *fuuuucked* up! I'll be right back."

Her brother ran inside, and he paused in the living room to show the text to their mother. Helen jumped up and circled Amir's neck. Then, they danced. Charles was looking at them with a smile. Aisha watched them for a moment. Her mind was still, and her heart was full.

She turned around to look at the stars.

ABOUT THE AUTHOR

BIANCA PENSY ABA was born on May 27, 1993, in Yaoundé, Cameroon. She lived in her native country until she turned eighteen. She graduated from Graceland University in 2017. She was a college athlete who played sports most of her life. Her second love was basketball. Her first was writing. She is the author of *Across Both Sides of the Mirror* and *52 Weeks a Party of One*. She lives in Allen, Texas, where she enjoys picnicking, reading, hiking, watching terrible dating shows, sipping a glass of wine on her balcony, and doing whatever else she is in the mood for. You can learn more about Bianca and her upcoming projects at *www.biancapensyaba.com*.

Connect Online:

- *www.biancapensyaba.com*
- *biancapensyabawrites*
- *Bianca Pensy Aba*

Thank you for reading *52 Weeks a Party of One*. I hope you enjoyed it. If you have the time and inclination, please leave an honest review on your chosen platform(s) and tell a friend about this book. Thank you so much for the support!

Bianca Pensy Aba

Also by BIANCA PENSY ABA

Across Both Sides of the Mirror